The NIGHT of the FIRE

The NIGHT of the FIRE

A MYSTERY

Kjell Eriksson

Translated from the Swedish by Paul Norlen

MINOTAUR BOOKS

NEW YORK

First published in the United States by Minotaur Books, an imprint of St. Martin's Publishing Group

www.minotaurbooks.com

Library of Congress Cataloging-in-Publication Data

Names: Eriksson, Kjell, 1953– author. | Norlen, Paul, translator.
Title: The night of the fire : a mystery / Kjell Eriksson ; translated from
   the Swedish by Paul Norlen.
Other titles: Skrattande hazaren. English
Description: First U.S. edition. | New York : Minotaur Books, 2020. |
   Series: [Ann Lindell mysteries; 8]
Identifiers: LCCN 2020026247 | ISBN 9781250766144 (hardcover) |
   ISBN 9781250766151 (ebook)
Classification: LCC PT9876.15.R5155 S5813 2020 | DDC 839.73/74—dc23
LC record available at https://lccn.loc.gov/2020026247

Our books may be purchased in bulk for promotional, educational, or business use. Please contact your local bookseller or the Macmillan Corporate and Premium Sales Department at 1-800-221-7945, extension 5442, or by email at MacmillanSpecialMarkets@macmillan.com.

Originally published in Sweden by Ordfront förlag under the title *Den skrattande hazaren*

First Minotaur Books Edition: 2020

10 9 8 7 6 5 4 3 2 1

The NIGHT of the FIRE

One

Regina Rosenberg was a new hire, and this was her third day on the job. But that didn't make her a dimwit.

"Lindell."

"Excuse me?"

"I want to speak with Ann Lindell."

"There is no Ann Lindell at the department," Regina Rosenberg stated after a few quick finger taps and a glance at the screen in front of her.

"Of course there is. Are you new, or what?"

That couldn't be denied, so for that reason she did another search, but just like before she found only one: Lindell, Leif Torsten, in Lost and Found.

"I'm sorry, but there's no Ann Lindell in the building. What does this concern?"

"Knock it off, damn it! I've got to talk with her. Does she want to be anonymous, or what?"

"That tone isn't much help," said Regina, who was from a village in north Uppland, where people talk that way.

A few seconds passed. The man was breathing heavily into the receiver, as if he was jogging with the phone in his hand. Regina heard a clanging tone in the background, like the insistent, disquieting sound when the gate goes down at a train crossing.

"It's . . . Someone may die."

The alarming clang became more and more intense.

"I have to talk with her. She's the only one who listens. Someone may die."

"I'll transfer you to the Violent Crimes Unit."

✦

Two

Stefan Sanberg was not a good person. That was common knowledge. Essential features in his set of social skills were lacking. He had probably never watched a romantic comedy with enjoyment, or voluntarily listened to a peaceful ballad.

Even his grandmother, who'd had the sense, or the weakness some might say, to overlook and forgive a lot throughout her life, was forced to agree. "He's mean," she would say, "because he only thinks about himself."

For Evelina Sanberg, that characteristic was the most despicable, because she was familiar with circumstances where generosity was the only way to make life more or less bearable. She could even use the word "solidarity" without it sounding strange, having grown up in straitened circumstances in farmworker barracks in the village of Rasbokil. At that time in such quarters new ideas were circulating that the poor did not have the slightest problem accepting. In reality they were the ones who made the solemn proclamations meaningful, not least because they put force behind the words.

"Now it's just claptrap," she would exclaim when the talk turned to politics.

"But, Evelina, aren't you happy here?" replied Aamino, who was a nursing assistant at the home where Evelina had spent the past few years.

"I'm just saying," Evelina said, flashing her best crocodile smile, and the woman from Somalia smiled back, even though she had no idea what she meant.

Stefan was about seventy years younger than his grandmother. It was during that three-quarters of a century that Sweden was transformed in a strange pendulum movement: from building up, which Evelina took part in, to tearing down, which in the autumn of old age she could observe with increasing consternation. "There are documents for everything," Stefan's father, Allan, maintained, but that wasn't really correct, because in his work as a self-employed carpenter there were quite a few under-the-table jobs. In every election he'd voted like his mother, but now he was having doubts.

The pendulum movement had contributed to making Stefan Sanberg a heedless young man who could not spell "concentration camp," much less Auschwitz, but eagerly posted pictures on the internet of ovens from there, as the final solution to the problems that tormented him and his friends. All born in the nineties. Obviously they had never experienced carpet-bombing, snipers, or boats that capsized. The most dramatic event during their childhood was when the school bus slid off an icy road and ended up at an angle, fortunately caught by a spruce tree so that no one was seriously injured.

Hate was their primary occupation. It was exhausting, because they hated so much, and so many.

"I'll take them one by one," Stefan Sanberg said, making a sweeping gesture toward the opposite side of the road, where the old school was fully lit up in the falling twilight. Advent stars were hanging in the windows and dark shadows could be glimpsed inside. There were those in the village who thought it looked cozy, like an exhibit in the local history museum.

The whole gang had gathered for a party at old man Ottosson's run-down house. The old man himself was languishing in a nursing home, but a grandchild had a key, and the gang usually met there. Beer and liquor had flowed, and no one really believed Stefan's bluster. They'd all heard him carry on before. A few listened more carefully, and perhaps were influenced, while others sneered.

One of those who was listening was Sebastian Ottosson. He was a listener, who often sat quietly. For that reason he could pick up on judgmental, meaningful glances, and not least become aware of suppressed emotions that could take the most peculiar expression. He read between the lines, knew to take the right position, and there was probably nothing wrong with that. He did like the rest. The problem was his surroundings.

Sebastian stood by the window, observing the old school. He went there a couple of years before it was closed down, but that was not anything that influenced him. There was no nostalgia, no memory that could counterbalance what he felt before its illuminated windows.

If darkies are going to live there, then it's completely worthless, he thought. He knew that he would inherit the house, his grandfather had told him that. Sebastian had ideas about what he would do. A few acres of pastureland were part of the property, and Sebastian had fantasized for a long time about raising sheep and goats. It was a dream that few knew about, but he had figured it all out quietly. He knew that there was a market for goat's milk. He could manage it, maybe by working extra at Sandvik to start with or somewhere else. But blacks as neighbors? They would surely steal his milk and animals. People like that eat goats, he'd heard. What was it called, hammal butchering or something?

It was a blindingly beautiful New Year's Eve. In the days after Christmas it had snowed heavily before clearing up on the last day of the year. The whole village, even the properties with dilapidated fiber cement facades and moldy verandas in shadow, and the farms stained with rural melancholy, was embedded in a conciliatory white blanket. Abandoned farm machinery looked like prehistoric animals dressed in white fur. The roads were edged by snow-burdened spruce and over the fields the ice crystals sparkled. At the edges of the fields, surrounded by inhospitable thickets and invasive aspen trees, deer stood, hesitant, before they stepped out in the open to scratch out a rotting potato under the blanket of snow on Waldemar Mattsson's parcel. The wind was stiff and it would pick up during the afternoon.

And naturally that made the firefighting harder in the blaze that would later light up the whole central village.

"They can't even shovel snow, damn it," Mattsson's youngest son, Daniel, said. His father had a municipal contract, so snow removal was Daniel's specialty, which he liked to talk about, especially after three days of intensive plowing on squares and parking lots and cul-de-sacs in a residential area in Gimo. In other words he was worn out and therefore susceptible. The weather forecast had promised that New Year's Day would also be clear, so he'd gotten permission from his father to go to the party and even drink some alcohol. He maintained that he fell asleep a couple of hours before the old year turned into a new one, and would therefore be freed from all suspicions about participation in arson.

For arson it was, everyone was convinced of that, even if the investigation could not prove it unambiguously. There was talk of lit candles that were left in the kitchen, covered heating elements or overload in the electrical system in the antiquated school, which had not been maintained for several years but could now serve as a residence for seventeen men, thirteen women, and nineteen children. All victims of persecution and war. All in flight.

That night the temperature was eight degrees Celsius. The sky glistened with starlight, but who could appreciate that when the rays were hidden by grayish-white smoke in the freezing wind?

Gösta Friberg stood as if petrified, supported by the kitchen table, on trembling legs, with his feet stuffed in sheepskin slippers and with a damp spot that was growing on his flannel pajamas, a kind of afterbirth to his visit to the toilet. The glow from the burning school created a ghostly fluttering in his kitchen. The rain of sparks came like swarms of countless fireflies.

He had seen everything, or had he? It had happened so quickly, when as was his habit after a trip to the toilet he looked out from his upstairs window. The shadowy figures that were outlined against the snow had moved quickly, there were two or three of them, at first he couldn't decide.

They came from the storage shed and were heading for the south end of the school building, the one that faced toward his house. The view was partly hidden by the lilac thicket that had always served as the boundary between the school property and his own. They moved ahead clumsily in the snow, one of them fell down, but was quickly helped up. But there had definitely been three of them.

It was not just the darkness and their hurried movements that confused him, the whole scene was like a hallucination. Sometimes he hallucinated, especially during the nocturnal trips to the toilet when in the borderland between sleep and waking he thought he saw and heard things. Irma had laughed at him many times when in the morning he told about his nocturnal experiences. "You should write a horror novel," she'd said on one occasion, and Gösta had felt offended, even though he knew she didn't mean anything bad. For him it was almost reality, and he didn't like that she belittled his revelations. It was as if things really did happen, or could conceivably happen in the future.

That was the kind of feeling he got as the shadows were moving in the night. On the days that followed he would recall the sight in his memory, and the outlines gradually sharpened. At last he knew what he had seen and that what he'd seen was reality. He was still a little uncertain about who it was, but fairly sure. The one who ran first, leaning forward like a soldier in battle, Gösta had seen so many times that despite the darkness and the pulled-down cap, he was rather easy to identify. Even so he doubted himself and his impressions.

Flames started greedily licking the facade, at several places at the same time. The blaze quickly took hold in the century-old timber. Soon the whole school was on fire, burning along the full length of the facade. The top floor, which housed a schoolroom and the old teacher's apartment, was already in flames. A broom of fire sprayed in the brisk wind like a blowtorch from the roof, which had partially collapsed. Everything happened so fast. He understood that nothing could be saved. Through the thicket of bushes he could see groups of people. They stood strangely quietly, as if they were attending a bonfire.

Gösta sank down on a chair. Naturally he should have called for the fire department and then gone out to see if he could help out, but the paralysis would not let go. "There is nothing to do, the school is lost," he repeated again and again to himself, mumbling, "fire always wins." Then, during those ghastly hours in the kitchen, it did not occur to him that people could be injured. That was of course an incomprehensible error, a self-betrayal that was grounded in his own panicky terror of open fire.

✦

Three

For a moment he stood completely still, staring down at the snow. He closed his eyes and tried to disconnect what was happening: the screams from the camp, the flames that created a restless fluttering across the sky, the smoke, the cold, and not least the terror.

It didn't work, of course. He would never forget. There was only one thing for Omid, flight, once again flight, his whole life this feeling of shame of not belonging anywhere, forced to take to the roads, to flee. He extended his arm and with his bare hand stroked a tree trunk striped with snow. For a moment he wanted to turn around, but realized that it could be danger-ous. Perhaps the crowd of people would kill him. They didn't wish him well in any event. He knew what people in groups were capable of.

He looked around and returned to the road, hoping that no more cars would drive past. His feet were frozen stiff. His hands likewise. His head was bare. The only warmth was the jacket that he had grabbed in passing. He stamped his feet, waving his arms like his grandfather had done, and then set off at a rapid pace, away, away. The fire behind him was raging, the fire inside him was raging, driving his legs to keep moving.

After a few minutes he saw the glow of headlights, and realized it was a car. A short distance ahead was a narrow side road in between the trees. Not far away lights were shining in the windows of a house. He ran onto the road; clomping around in the deep snow was not an alternative, if he didn't want his feet to freeze.

The car passed on the main road and clearly more were coming, head-lights played between the trees. He headed for the solitary house. A dog barked. He picked up the pace and passed the house. The barking continued but grew quieter. The forest was dense, denser than any he had experienced. The darkness meant nothing. It was the fire that frightened him. The memories of consuming fire.

What had happened to Hamid? He had seen how his cousin had helped the woman from Syria with one of her children, how he carried the child in his arms wrapped in one of the red tablecloths that were on the tables in the meeting hall. He himself had helped Reza, who had a bad leg. The pain made him quietly moan a little, but Omid hurried him, almost shoved him ahead, out the door and stumbling down the steps.

Outside the Swedes had gathered. Silent. No one made an effort to help out. They just stood there, close together, without a word, staring.

It's not my fault, he wanted to scream, but knew that silence was better, to not be seen and heard.

He started crying against the wind. Burning fire or paralyzing cold, always like that, never in between, then the body could relax. The dog unexpectedly resumed barking. A door opened, an oblong rectangle of light burst out on the farmyard. A shadow figure was outlined in the entry. The dog barked. "Shut up!" a man shouted, and those were words that Omid recognized.

For a moment he thought about making himself known. The light that radiated from the open door promised warmth, but he kept running. The snow muffled his steps. Soon he was swallowed up by the darkness. The dog kept barking. The door slammed shut.

✦

Four

Almost five months had now passed since the fire. The police investigation was officially still open but in reality shut down. The remains of the old village school were removed. All that was left was a shed that once housed an outhouse and storehouse, and then the blackened ground, a rectangle twenty-three meters long and eight meters wide, with a sooty chimney that rose like a macabre monument to an arson that took three lives, perhaps four. The rough-hewn granite plinths were carted away by Mattsson's sons.

Especially for those who had attended the school it was of course a disheartening sight. Generations of villagers had been pupils in the hundred-year-old building. When they passed by they recalled episodes from another time, both kooky and clever. They thought about their own childhood, they recalled the two teachers, Edlund and Gauffin. One gruff and the other understanding, but both respected, in any event by most and now in retrospect. Åke Edlund died long ago, that was known, but no one knew where Alexandra Gauffin might be, if she was even alive, so there was great surprise when she showed up one day.

She knocked on Gösta Friberg's door and introduced herself, which was completely unnecessary. Gösta had a hard time holding back the tears as he observed his old schoolteacher, who with her inimitable smile and still gentle gaze was standing so unexpectedly on his stoop. He quickly calculated that she must be over ninety.

"The school burned" was the only thing he could say.

"I heard that later," Miss Gauffin said in a voice that had preserved its timbre. "I was in Odense visiting my sister over Christmas and New Year's, and wasn't really keeping up with what was happening in Sweden."

It's strange how some people go through life unbroken, Gösta thought.

"You look so spry, miss . . . like before," he said, and was immediately embarrassed by his words, which perhaps could be perceived as intrusive, because she was still his teacher.

"You do too, Gösta. The same fine cheeks and glistening eyes."

Then Gösta sobbed. Since his wife died, no one had said anything so beautiful to him.

They had coffee, sitting in the sun against the south wall, but with their coats on. It was spring. The hedge was about to flower over and the buds of the lilac were brimming with longing, or even blossoming, but it was not long since it had snowed. For that reason the spring flowers were somewhat stressed, they did not want to be passed up by the summer flora.

"You live alone now?"

"Yes, Irma passed away a year and three months ago. It still feels strange."

Not a day passed that he didn't think about her.

"Was it cancer?"

Gösta nodded. "She struggled for a long time, and we tried everything. We even traveled to a special clinic in Florida, and stayed for almost two months, but nothing helped. She died late in the winter."

"That must have cost a pretty penny."

"Yes, it was frightfully expensive, over ninety thousand dollars. And as a carpenter you don't exactly have any reserves. I had to borrow most of it."

"It's good that the bank helps out in those situations, but the interest rates must be high."

Gösta's face turned bright red. Miss Gauffin observed him for a moment before she changed the subject.

"And the police don't know anything?"

"No, they have no answers. You know how it is."

"So what are people saying? In the village, I mean?"

"Folks don't want to talk about the misery."

Should he tell what he knew? He'd asked himself that question hundreds of times, ever since the day when the last remnants of the school were still smoldering and the police investigators knocked at the door.

"There's so much talk," he said at last, thereby contradicting his own statement a moment before.

"I was thinking about sticking around the area for a while," Miss Gauffin said, "so we'll have more occasions to discuss."

"Sticking around?"

"Yes, I write a little. My memoirs, you might say, and it struck me that it would not only be pleasant to meet some of my pupils, but also valuable so that my recollections would be richer. We remember things so differently."

"So you're going to interview people?"

"That's going a bit far," Miss Gauffin said.

"How will you get around?"

"A great-grandchild of my brother drives me. He's unemployed and I'm paying him. He forgot his snus and went for a drive. It will probably take a while, because I saw that the store is gone."

The two of them, teacher and pupil, conversed a good while; it got cold around their legs. They went over who was still living in the area, who had died, and what might otherwise be of interest.

"There's a boy missing, isn't there?" she suddenly interrupted the review of old pupils, bringing him back to those horrible days in January. He nodded.

"And nothing new has come out?"

"No, nothing new."

He wondered how much she knew. Two cousins had disappeared. One was located. It was Gösta who found him. It did not seem as if she knew about the circumstances, even though it had been reported, and Gösta found no reason to tell. He did not want to tell. He did not want to even think about the terrible sight that had met him early on the morning of the third of January. It was as if he was an accessory to the boy's death. There were those in the village who implied that too.

The young relative showed up and turned onto the driveway a bit carelessly. He nodded at Gösta but made no effort to leave the car.

"It's a reliable car," Miss Gauffin said, and you could hear that she also included the driver in that assessment. She placed her hand, as if consolingly, on Gösta's knee before she stood up.

Long after the car had disappeared behind Efraimsson's workshop, Gösta remained standing under the mighty maple that his grandfather planted perhaps a hundred years ago. The visit had had a double effect; he had been enlivened, but he also felt melancholy and a trifle anxious. Unconsciously he reached out one hand and stroked the smooth trunk as if it were a woman's skin. He ought to go in, but he knew that fresh air made it easier, as if the anxiety could be aired out.

"Go up to Bertil's," he said out loud and challengingly, and obediently trotted off. It was a walk he had made thousands of times. Bertil Efraimsson was born-again, while Gösta was a dogged atheist, but they were good friends anyway and had been since they were kids. They were a week apart in age, sixty-six years old in July, and had been playmates and classmates as well as neighbors. Bertil had taken over the workshop from his father and uncle, and continued repairing everything from clocks to combines, but when the mechanics were increasingly replaced by computerization he closed down the operation. The decision was made on a Friday. He completed the few tasks he had, and on Tuesday he nailed up a sign that said

CLOSED and then drove to the state liquor store in Öregrund, where he didn't think he would be recognized. There he bought a bottle of cognac of the sort his father and uncle used to drink, the only alcohol he could identify with certainty. It was the first and so far the only time in his life he got intoxicated and boisterous. A strange and in retrospect inexplicable act, which should have led to remorse, but Bertil shrugged off the criticism and surprise of his surroundings, and in Gösta's eyes the Pentecostalist became more human. He saw it as an act of reverence for the generation that preceded him. Bertil's father, who was the son of a blacksmith from Lövstabruk, had slowly built up the workshop from scanty resources and it had supported two families.

Bertil was standing in the yard talking out loud to himself, unaware that his neighbor was approaching. Gösta stopped but his hearing was too poor to make out more than scattered words. Bertil had changed recently, becoming withdrawn and taciturn, even if he had never been a vivacious joker. "Secretive" was a word that occurred to Gösta, as if his neighbor was unwilling to share. Had he also seen something during the night of the fire? Over the years they had always talked with each other, had discussions, supported each other, but now it seemed as if the line was broken. Bertil was increasingly unwilling to socialize, the joint coffee breaks in his kitchen had unexpectedly ceased. He became contrary and strange, and yet another bewildering matter was Bertil's new evening habits. Before he always used to turn off the lights after the nine o'clock news, now the lamps might burn until midnight and even later. Sometimes he could be glimpsed passing like a shadow in one of the windows. Gösta had not wanted to ask what he was doing up so late, but it was strange that a creature of habit like Bertil started behaving in a completely new way. Was it perhaps some illness that was sneaking up?

And then these frequent trips with the car, even into Uppsala, which he previously despised visiting. Now he took off all the time and returned with bags and boxes with unknown contents. Once when Gösta openly showed his curiosity, Bertil said something to the effect that he was "in the process of inventing something."

Bertil was tall, and he still looked imposing, standing there in his yard. Next to him, Gösta had always felt like a leprechaun at five foot five in stocking feet. His profile was like a Mohican, with an aquiline nose and sturdy forehead, his dark hair combed back. In his youth he was called "the Indian." There was a time when women happily stopped by Efraimsson's, on the pretext of buying eggs from Bertil's mother or some other every-day errand, and if possible exchange a few words with the son. He mostly stayed in the workshop, however, and was unapproachable. In the congre-gation too he kept his distance from women, and gradually the courting ceased. He remained a bachelor.

Gösta coughed and Bertil turned around.

"You scared me," he said. "It's not often—"

"We're still alive," said Gösta, "but it's starting to thin out."

They shook hands, a custom they'd had since their youth. After that they stood silently a moment and observed the road and the few cars that passed.

"It's strange," said Bertil. "The blackbird that always stayed at the top of the spruce has fallen silent. This year I haven't heard a single warble."

"Either your hearing has gotten worse or else it's dead," said Gösta.

"My hearing is worse, I know that, but I hear other birds. And dead?" He snorted. "New generations come, they always have, but now it's prob-ably over."

Gösta changed tack. "I had a visitor."

"Who might that be?"

"Miss Gauffin."

"It's not possible."

"Old as the hills."

"That was strange. What did she want?"

"She's going to write her memoirs, as she said."

"And then you'll be included?"

"Well, it's probably more the school and such. She came of course as a brand-new teacher and stayed until retirement. There's quite a bit to re-member."

They both looked toward the scene of the fire.

"I saw the one who set it, in any case one of them," Gösta said quite un-planned, immediately bothered about what had popped out of him. Bertil stared at him, speechless.

"And you're saying that now?!" he exclaimed at last. He seldom raised his voice, but now was such an occasion. "But you told the police that you were in bed asleep."

"Yes, I misspoke."

"Misspoke? That's the dumbest thing I've ever heard."

Gösta turned away; he couldn't bear his friend's agitated expression. He knew himself that it was an extremely idiotic statement.

Bertil took hold of his shoulders, shook him, and forced him to raise his eyes. "You know who it was, don't you?"

"Let go of me," Gösta said. "We've never quarreled and there's no reason to start now."

"It was arson. People died."

Gösta nodded mutely.

"It's someone you know," Bertil observed. "Someone from the village, isn't it?"

"I don't want to talk about it right now," Gösta said, releasing himself and fleeing with big strides. He cursed his own indiscretion. Why in the world he'd blurted out something he'd kept quiet about for months, he didn't understand. Was it perhaps, in some strange way, Miss Gauffin's influence?

Bertil was shouting something after him, but he couldn't make out what. He didn't want to hear, didn't want to look back. It was painful to be at odds with his friend, and he understood that the matter was not over and done with. Bertil was stubborn and would go at him again, try to get him to speak up.

"Maybe it's the only right thing," he muttered as he passed through his gate. It was a sentence he repeated numerous times, but the fear of having to come forward and testify was too great. He knew that he would lose everything. Now admittedly he had lost his honor and had to live with a burning sense of shame, but he could still live in the village and in his house. And what good would it do if he testified? It wasn't a certainty that the arsonists would be convicted anyway. Clever lawyers would be sure to question his credibility and do everything to decimate his testimony, even more so if he came forward five months after the fire.

✦

Five

Sammy Nilsson was puzzled. He thought he recognized the voice, but he just couldn't place it in either time or space.

After the brief conversation, when he repeated the receptionist's information that there was no Ann Lindell in the building, he took the elevator down to Regina Rosenberg to hear what she had to say. She reported what the man had said, that it was Ann Lindell he wanted to speak with, that she was the only one it was possible to talk with.

"He didn't say anything about how or where he got to know her?"

Regina shook her head.

"Lindell is a former colleague, I understand."

"She worked in the building. One of our best."

"And now she's sitting in meetings in Stockholm every single day."

Sammy Nilsson laughed. Regina had learned quickly.

"No, on the contrary you might say."

Regina waited for him to continue, but Sammy Nilsson thought it was a little embarrassing to tell what his former colleague worked with, and he was ashamed that he felt that way.

He missed Lindell. She was good, a little uneven perhaps, and he blamed that on unhappy love and wine, but she had added something, a kind of awareness of vulnerability. She never got thick-skinned; on the contrary, she was constantly surprised and upset about the abominations they had to deal with. She had shared this with Ottosson, onetime head of the unit and her protector. There were those who whispered that he was a dirty old man and for that reason looked the other way when her missteps became all too obvious. He wanted everyone to "get along" and for the atmosphere in the unit to be "convivial." And the fact was that it often worked. During his regime personnel turnover was remarkably low.

And then there was Berglund, the most experienced of them, with an extended, fine-mesh network in the Uppsala he knew so well. He had a way of talking that got people to listen and then talk themselves, perpetrators as well as crime victims and valuable witnesses. He could dig up some superannuated school janitor who could contribute a few puzzle pieces in a "rowdy" student's youth, pieces that might give a hint about where the police should search for answers. Vital information could be obtained from a construction worker with a father who, like Berglund's, had worked at the Ekeby mill, and that solely thanks to the phrasing in his distinctive Uppsala dialect, and with a common circle of acquaintances that was thoroughly thrashed out over a couple of cups of coffee. He did have a weak point and that was the opposite sex; what he so masterfully executed in his contacts with men he never really succeeded in where women were concerned.

Ottosson and Berglund were gone now, both from the force and from earthly life. Sammy thought that had contributed to Lindell quitting as a police officer. She had been dependent on those two father figures, in many people's opinion.

The Violent Crimes Unit had gotten younger. He himself was one of the veterans, but he didn't feel any more secure because of that; on the contrary. These were new times, a new language, new codes for how society and the mutual relationships of people could be understood. Berglund would have immediately embarrassed himself, and the fact was that Sammy Nilsson had thought about resigning. But where would he go?

"There was something in his voice that made me scared," Regina said, interrupting Sammy's train of thought. "It was serious, maybe someone would die."

"How old do you think he is?"

"Between twenty-five and thirty-five, no older. It was the way he talked, this was a young person. A desperate young man. Certainly born, in any event raised in Sweden, in Uppsala actually. No dialect, no accent."

Sammy Nilsson agreed. That was his conclusion too.

"Someone is going to die," Regina said, and he understood that she would brood a lot about that call. She would receive more, she would get to hear a lot of frightening things, but this was her first truly scary call, one that suggested a future violent crime and a person's death.

They listened to the short exchange of words together, one time, twice.

"Maybe that Lindell woman will have an idea."

"I'll talk with her."

"Does she still live in town?"

Sammy only smiled in response.

"Can you make me a copy of the call?"

✦

Six

She sniffed the bare skin on her forearm to confirm that she was no longer a police officer. It smelled different. Everything was different. Sammy Nilsson's call hadn't changed that, of course, but even so it felt a little strange. Like in the past, a message on the phone, a colleague who peeked in and told her something. Ottosson asking her to come to his office. A new investigation, fresh excitement, worry. She'd loved it. Until the love ended, and she went her way. Now it was there again, the curiosity and along with it the worry. Sammy would come out in the afternoon and have a voice sample with him. He didn't want to say what it concerned, other than that someone had been looking for her, and only her.

Outside the window spring was singing; she had also experienced it that way the first time she was here. Then a real estate agent was standing behind her, talking uninterruptedly. She asked him to stop, said that she wanted to observe the view for herself, in silence. The whole landscape was singing. She understood immediately, after a lengthy search, that this was the cottage she had to buy. At first it was a summer cottage, before she moved there for good. Then she'd received a half promise of work, 528 steps, and 22 mailboxes in a due-north direction.

She put a post in the ground, set up her own mailbox with her name in red: *Ann Lindell.* The moving truck came, the three Estonians loaded her household goods in no time. She lit a fire in the newly inspected and approved fireplace. "This is probably the twentieth fireplace by the same mason," the chimney sweep said. "Lundin was his name. My name's Sundin." It was these kinds of contexts and information she liked and had missed.

The first evening the loneliness struck her with full force, but she knew that she would manage it. Maybe. The clock was ticking toward ten when she opened a bottle of wine, even though she'd promised herself to abstain.

Sometimes she thought about Edvard, in some periods fairly often. He'd come to visit a few times. "You can spend the night" had come out of her mouth the last time. Then he was in a hurry to leave.

They were both free to do what they wanted. He hesitated, looked lost the way he had fifteen years ago, but departed, under the pretext that he had things to do on Gräsö early the next morning.

The other day she'd sent a message, asked if he might be in the neighborhood. He had replied that he would come on the weekend. "I'll bring Baltic herring," he'd added, and she had herself a good laugh. That was typical Edvard, who always had to see to the "use" of a trip, or a visit.

Love was hard, lots of things were hard, but work was a success. The 528 steps were easy to take. When after 300 steps she passed the burned-down school, she was returned for a moment to her old profession, as a police investigator. Like all the villagers, she had wondered about what happened, if it was an accident or arson. At the scene she had met some of her old colleagues, including from Forensics. They were convinced that a crime had been committed, not least because camps and refugee housing had a tendency to catch fire—two out of three fires are set, Olle Wikman maintained—but they could not speak with certainty based on the technical investigation.

They stood there and discussed the case like they used to. Suddenly Wikman started laughing. "Are you on duty again now, Ann?" He was one of the few who called her by her first name. The next day she'd brought him a couple of cheeses. She knew that he would never gossip at work, about what she'd said, what she looked like nowadays. There were colleagues she missed. And now perhaps her closest ally of all was coming for a visit, Sammy Nilsson.

Should she tell him about the birds? Sometimes he could overreact, and actually there was not much to talk about. First a dead bird in the mailbox, and to be on the safe side one more the following day, if she had the idea that the first one had squeezed down into the mailbox on its own and died there. She had photographed the second one, a dove, but it was definitely not a dove of peace. The neck was broken.

There was someone or more than one who did not wish her well. She was a stranger. A cop, admittedly a former one, but someone who asked around, didn't sidestep old obstructions and considerations.

Matilda at the creamery had warned her about being too inquisitive, but there was actually nothing that linked the dead birds to her interest in arson. Maybe it was kids who wanted to play a joke and chose an outsider for their tasteless prank?

"Of course I'm curious," she said.

"Shall we listen to how he sounds?"

They listened together. Three times. "No," she said every time after the final words "someone may die."

"Nothing? You have no idea?" Sammy Nilsson's voice sounded doubtful. Maybe he'd seen hesitation in her face. She was bad at lying and Sammy was skilled at seeing through liars.

They sat in the kitchen. Sammy had praised the cottage, which he had only visited a few times previously, how nicely she had furnished everything. And it was nice, both inside and out. Against the south wall the first lilacs had started to bud, the summer flowers were planted even though the risk of frost was not over. But every time she got praise the thoughts of loneliness came, also when Sammy made a quick house inspection.

She thought she was doomed to live alone in the nice cottage with its fireplace and its lovely ceramic stoves, scrubbed wood floor and frosted windows in a neat porch, and a garden with flowers, fruit trees, and a potato patch and everything else that was simply there or that she had constructed and planted. A villager, Gösta Friberg, had helped her a lot. He was a retired carpenter and also handy when it came to cultivation.

Erik lived in town, and that was probably the right thing. He was in his first year of high school and had protested about having to change schools, and friends along with it. Now he was living at the home of an old colleague of Lindell's, with a five-minute walk to school. On weekends he could be convinced to come out to the cottage. Gösta had helped her to renovate and furnish an old shed as a guesthouse. He stayed there, and seemed content. Sometimes he brought friends along from Uppsala. They looked at her and treated her with respect, which she liked.

"I'll put coffee on!" She stood up and started filling the coffee maker. She felt his eyes on her back. Her cheeks got warm.

"Have you heard anything about the fire?"

"No," said Sammy. "You're the one who's more likely to hear anything exciting, I mean, since you live in the village."

"Do you think it's a local arsonist?"

"We got that feeling early on. We did bring in a gang from the unemployed, young guys, and none of them seemed squeaky clean. It was New Year's Eve and many of them had been drinking."

She was grateful that Sammy accepted that she changed tack just like that.

"Things can easily start burning, you mean?"

She turned around.

"It's an acquaintance, isn't it?" he said, mercilessly.

"What do you mean?"

"The caller."

"You don't give up, do you?"

"Can this have something to do with the fire? Was it someone from the village who called?"

"How should I know that?"

"I think I'll skip the coffee."

He stood up and Ann knew that there was no possibility to get him to stay if she didn't get involved in a discussion, one of those that once upon a time they used to have with complicated occurrences where the questions were piling up.

"Okay," she said, turning around and turning off the coffee maker.

"Maybe it was someone from that mold factory where you work."

"If that were so, why would he call?"

"Yes, that's true, but maybe he's not at work, maybe on sick leave."

"Jesus," said Ann.

"Yes, that was a long shot." Sammy reached over and pressed the button and the coffee maker responded by immediately coughing to life again.

"Go out and sit on the porch, I'll be right there," she said. He obeyed, naturally.

"No, I don't know who it is, not sure at all, but the voice reminds me of someone, something." She made that admission solely for tactical reasons. The question was whether he would let himself be fooled.

"Many years ago?" Sammy Nilsson asked.

Lindell nodded and raised the coffee cup in a toast. She had to watch out, she understood that, they knew each other well and he was an experienced investigator.

"Far too many years ago," she said.

"An investigation, but which one? A witness? A crime victim? But that . . ."

"You thought it had something to do with the fire. Is that just because I live here? It may very possibly be so, everyone knows of course that I'm a police officer, was one. You saw that *Upsala Nya* even published a picture when I was standing by the school making small talk with Wikman, only to get attention and speculate that I was on my way back."

Despite everything she was glad that they hadn't mentioned that she lived in the village.

He observed her thoughtfully. "Think about it, listen to the voice. You can keep the USB stick with the call."

"I'll listen," she said and knew that it was both true and false. The conversation was very brief, and there was not really much to brood about, but perhaps there was something hidden to pick up on. Something that wasn't obvious at first.

"But what old investigation would it be? If the voice belongs to a relatively young man, thirty at most."

"I don't know," said Lindell, cursing her passive tone of voice.

"Someone who trusted you."

"There are probably a few," said Lindell.

"A young person."

"I'll listen, I promise. If I think of anything, I'll call you right away. Okay?"

"How's Edvard doing? Does he still live out there on the island?"

"It wasn't one of his boys who called, if that's what you're thinking!"

"Which one of his boys? One of them has had a few interactions with us, perhaps you know that?"

She did not reply. What was there to say?

"He's involved in one of those acronyms, NRM, or was it the Swedes Party? They change names all the time. He was involved in beating up a guy in the middle of town."

"An investigation that wasn't one."

Sammy Nilsson smiled. "Fortunately the local press got involved, so we had to pick it up again."

She knew that they shared an understanding here, that the whole thing had been mishandled from the first moment. It was an obvious case, there were willing witnesses, it happened in public and even cops were filmed. It was only after *Upsala Nya* wrote about it all that things started happening and the investigation was opened.

"He wasn't one of those who were convicted, but he was involved in the group, you can say."

"Bad enough," said Ann. She knew that Edvard was ashamed as a dog at his son's involvement in various racist and Nazi groups. He himself was raised in a Social Democratic farmworker home, and like his father and grandfather was active in the union. His sons' mother blamed their political wandering in the desert on Edvard, that he abandoned the marriage and home and thereby left Jens and Jerker adrift. There was a grain of truth in the criticism, he hadn't been a good father, or rather: He had been a fairly good father, until Ann Lindell showed up and unraveled his life.

He'd been seduced, they had been seduced, and it was probably not so strange, but the force with which the collision happened was baffling to those around them. He broke off from everything, left the work that he'd inherited, his family and house, and rented a room on the top floor of an old estate on Gräsö outside Öregrund. Viola lived on the ground floor, an old archipelago woman of a rare caliber. When she died he inherited the property and a little land, mostly stony hills, meadows, and overgrown ditches, a number of small islands and rocks and fishing rights.

Slowly but surely he became an islander and during that journey he lost his sons. Lindell had seen that early on, but there was not much she could do.

Sammy's theory that it was Jens or Jerker who called was unlikely. They had never liked her.

Ann played the call again and felt that she had to struggle against the tears, looked at the hand resting on the table, the cheese hand, as her son Erik called it. Everything had turned out so different, but now the old days came rushing toward her and from all directions. She turned the hand, studied the lines, the police hand. Her colleagues stepped forward, first the old ones, but also the others, Haver and Fredriksson, even the sly Evert Lundkvist with a past in the secret police, with whom she worked in the investigation where Edvard tramped into her life. He had found a young man in the forest, murdered and barely concealed under a spruce tree, and the macabre find started a process that he was never really able to explain to her. Ann had come to the insight that Edvard lacked the tools for analyzing that journey. There was nothing like that in his family, in his culture. There you worked, suppressing everything that could obstruct your livelihood. For that reason many times he was incapable of stepping right. That he nonetheless didn't stumble all too many times was due to a kind of morality and pride that also was part of the Risberg inheritance.

"That's how you travel," he'd said once, when he had been lured out into deep water by Ann, "without knowing where to. Some are built for outings, carefree in a way that I can admire. I'm not. I was happy as a worker on a farm, proud of my father and grandfather, but suddenly it was as if we weren't worth anything. Our efforts, I mean. It was enough to read the headlines, or look at all the damned game shows on TV, to get that. I was active in the union, but then the local division was suddenly shut down. I was happy with Marita, but we went our separate ways. Can you understand?"

Then he fell silent. *Go on, continue!* Ann wanted to shout. *Talk with me!* But he fell silent.

"You still loved her when you moved to Gräsö, is that it?" she asked, but got no answer. She wanted to hear it, wanted to get him to take on part of the guilt that things went the way they did between them.

She listened to the audio recording one more time, like someone who can't stop picking at a scab. Should she tell Sammy? No, she decided for the umpteenth time, that would be betraying a confidence. She had to search for the boy herself. Well, not "boy." Now he was a young man.

Her free afternoon was ruined. She had looked forward to cleaning up in the flower beds, perhaps plant the perennials she had bought. The bags had been standing for several days outside the porch, with the blossoming bleeding heart that waved seductively, but she stayed sitting in the garden, rocking back and forth. Edvard had a good laugh when he saw that she'd bought a hammock, and she felt a little ridiculous, but mostly wounded by his merriment. She could not say why she'd bought it. In a hammock you rock, and in motion it's harder to drink wine. And it's impossible to place a table in front of a hammock, in other words there's no place for a glass.

In the trees and the thicket the finches were talking away. Ann went in and poured a glass of wine, took a sip, but left glass and bottle behind in the pantry. She brought the phone with her to hopefully find the desperado, as Sammy had called the man who was looking for her.

✦

Seven

"Stay with me, linger here, while I still have hands, skin, and body." With one hand she stroked her belly, the other was raised in front of the window. Her whisper was inaudible to Edvard, but even so he turned around where he was crouching by the potato patch. His one hand rested flat on the ground, his eyes were closed. Was he gauging the temperature, or what was he doing? Was it a kind of primitive ritual, where contact would be established? She knocked on the windowpane.

"It's time," he said when he came into the kitchen. "I can help you trench. It won't take long."

Let it happen slowly, she almost blurted out. He smiled; maybe he was thinking about potatoes, maybe he was thinking about her. Did he see something in her eyes and movements? Perhaps she emitted an aroma, which she'd read that butterflies do when they want to attract a partner.

"It's a good variety," he said.

"What's that?"

"Maris Bard," he said, taking one of the sandwiches she had made. He had dirt on the back of his hand. "But you should have pre-sprouted."

"I did," she said. "The pantry is full of egg cartons with potatoes."

That was Gösta the carpenter's idea.

"I'll be damned," he said, taking a bite. She took it as a compliment and felt how she blushed, and got irritated at herself, but not really. She wanted to be there, in the borderland, like a half-grown young girl, on her way to conquering something. Something big, significant, even essential.

"There's room for a late variety too. Asterix is good. Red-skinned. I plant it every year. It likes the soil you have."

"What kind of soil do I have?"

"Light."

He smiled at her. "And you should be happy about that," he added.

"I am."

Something in her voice betrayed her, because he looked up. He was often insensitive to moods, but sometimes he was like a finely calibrated seismograph, whose needle shook a little at the slightest tremor.

"Asterix," she repeated, to hide her embarrassment.

He finished the last of the sandwich and licked his fingers. "Egg and caviar," he said contentedly.

While they planted potatoes she told him about Sammy Nilsson's visit and the audio file he brought with him. Edvard had met him on several occasions and Sammy was the colleague of hers he liked best.

He made the final furrow straight as an arrow before he commented.

"Do you know whose voice it is?"

"Maybe," said Ann.

"What will you do?"

"I don't really know. That's a life I've left behind."

"Didn't you play private detective a little when the school burned down?"

"I just asked around a little."

"And what did you come up with?"

"That the arsonist is in the village."

"Maybe the call was about that?"

"Sammy was thinking that way too."

She placed the last potatoes in the final furrow. She did it with care and strove to keep an exact distance between the tubers.

"There now," Edvard said, picking up the rake.

She remained crouching a moment before she straightened her back. She studied the grip of his hands around the shaft and was struck by how easy, almost unresisting, everything seemed to be for Edvard, in any event as long as it was about tools and gear. And he did it nicely, stroking the rake with precise movements over the hills of earth, sometimes tapping a little clod that willingly fell apart, covered the seed potatoes with careful pulls so as not to injure the sprouts, evened out and left a completely flat surface behind him.

"Water in two days," he said.

He picked up the egg cartons that had held the seed potatoes and carried them over to the trash barrel by the road, while Ann let her thoughts wander to the man who had called. If it really was who she thought it was, he had nothing to do with the village. She had a hard time seeing him in the country at all. How many years ago was it, maybe fifteen? They had met a few times since then, most recently four years ago. That was before she resigned from the force. He had looked a bit scruffy, resembling his uncle in that respect, but said he'd gotten a job after a period of unemployment. They're building, he had commented. He lived in the same neighborhood where he grew up. Safest that way, he'd said with a laugh. Safety wasn't exactly something you associated with him.

A light soil, she repeated silently to herself. *A light life with a light soil*. She knew that the season was far advanced. Gösta had got his Early Puritans in two or three weeks ago, but that didn't matter. It really didn't matter if any tops came up, or if there was any harvest to brag about.

Wrong! She changed her mind immediately. It would be great if their joint exertions could produce an amazing outcome. Something to talk about, even remember.

It felt strange to work together with Edvard. As if they were a couple, like many years ago. They had collaborated nicely, but she couldn't say anything about that, so as not to appear childish, or rather, because she and no one else had seen to it that the collaboration was broken.

Edvard returned, picked up the rake, but rested on the shaft, looking around, as if he was searching for more tasks.

"Listen, Ann," he said in a strangely serious tone, and she started, fearing the worst. Now he would tell her that he'd met a woman on his damned island and for that reason couldn't visit anymore, because that woman on the island, or in Östhammar, or in Hökhuvud, or wherever he'd met his ladies over the years . . . because that bitch was jealous. She recalled one of them, an artist who moved up from southern Sweden, red-haired and big. She'd seen them outside the state liquor store at Gränby Center. *That's the kind of woman he wants,* she'd thought, *with large breasts and a capable pelvis.*

"Yes?"

"I met a woman last winter."

"I don't want to hear."

Damn you! she thought about screaming, but her jaws were locked.

"I putter around in my Gräsö place. My habits are somewhat eccentric, and even though I might long for a little company sometimes, I'm used to being on my own. During the winter it gets especially gloomy. It's dark and dreary."

Jeez, she thought, *coming from Edvard this was like a whole novel.*

"She still calls, pretty often actually."

"Why are you telling me this?"

"Spring and summer there's always the sea. You can get out, scatter your thoughts."

"You trawl for herring or set out duck decoys when you get horny, in other words."

He looked at her in surprise and then burst into laughter.

"I've shot birds a single time in my whole life. It wasn't fun."

"It was also illegal."

"I didn't know that," he said with a smile.

Ann snorted. He was scared, it was that simple. Scared that he could fall in love with her again. Why did he even come to visit? To deliver herring and plant potatoes? She wanted to ask flat out, but was just as afraid as he probably was, injured as they were by life, by each other. By her betrayal, when she went to bed with an unknown guy, and that probably could have been overlooked, but against all odds she got pregnant. How many times hadn't she looked at Erik and thought, dreamed about, wished: *if Edvard were your father anyway,* and then immediately regretted it, because it was somehow like rejecting her own son.

Did he want to make her jealous? Or were his nonchalant comments about women a primitive way to get back, to show that he truly was desired, but not particularly interested himself? As if intimacy and love were all the same, he had his homestead on Gräsö and the sea.

He smiled! That alone. The feeling of happiness made her ashamed, but she loved his smile.

"Shall we set up the greenhouse?"

She had mentioned that she'd bought a greenhouse by mail order, which now lay in a pile of unopened packages under a tarp.

"A neighbor has promised to help out."

"Is that the carpenter?"

"He's sweet and helpful, but he's gotten a little sad since the fire. He found one of the missing refugee boys. It took a toll on him."

"How did that happen?"

"The boy got into Gösta's car, and he froze to death there. He was lying curled up in the backseat with a blanket around him, but it was almost ten degrees below freezing that night."

"Was he going to steal the car?"

"No, they think he was seeking shelter. He probably got scared and ran from the fire, it was chaotic. Gösta doesn't use the car much in the winter, so he didn't discover the boy until a few days later. Then the car was completely snow-covered. Imagine what a shock, you start to brush snow and scrape windows, and discover a dead boy on the other side of the windshield."

"Poor thing," Edvard mumbled. "Where did he come from?"

"Afghanistan, I think," said Ann.

"Many years ago I was forced to open Viola's old atlas and look for all the countries they were talking about on the news. You want to understand a little in any event. All the wars, all the refugees. And now it's even worse."

Ann was forced to turn away. Edvard's innocent expression and the humanity in his comments, wanting to know, touched her. She knew his worry, even anxiety, so well, where people who suffer was concerned. And who used an atlas these days to get oriented?

"Then he sold the car," said Ann, "and bought another one."

"I'm out there on my island . . . they talk about the climate, refugees, and all the misery . . . I have no connection to anything, other than the little jobs I get, patching a foundation, excavating some pipe, fixing a veranda, or whatever it is. It's a world that rolls along on its own. People are nice, we shake hands, I excavate, they pay, we shake hands again. Then I go home. Make dinner. The next day I take the boat out to the skerry. It goes around like that. There are so many pages in this atlas that I've never visited."

"Are you happy on the island? You saw more people before, didn't you?"

He shuddered at the question, shied away immediately, and she regretted it at once.

"You were pretty active before, in the union, I mean," she threw out to smooth over her question.

"I was," he said, without taking the thread further.

"Where I work no one is in the union, except for me."

"Are you in the union? In the confederation?"

Ann nodded. "The food workers' union."

He looked at her, laughed, and gave her a tap on the shoulder. It was intended as a friendly gesture, she understood that, but she almost lost her balance.

That was the closest to physical contact they came. While he helped her to clean the herring—he'd brought a whole bucket with him—she contemplated her hopes prior to his visit. She had changed the sheets. Admittedly she did that every Saturday, but not with such cool sheets as this time. She had brought home wine, which she also did every Saturday, but seldom such a good, expensive wine. In the fridge there was veal entrecôte and packages of various delicacies that she bought over the counter in Uppsala.

"Maybe the carpenter would like a little herring," he said when she saw his expression.

"I'm sure he'll be happy," said Ann.

"Plant Asterix too, so you have potatoes this fall" was his parting line.

She looked after him, like always his upper body swaying a little, his back a bit more crooked, his hair a bit thinner, straggling in all directions, but basically the same Edvard that she got to know many years ago. She had also changed, of course. The move to the cottage had improved her physical condition, however, and helped her lose twenty pounds. She was moving more, eating more sensibly and at certain times, she was happier and for that reason drank less. She often felt fresh, with a litheness in her movements like seldom before. Didn't he see that she was a different person?

Without turning around he climbed into his pickup and took off. Where was he going, home to the island, or to some red-haired bitch in Norrskedika? What would he do on a Saturday evening? Should she have said something about the filet and the other goodies in the refrigerator? Should she simply have said something about her longing?

"The hell with you," she mumbled, casting a glance at the potato patch. She took the bucket of cleaned herring and trotted off. Gösta would probably want some, likewise Bertil and maybe his sister a little farther away.

Three villagers, three testimonies that she was going to take, not document on tape or in a notebook, but even so. She was still an investigator.

✦

Eight

First up was Bertil. She thought that Gösta would talk as usual, and for that reason it was better to take him last. But Bertil also wanted to get something off his chest, she realized that almost immediately. He was sitting apparently idle on a bench, leaning against the wall, but stood up immediately when Ann arrived.

"A welcome visitor," he said in a voice that betrayed a cold coming on.

"I thought maybe you'd like a little herring." Ann held out the bucket.

He went into the house and came back with a plastic bag. "Gladly," he said. "Cleaned and ready besides."

After the completed transaction they stood there. Bertil looked at her and smiled.

"How long have you lived here now?"

"Two years."

"You like the job?"

She nodded. *Out with it now,* she thought, setting down the bucket.

"Yes, it's a nice village, but a lot has changed," he said. "Before there was more solidarity."

She'd heard that before, how community parties and arrangements had gradually disappeared.

"Since the school burned it's gotten even worse."

"Of course that has an impact, a school means something."

"It was arson," he said suddenly.

"Did you see something that night?"

"Not me, but now I've heard two people say that. Who saw."

"Independent of each other?"

"What do you mean? Yes, now I understand, yes, they don't even know one another!"

Bertil swung the bag of herring. A car passed on the road and reflexively he raised the other hand in a greeting. Ann waited for him to continue, but he said no more. She suspected that Bertil was good at keeping quiet.

He'd lived alone ever since his parents died, about twenty years ago. Gösta had told her a little about his friend and neighbor, that he could be uncommunicative and sometimes a little blunt, but the latter was not something she'd noticed.

"Have you talked with the police?"

"You're the police, aren't you?" he said with a mournful smile, as if that was deplorable.

She didn't comment on that, but instead made an attempt to wait him out, but in vain. Bertil Efraimsson kept quiet, hummed a little, and swung the bag of fish, as if he were a thoughtless child.

"I'm going over to Gösta, but do you think your sister is interested in herring?" Ann had shamefully forgotten her name.

"I would think so," said Bertil.

Her name was on the mailbox: *Astrid Svensson.* They hadn't had that much contact, talked a little about everyday things when Ann passed on her way to and from work. She opened the gate, which was taken from an old railroad car. Ann knew that her husband had been a railroad worker. She was considerably older than her brother, but gave a livelier impression.

Ann hadn't taken more than a few steps on the gravel path before Astrid opened the front door. "You're coming with a bucket," she observed. "It's too early for cherries and not the season for potatoes or mushrooms."

"Herring," said Ann. "I got a lot, so now I'm going around and sharing."

"That was a nice thought, but shouldn't I pay something?"

Ann shook her head. After she had tipped over a couple of kilos into a bowl, they remained standing awhile. Ann was fishing for information; perhaps Bertil had spoken with his sister? But she seemed completely uncomprehending when Ann mentioned that evidently there were witnesses who had seen someone set fire to the school.

"Lord have mercy," Astrid exclaimed. "Is it the police who are saying that?"

"No, there's talk about it in the village," said Ann, feeling like a real gossip going around with loose rumors.

"You were over at Bertil's too, I saw. He loves herring. When he was young he could tuck in twenty at a time. He loved to eat.

"You should know," the woman said at last, as Ann was preparing to continue her herring tour. "There's been a lot of talk. There are those who say that it's folks from outside who set it. There's talk of foreigners, gypsies."

This was the most imaginative Ann had heard till now, but she wasn't particularly surprised.

"And what do you think?"

"You can say a lot about those beggars, but they don't burn down schools. No, I think it was Mattsson's boys. They've never had any sense. Like their father."

"You mean the farmer?"

"Waldemar, yes."

Ann had met him just once, when she had stopped by to see Gösta. Mattsson drove up, stopped and parked a little carelessly by the side of the road, and got out. A sturdy fellow, the archetype for a successful farmer with a kingdom of his own, limited to be sure, but nonetheless a self-appointed local chieftain. He had waved Gösta to him. "I'll wait here," said Ann. They had been talking about payment for his work on the storeroom. It took a while, Gösta had a hard time squeezing out how much it would cost, but she insisted on paying, and for that reason stayed put.

The two men had talked for several minutes, Mattsson leaning back against the car, a pickup striped with clay and dust. Gösta stood with his hands hanging along his sides, seemingly taciturn, as the farmer was doing most of the talking, gesturing in the air with one hand like a one-armed conductor.

She didn't know much about the Hamra farm, the farmer, and his family. She had no concept at all about his sons.

"I knew his mother well, we were good friends you might well say. She was shy, a bit delicate, if you understand, and had difficulty with Albin, her husband. He was too big for her, if I'm going to be frank. They're gone now, so it can be said."

He was too big, what might that mean? In bed, or what? Did he hit her?

"He was big?"

Astrid made a face, where distaste was mixed with anxiety.

"Was he violent?"

"He was hot-tempered, if I may say so."

Ann couldn't keep from laughing.

"Yes, we said that before, when we wanted to joke about it a little."

The old woman smiled. Ann felt as if she'd gained a confidant, who could subtly shift perspective with a change in facial expression or by using words that sometimes concealed, sometimes pointed ahead.

"I'm turning eighty. There won't be anything remarkable, but there'll be a little coffee anyway. Next Saturday if that's good. At noon perhaps."

"I'll be happy to come," said Ann. This was the first birthday party she'd been invited to in the village.

"If the boy is here, he's welcome too."

Ann's first thought was Edvard, but then she understood that it was Erik she meant.

She took the main road back. After the "long curve" she saw her cottage, and when she turned around her workplace was visible behind the groves of young birch trees. Straight across the newly sown fields, the shoots like a light green sea, the red-painted outbuildings at Hamra farm shone, and over the roof tiles of the cream-white farmhouse a flock of birds, perhaps starlings, was flying. It was an idyllic rural scene, a sunny Saturday afternoon in May. Her world these days. When she met Edvard she could not fathom that he wanted to live in the country. In her youth she had longed intensely to get away from Ödeshög, which was still a fairly large community, and moved as soon as she got the chance. She wanted to be in a city, the bigger the better. During her time at the police academy it was Stockholm, then service in Uppsala, and then at last a real backwater with a closed store, a burned-down school, a community center, and a decaying wooden bulletin board up by the "big crossing."

A steady stream of cars passed, probably on their way home from an auction or an estate sale she'd seen advertised, but Ann stood there, as if her thoughts had slowed her down and the growing melancholy made the machinery stop completely. It wasn't Edvard, she was so used to that wrestling that she'd learned it wasn't worth being paralyzed for his sake. Instead it was a sense of aversion and irritation that had slipped up on her, like the one that haunted her during her years as a detective. When something didn't fall into place. It was obviously the fire, it was no more complicated than that, the fire that remained a wound in the village and insisted on a solution. And now the call to the department, where someone had been looking for her, but that riddle was easier to solve. The simplest of course would be for her to call and get this resolved, but did she want to be dragged into something, where "someone may die"? Did she really want that? "No" was the obvious answer. *But I can always pass it on to Sammy,* she thought, and headed for Gösta's house. In the bucket there was no more than a kilo of herring left.

As usual he was working on something. "I'm puttering around a little," he always said, even if it concerned fine carpentry. Like this time. He was standing at his workbench sawing thin rods of an unknown type of wood, and looked up when he noticed her shadow in the doorway. She stepped in and to the side.

"These will be inlays for shutters," he explained without being asked. "It struck me that it would look nice on the little cabin," he added, completing his work without letting himself be disturbed.

"Intarsia?"

"Intarsia, we can call it that," he confirmed with a smile, and Ann felt a bit pleased at knowing the right word.

She observed the fine-toothed saw that he held in his hand, as if it were an extraordinary object. Then a shadow passed by; this time it was a memory.

"It was actually in school that I got interested in woodworking. One of the old teachers, Edlund, did carpentry in his spare time. In the shed he had a workbench and a cabinet with tools. Some he'd inherited from his father, vises, a jointer plane and other planes, worn-out iron that could still chisel out the finest details, and with wooden handles worn smooth. I got to hang out there, he noticed that I thought it was exciting. That was where I became a carpenter."

School again, thought Ann. "What did he make?"

"All kinds of things," Gösta said in a tone that Ann perceived as reluctant. "You had to have met him to understand what an artist he really was."

In order to be a native you had to have met Edlund was her conclusion.

"What about Mattsson? Is he an artist too in his own way?"

"Waldemar?"

"Exactly."

"Why don't you ask him?"

"He seems to be important in the village."

Gösta did not reply. He set aside the saw and started cleaning the bench with a minimal brush, which had been around for a few years.

"What did your father do?" Ann asked, making use of her old slugger tactic, to unexpectedly change the subject in order to create a vague feeling of uncertainty.

"He was a country mail carrier, not here, but over toward Österby. He didn't want to deliver mail to neighbors and people he knew. Over the years a mail carrier learns quite a bit about the customers, especially here in the country. A person should think about that."

Gösta continued talking about the conditions of the country mail carrier, while he made his way out of the workshop, forcing Ann to follow. Ann was convinced that out there he would surely find new threads to spin further on.

He's skillful, she thought, listening with half an ear, while she wondered about his discomfort when there was talk of Waldemar Mattsson.

"It'll go fast now," said Gösta, pointing toward the apple trees, whose rose-white petals created an insubstantial veil on the ground.

"I'm thinking about the village," said Ann. "And . . ."

"Don't do that," he interrupted. "Live here, work and live here, but don't think! And stop asking everyone about everything."

"You mean the fire?"

"This village is doomed to go under, it has gone under!"

She did not say anything, waiting for a continuation that didn't come, before he returned to the workshop, bolted the door, and closed the padlock.

"They won't leave anything alone these days. Edlund never closed his door and didn't lose a single tool. Now they steal everything! Bicycles, copper gutters, lawnmowers, mailboxes, and even the flowers on the grave."

"Your wife's grave?"

He nodded. "Ice begonias. I had planted white and red ones. They're simple, but she liked begonias. And then they stand up well against rain."

He was truly skillful, if the talk about the grave was an evasive maneuver. How could she bring up Mattsson again?

"Who stole them?"

He gave her an angry look in response.

"Would you like some fresh herring?"

She held out the bucket.

"I'll bring the bucket back later," he said while he viewed the contents. "Thanks," he added, but did not look the least bit grateful.

All the herring was doled out, and that felt good. If she got hungry there was filet. She plopped down in the hammock with a notepad of the type she'd used as a police officer. Blank pages. A sudden gust of wind passed through the garden and brought with it a scent of the sweetness of spring. "It'll go fast now," she said, repeating Gösta's words.

"I want someone," she mumbled, but expertly suppressed the thought. "Two witnesses," she wrote. She tried to remember how Bertil had put it. Didn't he say that the two didn't know each other, or else that they didn't even know about each other? What did that mean? Two who didn't know each other and who were in the school, or outside the school, on New Year's Eve. An outsider, in other words. There were actually only two alternatives. Either it was one of the refugees, or else it was a temporary visitor, maybe one of the young people who'd been at the party on the other side of the road. How many were there? Ann had no idea, but she'd heard that the party started early and went on until the school was in flames. She got the impulse to give Sammy a call, but decided to wait. It was still Saturday. He ought to be able to produce a list of the partygoers. But how could Bertil know about the person and what he had possibly seen? There was only one answer: They had run into each other in the crowd of people that gathered on the road outside the school, and perhaps intoxicated, perhaps confused and in shock, he had told Bertil what he'd seen. Was it a "he"? Probably. A young guy who then, when he sobered up and realized the consequences if he snitched, did not want to tell the police anything.

Okay, I'll call Sammy on Monday, she continued her inner dialogue. The other one then? Was it Bertil himself? No, she decided. Was it Gösta? He lived next door to the school and was the person with the best view of the back of the schoolyard. But the carpenter had maintained that he was asleep and that as usual he woke up at five o'clock in the morning, and by then the whole thing was over. His bedroom faced south, the school north, so it wasn't impossible, but how likely? There must have been a lot of commotion. She herself had been at a party in Uppsala, but thought that she would have woken up when the fire department showed up much later, if not before. They had driven with their sirens on, Astrid had told her that, how she sat up terrified in bed, thought she'd woken up from a bad dream, but then realized that the bellowing of the sirens was reality. Shouldn't Gösta have woken up too? In principle it was then too late to witness how the fire started, but this stubborn assertion that he slept heavily the whole night, which Sammy had revealed that Gösta had testified, did not give a good impression.

But if he really was telling the truth and slept through the night, who was the witness that Bertil talked about? Yet another question mark. There wasn't much to write down on the notepad. "Sammy Monday," she wrote a bit superfluously.

Now it was time to confirm what she believed. She looked for his name on the internet. There were two of them, one of whom was on Molngatan in the Gränby area, where she seemed to recall that he lived. Could she call on a Saturday? She realized how silly the thought was, but perhaps it was a way to try to postpone the whole thing.

She entered the number. He answered on the third ring.

"Hi, this is Ann Lindell."

There was a rattling sound as if he'd stumbled on something, and a swear word was heard.

"Have you been looking for me?"

It took a few seconds before he answered. "It may be too late." It was obvious that he was drunk.

"What's too late?" That old tiredness, the police tiredness, suddenly came over her. *Why must it always be so tough?* she thought.

A drawn-out sigh came in response, and then nothing. She waited.

"Ann, it's been a long time."

"How are you doing?"

"I think about Dad sometimes. You know Dad."

"Me too," said Ann, and let the whole thing go as it would. She was no longer a police officer, nothing was documented, she couldn't be criticized after the fact for anything, and she was aware that sometimes it was good to lure the other one out onto thin ice. Sometimes then everything could burst. Berglund had worked that way, borderline sensitive, but with a different form of address. But then he also had a different weight. Maybe he was the one who inspired her, not hesitating for what was low or elevated, where moods were allowed free play.

"And about you too," she added.

That boy, she thought, *Justus, that little guy.* She remembered his despair, his incredible sorrow and longing for his murdered father, Little John. The two of them had nurtured a dream about opening a store for aquarium fish, his father's great interest. He was an expert on cichlids, one of the foremost she'd understood later, but he had supported himself as a welder.

It had been a difficult investigation, where she learned an incredible amount about Uppsala. The tragedy seemed fated. Berglund thought that there were doomed families, who slowly but mercilessly were broken, ground down by the state of things. Justus's family had been like that.

"How is Berit doing?"

He sobbed and let out a hiccoughing sound. Was he too drunk to talk? Maybe it wasn't a good idea after all to call on a Saturday.

"Mom's not doing good," he said in a sharp voice, as if he wanted to accuse someone of having inflicted illness on her. Ann didn't want to hear. Not now.

"You called," she reminded him. "It was Sammy Nilsson you spoke with. You don't remember him."

"No."

"He's good, you could have talked with him."

"Listen! What do you think about all this?"

He moaned as if he was stuck in a vise.

"What do you mean?"

He did not reply.

"Shall we meet on Monday? I'm going into town."

"Where the hell do you live?" Ann was not in any publicly accessible register, could not be searched for on the internet with information about date of birth, telephone number, or address.

"In the country. Shall we meet at five o'clock?"

"But, I can't . . . we can't . . ."

"You don't want to be seen with a cop, even if it's a former one, is that what you mean?"

"Something like that."

"Come to the Linnaeus Garden at five o'clock, I'll be sitting there on a bench. I don't think any of your buddies go there."

"A garden? Where the hell is it?"

"Svartbäcksgatan. You'll have to look it up. Shall we do that?"

She got him to repeat the time and place, clicked off the call, and got up from the hammock.

It was an at once familiar and strange smell that struck Ann when she went back into the house. The herring trimmings, it struck her first, but hadn't she wrapped those in newspaper and then put them in a garbage bag? It was still in the kitchen, but the strange thing was that in the kitchen the odor was considerably fainter than in the hall. She took the bag, looked around, went into the living room, returned to the kitchen, sniffed, looked around again. An indefinable feeling of discomfort came over her. If there was anything she disliked it was unpleasant odors. That was one of the things she had a hard time with in police work, the smell of unaired, stinking apartments and houses, with ashtrays filled to the brim, rotting food scraps, even a corpse in more or less decomposed condition. In that respect Sammy, but Berglund too, had been better, and many times they'd taken over and sent her out in the fresh air.

There was no cat in the house, so she went to the trash barrel. Back in the hall she noticed the smell again. A mouse, she decided. After finding droppings in the kitchen a week earlier she had set out rat poison, which now had evidently produced an effect.

✦

Nine

Ann had extremely diffuse memories of the man who became her son's father. It was a one-night stand. She remembered his first name, and that he was an accountant, or claimed to be. Was he good in bed? No, not particularly. Was he handsome? She didn't remember, thin-haired maybe, fairly tall, light trousers that he had problems getting down and off. They were drunk. She was horny, or something like that. That was all.

She hated him. Maybe a bit unjustified, but she couldn't escape that feeling. She didn't want to hate, not even loathe, simply forget. She was convinced that he didn't know that he was a father.

Now she was waiting at the bus stop for their offspring. Erik. He was strong, that was the word that came to her when friends asked. Because they knew, but thank God not all of it, about what he had to experience when she was down on her knees, burdened by guilt, work, and out-of-control alcohol intake. It was a miracle that he still wanted to have contact with her, but he'd always been loyal. On the other hand, what alternative was there? He had obviously wondered about his father, but it had never been particularly dramatic. "Everyone has a dad," he'd say, "even if they don't show up." Ann waited for him to confront her in earnest. She was convinced that moment would come.

When he was fifteen she had presented the proposal about moving. He put his foot down at once, quite vocally too, and explained that he never wanted to move to "the sticks." She understood that very well, but he couldn't live alone in Uppsala. "I'll drive you," she said. He was in ninth grade, he had lots of friends, and played junior hockey in Sirius with some success.

"Every day?"

"Every day. So you won't have to change schools. And you can keep playing hockey. Then, when you start high school, we'll figure something out."

"There are practices too, not just matches," he said.

"As if I didn't know that, I drive you quite a bit already."

"Okay," said Erik.

So that's how it was. It was tough, but it worked. A win on points. She drank less too, when she had to get there on time or pick him up in the evening. She was often completely beat, the new job was also physical in a way that she wasn't used to, but she gained his confidence that year, it felt that way. They were doing well together, and Ann could feel a bit of happiness and peace for the first time in a very long while. The fact was that Erik's grades improved considerably. The "sticks" were so boring that for lack of anything else he studied a bit more.

She thought that he liked the arrangement. That slightly meditative feature that he'd always had was reinforced. On the other hand he was happier, he dared to trust his mother, avoided anxiously watching and adapting to her moods.

Now he was living in the city, and came out when he wanted to and stayed in his own cabin. Sometimes he showed up unannounced, and then he walked from the bus stop. It struck her that he did that solely to please her, as if to say: *I like you after all.*

All young people should have that independence, she thought, when she saw the bus appear on the highway. She understood that it was also a kind of freedom from her, but she told herself that it didn't hurt anymore. Sometimes she felt that she gave him too much freedom, but she dismissed that thought.

He was the one who had called unexpectedly and said he was coming out. "Is there anything in particular?" she had asked, but he simply said that he wanted to get a little fresh air. Then he'd laughed, as if to play down his statement, which could be interpreted as that he wanted to see her.

"What's that smell?" was the first thing he asked. The stench in the house had increased.

"Maybe a mouse that died," said Ann.

"A mouse? More like a dead hippo that's rotting," Erik said. He walked around in the house, simply to decide that it was worst in the hall.

"Have you checked upstairs?"

Ann shook her head. It didn't feel good. Something was wrong. She realized that it couldn't possibly be a mouse.

"Mice that eat poison dry up," said Erik.

Ann peeked up the stairs to the top floor, where her bedroom was.

"Yuck," she said. "Stow away your things now, and I'll make something to eat." That was a signal that made him respond. He was always hungry. He took down the key to the cabin.

She unwrapped the veal entrecôte, which she had taken out earlier, and set it on the cutting board. A neat little 450-gram piece. Erik stood outside his cabin with his hand on the doorknob. It struck her that he was a handsome boy. She pulled open the kitchen drawer and saw immediately that the knife was missing. The best one, which she'd bought in a specialty shop in Lisbon, the one she always used for meat. Now it wasn't in its place. She looked up and out the window. Erik had gone in and shut the door. Now he was no doubt sitting in front of the computer. She searched through the drawer again, took out the few kitchen utensils, eyeballed the counter and the sink. The knife was gone. She was always careful with that knife, she washed it by hand, dried it off, and stored it in a cork case, advised by the salesperson not to let it bump against other utensils unprotected. "This knife is the most important tool in your home," he'd said. It had been priced accordingly, 105 euros.

She turned around. Someone had moved the knife, maybe stolen it. The front door had been unlocked while she went around doling out herring. An hour's absence and that was more than enough for an intrusion. Someone had seen her leave the house and taken the opportunity, was that it?

A freezing cold spread in her body, as if a contrast fluid was being pumped into her veins. Her muscles tensed. The anger would come, she knew that, but now it was only a budding terror that was growing ever stronger. A knife, why would you steal a knife? The computer was on the table, the thief hadn't bothered about that. A knife.

Was the intruder still in the house? She took the vegetable knife down from the knife holder on the wall. It was far from as imposing as the Portuguese meat knife, but the blade was about ten centimeters long in any event and well sharpened. She had been a lone wolf in her work with the police, going her own way many times, and she had nearly paid with her life. Now she was in her own home, surrounded by an increasing odor of decomposition and obliteration, because of course it was death that stank. *I'm calm*, she told herself. *I'm calm, nothing can make me paralyzed.*

The stairs creaked as usual. The smell increased with every step she took. The bedroom door was wide open. The door to the other room, which was mainly used for storage, was closed. Centuries ago she had taken part in an exercise at school, how you go in and search a house. Twenty-five years later none of this actually had any significance. Now it was just her, alone with a vegetable knife. She breathed deeply, tested the blade against her left index finger, squeezed the handle, feeling the sweat beading on her hairline.

It was on its back, and strangely enough gave a human impression. The four legs stuck straight up, as if it were participating in an exercise session. The belly was cut open and in the middle the knife was thrust in. This was perhaps what made her the most upset; how would she ever be able to use it again? How would she be able to cut up a piece of meat without thinking about the dead badger in her bed, without associating it with the stench? The hell she could!

She took out her phone and photographed it from all angles. It struck her that perhaps she had seen the badger earlier; could it be the one that was lying a bit down the road the other day, right at the edge of the ditch, swollen up with its paws in the air? Someone had picked up the badger, dragged it into her house, set it on her bed, and stuck the knife in it, releasing a loathsome stench.

After a minute or so, while her disgust and agitation had free rein, she wondered whether it was worth the trouble to call Wikman at Forensics. But she abandoned the thought; they had other, more important things to do.

In the kitchen she retrieved garbage bags and plastic gloves. She hesitated a moment before she took hold of the bed linens and rolled the badger up in them, leaving the knife where it was, and consigned the package to the garbage bag. The pillows went into another bag. The mattress was bare. Should she throw it away too? She postponed that decision. She could spend the night in the other room, where there was a bed already made.

She would never tell this to Erik, not to anyone! It was not just the stench, the whole thing was dirty, as if someone had shit on her and her cottage. The danger involved that someone so explicitly threatened her with this Sicilian action receded for the mental assault that had occurred, and she felt shame. She was the one who was ashamed! It was not just a crime, it was also an assault on her peace of mind, on her right to live undisturbed and peacefully in a little village in a backwater.

That evening she did something she'd never done before. They were sitting in the hammock, the entrecôte was consumed along with some of the vegetables she'd bought. She'd had two glasses of wine, which was the unstated daily ration when Erik was at home. Most often she could hold herself to that. Erik had made popcorn, which he was eating with rare fervor.

"When the school burned," she started, "most people thought that someone started it."

"An attack," said Erik.

"You can say that," she said, wondering about the choice of words, but found it striking.

She told him what the CSIs had unofficially concluded, that it was arson, and after that about the neighbors and their talk.

"You've never talked about your job," he said. "Not even when I wanted to know."

"I couldn't, it was that simple. But now I'm no longer a police officer, and I can gossip as much as I want, with whomever I want."

He observed her in that penetrating way that Ann somehow found embarrassing, as if he was searching for something unstated, while he carefully ate his popcorn. It lasted a couple of seconds, but it was enough, she recognized the expression in his young face. Then he smiled and tossed another handful of popcorn into his mouth.

"And yet it feels strange, as if I'm doing something wrong."

"And what do you think? About the fire, I mean?"

"Attack," said Ann.

"Wonder how it feels to murder a person."

"One time I asked a murderer."

"And what did he say?"

"It was a she, and she said that it felt like she'd done humanity a favor."

"She didn't regret it?"

Ann shook her head.

"Creepy."

Ann did not want to mention that she could partly understand the woman, because murder must be condemned, even if the victim was a thoroughly rotten human being, and a violent rapist.

"Maybe the person who set the fire thinks that too, that he was doing humanity a favor," said Erik, after a long moment of silence. "Someone who hates immigrants. We have a few at school, they've started an association, they call themselves National Swedes."

"National Swedes," Ann repeated, tasting the words. They didn't say much.

"You know that the Nazis in Germany were called national socialists," said Erik.

"Would they be able to burn down a school?"

"Some of them maybe. Sigvard is in it."

"Sigvard from Årstagatan, your old classmate?"

Erik nodded.

"But he was so nice."

"Not anymore. If you knew what he says about the police."

"I don't want to hear," said Ann. She didn't like the turn the conversation had taken.

"They hate everything," Erik continued, after another load of popcorn.

"You'll get a stomachache," said Ann.

"How did she do it?"

It took a moment before she understood what he meant. "With a frying pan," she said, and remembered with horror the sight that met her and Fredriksson when they stepped into the couple's bedroom. The woman was sitting straight-backed on a chair in the kitchen, with her gaze stubbornly fixed on the counter, mute before their questions. It was only after a couple of days in jail that it all came out, and she recounted coldly and factually about a fifteen-year marriage which for her entailed mental and physical abuse.

"The strange thing was that her mother was probably an accessory, but we could never prove it. There were two frying pans, one with the mother's fingerprints. Both she and her mother maintained that they'd been put on the handle after the murder, when her mother was going to hide them."

"What story did they come up with, that she used both frying pans herself?"

"Just what I asked. She claimed that she struck her husband alternately with two pans, one in each hand. They were of the old model, cast iron, heavy. We have a similar one from Grandma and Grandpa. Both maintained that the mother was asleep in a guest room when the murder happened."

"They stuck together," Erik observed.

"That they did, and it was for the children's sake. The couple had two boys, that the grandmother had to take care of. If she'd been convicted too, well, then there was no one for the kids."

"How many years did she get?"

"Seven, if I remember right. There were extenuating circumstances, after all. He'd abused her for years. But murder and arson, can't we talk about something else?"

"I'm going to Berlin, we can talk about that. I talked with Lyset and Viggo yesterday, and there's room for me too," Erik said, and Ann understood that this was a reason, perhaps the main one, that he had come out. He wanted to get the plan approved.

"This summer?"

"July."

It would be the first time he had traveled abroad without her. What did she know about Berlin? Absolutely nothing. She knew that David Lys had an older brother in Berlin.

"How fun," she said. "But do you have the money?"

"I've been saving," he said with a smile, and that did not surprise her at all. Erik was careful with money, not to say stingy.

She had vacation in July herself, and it struck her that she wanted to travel somewhere. It had been a long time since she'd been abroad.

"I've thought about Greece this summer," she said.

"Alone?"

"We'll have to see," she said evasively, unexpectedly embarrassed by the thought of a hotel room with a view of a blue sea, a made bed.

"Oh, how secretive."

"A little heat would be nice," she said, mostly not to feel so awkward before his grin.

"You don't like it when it's too hot."

"This woman with the frying pan, I actually saw her not too long ago."

"Where was that?"

"In the city. Now she's free."

"Fifteen years with violence, approximately like you," said Erik, "and now you're free. You can even go to Greece."

Their eyes met. He'd said it with warmth. *We allow each other,* she thought, *we allow each other to live.*

✦

Ten

The echoing calls came from far away, as if someone was standing on a distant hill, crying out over a valley. That was how Ann perceived it before she woke up properly.

"It's burning!"

She leaped out of bed, glanced at the clock, which said 2:13, pulled on her bathrobe, and hurried downstairs. Erik was standing in the front door.

"Where?" she screamed. "What's burning?"

When she looked in the direction he was pointing she saw an orange-yellow flickering glow at the edge of the forest, about a kilometer away. The sun had gone down a couple of hours before but you could already sense the first light of dawn.

"Did you call the fire department?"

"I called 112."

"Did they know there was a fire?"

"I don't think so. What is it that's on fire?"

"I don't know. There's a farm over there, but it's more to the left, you can glimpse the silos. What address did you give?"

"I said that they should drive to Tilltorp, the same village where the school burned last winter. From there they would see the fire."

She reached for the phone, which was on the hall table, and entered Gösta's number. After a short time he answered in a confused voice. "Friberg here."

When she explained that there was a fire he let out a moan.

"You have the Mattssons' number, don't you? Call them! We've called the fire department." She clicked off.

"We'll drive there, let me just put some clothes on."

She suspected that Erik hadn't gone to bed, but had been sitting in front of the computer instead. *Fire extinguisher,* it occurred to her as she pulled on a pair of jeans. *I don't have one. There isn't one in his cabin either. Not even a smoke alarm.*

Soon they were on their way. Ann saw that the lights were on at both Gösta's and Bertil's. Erik didn't say anything, but she understood that he was shaken. She herself felt a little of the old excitement, a kind of expectation, even though she knew that something unpleasant, even terrible, was waiting. It was that characteristic a police officer has to have. Ola Haver, a colleague from Violent Crimes, didn't have it. They'd discussed that issue many times, and finally he had to quit the force, even though he was actually a good investigator.

She had passed the *Hamra* sign a number of times, but never had any reason to visit the farm. Now she turned onto the recently graded but still bumpy road, even though she was not certain it was the right way to the scene of the fire. Before long they reached the farm, a sizable two-story farmhouse with a couple of smaller buildings as wings. A barn was nearby and what she thought was a pigpen a little farther away.

Everything was dark, except for the farmyard light. Ann honked. "There's probably no one home," Erik commented.

A dog started barking, hard to tell from where, but no lights were turned on, and no person appeared. The first light of dawn had gradually scattered the darkness, but the cool night air remained as fog over the fields. They drove on, rounded one of the wings, where the doghouse was, and continued on a narrow gravel road that led into the forest. They saw the glow of fire between the trees. The car bounced on the winding road and the dark tree trunks were much too close. For a moment Ann got a sense of déjà vu. Some time in her former life she had driven in a similar way, too fast, but still not fast enough.

"When we get there you'll have to stay in the car until I say so."

With a hundred meters left, as they rounded a grove of trees, for the first time they got an overview of the fire scene. It was a small building. In flames.

Ann drove as close as she dared. She got out, Erik too. She made no attempt to stop him, realized that there was no point.

"It hardly seems to be a residence," said Ann. "It looks more like an old workshop, maybe a smithy. You see the chimney. They located smithies away from the farmhouses just because of the risk of fire."

"The things you know."

"I've investigated fires in the country," Ann said curtly, because now she'd caught sight of something that worried her. A bicycle was leaned against an apple tree, and behind a container a vehicle was visible. It appeared to be an older Toyota pickup.

"What's making that sound?" Erik asked.

Ann had also heard the whining sound. "It may be that way," she said, feeling a little stupid, uncertain herself what she meant.

"It's a dog howling," said Erik.

"Do you think so?"

"A dog is dying in there."

Maybe someone will die, she repeated silently to herself. She was seized by the loathsome thought that it could be a person moaning they heard, but told herself that he was right.

"We can't do anything."

"I understand that too," said Erik.

Helplessly they observed the fire for a minute or two. Sparks flew toward the sky. Shouldn't the fire department arrive soon?

"Wait here, I'll look around."

"And what if it's a crime scene?"

"You've watched too much TV," said Ann. She kept her eyes on the truck and at the same time fished out her phone, using speed dial to make a call. It was a woman who answered.

"Hi, my name is Ann Lindell, a former colleague . . ."

"I know who you are. My name is Regina."

"Hi, Regina," Lindell said, feeling how unnecessarily irritated she got. "I'm at the scene of a fire, it's all in flames."

"We've gotten a call about that, an Erik Lindell called. If that's the same fire."

"It is. Is anyone coming, and when?"

"The fire department is on its way, and a colleague from Östhammar. It's a ways to drive. Do you live out there in the wilderness? Was it your son who called?"

Lindell overlooked the impertinent questions, thanked her for the information, and ended the call.

The truck was unlocked. She opened the door and was met by a strange combination of smells, heavy and oily mixed with sweet perfume. As she guessed it was a Toyota, at least ten years old. She leaned in, careful not to leave any prints. The backseat was full of boxes, a helmet, various tools, and bags from a hamburger chain. A working vehicle in the countryside, she thought, and backed out into the fresh air.

A car approached. She thought at first it was the police or the fire department's command car, but it was Bertil who came bumping along. He parked beside Ann's car and with some difficulty got out of his ancient Simca.

"Hi, Erik," she heard him call. "Is your mother here somewhere?" She was happy that Bertil remembered his name. They hadn't met very many times, after all.

Erik pointed toward Ann. Now there was no hesitation in Bertil's movements. "Does anyone live here?" she asked immediately.

"Yes, Mattsson's youngest, Daniel."

"Is that his truck?"

Bertil nodded mutely.

"Does he have a dog?"

Bertil shook his head.

"Not as far as I know. He's not exactly an animal lover."

"Where's the rest of the family? The big house is completely dead."

"The whole gang was going to Stavby. Gösta forgot to say that when you called. Maybe he was confused. He never called Waldemar. He wanted me to do it."

"Why isn't Gösta here?"

"He's afraid of fire. He hates fire."

"Is he afraid of Waldemar Mattsson too?"

Bertil observed her for a moment before he replied. "What have you heard?"

"Nothing, I'm just guessing."

She suddenly became aware of Erik, who had slipped up and was standing right behind her. She ought to let go now, she realized that. He was young, after all, sixteen years old. It was night, perhaps it was arson. Perhaps there was death. But she was forced to go on.

"Bertil, who set this?"

"You think it's arson?"

"Of course," said Ann.

"That was an easy calculation," Bertil said with an unusual sharpness in his otherwise well-modulated voice.

"Who did it?"

Bertil turned his head and observed the fire. At the same moment sirens were heard in the night, such a familiar sound for Ann, but in her new environment so foreign.

"It's the old smithy," said Bertil. "My father worked the bellows here when he was young."

Why must everyone in the village sound like ancient monuments? Ann thought.

"Erik," she said, suddenly moved by the fire and the darkness that surrounded them. She turned around but didn't know how to continue, what she wanted to or could explain to her son. *I ought to be terrified of the fire too,* she thought. She had never told him about the crazy woman in Kåbo, an encounter that nearly cost Ann her life.

"Yes, Mom," he said, meeting her gaze. She heard that he actually didn't expect her to go on, but instead wanted more to mark his presence. He rarely said "Mom."

"We should probably move to our cars." She wondered how many possible tire tracks they had disturbed. She should be ashamed.

"What did Mattsson say when you called?"

"They're on their way," said Bertil, and now his voice had lost its edge. On the contrary, there was something very resigned in his voice, so much that Ann turned around.

"Do you think that Daniel is in the building?"

"I don't know," said Bertil. "Waldemar said that he didn't go with them to Stavby, he was going to see a friend."

"And stay there?"

"Not a clue."

"The truck is here," said Ann.

"That's just it," said Bertil.

"There are those who say that Mattsson's boys were behind the school fire."

"I understand where you're going," said Bertil.

"Stop now!" Erik exclaimed. "You're not a police officer anymore. Why should you get involved?"

"The stripes never go away," Bertil observed.

"And the other son, Andreas, right? Where is he, does he live at the farm?"

Bertil turned away, it was obvious that he didn't want any more questions.

"I think it would be good if you took it a little easy. The world is big, but this is a small village, and there are those who get irritated," he said without taking his gaze from the fire.

It did not take long for the firefighters to subdue the fire and at last put it out completely. They worked in silence. A handful of curiosity seekers had shown up; they too stood silently. Everyone awaited Waldemar Mattsson with his wife, Wendela. They came at last. If Ann had understood Bertil right, double-W, as he called the farm couple, had a great deal to drink during the evening, and for that reason had to find and waken someone sober who could drive them home. The chauffeur got out and observed the fire for a moment before he got back in the car to return to Stavby.

Ann did not think he was acquainted with the Mattssons. He was sober and a driver and nothing more. She shivered; the early morning hour was damp. Streaks of fog mixed with smoke from the smithy.

Wendela Mattsson was supported by her husband. She gave a fragile impression. They went as close to the burned-down building as they could. By their side were the fire commander and a police officer from Östhammar, Ann thought his name was Åke Brundin. They had met briefly in connection with an investigation of the murder of a young Thai woman in the archipelago, but were not well acquainted. He nodded at her, no doubt a bit surprised at meeting her there. Wendela reached out a hand toward the burned-down building, a gesture of helplessness.

The farmer's sturdy figure made Ann think about what Astrid had said about Waldemar's father, Albin, that he was too big for his wife, and she wondered whether it was the same a generation later. They were talking with the fireman. Whether his task was easy or not naturally depended on whether the couple had made contact with their son Daniel. Åke Brundin stood quite still, but observed Waldemar from the side with a strange expression on his face, as if he distrusted the farmer's words, or in any event was very skeptical about what was said.

"Shall we go?"

Erik nodded. They said goodbye to Bertil. Brundin looked up when he saw that they were leaving. He gestured that he wanted to exchange a word. Ann went up to him.

"What are you doing here?" he asked without further ado.

"I actually live in the area. It was my son who called the fire department."

"So that's how it is. What do you think?"

Ann could not keep from smiling. Brundin was a policeman, not the bullshitting type that beats around the bush with small talk.

"Wouldn't you say it burns a bit too often in this village?" Brundin continued when she didn't react immediately.

"That it does" was all she had to say.

✦

Eleven

It ended up being a strangely late night and early morning for Ann Lindell. Erik had collapsed in bed, incapable of commenting on what they'd experienced, but she found it impossible, if not immoral, to go to bed a second time.

She stood by the kitchen window, her primary lookout. She was a little tired, but not at all drained like before, more like clearheaded, sober, sharp-minded as she herself thought. The morning light created a strange shimmer over the lot, the fields, and the edge of the forest. Or was it strange? It was divine, she caught herself saying out loud. "Divine" was a strong word for a nonbeliever, or did she believe in something higher? Who created all this? The answer came immediately: all the generations before, she herself, Gösta a little, and then Edvard, who arranged the potato patch with such finesse and precision. That was the creation story.

"It doesn't matter," she continued her monologue out loud.

Her next thought was poignant. It was Erik she was thinking of. This wise boy, soon a young man. Life tumbled toward her with all the force the years and experiences gave.

"Blame it on the light." *Edvard would laugh at me,* she thought, not without pain, but then the thought turned to its opposite: He would envy her. Be silent. He had his own baggage. Experiences both new and old. Once, a single time, he had talked about his grandfather, a key figure in his home district, a "man with stature," as the minister had said at the funeral about the atheistic farmworker. What the minister didn't know was that Edvard's grandfather had killed a man. It had happened in Paris sometime in the forties. Edvard was the only one who knew about the incident. He had come across a kind of diary in his grandfather's posthumous papers. It was a pimp or possibly a cuckold, it depended on how you wanted to interpret his grandfather's somewhat contradictory notes, who had surprised his grandfather with a woman. "Black as soot," it said in the notes, but it wasn't clear whether that meant the woman or the murdered man. There was a notation that Edvard remembered in particular, about blood in a sink, dark red against the white porcelain.

An hour passed like that. She thought about the present, or what had happened the past few years; memories from her childhood and youth never tormented her. Of course she could call to mind what her parents had said or done, remember schoolmates or neighbors in sleepy Ödeshög, but it never made her anxious. She often thought that it was boring and monotonous when people talked about their early experiences. *So what!* she wanted to exclaim when her few girlfriends harped on perceived or alleged injustices. She would have fallen asleep on a Freudian couch. And probably dreamed about sex.

She thought about where Daniel Mattsson might be, burned up in his simple cabin or sleeping it off at a good friend's place, unable or unwilling to answer his phone.

Perhaps the answer would come sometime that morning. She entered the same number she'd called during the night. Regina answered again.

"You work long shifts," said Ann, trying to sound friendly and relaxed.

"Better paid on the weekends," said Regina, whose voice still sounded perky.

"Who's on duty in Homicide?"

"Bodin and Olsen" was the immediate reply.

She had worked with Olsen for a few months before she quit, but the other officer was an unknown card. Then it struck her that perhaps Regina could help her.

"Can you check on something?"

"It depends."

Ann rattled off the license plate number that she had automatically memorized during the night. The answer came after just a few seconds.

"It's registered to one Albin Daniel Severin Mattsson, with two tees and two esses, registered at Hamra farm. A 2006 Toyota pickup. It hasn't been inspected or taxed and has had a driving ban since early March."

"Driving ban," repeated Ann, who thought she'd seen the pickup drive past her house as recently as the other day.

"Is he a victim or a suspect?" Regina asked.

She's almost too quick, Ann thought, and avoided the question.

"Is he in the crime register?"

"Should I answer that?"

"If you can produce the information and if you want to. It was his house that burned."

It took a moment before Regina answered. "He has a minor assault in 2016 and was questioned for informational purposes in connection with the school fire in Tilltorp. That's all."

"What was the assault about?"

"Now the questioning period is over," said Regina, but without sounding abrasive or cross. Ann understood that there was no point in nagging. She could bring it up with Sammy.

"You're quick, Regina," she said. "Thanks a lot."

"A person needs a little variety and excitement in life."

"That's so true," said Ann.

"Did you recognize the voice? The man who was looking for you."

"Maybe," said Ann, who felt the need to be a little accommodating. "But I'm not sure."

"I thought he sounded nasty."

"He was probably a little drunk."

"No, it wasn't that. 'Someone may die,' he said."

"Yes, he said that, but I thought it sounded like he wanted to prevent that."

"Maybe he got cold feet," said Regina.

They ended the call. Ann left the kitchen and went out in the yard. She peered toward Hamra, but everything was quiet, besides a bird of prey that came sailing over the edge of the forest to the south. She suspected that the technicians had started their work, if the scene of the fire had cooled enough. If someone had been trapped inside, the body would have been found at this point. *Don't go there,* she had to persuade herself.

Instead she carried the bags of perennials to the water faucet on the wall and gave the plants a much-needed soaking. Today they would go down in the earth! She walked around in the yard, inspecting how the beds were sprouting, finally decided where the greenhouse should be placed, walked along the fence toward the road and counted how many stakes had rotted and for that reason had to be replaced. All of this was to scatter her thoughts and keep herself from getting in the car.

Two contrary characteristics were demanded of a police officer, her colleague Berglund had thought. First and foremost empathy for crime victims and their families, and sometimes actually for the criminal too. But a full measure of superficiality was also required, the capacity to overlook the human, the deeply tragic, and be carried along and away by the tension in the crime, the mystery. It's the same feeling as with a fire, he'd maintained. The terror, and the fascination.

That Berglund showed up in her thoughts once again was not that strange. It was the sound they had heard outside the smithy that created the association to her colleague, the howling that could come from a human being, or a dog, or simply some kind of draft that appeared when air was sucked away.

As a young policeman Berglund and a colleague named Styhr had responded to a fire on Lindgatan in Petterslund, a multifamily building that was in flames. He did not remember much, basically only two things: One was how a collie, trapped by the flames, howled, then whined, and finally fell silent. The dog's owner collapsed screaming on the street, but it was the dying dog's howl that had moved him the most. The other was how a little baby, a babe in arms, as Berglund put it, was thrown from the fourth floor and capably caught by a man on the street, and whose life was saved that way. "We were slightly acquainted," Berglund had said. "He was a painter. I remember his hands, stained with paint, holding the child."

* * *

Erik had not appeared. Ann was accustomed to the solitude and the silence, especially on Sunday mornings. But this morning was different. She could not really appreciate the stillness, and she thought she understood why. She needed the excitement, the unexpected, what she got a taste of during the night. It was a macabre thought, she knew all too well, but that was nothing to lie about. She wanted to go up to the edge, lean over the abyss, peer down into the darkness, even throw herself over. "I'm no better than a pyromaniac," she muttered to herself. But she was not at all ashamed, more like the contrary, she had a tingling contentment as if she was about to seduce someone. *Give me a violent crime or two and I'll perk up,* she thought. That was probably what Erik had seen as they stood before the old smithy, when he admonished her not to get involved.

The sun stood high when Gösta Friberg came walking over. Erik had not woken up yet. Ann was sitting in the hammock with a third cup of joe. Gösta said hello and turned down coffee. He was stepping in place, perhaps because he was a little ashamed about his behavior the last time they met, but more likely because he did not want to openly demonstrate his curiosity. Ann was amused by his irresolution and at the same time felt a little contempt for him. She went on about the greenhouse, and when he did not show any great interest, she changed to questioning him about what type of paint was best for fence posts.

At last he could no longer contain himself, but instead blurted out what he'd come for, if she'd heard anything about the fire at Hamra.

"Well, I thought about going there, but I didn't want to disturb my old colleagues. There are probably more than enough curiosity seekers to shoo away."

"And Daniel?"

"I really don't know. How is he?"

"What do you mean?"

"I mean as a person, I don't know anyone in the Mattsson clan."

Gösta did not answer immediately, as if he wanted to get back for her unwillingness to communicate. He stepped a short distance away, pretended to observe the patch of ground where Ann had said she wanted to put the greenhouse, took off his cap and scratched the top of his head, as if the placement were a tricky problem.

"Maybe it will be fine," he said. He returned and stood by the side of the hammock. "He is the way he is."

"And how is that?"

"Hot-tempered, you might say."

"Tell me about it."

"One moment this, the next moment that."

It was ridiculous. *Grumpy old man,* thought Ann, striking herself on the knees as if she'd made a decision, and quickly stood up. "If you don't have time, an acquaintance offered to help out." Gösta looked completely bewildered.

"He's coming this week," which was wishful thinking on her part, but a lie. "He said it wouldn't take long to put up a little greenhouse," something Edvard had not said a word about. "Was the herring good?"

Just then the door to the guesthouse opened and Erik came sleepily out, as if it were choreographed.

"Time for lunch," said Ann. "Then he shows up."

Gösta said a curt "Bye," with an expression that could be interpreted several ways. She watched him. Gösta hates fire, Bertil had said, and maybe that was true. Fires were not good for his peace of mind, that was evident in any case.

"What was up with him?" Erik asked.

"Male menopause," Ann said in an attempt at a joke that even she didn't think was amusing. Instead for the first time the bile of the village came up and burned in her mouth. It was a small village, she was aware of that, but now it stood out as more limited than ever. If you only have a handful of neighbors, you become cut off by your surroundings in a way that she never had been before, not in any event since childhood. She could not conjure Gösta Friberg away. Not the Mattssons, Astrid, or Bertil either. By moving to the village she had chosen them, and that could not be undone. The villagers on the other hand had the possibility to exclude her.

"Don't be so crabby to people," said Erik.

✦

Twelve

The body was a woman's. It was severely burned, except for a triangular section from the left hip down to the right knee. An area of the throat and neck had also been preserved; some patches of skin stood out like a light, flaky collar against a sooty background. She was lying on her side, with her legs pulled up as if in anxious protest, in what had once been a kitchen. None of the furniture remained, all possessions were burned up or severely damaged, almost carbonized. Water that had collected in small pools still glistened. The CSIs thought that some charred bones in the vicinity of the woman were from a small dog.

"How old is she, do you think?" Sammy Nilsson asked. Bodin had called him in already at six o'clock in the morning, with the justification that he'd been part of the investigation of the school fire and knew the circumstances in the village. Olsen was feeling a little under the weather besides, as he often did, Bodin suspected. Recently relocated from somewhere in Västmanland, he himself had never been northeast of Uppsala. Without complaints or protests Sammy got in his car, stopped by Bodin's house in Gamla Uppsala, and picked up his colleague. They left the city in silence, and it was not until they reached Rasbo that Bodin told him that it was a son of a former colleague who had called in the alarm. Sammy realized that it must be Erik. It pleased him that the kid visited Ann. That was how she had expressed it with a crooked smile: *Erik visits me sometimes.*

The medical examiner sighed. "Young," he said. "She probably hasn't given birth."

Sammy did not ask what he based this on, but instead took it for granted that it was true. Too much talk could cloud their view. Instead he looked around. The old chimney still stood straight. The forge was also preserved, even if part of the brickwork had cracked from the heat. It had experienced heat, but never anywhere close to the past night. From what he could understand the old smithy had been sparsely furnished. A bachelor pad, Bodin said with a sardonic smile. The impression was dominated by the remains of roof tiles that had fallen down and were now spread out across the floor.

What had happened? How had the fire started? In the same village and with the same explosive development as five months ago, a nighttime fire that harvested human lives. Was it set? What could the motive be? These were the same questions they had asked last winter. Would they be any wiser this time?

"My bet is smoking in bed," the doctor said, as if he had read Sammy's thoughts. He pointed at a scorched, cracked saucer on the floor in the middle of the room, where two bedposts testified that a bed had stood there. Sammy recognized the plate's blue-flowered pattern from his grandmother's kitchen.

"Ashtray," he said.

"Or nighttime snack," the doctor said.

"There's not much I can do. You and the technician should get to work in peace." With long strides Sammy left the remains of the house, squeezed through the drapery that had been set up as a screen. The whole area was cordoned off, with a radius of perhaps fifty meters from the smithy. There was nothing to see, but even so a dozen curiosity seekers were hanging around outside the blue-and-white tape.

While he pulled off the shoe protectors he glimpsed a movement in the thicket behind the house. It was Bodin, leaning forward and sniffing like a tracking dog. Sammy had the idea that he had a hard time with the sight of the burned, killed, and maimed. A new Ola Haver, he thought, scared of the dead, but really good at context and surroundings.

Sammy walked in the exact opposite direction, came up to the barricade, and took a look at the farm. He knew that his Östhammar colleague had spoken with the Mattsson couple during the night. Sammy had run into them earlier and was not overly pleased. The husband, Waldemar, had an assertive style, like the local pope he was. His wife, Wendela he thought her name was, was not completely healthy, he recalled. Neither of them had then had anything to say about the school fire.

They had been informed earlier by the fire commander that the body of a woman had been found. "Thank the good Lord," Wendela had exclaimed.

Now it was time to talk in a bit more organized and precise way. Halfway to their house Sammy Nilsson stopped, went back, and searched for his colleague in the thicket.

"We should question the boss himself," Sammy said and informed him briefly about the situation, but refrained from telling him about his previous experiences and impressions of Waldemar. Bodin could form his own understanding.

"Have you found anything exciting?"

"No, I can't say so. I see this as an initial search, then others will have to search the area, won't they? It's pretty difficult terrain."

"That sounds sensible," said Sammy, who found his colleague more and more reasonable.

"Who is she?"

"No one knows. Probably only Daniel Mattsson can answer that question, and God only knows where he is."

"Hope the smoke fumes took her first. It's usually that way, isn't it?" said Bodin, kicking at a stone so that it flew off noisily.

Waldemar Mattsson looked anything but fresh. Tired and hollow-eyed, maybe still a little hungover, with grayish beard stubble over his puffy cheeks, he was standing apparently idle in the front yard of his house. Perhaps he was observing the somewhat unsuccessful circular planting in the middle of the yard, which surrounded a flagpole that was much too short. No flag was flying. He threw out one hand, as if he were involved in a discussion. His mouth was moving.

Sammy Nilsson placed a hand on Bodin's arm to get him to stop. They observed Waldemar Mattsson, fifty-six years old, sole owner of more than a thousand acres, a small part of which was cultivated, the rest forest or nonarable, and a lake full of fish, married to Wendela, née Sigman, a few years younger than her husband, with two sons, Andreas and Daniel, thirty-two and twenty-six years old respectively. Together with his sons Waldemar owned three trucks, a trailer, and an unknown amount of construction machinery in a medium-sized haulage firm.

All this was in the public record. Sammy and his colleagues had routinely mapped Mattsson in connection with the school fire. He did not recall the details, but found the farmer a typical representative of a kind of arrogant citizenry in the Swedish countryside; tough, expansive, and successful, with influence in their own parish, but perhaps not too far beyond.

When the rumors that his sons had been involved in the arson started circulating, the father had laughingly dismissed all the talk. "They want to get at me" was his only comment. "The gossipmongers want to get at me."

He was almost a caricature of a conceited estate owner, a bit reminiscent of a former prime minister. Sammy did not like him then, and there was nothing that suggested he would do so now.

"Mattsson!" he shouted. The farmer turned around.

The two policemen went up to him. "Have you gotten any sleep?"

"What the hell do you think!"

"I don't think so," said Sammy. "You've thought of course about who the woman is."

"I have no idea."

"And Daniel, he hasn't been in touch?"

The farmer stared toward the driveway into the farm.

"His brother, Andreas, shouldn't he be here?"

"Someone has to take care of the work. We're driving for the Peab construction company, and we're damned far behind. Then you can't cancel just because it's a Sunday."

"Not even with arson?"

Mattsson did not reply.

"Why have you taken out a Winchester?"

Bodin's question surprised Sammy, but Mattsson just sneered. A rifle was leaning against the closed lower door to the house. Sammy hadn't seen it earlier. *There you go,* he thought, *talk diverts attentiveness.*

"Are you satisfied with it?" Bodin continued.

"We'll have to see," said Mattsson. "Are you a hunter?"

"I have the old model," said Bodin.

"M70?"

Bodin nodded.

"Yes, let me tell you this," Mattsson said, turning demonstratively toward Bodin. "In these times it's best to be armed. You never know what's waiting around the corner."

"Has someone threatened you?"

"Not just me. Look around you. What does it look like?" The farmer had lowered his voice, as if he wanted to whisper a confidence. "What? Turn on the TV and it's nothing but disasters, and now we're importing them, as if we didn't have enough problems of our own. Would you want that Gaddafi as a neighbor? That's what threatens me—and you. These days those who like to move in God's free nature can't be secure."

"He's dead," said Sammy.

"Yes, you see!"

"But . . ." Bodin tried to interject.

"No buts! When Wendela and I were picking mushrooms last fall," he swept his arm out in a vague direction, "we met a whole pack of blacks. At the head of the line were two perky do-gooders. The blacks should be introduced, as they said, or whatever the hell word it was they used."

He waited for a reaction, but when none came, he continued. "In our forest. They should be introduced! What will the next step be?"

"You have no idea at all where you son is?"

Mattsson turned around and stared at Sammy Nilsson.

"He's an adult."

"Your wife doesn't either?"

"Don't drag her into this."

"Her son is missing, his house burned down, his girlfriend or buddy burned up inside, so she's already dragged in."

"When I know where he is I'll let you know."

Perhaps it will be the other way around, Sammy Nilsson thought, but nodded. "Do you mind if we look around the farm a bit?"

Waldemar Mattsson muttered something, turned on his heels and walked toward the house, took the steps in two quick strides, seized the Winchester with his back to the police, and lifted it with one hand in the air before he disappeared through the open door.

"The free man's gesture," Bodin said without an ounce of irony.

"Shane," Sammy Nilsson answered with a grin.

"Richard Widmark," said Bodin.

"It was Alan Ladd."

"It's all the same, isn't it?"

Afterward Sammy Nilsson could understand very well how the two of them made associations to American film culture. Mattsson was "American," it was not just the presence of the rifle and what it symbolized. There was also the narrow-minded self-importance mixed with a large measure of pride, bordering on self-satisfaction. He guarded his land, his acres and his farm, his family, his porcini mushrooms.

"What could get someone like that to change?" Bodin wondered. They were still standing on the farmyard, thoughtful about where Waldemar Severin Mattsson could be redirected. "I mean, get involved with the Red Cross, become a refugee guide, or mushroom guide, light candles for those drowned in the Mediterranean, anything at all that might refer to a life outside the village."

"Nothing, I think. Possibly a religious conversion or a rap on the skull."

Bodin broke their passivity by heading for what Sammy thought was a machine shed. Large doors of corrugated sheet metal rattled faintly with the slightest gust of wind. He observed his colleague. *Wonder what he hunts?*

They strolled almost carefree past buildings, some weathered by age, with logs on the shady side discolored by shimmering blue mold and striated pale red on the south side, and with roof tiles that had crumbled from decades of sun and rain. The doors were fastened with iron bolts inserted in crude latches, some of which surely forged in the now-destroyed smithy. Other buildings were newly constructed, and there sheet metal, aluminum, and functionality dominated. The locks were sturdy, all of the same manufacture, probably with similar locking mechanisms. It looked reasonably clean and orderly; the whole farm exuded entrepreneurial spirit and a certain measure of affluence.

Bodin moved around familiarly. It was noticeable that this was his environment. He looked around and no doubt registered details that Sammy Nilsson himself missed or simply did not understand.

"No animals," observed Sammy, who wanted to contribute something anyway.

"Too little profit and too much tending. They've had hogs, but no longer, and even earlier dairy cows" was Bodin's concise reply.

The survey produced absolutely nothing, in any event not anything that visibly led the investigation forward. Despite the poor outcome they wandered quietly back toward the scene of the fire. It was a lovely morning at the end of May, and they had something to think about. The closer they came, the stronger the smell of fire became, and their thoughts acquired a different, more mournful direction.

"I called for a dog," said Bodin.

"You think there's anything to search for?"

"There always is."

"I think I'll go for a drive. Maybe Lindell has something to contribute. She lives here, after all."

"It's okay, I'll take care of Fido, or whatever his name might be, and his master."

Sammy Nilsson jumped into the car and bumped back on the gravel road. He thought such a poorly laid and maintained road was strange when the farm had access to all kinds of machinery. As he turned onto the highway he peered back up toward the farm. Everything looked idyllic, the birch trunks with the rich flora at their feet, the moss-clad stones sticking up and the birdsong with calls of every type, but he knew from before that idylls often concealed atrocities. It was when humankind took possession of the landscape that everything was soiled. That was also something Bodin talked about, although in different words, and Sammy sensed more than knew that his colleague was brooding about something. In due time he would probably blurt out what this was about.

Ann Lindell was on her knees, planting flowers in a ring on the back side of the house. It was such an odd sight that Sammy observed her awhile before he coughed.

"You'll never be a spy," said Lindell, and he understood that she had heard him coming.

"Nice" was all he said.

"I thought Bodin and Olsen were on duty."

"How do you know that?"

"I talked with our mutual friend Regina."

Ann stood up and inspected the result of her work.

"She told me that Daniel Mattsson was living in the cabin and that his truck had a driving ban."

"I didn't know that," Sammy said without hesitation.

"I've seen that pickup driving on the road all spring."

"We found a body, a young woman."

"What!" Lindell exclaimed. "I'll be damned."

Sammy could not keep from smiling.

"No trace of Daniel?" she continued.

"No, but no one seems worried. Or rather, his father, Waldemar, doesn't seem to think that anything has happened to his son. And it bothers me that he can be so dead certain. He doesn't know who the woman is."

"And everything is burned up? I mean . . ."

"There is nothing that says anything about anything. In any case not yet. Maybe they can find something."

"Whose bicycle is it?"

"You saw it? Don't know. It struck me that maybe the girl came to the smithy by bike."

"Then Waldemar ought to know who it is, if it's a local girl who cycled to Hamra farm."

Sammy was getting more and more pensive, but Lindell forged ahead in her good old style.

"Daniel's minor assault in 2016, what was that about?"

He didn't want to show Lindell that he was surprised about how well-informed she was, but instead tried to adopt an indifferent expression and tone. "A Somali that Daniel head-butted outside a sausage stand in Gimo. The boy fell badly, cutting himself on an aluminum strip. A lot of blood, but no permanent injuries."

"More than in his skull perhaps. Wonder where he is?"

"I'll check," said Sammy, but he did not think this would lead anywhere. "How's Erik doing? I heard that he was the one who called about the fire."

"Good, I think. He slept a long time, wolfed down an early lunch, and now he's probably sitting in front of the computer."

"Is he going to keep playing hockey?"

"I think so. He hasn't said anything different."

Sammy noticed that she was pleased. He was too.

"Like before," he said, and Lindell picked up on what he meant immediately.

"This is what I miss. When we had time."

"You were good," said Sammy. "But I think this is even better."

Ann smiled and leaned down to brush off the soil from her knees.

"And there'll be less wine now, right?" he said. She looked up, met his gaze, something that was inconceivable a couple of years ago when he brought up her drinking.

He observed her. She closed her eyes, but there was something alert, even clearly beautiful, about her face. She looked healthier than ever. The spring sun had also contributed.

"Good. The country and the cheese. The flowers."

"The country and the cheese, and the solitude," said Ann. "There were too many people."

"Wrong people."

"So it is. I missed Ottosson and Berglund, but that wasn't decisive. It felt as if everything was running between our fingers."

"Results weren't good enough, in other words."

"Yes, now a lot is being written about that, I've seen. Your new boss Stefansson is really going all out. The shootings are blamed, but I think it's been in the works a long time, a kind of impoverishment."

She pulled off her gardening gloves.

"New types of crime, new types of police," said Sammy.

"There must be some good examples? Where the force is functional."

"Do you know how many cars we confiscated last year?"

"How would I know that?"

"To be exact, three hundred and nineteen with connection to criminal gangs. Sentences of more than seventy years imprisonment. We've put a blowtorch on them. But forget about that now, what do you think, was the smithy fire set?"

"The smithy fire, is that what they're calling it? Yes, it was. But now I want a glass of Chablis. Sit down in the hammock and rock a little, but don't fall asleep, I want to tell you something."

He obeyed, curious about what she had to tell. After ten minutes she showed up again. She had changed her shirt, from a big checked one, perhaps Edvard had left it behind sometime, to a white, ironed, secretarial one with starched collar, a choice that surprised him. The stained work pants had been replaced by a pair of skinny jeans. She had clearly lost weight, he noticed.

She sat down beside him, a glass in hand. A scent of soap and perfume, she'd had time to shower too.

She raised the glass, took a mouthful, and then resumed her line of reasoning about the fire. "It's not by chance that there are fires in the same village in the course of a few months. And what is the common denominator?"

"Daniel Mattsson," he said, like a compliant schoolboy.

"Exactly, that's the circumstance that makes me distrust chance. Find that young man, you've solved the whole thing. Maybe. It depends on Daniel's specific gravity. Another thing: Can you check whether there was anyone from outside the village at the New Year's party, buddies of Daniel and the other local talents?"

"What are you thinking?"

"Just an idea," said Lindell.

"Partygoers who perhaps are not that loyal to the village, you mean?"

"Something like that."

Sammy did not get a chance to expand on that as his phone rang just then. He answered. It was Bodin.

"We've found him. Dead."

"Daniel?"

Lindell looked puzzled while Bodin told him that it didn't take Freja more than ten minutes to nose him up. That it was Daniel Mattsson was probably the most likely.

"Who the hell is Freja?"

He got out of the hammock, while Lindell took another sip.

"'Fido' was a bitch," said Bodin. "The body was lying squeezed between a couple of boulders, hard to get to. I did say that it's a difficult terrain."

"Someone else's handiwork?"

Lindell looked at him. He thought he saw something expectant, even ravenous, in her face.

"Yes, you can easily say that. It seems like a sharp object was poked into one eye."

"Listen," said Sammy Nilsson. "Now we have to get the big machinery going. I'm coming over. Will you call Stefansson?"

He clicked off.

"Albin Daniel Severin Mattsson's specific gravity is falling, I understand."

Sammy nodded in response, already on his way. Suddenly he cursed himself, why had he so willingly volunteered on a free Sunday? He recounted what Bodin had told him.

"Holy shit," he exclaimed. "I'm the one who has to have the talk with the awful farmer and his wife." But he regretted it at once. "Excuse me, they have actually lost a son."

Lindell extended a hand in a calming gesture. Erik had come out of his cabin. Maybe he'd heard Sammy's outburst.

"Now there's both arson and murder," Lindell said.

"What?"

"I'll tell you," she said, putting her arm around Erik.

Sammy stopped. "Yes, exactly, you were going to tell me something?"

"We'll deal with that later," said Lindell. "I'll know more tomorrow."

✦

Thirteen

"You understand, he was my son."

The big hands, marked by labor, rested on the garden table. His hair stood on end, his eyes beyond all rescue, his face heavy, not to say destroyed, from fatigue. Waldemar Mattsson had explained that he could not be inside for more than a short time, he felt like he was suffocating indoors.

"My son."

Sammy Nilsson observed the farmer. Gone was the arrogance, gone the forceful impression.

"I'm sorry," said Sammy.

"What is it worth?" said Waldemar, raising one hand in a feeble gesture. Sammy sensed that this was about the farm, perhaps about life as such.

"I was proud."

He got up, but remained standing in front of the table, as if he was giving a speech. "You, the hunter," he said, turning to Bodin. "You know. That feeling on an early autumn morning, there is silence, no birds are in motion, most of them have flown away or are busy fattening up, the morning chill is nothing because you're dressed to meet the mist over the clearing, and you have coffee in your thermos. Maybe you've had a shot, but only one. Everything is familiar, I mean, you recognize everything so well. It's home. Nothing more is needed. You don't need anything else."

"Did the two of you hunt together?" Bodin asked.

"He was at his best in the woods. He was no driver or machinery operator, if I'm going to be honest."

"Was he an arsonist?" Sammy asked. "I have to ask, because there can be a motive, whether or not the rumors in the village are right. Someone may have gotten the idea to take revenge."

Waldemar Mattsson sank down on the chair but his expression did not change. They sat silently a good while before he brushed his hand across the tabletop. "Pollen," he said with a sigh. Is that how you think it happened? Someone sets fire to the smithy, Daniel manages to get out, the arsonist runs into the forest, Daniel runs after and catches up, and is beaten to death."

"It could have happened like that, right?" said Bodin.

"He was no fighter," the farmer said.

"He was convicted of an assault in Gimo, I'm sure you remember that?"

"That black tried to cut in line, and what business does a Muslim have at a sausage stand?"

"There are vegetarian alternatives," said Sammy.

"Have you ever been in Gimo?"

The farmer observed him with a contemptuous gaze, as if Sammy were an inferior person you didn't have to take seriously.

"And Andreas?" said Bodin.

Mattsson took his eyes off Sammy and turned his head.

"What are you getting at?"

"His brother dies and he's driving gravel for Peab."

"Fuck you!"

"I want to solve a crime," Bodin said calmly.

"I have to go in to Wendela. Her sister has to go home to her husband, the professor who can't even tie his shoelaces." He stood up and walked away, stopped after a few steps, turned around and looked at the two policemen with an expression that was hard to decipher. "She despises me and she'll gladly tell you why. The sister that is, but don't believe everything she says."

"Okay," said Sammy.

"One thing," said the farmer. "My wife is a little . . . She forgets things, she can answer a little wrong sometimes, but that's nothing to worry about, in any case not for you. You don't have to treat her disrespectfully."

"Why would we?" said Bodin.

"As I said, she can say crazy things sometimes."

Waldemar Mattsson disappeared through the doorway. No Winchester, no victory gesture this time. A few minutes later a woman came out, headed for her car without giving them a glance, but changed her mind and made a ninety-degree turn. If Wendela stood out as pale and shaky, her sister gave a completely different impression. Sammy thought she was between forty-five and fifty years old, but she moved like a young woman, and walked quickly toward the garden chairs where they were sitting, stopped a few steps away from them and inspected first Bodin, then Sammy Nilsson.

"How are you going to solve this?"

"With honorable and careful police work," said Bodin, and Sammy could not help smiling.

"You haven't exactly distinguished yourselves before."

"Do you live in the village too?"

"No, thank God."

"What's your name?"

"Ananda Frykholm."

"What do you think happened?"

She looked around. "Daniel ended up in bad company."

"How bad?"

"He's dead," she said quickly, as if that was an answer to the question. "He was a good kid. For a long time he was quite wonderful."

"Was Daniel an organized Nazi or something like that?"

Bodin's question would worry anyone, but Ananda Frykholm did not bat an eye.

"He wanted to be a forester, but Mattsson flatly refused. He thought that Daniel didn't have any aptitude for study, and maybe that's right, but he would have managed it. Then everything would have been different. Instead he had to drive dump trucks and machinery. He felt inferior, always in the shadow of Mattsson."

"By Mattsson do you mean Waldemar?"

"There's only one Mattsson."

"Is he domineering?" Bodin asked.

"Have you studied psychology?"

Bodin explained that it was his major interest, right after glider flying. At first Ananda Frykholm looked startled, but then she smiled.

"Daniel compensated, he became loudmouthed, wanted to show off. It didn't always work out that well."

"His brother then, Andreas. What's he like?"

"He's . . . different, of course. You'll have to form your own impression."

"Are you and your sister close?"

"Not particularly."

"Is she sick?"

"She's going to be, Alzheimer's or something. But she's always been a bit feeble and confused."

"But you have a good memory, I understand."

Ananda Frykholm overlooked the comment. "She was that way already as a child. Now she's collapsed."

"Daniel set fire to the school, people say," said Sammy Nilsson, making it sound as if it were a general understanding, an obvious truth.

"That may be, but where he is now there are no prisons."

"What did he say to you, about the school, I mean?" Bodin added.

"Why would he talk with me about the fire?"

"You were close to each other," said Bodin, who actually was interested in glider flying and psychology.

For the first time a breach could be glimpsed in Ananda Frykholm's facade. She turned toward the farmhouse. "I have to leave," she said.

* * *

"Okay," said Bodin when the car started. "A one-and-only Mattsson, a confused Mrs. Mattsson, and a cocky sister-in-law who felt sorry for her nephew."

"It was wrong to let Wendela see the body," Sammy said, studying the cloud of dust that hovered over the driveway from the farm.

Bodin showed his agreement by humming, but his thoughts were elsewhere. "There was someone who was extremely angry," he continued. "He was thoroughly beaten to death."

"Why does someone kill?"

"Passion, money, or revenge," said Bodin in a mechanical voice, as if the answer was programmed in.

"Confusion and obsession," Sammy added.

"Is religion a sign of confusion or an obsession?"

They were chatting, Sammy felt, but they were both occupied by Ananda Frykholm.

"Strange that she has a man's name."

"I think it's lovely," said Sammy.

"Ananda was Buddha's assistant, known for his good memory."

"Historian of religion, really?"

"My wife's fault," said Bodin, but did not explain further. Sammy thought that perhaps it would come out later. His colleague liked to release information a little at a time. Sammy nonetheless felt satisfied. Bodin could gladly be his permanent squire. Their dialogue reminded him of what he'd had with Lindell.

"There is only one Mattsson," he said.

One of the CSIs was approaching. He and two colleagues had spent the whole day around the smithy, which was now also considered the murder scene, and a gang of uniformed colleagues had fine-combed the surroundings without finding anything sensational. A pair of shoe prints had been secured on a road a few hundred meters from the smithy, but no one could say whether it had anything to do with the murder. Some thirty objects had been collected, including a picnic basket, a gym shoe, and an empty Marlboro cigarette pack. In other words it was as usual, many impressions and conjectures, but no certain results.

Journalists and photographers had flocked around the farm and the surrounding area since before noon, and despite the barricades by the highway some had made their way up to the smithy. Blowflies, the otherwise balanced Bodin had scolded them in an outburst, which Sammy believed was caused by the strain. Bodin did not want to let on, but it was obvious that he was not feeling well.

"Should we give them anything?"

"Let Westin take care of that," said Bodin. Westin was the police spokesperson. A bore, some thought; others said efficient and factual.

"I'll give them basic facts, then he can take the rest tomorrow, okay? If they're going to have time for anything sensible for tomorrow, it has to come out now."

Bodin shrugged. Sammy went up to the group of journalists, two of which he recognized, and introduced himself.

"Fire last night," he started without any ceremony. "A young man lost his life a hundred meters from the scene of the fire. He's been identified." It undeniably sounded dry and factual, but the message could not be conveyed in that many ways.

"Is it arson?"

"Too soon to say."

"Who is the young man?"

"We are waiting to release his identity."

"Is he a Swedish citizen?"

Sammy nodded. He understood very well what the next question would be, and it was the young reporter from the Uppsala paper who asked it.

"Does this fire have anything to do with the school fire last winter?"

"We can't see any connection. At the present time."

So it went for a few more minutes. He did not think he could say anything about the woman who died in the fire, not as long as she was not identified. The group of journalists wanted more, that was obvious. They had waited a long time for a few morsels and admittedly in an environment that was arrayed in spring garb, but it still felt unnecessarily rural.

"Is the young man connected to Hamra farm?" The Uppsala reporter did not give up that easily.

"What's your name?" Sammy countered.

"Jonas Fälldin," the journalist said with a smile.

"I read your reporting last winter."

"How nice."

Sammy felt inside that he shouldn't go further, but did so anyway.

"I liked your description and survey of how refugee facilities have a tendency to burn up."

"You didn't answer the question."

"At the present time we are not releasing the identity. I'm sorry, but that's how it is." Sammy made a gesture with his hands, which could be interpreted as resignation, to suggest that it wasn't his decision to make.

Jonas Fälldin did not look resigned, more the opposite, as if he'd received a suggestion for a new series of articles. Despite his youth he seemed to be the most experienced in the group. He closed the worn notepad he'd taken notes in. It surprised Sammy that journalists still used such an outmoded technology as paper and pen.

The work was over, in any event at the scene. Bodin and Sammy would return to Uppsala after a long shift.

"It's my birthday today," said Bodin when they got in the car.

"Congratulations," said Sammy. "I'll drive you home directly so you can have cake. I'm going to stop by the office."

"That was nice, but the party is over."

Sammy sneaked a glance at his colleague to discern if there was possibly some double meaning in his laconic comment, but saw only an expressionless face.

He called home and told his wife that there was still a little to do. "Internal surveillance," she said in a voice that dripped with acid.

"Exactly. Ann gave me a few suggestions."

"Ann?"

"Her son called in the alarm. They live out there, I'm sure you remember that."

That was his response to her poison. Angelika was no fan of Ann Lindell. It was childish, but he didn't have the energy to once again defend and explain why he worked all day on a Sunday.

"When are you coming home?"

"At nine o'clock or so."

"I see," said Angelika.

Nothing more was said.

✦

Fourteen

The beaters were in motion, round and round in the cheese vat, which held five hundred liters of cow's milk. The thermometer showed thirty-three degrees Celsius. Everything was as it should be. But somehow not.

The sounds on the other side of the glass wall disturbed her, where Matilda was talking with Anton about God knows what. How chatty that old man could be; Ann heard in Matilda's voice that she was tired. The voices blended with the music from the loudspeaker on the shelf. Then came the news, P4 Uppland. The fire at Hamra farm was the lead item. The reporter sounded dissatisfied somehow. Lindell got the idea that he would like to say "suicide vest" or something like that, perhaps "Islamists" or "terror," something alarming that measured up to the reports from the hot spots in the wider world. He recalled the school fire and speculated like everyone else about Saturday night's fire as a revenge action, spoke about the rural idyll that had now been lost. "Is Tilltorp going to be a concept all over the country, more or less like Knutby?" he asked, and answered with an unhesitating "Yes." "The area will always be associated with a changed Sweden. A new country is emerging, a country that many don't recognize," he continued in an attempt to sound ominous.

"What an idiot!" Lindell exclaimed, so loud that Matilda looked up. Their eyes met through the glass wall that separated the rooms. Maybe she thought that Lindell meant Anton, because she gave a thumbs-up.

She checked the clock: Half an hour until the rennet would work. There was time for a little coffee. She left the white-tiled room with the monotonous circular motion of the beaters.

Matilda Wiik resembled a sweet champignon in her bonnet and white protective coat. She smiled, which she often did. She was the one who had initiated Lindell into the mysteries of cheese production. Her father had grown up in Burträsk and made Västerbotten cheese for decades. Matilda inherited much of his skill, but left her home region and married Anders Hedman, born in Skebo in Roslagen. They met at a course in Jämtland and made an immediate connection. Ann Lindell could see, with admiration and sometimes a bit enviously, how they still seemed newly in love.

Anders could not imagine living in "Lapp hell," and Matilda had given in, so they moved south. The idea was that they would start their own business. By chance they came across a property in Tilltorp, and there they started their creamery. That was ten years ago. Success came quickly, locally produced organic cheeses had started to be popular, and it did not take long before they were supplying cheese to shops and restaurants all over central Sweden.

"What was Anton yacking about?"

"He's still mad as hell because he doesn't get to come with us."

Ann was supposed to go with Matilda and Anders to a cheese fair in England at the end of September. Anton was not part of the plan. He was retired, they reasoned, and worked at the creamery mostly as therapy, a way to get out of the house, and Ann understood that Matilda had reminded him of that.

Matilda suddenly looked serious. "What is happening?" she said. Until then the two of them had not had time to talk about the fire at Hamra.

Ann told her what she knew, which wasn't much. A relaxed silence arose between them, and that was something Ann appreciated in Matilda Wiik, that she had the ability to stay silent, without it feeling awkward.

"Ask Bertil Efraimsson, I think he knows something," she said at last.

"What makes you think that?"

"We belong to the same congregation."

Ann knew that her boss came from a deeply religious background, even if she never talked about it.

"He's been worried all spring, convinced that the school fire was set."

"Did he see anything?"

"Bertil is a man who keeps a lot inside. He's a strong person, who doesn't have that need to babble about everything and everyone."

"Like Anton?"

Matilda looked serious. "Have you checked the time?" She nodded toward the cheese vat on the other side of the glass window.

"I set the timer," said Ann.

✦

Fifteen

A country girl in the city, that's how she felt. But that passed quickly. She was standing in Gotlandsparken, playing bird-watcher. The ducks looked like they too had spring plowing to do. Then she raised her eyes and looked toward Åkanten, the restaurant on the other side of the Fyris River, and immediately felt famished. It was crowded there on a Monday, but the sun was out and it was spring. She smiled and had good thoughts, because she wished them well, those who ate and drank, babbled and laughed, or simply soaked up sun. As long as they weren't sticking knives in each other, or hitting their table companion over the head with a bottle, she was content with her fellow humans, in any case on a day like this. She took out her phone; new message. Maybe Justus had got cold feet and changed his mind, but it was Erik: "July 7: 10 days." He had decided on Germany. *Ten days*, she thought, *has he saved up that much money?*

She left the park, followed Sankt Olofsgatan to Svartbäcksgatan, and turned north. The pub that had been there for years was gone, now it was a restaurant. There too the guests crowded the sidewalk tables. She associated the street with her old job; how many times had she walked from the police station down toward the city center, and vice versa? Before the intersection with Linnégatan a police officer had been murdered, Ann recalled that Jan-Erik Hollman was his name. It was an act of insanity that happened at the same time as they were chasing the person who murdered Justus's father.

Outside the bakery café she saw a familiar face, but couldn't recall from where and for that reason chose to look away and hurry ahead, even though she didn't need to feel stressed. The garden was open. She walked right in, neglecting the sign about an entry fee. Parks should be free, she had always thought. There was a police memory here too, the city was stalking her! It must have been in the early 2000s, all investigations flowed together over the years into a single fog. A young mother and her daughter had been found run over by Uppsala-Näs church. The case led in many directions, even abroad, to the Caribbean and southern Spain, but the solution was found at last in the home district. During the investigation she had met an informant in the Linnaeus Garden who had important information.

She chose the same bench as that time. It was ten minutes to five. She was completely calm. There were not many visitors, and they were walking between the herb beds with bowed heads, as if submerged in prayer or deep thought, but it was probably to be able to read the squiggly handwritten signs with the names of the plants. A child came running on the path and with her laughter and playfulness created a certain disorder in the otherwise gloomy Linnaeus system.

Justus Jonsson had not yet arrived. This did not surprise her. He was just as likely to show up as not. And she herself was divided, on the one hand curious about what he had to present, while on the other hand it would be a relief to escape being taken back to a different time, reminded of what had been.

There was movement by the entry. A group of tourists were flocking around a portly man outfitted in period gentry clothing and a wig. Were they Korean or Japanese, she could never tell the difference, even though she'd been told that Koreans weren't as well-dressed. She understood that it was the guide who would portray Linnaeus himself, a man she'd seen numerous times. He appeared in the most varied contexts, showing up like a green-clad chameleon and letting his voice resound over everyone, regardless of dress and nationality. The Japanese, as she decided they were, moved obediently according to the guide's instructions. He pointed and gestured, spoke convincingly and knowledgeably, provoked smiles and laughter. She snapped up some of the words and sentences. He was to be envied, he had his Linnaeus, he knew his character and his garden, his program, his phrases and jokes practiced through the years. What could happen to him? A bad day? An occasional lapse? Even so. New Japanese and Koreans, Americans and Germans were constantly arriving. His clearance rate was far superior to the police's.

Justus freed himself from the group of Japanese. He had seen her, she understood that, but he gave no sign, did not smile. He walked neither quickly nor slowly, did not look around. His clothes were Korean, in the sense that they seemed cheap and simple. There was something vaguely hostile about his figure, an impression that was strengthened the closer he came. He had changed since they last met. Exactly in what respect it was hard to put her finger on. In terms of appearance there was no obvious difference, but perhaps it was the way he made himself known to his surroundings. Like a man without hopes about others. He made way instinctively for the group of Japanese tourists, flower lovers, and the happy girl in the path, without actually seeing them, without caring.

Even so she got a smile when he was standing in front of the bench.

"Hi, Justus," she said, standing up, perhaps to create a little balance. She took a step closer, perhaps to give him a hug, perhaps to take a sniff test, determine whether or not he'd been drinking. He jerked his head, shrugged his shoulders, and feinted with his body like a boxer. It was a movement she recognized from his uncle, Lennart, the petty criminal with a big heart but shaky judgment, as she had perceived him then. It was a dismissive movement, she understood that, he did not want to be hugged. It might be noticed, someone could see him giving a cop a hug, was that it?

She sat down and signaled with her hand that he should do the same. They sat in silence for a few seconds. "You came at last."

"Listen, I'm in a bit of a bad way."

"How is that?"

Without any qualms Justus fished a beer can out of his jacket pocket, but did not open it. He looked around, as if it occurred to him too late that perhaps it wasn't appropriate to drink in a public garden.

"You said that someone might die. Who?"

Justus smacked his tongue, as if his mouth was completely dry.

"It's a long story," he said at last. That was a line she'd heard numerous times. Often it was to gain time, sometimes it was an attempt to wriggle out of a difficult situation through a stream of words. She answered like she always did, that he should take it from the beginning.

"I have an old buddy. We hadn't seen each other for a while. We went to Boland together, the idea was we were going to be masons."

"And you did."

"Both of us. Got jobs at NCC. That was a good time. Smulan met a girl, they had a kid, then . . . Then things went downhill."

He glanced at his beer.

"My grandfather was a sheet-metal worker, and he fell down from a roof. The funny thing, even if it wasn't that funny, was that the same thing happened to my buddy's grandfather. We thought it was a little . . . well, what should I say . . . exciting. Do you get it? Sheet-metal roof it was, damned slippery. They were careless, maybe loaded."

A stream of words, she thought, but nodded.

"My buddy . . ."

"What's his name?"

"He goes by Smulan. Last name Edman."

Now she needed Berglund. He would have wound this up in no time flat, said something along the lines of "I see, that must be Kalle Edman's grandson, and didn't his old man work at the stove factory?" and Justus would laugh, or at least smile, and say something about Smulan's old man, and then the talk would flow like a spring flood.

"Why aren't you in the phone directory?"

"I was a police officer."

"So you've quit?"

"For good."

"But not completely, right?"

"What do you mean?"

"I saw how you looked at the beer."

"No, I still drink wine."

"You were good, I remember that. You had a little kid." He marked the size with his hands.

"He's a teenager now," she said, and measured like a fisherman. "Do you remember Berglund, my colleague and coworker?"

"The guy with the hat?"

She nodded, looked down at the ground, and hesitated a moment before she continued.

"He told me what it was like when Lennart died. He fell from a roof too. Berglund's gone, but he sometimes talked about the two of you."

"Why is that?"

"I think he liked your family, it was that simple. He knew your grandfather, the blocks where they lived, where Little John grew up."

Justus raised his head and looked toward the sky, as if he might catch sight of his father. "I've driven there a few times, parked the car, and walked around the block. Pop used to talk about Ymergatan, what it was like for them, but it doesn't really look very special. Smulan Edman grew up there in the neighborhood, on Väderkvarnsgatan."

"Yes, what happened with him?" She asked the question as if she'd known him for years. "What's he doing now, I mean?"

Justus shook his head. "It's gone to hell. He's part of some Nazi front. He's a good guy really, but he just gets more and more strange. It started when his dad died a few years ago. The old man was an alcoholic and died in a drunk tank. Maybe you remember, wasn't there a lot about it in the news?"

Lindell hummed, but didn't recall anything about an Edman who died in a cell.

"He started hating everything and everyone, especially cops. Now it's mostly talk about refugees."

"Is it political?"

"He got a little strange. All the talk about darkies and such. And that fucking music he played. He's basically stopped that, but the talk just gets worse and worse."

Justus leaned over and picked up a fistful of gravel, let the pebbles slowly sift through his fingers before he quickly closed his hand around the last pieces, as if he were afraid of losing them all. His hands were rough and angular, a couple of his knuckles scraped. Ann remembered the photographs taken at the Libro snow depository, where his father was found. Little John had been tortured, his fingers cut off. Did Justus know about that, had he read the documents and seen the pictures?

"Were your mom and dad rich?" he asked suddenly.

"No, far from it."

"Did you live in a villa?"

Ann nodded, and Justus hummed, opened his hand and let the stones fall to the ground. *Single-family house,* she thought, *a home of your own. We had that, on a boring cul-de-sac.*

The group of Japanese, with the constantly talking guide in the lead, was approaching. Justus squirmed from worry or aversion.

"I've never been in Thailand, like everyone else. Some of Smulan's Nazi buddies are living there. He wants us to go there, he has a house in the works. He talked about heat and freedom, and that I can understand, compared with this shit. But what then, who the hell needs a mason in Thailand? And the ones who hate darkies . . . they pick up seventeen-year-old Thai girls. It doesn't add up."

"Do you have a job?"

"I just came from work."

She wanted to ask if he was happy, if he was dating anyone, what he dreamed about, but none of that was said.

"We're marked."

"What do you mean?"

"My old man was murdered, Lennart fell down from a roof when the cops were chasing him, their little sister was run over when she was little. Their old man, my grandfather, died on the job. It's as if we have a stamp on our foreheads that says, *Die, you bastard!*"

"Are you scared that it's your turn now?"

The Japanese tourists were getting closer and closer. The guide leaned down, pinching off a vine that he held up and said a name. Justus seemed to be listening.

"I worked on Thunbergsvägen last year," he said. "I don't know who Thunberg is, but he's probably one of those." He made a weak, vague gesture with his hand over the garden.

He sighed heavily. *Jeez,* thought Ann, *he's a compendium of all the markers of depression.*

"That old guy probably knows everything," said Justus. "But think how tired his brain must get, going around talking flowers for days on end."

"When you called the police you said something to the effect that someone may die. Who is that?"

"It's not anyone you know."

"Well, I get that. What does he have going, this 'Smulan' Edman?"

Justus stood up from the bench.

"You want to talk but somehow not, is that so?"

"I don't like crowds," he said.

"They'll be gone soon."

"I know that he swiped explosives."

"For what?"

"One thing is certain, he isn't going to help a homeowner blast stones."

"Where did he steal it?"

"An installation in Almunge, a few months ago, I think he said. A buddy of his works there."

"That's why you think someone is going to die?"

Justus nodded.

"Get blown up?"

Justus made that boxing movement again, jerked his head, feinted with his body.

The group of tourists scattered. The guide dressed in green stepped away. Ann could see the relief in the man's face. He didn't seem to like crowds. The playing girl had now been caught by her father. They walked hand in hand toward the exit.

"You're still a cop."

"That's probably true," she admitted. "What is he going to blow up?"

He did not answer, perhaps because he didn't know, perhaps because for some reason he was hiding what he felt, perhaps because he thought that it was the job of the police to figure that out.

"I'm going to talk with a former colleague, do you understand that?"

He looked at her while he soundlessly formed the word "colleague" with his lips. Ann got the sense that he was testing how it fit in his mouth.

"You've got a name," he said, and she understood by his tone of voice that it didn't feel quite comfortable for him.

"'Smulan' Edman," she said.

"In the past his type became greasers, now they become Nazis," he said, and she was surprised by his brief analysis, which despite the simplicity was of Berglund class.

"Greasers are preferable," she said.

"My old man was a little like that. He told me a little. Big cars and such."

"Wasn't Little John too young for that? I mean, greasers, wasn't that more in the fifties?"

"There have always been big cars," Justus replied. "Lennart had a DeSoto. He sold it later. He had to."

"Did he lose his driver's license?"

Justus smiled. "They really liked each other, my old man and Lennart."

"That business with Smulan," attempted Ann, who realized that he was being carried away by memories, but Justus didn't want to continue. He took a couple of steps away, as an initial attempt to flee the field.

"Can I trust you?"

"If I run into Smulan I won't say hello from you, that's for sure. What's his real first name?"

"Erland. That's a shitty name, but they're all named Erland in that family. He named his kid Erland too. That was a shitty thing to do."

He nodded and went his way. Ann remained seated. The guide dressed in green had stayed behind. She noticed that every so often he looked in her direction. Then he came walking up, with dignified steps, as if he really hadn't left his role as Carl von Linné.

"May I buy you a beer?" he asked in a courteous voice. "You get thirsty from talking."

"Do we know one another?"

"No, and perhaps that's an advantage," he said. "We can go to Costa's," he continued unconcerned. "I don't like being alone over a beer."

"Where's Costa's?"

"Very close by. It's a lovely spring evening."

"Are you hitting on me?"

"No, I have a busload of Chinese seismologists, or else it was retirees from Eskilstuna, in forty minutes," he said. "But we have time for a beer, even if a beer seldom comes alone."

They left the garden together and walked to the Greek restaurant. They sat down at a table on the sidewalk.

"I recognize you," the guide said. "You've probably heard that before," he added when he saw her expression. "I remember the murder here on the street, that's why your face is familiar."

"I see."

"I've thought about something, this business of justice."

"Listen!" Ann Lindell interrupted him more brusquely than she intended.

"It's about my character, Carl von Linné, nothing else."

"Okay," Lindell said, taking a sip of the cold but ever-so-nonalcoholic beer. "But I don't think I want to hear it."

"Not me either, actually, but we can just sit here anyway, and pretend to be enjoying it."

✦

Sixteen

When the guide hurried off at the last moment to his waiting group—Ann could see that they were Chinese—she remained seated for a while outside the Greek restaurant. *This is the city,* she thought, *spring is beautiful even on streets and squares.* She was tempted to order a glass of wine, but immediately dismissed the thought. Her car was waiting on Östra Ågatan.

The group of seismologists disappeared into the Linnaeus Garden. In the same direction, north, was her former workplace. If she were still in service it was a few minutes' walk to the police station, where she would be able to check up on Erland "Smulan" Edman and the alleged theft in Almunge a month ago. Then she also could have found out more about the assault on the Somali at the sausage stand in Gimo, and not least produce the list of who had been at the New Year's party in Ottosson's cottage, the party that Daniel Mattsson had attended. Perhaps there was an "outsider" among them, who was prepared to speak more openheartedly, especially now when everyone had gained a little perspective on the school fire, the arson in the smithy, and Daniel Mattsson's death.

Instead of hurrying away toward the police station she lingered on the sidewalk outside a dry cleaner's on Svartbäcksgatan, and blankly observed the antique irons in the display window. Could she call Sammy? It was seven o'clock. Maybe he was still in Tilltorp, but the risk was that he had made it home. She sent a text message.

She got an answer a few minutes later: "Come to the fort, I'll pick you up down there."

* * *

Fifteen minutes later she was introduced to Regina Rosenberg. For Ann it felt like meeting an old friend, even though until now they had only talked on the phone.

"I see, so that's what you look like," Regina said with a smile, and the introductory remark reinforced the feeling. "I think Sammy boy has a little crush on you, but you probably know that already." Her words made all three of them laugh. Sammy actually looked embarrassed, while Ann felt at ease.

"It's nice to be here," she said. "It's the first time since I quit."

"It's good that you quit," Regina decided, "because only a lot of police work here, and what fun are they? What do you do now?"

"I make cheese, mostly blue cheese," said Ann.

Regina looked at her a moment, as if to decide whether that was a joke, before she took a step closer to Ann.

"Cheese . . . how nice," she said in an unusually quiet voice.

The silence that lasted a few seconds was interrupted by an incoming call. Sammy and Ann left the communications center and took the elevator up to his office. It felt as if she'd been picked up in a bar and now was on her way to a hotel room with a strange man in a strange city.

"Who was at the party in the house right across the road from the school?" she asked without any unnecessary introductory talk. She explained what Bertil Efraimsson had said about two independent witnesses who maintained that the fire was set, two witnesses who didn't know each other, didn't even know about each other. "Were either of them from outside the village?"

"We've questioned everyone who was partying in old man Ottosson's cottage," Sammy said. "You know that, but no one saw or heard anything. There was one who stuck out, Stefan Sanberg is his name, a rather unpleasant character, but he lives in the village."

"Bring them in again, and be sure to—" Ann said mercilessly.

"It's not possible," Sammy interrupted, without explaining why, but Ann could think of several reasons. "On the other hand there were a few outsiders, three if I remember right."

"Question them anyway."

"We'll have to see. Maybe if we have time."

We'll have to see, thought Ann. *How wrong he is.* She was convinced of the connection between the two cases of arson. That was where they had to dig, but she dropped that and changed tack.

"Can you check another thing, if any theft of explosives from a construction site in Almunge has been reported, roughly a month ago, maybe more."

"What's this about?"

Ann hesitated to answer before she decided to tell Sammy about Justus and his old friend Erland "Smulan" Edman. "You remember the murder of Little John, Justus's dad?"

"Of course. Almunge, you said, and Edman, Erland." He twisted his torso a quarter-turn, brought the computer to life, and tapped in the information he'd received. Ann observed his profile, and could see that he too had been subjected to the tooth of time.

"It was Justus who called, but you understood that, didn't you?"

Sammy nodded. "In early March, on the third, about ten kilos of Austrogel were stolen from a construction site in the Almunge area. Can that be it?"

"Could be. Was it an NCC project?"

Sammy smiled quietly while he scrolled farther. "The foreman at NCC was Björn Thomas Rönn."

"Ask him for a list of employees."

"It already exists. It's routine with this type of crime. No Edman, on the other hand twenty-one others. One Lindell actually."

"Can you print out the list?"

"Can, I can, but will I, should I?"

"Do a search on Edman," Ann Lindell recommended, quite sure that in time she would get a list. "Do you have anything on him?"

"We have nothing on Edman. What's this shit about?"

"Hate crime, I guess it's called," said Ann.

"Something that will be blown up. The mosque? Refugee housing? God, I get so tired of it!"

"Of what?" Ann straightened her back, suddenly struck by an insight that nothing was static, not even Sammy Nilsson. He had changed.

Sammy looked at her in a way she hadn't seen before, before he answered with a sobbing sound and a single word: "Everything." Ann waited; she knew from before that he often needed time to collect his thoughts. He had practiced. The first years they worked together he would sometimes blow his top, and then go around and apologize. It was sad and time-consuming.

"I'm so tired of the hate, this fucking hate. The loudmouths in all directions. I am tired of the idiots who throw rocks at ambulances, fire trucks, and buses."

"Where is that?"

"Sävja, Gottsunda, and Stenhagen, mention any damned area where the young bastards don't throw rocks. And what do their moms and dads do? Not a thing! They sit with their damned parabolic antennas and . . . They talk about honor and every other kind of shit, but then they should damned well be out on the streets when their kids are burning cars and shooting each other in the head. And I'm tired of all the Nazis, who are screaming from their side. Jesus, haven't they learned a thing?"

"What is it?" Ann interrupted.

Sammy took a deep breath. "I don't know," he said. "They talk about alienation."

"There must be support services. I read something about Gottsunda."

"Yeah, yeah," said Sammy.

"Little John and his brother Lennart, they were outsiders too, weren't they?"

"But they didn't burn cars."

"No, they stole the cars, and crashed them."

"That was different anyway," said Sammy.

"Their names were Lennart, Sture, and Hasse, and not Ali and Ahmed, that was one difference. There must be more, but John had a job, he was in demand, capable. Lennart too, when he was sober, that is. They had the opportunity, and they knew it! They knew there was a place. Berglund talked about this, you recall, about the gangs in the fifties and sixties? Working-class boys mostly."

"I'm probably just tired after a long day," said Sammy.

"But why is it going to hell for some?" Ann steamed ahead.

"Tell me."

The printer started up and spit out a sheet that sailed down to the floor. Ann reached down and picked up the list of the work crew at NCC in Almunge.

"Daniel Mattsson assaulted a Somali in Gimo, do you remember?"

"I asked Bodin to check up on that. The camel boy lives in Vara these days."

"Where's that?"

Sammy did not reply, instead kept tapping on the keyboard. Lindell eyeballed the list of construction workers: eleven names ending in -son, three of which were Anderssons, besides two Lindströms, one Lindell, one Bouveng, and a few other ancient Swedish surnames. NCC was lily-white.

"What do you see?" she asked, holding the list up in front of Sammy.

"A ballot for the Sweden Democrats," he said without hesitation.

"But Bouveng sounds foreign."

"Walloon ancestry," said Sammy. "They're approved." He resumed the amateurish pounding on the keyboard, as if he were sitting in front of an old Underwood typewriter with sluggish keys. "And Vara is far away, you hear that? He's been cleared. Saturday evening he was at a party in Kållandsö, wherever that is, some kind of holiday, some saint or other. At least thirty witnesses."

"Bodin checked?"

"He asked the colleagues down there for help. It's airtight. He's good, that Bodin, effective, but a Haver when it comes to corpses."

"It'll work out, there are colleagues who are afraid of the living. Are there saints in Somalia?"

Sammy looked up.

"The connection," he said. "Two fires, a kilometer apart."

"The village isn't talking, in any case not so I hear."

"Not the dead either."

"There are two old guys who ought to be squeezed. They're neighbors of mine."

"Maybe Bodin and I should make a home visit to the senior center?"

"One is a slightly cranky carpenter, the other one is religious, but not overbearing. The carpenter would probably get a little shaky."

"I've met them before, but Bodin and I will take them tomorrow. We'll bring the Spanish donkey along," Sammy decided.

"Who's that, a trainee?"

"Kind of," said Sammy.

"Good, then I'll make cheese all day."

Sammy turned off the computer.

"The list," said Ann.

"I'll put someone on it, I don't know if anyone's checked into this. Maybe it didn't get done, or was given lower priority. A few kilos of explosives, what's that these days?"

"Nice. Maybe there's someone among the white folks in Almunge with a black heart."

✦

Seventeen

"Is it here?"

"Let's sit down," said Frank Give, heading for the only vacant bench. Björn Rönn followed obediently.

Peppartorget was full of life, that was his first impression. The food store was a magnet, people streamed in and out in a steady flow. Many came from the subway, perhaps picking up something on their way home from work. The mandatory beggar was sitting on a box outside the entry. He was an older man who did not appear to take his task all too seriously. A stand with secondhand items was run by a black woman, who also looked relaxed. Outside the pizzeria a group of teenagers was hanging around.

"You see what it looks like. Lousy."

"You were born here?"

"Then there was style. We had the Finns of course, a few Yugoslavs, but otherwise it was calm." He had a crooked smile, and Björn Rönn could sense some of the old charisma that made Frankenstein, as he was sometimes called, a successful charmer. Where women were concerned he'd had it easy. Now a scar disfigured his one cheek, and tattoos over parts of his throat and neck did not improve things, but what definitely dragged down the overall impression was the bitterness he vented all too often.

He talked on about the Hökarängen of his childhood. Björn Rönn listened with half an ear while he studied the people on the square.

"Is it here?" he interrupted Frank's verbiage.

"Do you see the darkies? They've occupied the square with a fucking yurt to sell rotten fruit. That's how it looks in every single suburb."

"It's in Uppsala too. I think it's usually cheap." Björn said something about Vaksala Square.

"It's because they sell drugs too. And ISIS is there, you can bet your ass on that. Market trading is a perfect cover for the mullahs."

Björn checked the benches to their right and left. They were occupied by winos who howled and argued only to fall into each other's arms at the next moment. Winos, but no darkies. As far as he could see they were of Nordic origin.

"I don't know," he said. "Is it that smart, I mean, a lot of people of all types are here."

"A point has to be made," said Frankenstein.

"But children."

"They're in class."

"Infants in strollers don't go to school."

"Day care," Frank said, leaning back.

"But it's a Saturday."

"All the same."

Björn made an opposite movement, leaning forward, as if he felt sick, stealing a glance at his friend. He'd known Frank for several years. The first time they met was at a demonstration south of Stockholm. Frank had been just as crazy then, but the difference was that in Salem he carried a knife and now he had access to Austrogel-brand explosive sticks.

"Then it will be Alby."

"Where's that?"

"Further south," said Frank. "Looks a lot like this. There's a town center. We've selected a few more places."

Frank tried to give the appearance of energy, striking a clenched fist against the armrest of the bench while he counted up five suburbs: Skärholmen, Fittja, Flemingsberg, Rinkeby, and Hallunda.

"After Alby we'll take another square, then we'll wait a few days before we strike one more. That's how they do it."

"Who is that?"

"The ones who know how to create terror. After that the darkies won't dare to hawk a single tomato, and no one will shop with them. It's important to create insecurity and chaos, then half the battle is won."

Björn Rönn stared toward the fountain in the square, where someone had amused themselves by pouring in shampoo. It looked playful, he liked it, likewise the children who chased foam bubbles that flew away at the slightest puff of wind. At the vegetable stand there was no invasion exactly, but a never-ending stream of customers kept commerce going. There were both light- and dark-skinned people, women in shorts and fluttering tops, as well as in hijab. A bum was holding a concert and did it reasonably well with an old popular song, one that Björn's father used to whistle early in the morning when he was on his way to the barn. Björn tried to make out the words, but the distance was too far and the song soon died away.

"Shall we have a beer?"

"I'm driving."

"Whatever," said Frank. "Let's go to my place. I think Lena has fixed something."

He did not await an answer but instead got up from the bench. Björn hesitated, but followed. He had to pick up the car outside Frank's house anyway.

When they had walked awhile Frank pointed at the grocery store's sign with a sneer. "ICA Bomb. Fits fucking well."

Sjöskumsvägen, the street where Frank lived, was in a neighborhood that Björn guessed was built in the forties. He had helped renovate numerous similar areas, including several in Uppsala. They sat on the balcony with a view of an extended greenbelt where there was a wading pool, with swings, slides, and sandboxes visible farther away. Everything was worn, but still marked by the concept the planners once had, airy and functional. Children were playing in the pool. Their voices and shrieks echoed in the warm spring evening. That was something he missed, children's voices. It was silent in Rasbo, and had been a long time, in any event where he and his brother lived.

Frank Give talked on. His wife, Lena, had set out tacos. There was beer in a cooler on the floor.

"You can sleep over," she offered when Björn said no to a Singha.

He smiled and shook his head. His mouth was full of chips and some green mush. He didn't like that kind of finger food, but ate anyway, and tried to show something that resembled appetite. But the fact was that he felt nauseated.

"I have to get up early," he said, when he finally managed to swallow the Mexican slop.

✦

Eighteen

"I wish I knew," said Gösta Friberg in a wistful tone of voice.

The old man is bluffing, thought Sammy, not based on any certain indications, but perhaps mostly on the basis of routine mistrust. The old carpenter seemed calm and collected, not at all shaky as Ann had maintained.

"You see, I dream sometimes, and for a long time I thought it was just a dream. Irma, my wife who passed away some time ago, maintained that I walked in my sleep too, but that I don't know. She talked so much, she said I snored too. You know how it is, a person gets blamed for so many things." Then he went on, told about Irma and other things they hadn't asked about and reasonably had no interest in, turned toward Bodin as if to draw him into the conversation, but Bodin showed his stoniest face and did not say a word about the old man's harangue.

The silence that followed was heavy. Sammy went up to the window and peered out in the direction where the school had once been. Bodin focused all his interest on the old stove and whitewashed brickwork.

"Why do you have the Advent star up? It's May."

"It was Irma who set it up, and then it didn't get taken down. They probably think I'm nuts, but I don't have it lit, not until Advent, but that's a while yet. I took down the elves in the window anyway."

"Tell us now!" said Bodin, who wasn't interested in Christmas decorations.

"I thought it was a dream," Gösta Friberg repeated. "You all probably think I'm lying, but I didn't recognize any of them. They were like shadows in the night."

Bodin straightened up and interrupted the verbiage. "You said there were two of them."

Friberg nodded.

"We don't buy that talk about a dream." Bodin's voice was harsh, and so filled with contempt that it made Sammy turn around. "You already knew then, that night, that what you saw was completely real. It was arson you witnessed, and you kept your mouth shut."

Friberg shook his head.

"Why?"

"I was confused . . . everything happened so fast . . . I'm afraid of fire."

"So afraid that you let people burn up inside."

Sammy made a cautious gesture with one hand, but Bodin steamed ahead.

"Afraid of something else too, huh? That kid in your car, the one who died, did you see him too?"

Friberg took a step closer to Bodin, as if he wanted to attack him.

"You saw that he got into the car, but didn't do a thing. . . ."

"Stop!" Gösta Friberg screamed.

"He froze to death because of your passivity . . . because you're afraid of fire, my goodness."

"It wasn't like that," said Friberg, sinking down on a chair.

Bodin stared at him a few seconds, before he left the kitchen. Sammy sat down on the other side of the kitchen table.

"Tell me," he said.

"I didn't see him, I promise. Not until it was too late. Two days too late."

"I believe you," said Sammy.

"I think about him every day. It's a nightmare. He looked so young."

"They are young."

"But everyone says that they lie about their age."

Sammy wanted to ask who "everyone" was, but let it be. He could guess how the talk went around the village.

"What happened with his cousin?"

"I think he ran to the forest, and froze to death too. We have wolves in the area, and lynx."

"Who did you see?"

Gösta Friberg looked up. Sammy could see a hint of relief in the old carpenter's face.

"I don't know, but I'm glad that I told you that there were three of them, that the fire was set. There's no doubt about that."

"Were you born in the village?"

Friberg nodded and made a gesture with his hand, as if to show that he grew up there in the cottage.

"You know every pine cone in the area, isn't that so?"

"Yes, but it was dark and I was confused. It was night, everything happened so fast."

"You've said that before, but you've changed your story. Five minutes ago there were maybe two arsonists, now there are three. Who's been added?"

"I think that maybe there were three."

"Think about it. Protecting a criminal is being an accessory. People were trapped in the fire, froze to death. Do you really want to live with the knowledge that murderers go free?"

Sammy Nilsson did not wait for an answer, but instead stood up and left the kitchen and the cottage. On the front stoop he took a deep breath. It smelled of summer and for a moment he was transported. He thought about Ann, who in a radical move changed her life, resigned, got a new job, and moved. In other words it was possible, he thought, with a mixed bag of shame, euphoria, and anxiety. His own situation was different, he was married and his daughter had left home, and his bonds with Angelika had always been strong, even if they were now under serious strain. And could he truly become a crofter in the country and work in a cheese factory, with a cute hairnet on his head?

Bodin was standing by the car talking on the phone, but ended the call when Sammy was approaching.

"That was the medical examiner. He told me that they found a tattooed swastika on the neck of the woman in the smithy. There was a little skin that was undamaged, and at the hairline was an amateurish tattoo. About one centimeter in size."

"Swastika. Who the hell is she?"

"Nice village," said Bodin.

"Let's drive over to the farm," Sammy decided.

"No, I don't know who she is," said Waldemar Mattsson. "A passing acquaintance."

"The bicycle that was outside the smithy," said Bodin.

"I've never seen it before."

The farmer was sitting opposite Bodin at the kitchen table. Sammy had chosen to lean against the kitchen counter.

"Come on now!" he said.

"Maybe it's Friman's daughter," said Mattsson after a long silence.

"Who is Friman?"

"They live in the village, but now they're sailing at sea. They started a while ago and are going to the Caribbean, I think. They have a daughter who maybe showed up now when her parents are away. I have the idea that she was living somewhere up north."

"Did Daniel talk about her?"

"No, never."

"Why do you think it might be her?"

"She . . . got a little crazy, ran away. I know that Kalle Friman was really angry. I think the idea was that she would go along on the sailing trip. He'd planned that trip for a couple of years, and then she backed out at the last minute."

"What's her name?"

"Don't remember. I can call Andreas, he knows."

"Call him!" Sammy said. "And see to it that he comes here, we want to talk with him, even if he doesn't seem that eager."

"He's working."

"You said that, but this is murder and arson we're talking about," said Bodin.

Mattsson picked the phone up from the table, entered a speed-dial number, but couldn't reach his son.

"Maybe my wife remembers."

"Ask her." Sammy felt growing irritation at the farmer's slowness.

"She's sleeping," he said, making it sound as if it were a betrayal.

"Maybe you should do that too."

"Last night I got up and had the idea that I was a Negro. Silly, huh?"

"Were you having a dream?"

"I sleep with support socks, all the way up to the knees, and when I swung my legs over the edge of the bed they were completely black, and of course they are, the socks that is. But it was strange, becoming a Negro just like that, a feeling of suddenly becoming someone else."

"These days we don't say Negro, do we?" said Bodin.

"When did the police get sensitive about such things?"

"Do any colored people live here in the village?"

Mattsson twisted his head and aimed the bloodshot eyes at Bodin.

"Do you say colored? We have a Yugoslav, a Polish woman, a few Finns, and a guy from Bangladesh, that's all, I think. And then a Filipina, but she seems to be on the way out. As it sounds in any event. Otherwise it's as usual, like it's always been."

"Do you feel threatened?" asked Sammy, who wanted to get him to talk. Maybe something interesting would come out of this somnambulant babbling.

"The UN is barging in," Mattsson continued. "Not really, but I understand that people get angry. All the subsidies, and then we can't afford anything else."

"Are you feeling pinched?"

"Damn but you're nervy, you know that?"

Bodin smiled in response. "I just wanted to tease you a little."

"Go right ahead, but not in my kitchen. When the school burned many people were crying. And it was a fine school, that it was. I went there for six years. They say that Daniel set the fire, and it's probably that bloody nobody who talks a lot of shit, but he ought to keep his big mouth shut. I told him so."

"Which nobody?"

"The carpenter."

"Gösta Friberg, you mean?"

"Are there other carpenters?"

"And what did he say then, when you said that he should shut his mouth?"

"He's afraid, always has been, and since his old lady died it's gotten worse. He spent a whole fortune on Irma, but what did it do, not a thing. And then the preacher on the other side of the road, and his sister on the neighboring farm. What a lot of bullshit. Although he's capable, Bertil, I have to say that."

Sammy unconsciously took a deep breath. He was up to his neck in discomfort. The pettiness of village life stood out even clearer. At the same time he was smart enough to understand that the fine threads that bound the village and its history together were critical. Fragile threads, which were now strained and threatened to break. Perhaps some had already broken? If they could sit in Mattsson's kitchen for a few days a pattern would emerge, he was sure of that. If they could walk through the village, visit more kitchens, sit down, take the time to listen, then the two arsons and Daniel's murder could be solved, he was equally sure of that. The answers were in the village kitchens and bedrooms, on farmyards and in machine sheds, but police work was only like that in the best of worlds, because there weren't that many policemen. The slowness that was required was an absurdity.

"And then your bloody colleague, that Lindell woman, who is still playing cop. Tell her to shut down that operation and tend to the cheese instead."

"Tell us about the guy from Bangladesh," said Bodin.

"He came here and started at the creamery. He minds his own business, lives down at Nelander's. Now he has a different job. He's ugly as sin, but otherwise . . ."

"Does he threaten you?"

Mattsson did not reply, but instead stood up and opened the door to an old-fashioned pantry, with shelves from floor to ceiling, and rooted around among glass jars and cans before taking out a bottle with a syrupy content.

"I got this from Dacka, but it's damn well undrinkable. Made in his home village, he said. Arrack."

"Why did you get the bottle?"

"He drives a moped and isn't too good at it, so to speak. He tipped over one morning, I was behind him and stepped on the gas a little, so he probably got extra nervous. I had to help him up. I took the moped on the truck bed. Astrid bandaged him up."

"Dacka, is that what he's called?"

"No one can pronounce his name."

"Aren't they Muslims in Bangladesh, I mean, do they drink?" Bodin asked, evidently amused.

"If they get away from the mosque they booze like pigs, I've been told, but he's probably some other sort, Buddhist or something."

How does he manage, it struck Sammy, *he's just lost a son.* He had the dizzying thought that it was his own child who had been murdered, but dismissed it just as quickly as it showed up.

"Shall we have one?" said Mattsson, holding up the bottle, the dregs of which clouded the grayish liquid.

"Don't think so," said Sammy.

"I can have a taste, you're driving," said Bodin.

Mattsson reached for two shot glasses, which were conveniently on a shelf an arm's length away.

"A thimbleful," said Bodin.

Mattsson poured, and they carefully took a little sip, swallowed, and looked at each other with a slightly astonished expression.

"This is what they call multicultural," the farmer said.

"My God," said Bodin. "But this is probably revenge because you threatened him on the road."

"Dacka has a sense of humor," said Mattsson.

"Are you drinking?"

Wendela Mattsson had soundlessly slipped up behind them, and stood in the door wearing an old dressing gown. Her hair was disheveled and her features likewise, as if she could not really decide what expression to put on.

"We're tasting Dacka's cough medicine, if you recall," said Mattsson, but obediently set aside the glass on the kitchen counter at once. Yet there was something irritable in his voice, which perhaps did not have so much to do with her slightly impertinent tone but instead seemed to be a kind of routine everyday irritation, as when things have dried up between two people who've lived together a long time and the bearings are creaking. Sammy recognized it from his own marriage.

"Do you know anything?" the woman asked, and it took a moment before Sammy understood that the question was directed at him.

"No, not really."

"It struck me that it may be Friman's daughter," said Mattsson.

"Lovisa, you mean? But she lives in Ludvika."

Mattsson gave Sammy a look that could mean: *She clearly remembers that.*

"She had a swastika tattooed on her neck," said Bodin.

"That was why the Frimans wanted to get away," said Wendela. "They thought the girl would reconsider when she got to see a little of the world."

"The world is coming here," said Mattsson, but without actual edge, as if he didn't really trust his own nagging small-mindedness now when death had once again struck in the village.

"She got into bad company," Wendela said, making an effort to continue, but nothing more came, as if her energy were used up. She immediately looked very tired, leaned against the doorpost gasping for breath. Her husband stiffened and made a vague movement, as if he might be forced to intervene.

"I'm used up," she said, turned away and staggered off.

It did not take Bodin long to produce Lovisa Friman's personal data. From the passport office he got a photo, less than two years old. It showed a young woman with shoulder-length hair and a rather commonplace appearance; there was nothing to "hang on to," as Bodin put it. It was impossible based on the picture to determine whether it was Lovisa who had died in the smithy.

"Does she look like an orthodox Nazi?" said Sammy.

Bodin gave him a look, perhaps unsure whether he was joking. They were sitting in the Mattssons' garden chairs behind the house.

"What do they look like?"

"Like you and me," said Sammy.

"I'll go to Friman's," said Bodin, "if you'll wait for Mattsson Junior."

The Friman residence was a kilometer or so away. They got driving instructions from Waldemar Mattsson. Bodin took off and Sammy followed him with his gaze, and the feeling that they were doing something meaningful grew. He looked once again at the picture of Lovisa, which Mattsson had printed out in his farm office. "Nazi," he said tentatively. It seemed so unnecessary, such a fine girl, at the start of her adult life. Burned up. Sammy made an involuntary association to the Holocaust and everyone who went up in smoke there. Now she got to taste her own medicine. Perhaps it was an unjust thought, because of course he knew nothing about Lovisa Friman.

✦

Nineteen

A young man came walking across the lawn. Sammy understood that it was Daniel's brother, although it was hard to see any resemblance. Andreas was dark, as if he came from a southern European country, fairly tall, and simply good-looking, as Sammy spontaneously characterized Mattsson's oldest son. He was dressed in a pair of sturdy work pants and a reasonably clean T-shirt. *Put a suit on him and he would be a hunk,* Sammy thought.

Sammy stood up, and they looked at one another for a moment before shaking hands.

"Sad," said Sammy, wanting to add something traditional about extending his condolences, but there was something in Andreas's facial expression that made such a line unnecessary, even foolish. They had met very briefly during the investigation of the school fire, but another officer had done the questioning of the Mattsson family.

Andreas simply nodded, and sat down with a grimace.

"You're working," Sammy observed.

"What should I do otherwise?" He told Sammy unexpectedly verbosely who he was working for at the moment, driving for Peab in Dannemora. "You've got to take advantage, things are going well now."

"Do you know Lovisa Friman?"

"Was she the one who died in the smithy?"

"We don't know that, but it came up as a suggestion from your dad."

Andreas hummed and looked away. "It's not impossible. I heard some talk that she was back. And she's always been dense."

"What do you mean?"

"Dim-witted enough to go with Daniel."

"Was Daniel dim-witted too?"

Andreas leaned forward, put his arms on the table, and sighed. Normally a gesture of confidence, quite different from his father's blunt attitude and body language. "He was a dreamer," he said at last. "Someone who was always someplace else."

"What did he dream about?"

Andreas hummed again and closed his eyes. "I'm really tired."

Sammy repeated his question. Andreas opened his eyes, looked around, seemingly disoriented, as if he had to survey his surroundings.

"I can take it," said Andreas. "Driving gravel for days on end, eight hours a day, often more. I can take it, because I have to, but mostly because I can set aside money to get out of here. Then you don't have time to float in the air, like Daniel did. You just keep going, save up, and then leave."

"Where will you go?"

"The Philippines. Diving. I'm a diving instructor. In the worst case Thailand. There's always work. I spent a winter on Ko Lanta."

Something aggressive came over him. Sammy sensed that he sometimes had to defend his interest in diving.

"That would be something, learning to dive."

"Come down, I've had guys in their sixties get certified."

"I've thought about it," said Sammy. "And the farm and the hauling business?"

"Daniel would take that over, that was the idea. Or that's what Waldemar thought."

"And that wasn't something you were upset about?"

Andreas sighed, raised his arms straight up, and then clasped his hands and let them rest behind his neck, leaned back, and looked toward the sky. "Maybe at first, when I realized how it was, how everything fit together, but now it doesn't matter."

This was what Sammy appreciated about his occupation as a policeman: the privilege of being able to see the cards. Often it was not a complicated game. Every person had a price, and even if they raised the stakes it came to a point where the cards had to be put on the table. They weren't there yet, he realized. He had one card, or rather the edge of a card that was peeking out, maybe it was a low card, maybe a face card, maybe an ace.

Andreas Mattsson gave a dual impression, on the one hand open, childishly immediate, on the other hand strangely powerless. It was not just physical tiredness, there was something else that held him back and gave his gestures a resigned impression.

"What is it that fits together?"

Andreas sighed and looked unexpectedly embarrassed, but did not reply.

"And what happens now?" Sammy asked.

"I don't know. I don't know a damn thing about this farm."

"You dream about diving. What did Daniel dream about? You said that he was a dreamer."

"He could get really hotheaded. Even when he was sober. Some people got scared, but I mostly got tired of the game, because I knew that he wasn't doing well."

"Why?"

Andreas looked around again, as if he thought that someone was eavesdropping.

"Sometimes I got the feeling that he was gay. He had girlfriends and that, sometimes for a little longer time."

"There was a girl in the smithy."

"Yeah, yeah, he was with girls, I said, but I think he wanted to try something else."

"But you think he was afraid of it?"

Andreas nodded.

"You don't have a picture of the girl who died?"

"Yes, but she was severely burned," said Sammy.

"I want to see."

"We'll have to wait until my partner comes back."

"I have to go talk with my dad, but I'll hear when your buddy arrives. Is that okay?"

"It's fine," said Sammy, who had nothing against having a few seconds to himself. It was the talk about diving that disturbed his focus. Angelika seldom if ever wanted to travel anywhere. He always wanted to go, and it had only gotten worse with the years. He thought unbidden about Lindell, who went away, not that far, but still. It was a journey, a kind of flight, that she actually completed. When they were colleagues he had sometimes daydreamed, and a few times at night, that he and Ann would take off together, leave everything behind. It was when Ann started talking about how she had to get away, break her alcohol dependence, break with life as a police officer, that Sammy in his thoughts had followed along, let go. One time he'd asked "Where should we go?" and Ann had been upset. She later apologized and blamed her sensitivity on the fact that she'd been drinking, but they both knew that there was a reason for the tears, as if an underground river broke through for a few seconds. "Erik is everything," she said, as if she was excusing herself. Sammy knew that she struggled to give him a reasonable life, not least to maintain her son's respect for her. He guessed that without Erik she would have totally collapsed, her worry and fear about the past and what was to come had been so deep. Besides the work situation at Violent Crimes, there was the islander Edvard, who sat like a thorn in her heart. The fact was that Sammy sometimes felt jealous when Ann talked about how stupid she'd been to let Edvard slip away.

Bodin returned with a neutral expression, but his introductory remark, once he'd sat down, was anything but. "I think it's her, Miss Lovisa." He reported that no one had answered when he knocked at the Frimans', but that there were signs that someone was living there. There was a trash bag on the front stoop, and a few more in the garbage can.

"Did you find anything? In the bags I mean?"

Bodin shook his head. "On the other hand I talked with the nearest neighbor. He maintained that he saw Lovisa Friman most recently the other day, and then on a bicycle. There was no bicycle at the house."

"Had he seen anything else?"

"Both yes and no. The Friman house is very isolated, about four hundred meters from the road, where the neighbor lives, but he thought that cars had driven up to the house, in the evening."

"What's he like, the neighbor?"

"Nils Enar Andersson, eighty years old maybe, glasses with thick lenses, work clothes. Lives alone and always seems to have. Likes to talk. He has worked here at the farm, he maintained."

"Who takes care of the house? I mean if the Frimans are out on a long sailing trip someone must see to the house, bring in the mail and so on?"

"A relative, half brother to Lovisa, who doesn't live too far away, but his name isn't Friman. The neighbor didn't remember what his name was. He and the Frimans don't appear to have had that much contact. I got the impression that they didn't get along."

"We'll check that."

"The grunt will do that."

"Who is this grunt?"

"A trainee, who loves to sit in front of the screen, ideal for internal surveillance. I don't think it's completely impossible to trace the sailors either. I've put him on that too," said Bodin.

They digested what they had collected so far.

"This is a strange village," Sammy said, breaking the silence. "Open, yet closed. Idyllic, yet so full of shit."

"There are a few," Bodin commented, apparently with no great eagerness to expand on the subject.

"Sweden," said Sammy, but did not explain further what he meant, didn't think he needed to. Bodin seemed alert.

Andreas Mattsson walked slowly toward them. At the same moment Bodin's phone rang. He answered and hummed, clicked away the call.

"The sailors have a page on Facebook. The grunt has sent a message that they should call or message my phone. And the half brother is in progress."

"My God," said Sammy, thinking about the parents' worry.

"Listen up now, I have a few things on Andreas that you don't know about, but don't be offended, okay?"

"What do you mean?" Sammy asked, but Bodin did not have time to answer.

"A cheerful group," said Andreas.

Bodin observed him. This was the first time they'd met. He took out a small tape recorder from the shoulder bag he always dragged with him. "Do you have anything against us recording?"

"If it amuses you, then okay."

"It doesn't amuse us," Bodin said dryly. "But perhaps it will worry you. I have to ask."

Andreas Mattsson sat down. Sammy observed his colleague. They had not talked about recording the conversation. Now it resembled a regular interview, which Bodin also marked when he turned on the recorder and stated the time and who was present.

"You've spoken with our colleague Brundin, but we have to take this again: Where were you the night of the fire? You said that you usually sleep here, in the wing to the left, if I understood correctly, but that night you were with a girl, Therese Andersson, was that it?"

"Yes," said Andreas, "and . . ."

"She's unsure now."

"Of what?"

"Whether you were there the whole night or not. In any event that's what she says to our colleague Brundin, who questioned her."

"Bullshit. She just wants to mess with me."

"How long does it take to drive from Therese's house outside Östhammar to the farm here? You ought to know that."

"It depends on whether you observe the speed limit," said Andreas.

"Let's say that you don't."

"Maybe twenty-five minutes, a little more."

"She lives alone there?"

"She rents a cottage."

During the exchange Sammy had observed Andreas Mattsson. There was nothing to suggest that he was particularly shaken, or even nervous. Maybe you couldn't be if you were a diving instructor, a strong current that threatened to carry away a client could unexpectedly appear, or else a shark might be approaching.

"Okay," said Bodin. "Have you had a relationship with Lovisa Friman?"

"You're unbelievable," said Andreas. "Why are you asking me if you know? That ended several years ago. We were together for a few months."

"She was the one who ended it, huh?"

Andreas looked away.

"And now it appears that she preferred your brother."

"Can I see a picture of her?"

Bodin gave Sammy a quick glance. He nodded, and Bodin took out a folder. "It's a nasty picture," he said. "Do you really want to see?"

He handed over a photo, which Andreas looked at for a few seconds. "It's Lovisa," he said, and for the first time a crack could be noticed in his previously so self-assured attitude. He looked at the picture again. Motionless, absent for a few seconds.

"How can you be so sure?" said Sammy.

"I just know."

"Because you saw her on Saturday night by the smithy? Maybe you saw her coming? You said that you went to see Therese in Östhammar around five o'clock. When did Lovisa bicycle to the farm, do you remember that?"

"I don't know when she arrived, because I didn't see her. I didn't even know that Daniel was here."

"Where did you think he was?"

"I don't keep track of him."

"I see," said Bodin, after a long silence. "You went to Therese's at five, then you drove to Öregrund and ate at the Bojabäs restaurant, that's confirmed, and returned to her cottage. Are you a couple?"

"Kind of."

"We have to go to Östhammar and talk with Therese again, you do understand that?" said Sammy. He felt compelled to assist in the game, even though he didn't have all the information.

"You'll do what you want."

"You said that she wanted to mess with you. Why would she want to do that?"

No reply.

"I understand that you think it's annoying to talk with us," said Sammy. "But we must get this clarified. You've lost a brother . . . and an ex that perhaps you still have feelings for. That's heavy and we understand—"

"And now you doubt your girlfriend, Therese," Bodin interrupted. "That can't be fun." His language, which Sammy thought was downright boorish, underscored in a peculiar way the impudence in his conduct and teasing interrogation style.

Andreas showed no signs of worry, other than that his jaw was grinding, as if something was stuck between his teeth.

"Are you having a rough patch, you and Therese?" said Bodin.

"That has nothing to do with you."

"Yes, it does, if it influences her testimony, if she wants to put you in a jam, maybe get revenge for something you've said or done."

He's clever, Sammy thought, *and I don't even know what his first name is. I know nothing about his family or background, other than that he comes from Norberg or something like that.*

"Yes, things are a little shaky for us right now," Andreas admitted.

"Is Therese jealous? She knew that your old girlfriend had come back, didn't she?"

Andreas did not reply.

"You have a BMW, right? Speed yellow."

"How is that?"

"It's conspicuous, I saw it right away when I drove up to the farm."

"You're just trying to lock me up!"

"Yes, if you've done something illegal, that's my job."

"You have to find a scapegoat."

"Okay," Bodin said with a sigh. "Let's drop the car, let's drop Therese, and talk a little about the party."

"What party?"

"Yes, which one is it now? There are a few on that side."

"Which side?"

"You appear—"

"I've put that behind me, get it? Don't come here and talk about things that a person did years ago."

Now Sammy wanted to break in, but he couldn't think of a reasonable excuse.

"You've made an apology?"

"I don't need to tell you a thing. Am I accused of anything?"

"No, not at all," said Bodin and smiled, but in the context it stood out mostly as a promise of future difficulties. "But of course it's interesting. Does Lovisa have any tattoos?"

Andreas looked up. Now, if not panic, then in any event there was fear in his eyes. He looked at Sammy, as if he could clear up the situation.

"You're actually the one who did it?"

"On her neck," Andreas said barely audibly, because now he knew for sure that it was Lovisa who died in the smithy. The silence that ensued was only broken by a blackbird sitting at the top of a scrubby spruce. It spoke quietly at first about spring, but then sang out its joy. Andreas raised his eyes and observed it. Sammy and Bodin waited. If there was anything to admit, or even confess, it could come now.

"Did you burn down the smithy to create a little panic in the village? It would undeniably look like revenge for the school fire and the victims there. The party and the militias would come running and shout about retaliation. Facebook would be overflowing with hate."

Andreas did not seem to be listening, did not give Bodin any notice, but stood up instead.

"Maybe you didn't know that Daniel and Lovisa were there. He was supposed to go with the others to Stavby, wasn't that so?" Bodin resumed.

"It was like a contagion," said Andreas. "You know, plague. I was involved, I marched, there are pictures on YouTube. I was drawn in and I drew Lovisa in. Infected her."

Bodin pushed the tape recorder closer to Andreas.

"She became a different person. She went to Ludvika where there's a gang of crazies. I recognize a couple of them. They hang out in an old country store or something like that, they have weapons training in the forest and believe in the return of the Third Reich. She went there!"

"When was this?"

"Two years ago. Then she came back and started dating Daniel, left for England for a while and then to Dalarna again and then . . ."

They waited for him to continue but he left it at that. "She became a different person," Andreas Mattsson repeated at last. This worn formulation, which Sammy had heard so many times, and which was brought out when you uncomprehendingly faced the other person.

"And then back here," said Bodin, "only to get burned up." For the first time you could sense a bit of empathy in his voice.

Andreas sank down on the garden chair. Bodin reached over and turned off the tape recorder. Sammy felt relieved. It had been a strain to see Andreas's transformation, from powerful to crushed. He was no longer straight-backed, but had gradually been slumping more and more.

"I have to ask one thing, outside the protocol so to speak. What were you thinking, how would the racially pure Sweden be achieved?" Sammy asked.

Andreas showed no desire to answer the question. Sammy was unsure whether he even understood it.

Sammy's phone rang. "I have to take this," he said, getting up and walking away.

"Hi! I have an idea about who the woman in the smithy is," said Ann Lindell.

"Lovisa Friman," said Sammy.

"How did you know?"

"Classic police work. More interesting is how you guessed correctly."

"I did what Berglund would've done," said Lindell.

"And that is?"

"I sat down and had a chat over a cup of coffee with someone who keeps up on things. A former coworker from the creamery who came to visit. She's the same age as Lovisa. They were friends before."

"Do you have any more info?"

"Are you upset?"

"No, but I've just been questioning a guy who's falling apart."

"Big brother Mattsson, maybe? I saw him drive up half an hour ago. He didn't look happy, but he has a cool car."

"Listen, I have to talk with Bodin. We'll be in touch!" Sammy pressed away the call. He couldn't be angry at her, but he was a little irritated. He'd always had a problem with private investigators. He turned around; Andreas had disappeared. Bodin looked content, as if he were soaking up sun.

✦

Twenty

The two policemen lingered at Hamra for a while. The blackbird had resumed its concert. A gentle breeze carried aromas with it. If it weren't for murder and arson, it would all appear really pleasant.

"How'd you get the info?"

"The grunt called when I was on my way here. And then Nils Enar Andersson, the Frimans' neighbor, gossiped that Andreas Mattsson had been together with Lovisa, and a little more too."

"Have you checked whether Lovisa's parents have been in contact?"

"Nothing yet," said Bodin.

"Can we go into the house?"

Sammy already knew the answer, but tried the idea anyway. Bodin just grinned.

"We'll probably have to wait nicely," he said. "And I don't think the answers are there. I think she just became an unplanned victim, that the target was Daniel, and perhaps not even that. The smithy was the target."

"So where do we find the perpetrator?"

"Hard to say," said Bodin after a moment's thought. "But revenge is probably close at hand. You burn up our school, we burn down your house. Someone thought the smithy was empty, but then Daniel rushes out and the murder becomes a necessity to silence him."

Sammy was doubtful, but did not object. He had almost completely stopped doing that. Whether that was a sign of maturity or simply indifference was hard to say.

"Let's get going to Friman's! What time is it in the Caribbean? Maybe they've gone to bed."

"On the contrary," said Bodin. "They're having lunch now."

"Let's go there, check the terrain, so to speak, maybe exchange a few words with the neighbor."

Bodin did not look convinced, but hauled himself out of the garden chair.

The house was dilapidated. For some reason Sammy had expected a lovely villa, maybe it was sailing in the Caribbean that made him think that, but the money had probably gone to the boat and not to fixing gutters, paint, and window putty. Lovisa probably hadn't done much to decorate; it simply looked trashy.

Sammy walked around the house, peeking in through the windows. The kitchen was one big mess, with beer cans, pizza cartons, and glasses piled up, but the living room looked neat, with simple, nice-looking furniture and a well-maintained wood floor. One wall was dominated by a large maritime painting depicting a sailboat, from what Sammy could see under an Åland flag, perhaps en route home from Australia with wheat. He stood awhile and observed the painting. He heard how Bodin opened a door in a storage building, perhaps a woodshed. He was truly a lone wolf who liked poking around on his own.

On the back side of the house a stairway led down to the cellar. The handrail had rusted away. Trash had collected around a covered well. There was also a punctured soccer ball. He took the seven steps down with hesitation, because he had experienced this before, suspected mischief. The window in the door was broken and covered with a piece of cloth, which was also starting to give way to weather and wind. He pushed down the handle. It was unlocked. He went up, looking for Bodin, who was not visible, went down again, and carefully opened the door. A puff of unclean air streamed out. On the inside was a lone key. The room smelled enclosed, of sewage and old rotten garbage. Shit. Human shit.

"What are you doing?"

He ignored Bodin's call and instead opened the door wide, stepping to the side, as if he instinctively wanted to air out the bad smell but not get caught in the draft streaming out. A narrow corridor with a couple of doors on either side. A pair of skis leaned against the wall and a bucket with a lid was at the far end of the corridor, that was all. The bare concrete floor was stained. He turned his head. Bodin was standing at the top of the stairs. Sammy nodded.

"I think we have something here, maybe a crime scene," he said. Bodin's expression was hard to decipher.

✦

Twenty-One

How unimaginative was the first thing she thought, *a piece of wood thrown through the window.* She picked it up from the floor, twisted and turned it to try to make sense of it. There was a printed message. Black marker. Three words. The message was simple and could not be misunderstood: "Stop snooping cop."

It's Gösta was her second thought. That was probably mostly due to the piece of wood and not from any reasonable suspicion, because the carpenter wasn't the only one with access to a wooden joist. It was amateurishly cut besides, crooked in a way that Gösta would never allow himself to do.

Ann went out in the kitchen to get a plastic bag. Maybe someone at Forensics could find something interesting, but then it struck her that it wasn't worth the effort. She couldn't keep from calling Sammy, however. Maybe because she had to talk with someone, maybe to tease her old colleague a little, that it wasn't just Sammy who perceived her as a private detective.

He answered immediately and she told him.

"Where's the board?"

"I'm saving it for now. If there are more, then we'll probably have to do something about it." She avoided bringing up the stinking badger in her bed.

"This fucking village," Sammy said with emphasis.

Lindell smiled. "Yes, it sure is," she said.

She could hear someone talking in the background. "Could you take fingerprints from the woman in the smithy?"

"No, her hands were completely destroyed, but DNA is no problem of course."

"Are you still at the farm?"

"No, we're at Lovisa's house. We've made contact with someone who has a key, and he's given us permission to go in. He's on his way. We're doing that, even though the parents who own the house haven't called."

"You sound a little agitated."

"This may be a crime scene."

"How's that?"

"It's just a feeling."

"Okay, I won't disturb you. We'll be in touch!"

She knew better than to babble on and they ended the call. Lindell remained standing with the phone in one hand and the plastic bag in the other. She knew Sammy well enough that she accepted his conclusion. *Feeling?* How many times had she acted on a feeling herself? But what could have happened in the Friman home? Was there a connection with the two fires? The questions were obvious but almost unbearable to ask, because she wanted to investigate! With due respect to cheese, a crime scene beats most everything. Her curiosity was bubbling inside her. Then came the thought of a glass of wine.

She left the house, went to the back side to look for anything interesting, stopped, and peered out toward the meadow that bordered her lot. It was possible to sneak up there between junipers and blackthorn thicket, but there was always the risk of discovery. Who? She'd spoken with the old men, with Astrid, and at work. She'd been outside the smithy, and perhaps had been seen by some of the curiosity seekers who gathered that night. Talk went around, that cop Lindell was snooping around, asking questions, that sort of thing spread quickly in a village like Tilltorp. When had it happened? She'd been at work the whole day.

"Doesn't matter!" she exclaimed, but still walked along the fence to see if there were any traces of the intruder.

After that she had a glass of wine in the hammock. Now she only drank Portuguese wine, preferably from the Alentejo if it was red, from the north if it was white. It was still spring, an enchantingly beautiful day where the sun still warmed, and all sorts of insects, spiders, and birds were in motion. Now was when it should happen, building materials gathered, holes drilled in the ground and rotten trunks dug out, stumps and fallen logs ground down to powder, webs spun, eggs laid, hatched. The flirting and the courting. The eating. Reproduction. There was simply a lot of creeping and buzzing.

The thoughts of Lovisa Friman, fires and murder, and not least the piece of wood on the living room floor, slowly receded. The sensational aspects of life seized her. That called for another glass, the second and absolute last one for the day, but first the leftovers from the plates of delicacies should be taken out. She did it properly, as if Edvard were actually present, sliced, plated, and then solemnly carried it all out on Grandmother's enamel tray.

"Now you can come," she said out loud. And he came. A few minutes later he was standing there, as if conjured by a fairy.

And best of all, he did not make any silly comment about her arrangement on a late-spring afternoon, did not say anything about the wineglass, simply nodded and looked genuinely happy, and sat down on the other side of the garden table. He was not dressed for work, that was the first thing she thought. His hands were scrubbed clean.

"Short hair suits you," she said.

"I've been in Uppsala and I'm on my way to Gräsön."

"Nice that you stopped by."

She went to get a low-alcohol beer. "Don't you have anything stronger?" he said. She returned to the kitchen and came back with a different beer, a brand she knew he liked. She never drank beer herself. Beer makes you fat.

"One can won't be a problem."

"I have more," she said, feeling how spring was rushing through her body. He opened the can, pouring the beer into the glass so that it foamed.

She told him about the board and that she had no idea who might have done it.

"How big is the window?"

Ann measured with her hands.

Edvard got up and walked away, rounded the corner of the house, and came back after a few seconds.

"I happen to have window glass in the car. I can fix it."

Ann did not doubt that for a moment. *Say what he can't fix, where practical things are concerned,* she thought.

"But we'll have a few appetizers first." Ann dug in, while Edvard picked a little carefully from the plates.

"What were you doing in Uppsala?"

"Buying window glass," said Edvard, "and a few other things. I can probably have one more beer."

Why does he come here? Ann felt a kind of panic when she left the table to get more beer. Should she bring the wine bottle with her? Did he want to spend the night? She observed him through the kitchen window where he was leaning back in one of her new chairs with thick cushions. A little too comfortable, he'd laughingly commented. He had one hand around the beer glass and the other resting on the back of her chair, as if he was practicing to put his arm around her shoulders. *Don't be so silly! Relax!*

"I brought a little wine with me too," she said when she came back. He removed his arm from her chair.

"Does it feel good?"

He nodded.

"You don't need to fix the window."

✦

Twenty-Two

The name of Lovisa Friman's half brother turned out to be Sam Rothe. "Some people call me Sammy," he said, which evidently amused Bodin. He was short in stature, spindly, some would say. Sammy thought he was a living illustration of all the deficiency diseases he knew of.

"This here ain't cool, that is since Lovisa moved in. She's gonna wreck the whole house. You should see. She loves to wreck things. I'm the one who has to take the shit when they come home. Always me. She wants.

Everything. But never does anything good. She and her friends were at my place and stole animals that they were gonna grill."

"Did they take any?"

Sam Rothe laughed. Sammy thought it reminded him of a jungle bird's call, shrill and nervous.

"We think that Lovisa has been the victim of a crime," Bodin said. *That was probably more than enough of a euphemism,* thought Sammy.

"Robbery?"

"No," said Bodin, sneaking a glance at Sammy, who demonstrated his most effective stone face. "Do you read the newspapers? There was something about Hamra farm here in Tilltorp, a smithy that burned down."

Sam Rothe stared uncomprehending at the police. "What do you mean?"

"We think that she died in the fire."

"Lovisa?"

Bodin nodded. Sam Rothe turned toward Sammy. "What's he saying?"

"That your half sister is probably dead, that she died in the fire," said Sammy.

The half brother stared toward the house. "Burned down," he said meekly. The two policemen looked at each other.

Rothe had come on a moped, which was probably the same age as him, around thirty. Now he dropped the helmet on the ground, took a few steps toward the house, turned around. "Is she dead?"

"We fear that," said Bodin.

"Do you know if she had any tattoos?"

"Lovisa?"

Sammy nodded.

"Yes, on her neck, one of those Hitler crosses."

"Sorry," said Bodin.

"You live a few kilometers from here, I understand."

"Five kilometers if you take the usual way around. Or you can ride through the forest, that goes faster. But it's impossible in the winter of course."

"Have you stayed here in the house at all recently?"

"I'm not allowed to."

"In the cellar?"

"Why is that?"

"I'll go down in the cellar and look. Bodin, my colleague, can talk with you in the meantime. There are a few things to think about."

Sammy did not await any response, but instead quickly stomped off. He had a hard time with his namesake, even though he should feel sorry for him.

The air had eased up somewhat, but it was still a struggle to even go into the cellar corridor. Two doors to the right, two to the left. The first one to the left led to a boiler room, which was probably no longer used other than to store random junk: a pair of old loungers, blue IKEA bags with newspapers, and so on that the indecisive or unenterprising failed to discard.

To the right was an old-fashioned laundry room, with washtubs and the same type of centrifuge that Sammy recalled was in his grandmother's cellar. There was also a reasonably modern washing machine. He opened the door and the compartment for detergent, unsure why, but it felt essential to examine all the spaces.

The other door to the right was ajar. He pushed it open completely with his foot. There was a space of perhaps three square meters with a mattress on the floor, made with dirty sheets and a shapeless pillow in a dingy pillowcase. A carefully folded blanket was at the foot. On an old dresser paper plates were heaped in a considerable pile, and on the top were a knife and fork, still with dried scraps of food. On the floor below was a spoon. Along the wall were rows of opened cans. Sammy read the labels: Red cabbage, wieners, pea soup, and white beans dominated.

Someone had been eating and sleeping here, and for a longer period at that. And shitting. Sammy had drawn that conclusion after having peeked in the last space. There was a barrel with a lid, identical to the one that was in the corridor. He did not want to raise the lid.

He left the cellar. There were others who could inspect more closely, and he needed fresh air.

"I don't know anything."

Bodin was standing with his head bowed, as if he were trying to get energy from the ground with a prayer. Three times Sam had repeated his denial that he was aware of what had gone on in the cellar.

"When did Lovisa come back from Dalarna?" Sammy asked.

"On my birthday."

"And when is that?"

"Huh?"

"When is your birthday?"

"March tenth."

"Until then you were here to look after the house."

Sam Rothe nodded. He looked more and more scared, as if the two policemen were trying to get him to say something that could be used against him.

"How often?"

"Not every day."

"Every week?"

"Not that often," said Sam Rothe. "There was a lot of snow and no plows came here."

"And you saw nothing, no footprints in the snow or such?"

"Nah, nothing."

"You didn't hear anything, notice any unusual odors in the house?"

Rothe shook his head.

"You don't know anyone who may have gotten the idea to stay in the cellar?"

Another shake of the head. "They aren't going to be happy when they come home."

"You can count on that," said Bodin in a voice dripping with contempt. "Their daughter is dead."

Sam Rothe looked up. For the first time a hint of defiance was seen in his eyes. "She was a bitch!" Sammy was forced to hide a smile. It was clear that the word was foreign in Rothe's mouth, as if he'd practiced pronouncing it, but that he thought it sounded good, that it gave his otherwise spineless appearance an illusion of toughness.

"In what way was she a bitch?"

"She always wanted attention, always be seen and heard! Lovisa this, Lovisa that! But what about me?"

"And now she's dead, do you understand that?" Bodin asked.

"I have to go home. I have animals to take care of."

"What kind of animals?"

"Rabbits mostly. Hamsters too."

"Are you an AIK supporter?"

"Huh?"

"Forget it," said Bodin. "Just give us the key to the house, then you can go home to your gnawers."

It took them an hour to go through the house. They padded around in shoe protectors and with plastic gloves, avoided touching things. The only connection between house and cellar was a can of sausages in the pantry.

In the meantime the CSIs had shown up. It was Olle Wikman and his most trusted colleague, Holm.

"Have you contaminated everything?"

"Yep," said Sammy, but did not get involved in any discussion. It was just the usual whining. "What we suspect is that the woman in the smithy has stayed here. Most everything suggests that it was her, primarily the tattoo on her neck, but we need DNA. If we can link Daniel Mattsson here, even better. There may be traces of Lovisa's half brother."

"In the cellar there is shit, literally," Bodin added. "Someone has been living there, unknown who."

"Could it be the Afghan?" Wikman suggested. "The one who disappeared after the school fire?"

Sammy had had the same speculation.

"We have DNA from his cousin who froze to death in the car," said Holm.

"We've had worse situations," said Sammy.

The four policemen stood silently for a moment.

"Kabul," said Bodin.

Wikman left them and set off, but a few meters before he would disappear into the vegetation the technician stopped abruptly and stayed there.

"He does that sometimes," said Holm. "Probably needs to get away."

Maybe so, thought Sammy, *but it could just as well be the other way around, that he needs to come in somewhere.* He decided to test his theory, and walked down to the edge of the forest.

"How's it going?" Sammy asked, feeling as if he was stepping out on slippery ice. The two had met at many crime scenes, and respected one another, but they had never talked about personal matters. Sammy actually knew nothing about Wikman's life. For that reason he was surprised when the technician started talking.

"It's hardest at this time of year. You hear them, right?"

"Who?"

"The stock doves, the way they sound, like a short refrain that they repeat endlessly."

"The doves and spring," said Sammy.

"And the cowslips. It's worst now," said Wikman, and it seemed like an incantation that he did not direct particularly at Sammy, who now felt that they were starting to get off track. What did the technician mean? Was he completely exhausted?

"Do you have spring depression?"

"Today exactly thirty years ago a little girl was born who only lived a few minutes. She was born too soon, and probably never had a chance. I could hold my finger on her rib cage, just a couple of seconds, that was all, then I was pushed away by the nurses. It was the heart, they said. I've tried to imagine her little heart. We christened her . . . it doesn't matter . . . I mean . . . she got a few minutes, but everyone must have a name, right?"

Sammy stood as if paralyzed, immediately aware of the magnificence; the fingertip on the little one's chest was such a strong image that he had to struggle to hold back the impulse to go up and hug his colleague.

"Mari, that was my wife, never really recovered. We got a divorce later."

"You never had any other children?"

"No, never, neither me nor Mari. She never really got well. Twenty years ago she swam right out into the sea. She was a competitive swimmer, there was talk of the national team when she was a teenager, but at Arholma the distance was too great."

"So the doves and the cowslips remind you?"

Wikman nodded. "Always. Every year." He listened with his head raised toward the forest.

"Thanks for the confidence," said Sammy, who only now noticed that Wikman was squeezing a bunch of cowslips in his hand.

"What was her name?"

"Lovisa. We christened her Lovisa," said Wikman.

"It'll be fine," said Bodin, but didn't look like it, because he appeared worn out. "I'll ride with the technicians to Uppsala, so you can have a chat with Lindell, if you want. I want to look around a little, check."

Sammy observed his colleague. What was he going to check? Wikman and Holm wanted to work undisturbed, and would not gladly let Bodin into the house again. "There are going to be long days," said Sammy. Bodin nodded, but turned away.

✦

Twenty-Three

Sammy drove slowly up to the highway. He tried to understand how his colleague functioned. His moods were so changeable, sometimes he was relentlessly talkative and then he would abruptly clam up, but he dropped it. Sammy's necessary attitude was that if Bodin had problems he had to solve them on his own. He had neither time nor energy to be consumed by other people's lives.

There was a pickup in Ann's driveway. Sammy recognized it and kept going, suddenly dissatisfied, as if he'd been robbed of candy. Was it jealousy? No, not really. It was something else, and he knew inside what it was: lack of friends, of friendship. He and Ann had not just been colleagues, but also confidants. Now he understood that the situation had changed. She appeared to be successfully cultivating the relationship with Edvard, and that was no doubt good for her.

He crawled through the village, thought about talking with the carpenter, but changed his mind; that curmudgeon would not improve his mood. Instead he turned in to Bertil Efraimsson's yard. He got out of the car, unsure of what he wanted, and looked around. The sign that said *Workshop etc.* was still on the wall of what had once been a small barn. From there came a cutting sound and then the clatter of sheet metal. He went up to the open doors and took in the odor of cut metal. It took a moment before he discovered the rangy Efraimsson, who was standing in front of a workbench at the back of the workshop. In his hands he was holding a hammer, which he set down on the bench next to a piece of sheet metal.

"Visitor," he observed, taking off his protective glasses and going up to the door.

"Am I disturbing you? My name is Sammy Nilsson and—"

"I know who you are. And you're not disturbing me, I have all the time in the world."

Sammy extended a hand, but Efraimsson held his right hand up meaningfully, oily and dirty.

"I like to say that it's the only thing that separates me from a Negro. I'm white on my face, but black on the palm of my hand. In Africa it's the opposite, there they have black faces but white palms."

He held up his open hands, marked by labor and very dirty.

"That's the only thing," said Efraimsson. "That's how you have to look at it."

"So it is," said Sammy.

"Jesus Christ was black."

"You're a believer?"

"I was saved as a teenager," Efraimsson said matter-of-factly. "Shall we . . . ?" He pointed at the garden chairs. "On the other hand I can't offer you anything."

"That's fine," said Sammy. "We'll just sit down."

"It's going to be a lovely evening."

Despite the calm that prevailed on the farmyard, the only disturbance the sound of scattered cars that passed on the road, Sammy sensed the worry that was in the air. He stole a glance at the workshop owner, and a single look was enough to convince him that the man would not let himself be budged right away. Perhaps the tension he sensed came from inside himself.

"Have you made any progress?"

"Yes, we think we know who the woman is."

"The whole thing is a tragedy. The one feeds the other. Violence moves on."

"What do you know?"

"Not much," said Efraimsson.

"What do you guess happened when the school burned, when the smithy burned?"

The man took a deep breath, and Sammy expected a tired comment, perhaps a lecture, but to start with there was only a sigh, before he tonelessly accounted for what he believed. "Both of the fires were set. As far as the school is concerned there are witnesses. Where the smithy is concerned I can't be sure, but the murder of Daniel probably indicates that. The arsonist and the murderer are one and the same."

"Who, which?"

"But there doesn't need to be a direct connection between the two fires," said Efraimsson.

"You say that there are witnesses. Is it Friberg you're thinking of?"

The man nodded. "Did he finally talk with you?"

"'Witnesses' is plural."

"I can't say that much more in this matter."

"Is there some kind of honor culture here in Tilltorp, that you mustn't talk about what you know?"

Efraimsson smiled. "Honor is in decline. It started when Birger Persson was forced to close down his country store, a shop that had existed for eighty years, at least. Then it was the buses. Now there are only two runs per day, so soon they can point to a dwindling base and shut down the whole line. They canceled the bookmobile last year. And so it has continued. And when the authorities, or whatever they are, have cut back and shut down, declared us unnecessary, well, then they send a load of refugees here."

"You didn't like that?"

"You miss my point," said Efraimsson, but did not explain how.

"But there is some life in the village, I'm thinking about the creamery, and the Mattssons have a business that employs people."

"I've drunk alcohol a single time in my life, and it's not something I miss exactly, but sometimes I wish I could get really drunk, every day, year round."

"That would be something." *Talk with Ann,* Sammy was about to add.

"Those Afghan youths, Hazaras I've learned they are, are probably handy. From what I've seen they want to work. Put them to work then, so you can separate the wheat from the chaff. You see that quickly, who measures up. Work, that's everything. Does that sound sad?"

Efraimsson threw out his hands in a movement that came to encompass 180 degrees of the farmyard. "It's a small world, this." Sammy did not understand whether Efraimsson meant his own limited sphere or whether it was an expression that was meant to include the whole extent of the globe. "We wander for a short time. What do we know about what others are like, how they live, think, dream? I've never led a camel to water, I've never been higher than a hundred meters above sea level, and what perspective do you get then? What promised land, what world, have I looked out over? What did I know?"

He lowered his arms. "I'm preaching," he said with a wry smile.

"Hazaras," said Sammy. "You've read up on them."

"You have to."

"You've seen the cousin, haven't you? The one who disappeared?"

Efraimsson shook his head. "They say that the wolves took him."

"Someone was sleeping in Friman's cellar last winter. Do you have any idea who that might be?"

"Talk with Kalle Friman's stepson. He has your name, but not your sense, if you understand."

"I've met him."

"Yes, then you know. He breeds rabbits and has a couple of really crazy buddies in his rabbit club. Maybe one of them has stayed there."

"Why in the cellar?"

"Sam would never dare let anyone into the house. He's not just retarded, but also cowardly and servile. Kalle has never been nice to the kid."

"The rabbit club?"

"Yes, they trade rabbits with each other," Efraimsson said with a laugh, looking really amused. "Breed new ones."

"In what way was Kalle Friman not nice?"

"The usual, a son that he really didn't want to acknowledge. Stepsons don't have it easy with a domineering stepfather, if you understand."

Bertil Efraimsson laced his hands, soiled by oil and grease. The fingers nestled into each other in a resolute grip. A prayer, or a way to keep the hands under control. Sammy was unsure, perhaps just an old habit, but apparently worry had also consumed the old repairman and smith.

"Nice table," said Sammy.

"I like what's rough." Efraimsson stroked his hand across the surface of the table, which was made of granite. "A long time ago they blasted where the bus stop is, and maybe ten years ago I caught sight of this piece. One of Mattsson's boys helped me with a tractor."

"Andreas?"

"Exactly. I like granite, the ruggedness, the heat. A marble surface plays nice, granite never does. What is smoothed out is seldom beautiful."

Sammy smiled and imitated his host, pulling one hand across the ruggedness.

"What are you working on in the shop?"

"My sister has a birthday. She's having a party on Saturday and got the idea that she should grill. That's probably never happened before, but I'm simply making a grill."

"I'm sure it will be good," said Sammy. "Do you have other siblings?"

"An older brother passed away before. I'm like the afterthought."

Sammy felt how fatigue was coming over him more and more. He wanted to get away from Tilltorp, even though much of the old delight at going home had been lost. He stood up.

"Now I want to shake that hand, dirty or not."

Efraimsson stood up to his full height, put on his most beautiful smile and grasped Sammy's outstretched hand.

"It says 'Workshop et cetera.' What's the 'et cetera' for?"

"We sold eggs too."

Before he turned out on the highway he sat in the car for a while. On the other side of the road was the deserted school property, to his left the house where the New Year's party had been held. Then, less than five months ago, the snow-covered house had looked cozy. Now it looked run-down. The lilac hedge that separated Efraimsson's lot from "Ottosson's cottage" was pruned at waist height. Even Sammy could see how poorly the work had been done, the stems were split as if a gigantic, aggressive moose had wandered past and tore them off. A window stood propped open and music drifted from inside the house. It was not an old man's choice of performer. A section of HAKI scaffolding leaned against the end of the house; hopefully there was surface improvement in progress.

Sammy had questioned Sebastian Ottosson, who had hosted the party, and remembered a taciturn young man who clenched his teeth and did his best to conceal his emotions. From what Sammy could understand there was both fear and hatred. He had mentioned that the house and land would be his. That his grandfather was going downhill. Sammy suspected that the transfer had now occurred.

Fear and hatred were seldom a good combination. It was only to be hoped that the boy had so much to do with renovating the house that it would occupy his thoughts and time.

Sammy turned off the engine, got out, and stepped onto the lot where the lilac hedge was sparse. He called "Hello," but no reaction came from the house. The front door was ajar. He looked in, repeated his "Hello." From the top floor came a faint rumble. A head appeared from what Sammy remembered was the kitchen. Sammy immediately recognized one of the partygoers.

"Hi, do you remember me?"

"What do you want?"

"I just wanted to stop by. I'm investigating the fire at Hamra."

"Sebastian's in the can."

Sammy did not wait for an invitation but instead stepped into the hall and on into the kitchen. On the table were a couple of beer cans with the tops opened. "I'll wait," he said and sat down.

"You were at the New Year's party too, weren't you? I don't remember your name."

"Stefan."

"Sanberg, right?"

Stefan Sanberg reached over and lowered the lid on the computer. From the top floor a flushing toilet was heard, and immediately the sound of feet that quickly came down the stairs. When Sebastian Ottosson came into the kitchen and caught sight of the policeman, he jerked back as if he'd been slapped.

"Hey, Sebby, how's it going? Is the house yours now?"

"What do you want?"

"I'm just refreshing my memory."

"Do you have permission?"

"For what? Your buddy Daniel was beaten to death, what do you think about that? Did someone want to get revenge?"

"What do you mean revenge?"

"For the school fire, of course. Do you have any idea who he had with him to set the fire? There were three of them. Two left."

Sebastian and Stefan stared at Sammy, but they were wise enough not to bite at the provocation.

"Nice house you have," Sammy continued unconcerned, looking around the kitchen. "A little paint and it will be freshened up. Old wooden houses are the best. And an old Norrahammar woodstove, I see. Good when electricity prices go up, and it's fun to stoke, isn't it? But have you checked the chimney stack? It can easily start a fire if there are cracks. Don't forget to insure the house."

The silence was deafening. Sammy was not pleased with himself, felt no satisfaction over his crude style, even more so when there was no reaction from the two, but it was necessary to get out some of the gall that was burning inside him.

"Now I'm going home, but we'll meet again soon. Bye now!"

As expected he got no response. He left the house and squeezed out through the lilacs. In the corner of his eye he saw a movement in Bertil Efraimsson's window.

Sammy Nilsson made the mistake of not going home. But the encounter with the two in Ottosson's cottage had opened a door into his memory archive, where an image, a thought, or whatever it was was hiding, and it was necessary to get hold of it before the door closed again. Instead of ending the workday he wound up in front of his computer at the office. He looked up the list of partygoers on New Year's Eve. It struck him that women were lacking completely. On the list were the two young men Stefan Sanberg and Sebastian Ottosson, but also a Rönn, not a strange name, though not that common either. Rasmus Rönn, twenty-six years old, registered in Rasbo.

He changed folders, opened the one labeled "Explosives," clicked on "NCC," and went further to "Work Crew." At the top was Björn Rönn, age thirty-three, foreman, registered in Rasbo.

Two lists, one party and one work crew. Two lists, one arson with several dead, and a theft of Austrogel. And to top it off yet another arson, with a woman burned up and added to that the murder of Daniel Mattsson.

Rönn. That was the name of a tree. Rowan, white blossoms, right? Red berries. Jelly. Sammy let his thoughts flutter as best they could, while another part of his brain processed the new information, drew lines in the landscape, visualized roads and villages, linked towns together and built a network of people in the eastern and northeastern parts of Uppland. Sometimes he liked to compare the process to that of a chemist, who by means of different-colored balls joined sticks together in an intricate pattern, to explain a chemical compound's construction to the ignorant. Sometimes it all got too complicated, there were always many places and names, but he still thought he could see it all before him.

Uppland mining and mill towns: Gimo, Skebo, Harg, Bennebol, Österbybruk, Dannemora, Norrskedika, Lövstabruk, Herräng, Länna, Tobo, Ramhäll, Forsmark, and many more. Sammy had been in many of them, mostly to visit art exhibits, galleries, and handicraft shops that Angelika dragged him along to. Now it had been a while. He ought to call home but couldn't bear to hear any more acid comments, not on an evening like this, now when the investigation had taken a step forward, when he could sense connections between ostensibly separate events. He looked at the lists again, read the names. Only men. In order to crack the solid front of white, mostly young men, he needed to shake them up, put pressure on and get at least one of them to talk.

Rönn. Sour grapes, said the fox. He called Lindell. That was the only direct thing to do. He ought to contact his colleague Bodin, but the old connection was too strong, it took over, and the puzzle piece, perhaps the most important, was actually hers.

The phone rang seven times, but no response, and he guessed why. She was repairing, mending, and patching, revisiting something lost, something he himself should have done instead of sitting in a mostly dark police station on a lovely spring evening.

First to be questioned was probably the foreman Björn Rönn. He called Bodin, didn't matter if it was evening, but he didn't answer either.

"What the hell is this?" Sammy Nilsson muttered, getting up, cracking open the door. Not a movement, not a sound. The nighttime lighting had come on, so the corridor was in semidarkness. Was he the only one working? He returned to the desk, noted and saved addresses and driving instructions on his phone. He got the idea to drive out to Rasbo and pay a visit to Björn Rönn, but put that out of his mind. He would deal with him tomorrow instead.

He called home. She didn't answer.

✦

Twenty-Four

Ann had suggested that he should take it a little easy. They could have coffee in the morning together in the garden.

"I've got work," said Edvard. "And I have to go home first." She brought the coffee with her and followed him out into the yard. He did what Ann had seen him do so many times, taking in a breath through his nose, as if to smell the new day. "Have to pick up some things on the island," he said and left. Once at the truck he turned his head and smiled. She sat down on the bench by the east wall and watched him drive away. It was half an hour after daybreak and Ann had two and a half hours to herself before the cheeses were calling.

What did she feel? Some soreness in her body, of course, but above all an inner calm. She sat there long after the coffee was finished, thought about how simple everything seemed now, more than fifteen years since they met for the first time. Of course much had been lost, but maybe they could regain some of that terrain, mined to be sure, but if they took it carefully it could succeed.

The phone vibrated in her pocket. The inconceivable came to her: that Edvard had driven off the road, and that Brundin in Östhammar was texting her so that she would know. But it was another policeman, Sammy Nilsson. "Call me!" Relief was mixed with irritation that the morning devotions were over, but also with a touch of curiosity. The time was 5:20.

She called. "Has something happened?" Nothing had happened, he assured her, and then told her about the Rönn brothers. She caught herself smiling broadly, while he related all the details. He sounded calm, but had that sharpness that she recognized so well from their joint investigations, those moments when things fell into place.

"And yesterday I stopped by one of your village buddies, Ottosson, who had a visit from another local talent, Stefan Sanberg. Both looked capable of slinging a plank of wood through a window."

Ann knew that old man Ottosson had died and that his grandson had taken over the house, and was now a neighbor of the Efraimsson siblings, Bertil on the one side and Astrid on the other.

"Take little brother Rönn first," Ann suggested. "Give him a good scare. Then he'll be sure to call his brother, and when you show up at the construction site Dynamite Rönn will be properly shaken. Maybe he'll think that little brother tattled about the theft, if he even knew about it, or else the older brother's protective instincts will be awakened."

"You're right," said Sammy immediately. "Both are on Facebook. If you check you'll see what kind of wingnuts they are. They're real racists, but not that bright, not the younger one anyway."

"And therefore maybe dangerous," said Ann.

"If you swipe a box of explosives you're dangerous by definition."

"Is it him?"

"That we don't know, but my guess is: Yes, it's him."

"Take Bodin with you."

"No, he has other things to do," said Sammy, without saying what. "And I feel like going solo."

"You're up early."

"You too," Sammy countered.

"Hard to sleep."

"Did he stay?"

"You saw his truck, right? Edvard stayed, and had to leave early. You know how he is. In contrast to you he's a morning person."

She waited for a comment, but none came. "Are you there?"

"Good luck, Ann," said Sammy, his voice a little shaky. Now she knew that the early hour was not completely self-chosen. She could guess what it was about, but didn't want to ask.

"Thanks. And thanks for getting in touch."

She went in for another cup of coffee, remained standing a moment to digest the information, and then went to retrieve her laptop, paper, and pen.

The 528 steps became more than 550. For the first time she didn't want to go to work. It was underscored when she came up to Ottosson's house. There the two of them, the homeowner himself and his buddy Sanberg, were putting up scaffolding. She stopped by the gate. She had their attention, even if they pretended that they hadn't seen her.

"Hi there!"

They turned around.

"I heard about your friend. Terrible. And then the girl who burned inside."

"What do you have to do with it?" Sanberg said after a moment of reflection.

"You mean that I'm an old lady who should stop snooping?"

"He was our friend, not yours. You don't have that many here. On the contrary, you're despised in the village."

She got the impulse to storm onto the property, but the time was past when she could force gates and doors by waving a badge.

"What do you want?" said Ottosson.

"We all know that Daniel was involved," she said, nodding toward the school property. "And that there were two more who were there and set the fire . . . and that time is running out for the arsonists. But you understand that too."

The triumphant smile she tried to put on more or less came across. She resumed her march toward the cheese. *What am I doing,* she thought, a little shameful, but the fury at their arrogance and mocking grins took over. *I'll put them away, that will end the sneering.*

On the internet she'd found the Rönn brothers, not unexpectedly friends on Facebook. There were also Justus's buddy Erland "Smulan" Edman, Lovisa Friman, Daniel Mattsson, and some of the others who had been at the New Year's party, including Sanberg, but not Ottosson. A picture was emerging of a racist bloc, and the tendency of their posts was clear: They were about refugees, how they were ruining Sweden, consuming our common resources, and threatening the country's survival. There were many Swedish flags, incitement against unaccompanied youths, obvious lies about the increased number of murders in Sweden, that soon all women would be forced to wear veils, so as not to "insult the Muslims," and that it was forbidden to sing the national anthem and celebrate Lucia. Altogether it made for tiresome and gloomy reading. *How do they manage*, it struck Ann, *how can they bear to put such energy into hate, how do they manage to be so stupid?* Rasmus Rönn was an active member of several groups, including "National Left," apparently a collection of wackos, and "Stand Up for Katerina Janouch." Who she was Ann didn't care to find out, there were too many crazies.

She turned around and observed the collection of buildings, the village center you might well say, even if the store was closed, the garage likewise, the school burned down, and the houses dominated by those over sixty. The flaking silo at Hamra farm stood like an exclamation mark over the edge of the forest, or rather like a memorial over a livestock farm that had capsized and was about to go under.

As a child she had driven around with her father in a then still living countryside in Östergötland, when he delivered soft drinks and beer to country merchants, gas stations, and scattered restaurants. It was not until she moved to Tilltorp that she understood what those outings with her father meant. Then the memories floated up: the gravel roads, the excitement she felt before what was hiding behind the crown of the hill or at the end of the next curve; a cottage, a barn, an *ICAnder* sign, a GB clown at a gas station; out of the forest, across the fields, tractors and threshers, her father knew them all—John Deere, New Holland, Zetor, Case, she remembered how he rattled them off, and she could still name most of the models at a distance; people standing on front stoops and sitting on garden chairs, digging in the soil or picking cherries.

Now she was there again, in the countryside, on the periphery, but a lot had happened in forty years. "Soil." "Cultivation." "Milk." Those were words that came to her. She understood that the neo-Nazis were fishing in these waters. The dream of the idyll, the pure Sweden, with haymaking and hayracks, a functioning countryside with social and commercial service worth the name, the secure Sweden, the Sweden that was irrevocably gone.

It was just before eight when she got to work. Everything was as usual. The company car was parked at the door, a new delivery of cheese was in progress. Anton's bike was propped against the wall. The man himself was standing by the waste container enjoying a smoke. He smoked two cigarettes a day, one in the morning and one when he left work. Never at home, as his wife suffered from COPD.

Ann felt a wave of fondness at the sight of the simple and truly ugly shed that was her workplace. *This is good,* she thought as she opened the door and the tart, raw odor of cheese struck her. It was not the first time she'd had that feeling. Could she tell Matilda about Edvard? Maybe she already knew, or in any event suspected, because if she'd driven past last evening she would have noticed his truck. *No, I'll keep up appearances,* she decided, when it struck her that perhaps it was both the first and the last time he would spend the night. A one-night stand. He hadn't said anything, not even "See you later." It was a chilling thought, which in one stroke swept away all the warm thoughts, a terror scenario that forced her to take a deep breath.

Otherwise she could talk about everything with Matilda, but there was one thing she hadn't mentioned, and that was the badger in the bed, even though she thought about it every day. That was an act that soiled not only her home, but the whole village and its inhabitants. She understood for the first time the feeling that crime victims tried to explain to her before: impotence and degradation, mixed with fury and a kind of disconsolation at people's desire to harm others. She suspected Sanberg and Ottosson, felt that she'd seen it in their faces and posture, a mixture of cautious fear and contempt.

She thought about Ottosson, who had now taken over the house and a piece of land, about his dream of raising goats, which Matilda had told her about. *Couldn't he become a nice goat farmer,* Ann Lindell thought a bit childishly, *couldn't he live in peace with his surroundings?* He himself would feel better, even the goats would graze more harmoniously, be enticed to more generously give up their milk. She thought that deep down he was a good young man, she didn't know why, because nothing she had seen so far gave her any reason to believe that. Perhaps she was fooled by his surname, which was the same as her boss at Violent Crimes when she started at the Uppsala police. The man who had been niceness personified.

It struck her that she'd made a mistake. Instead of harping about the school fire, she should have congratulated Sebastian Ottosson on the house and the fact that he was renovating it.

"What an amazing spring!" Anton shouted before he slipped in through the far door. *How you carry on about the weather, old man,* she thought. *Cycle home and take care of your wife who is gasping for air in the heat.*

✦

Twenty-Five

He caught him in bed, or almost. A sleepy Rasmus Rönn answered the door in a pair of sky-blue boxer shorts with yellow hearts.

"Rasmus?"

"Who the hell are you?"

Sammy introduced himself. "We've met. You remember the first day of the year?"

"What do you want? I don't know anything."

"You've heard that there was another fire?"

"I have to pee."

"Do that," said Sammy.

There was a musty smell of unwashed clothes and cigarette butts in the little cabin, which mostly resembled an enlarged garden shed. Sammy chose to turn his back to study the surroundings. Some twenty meters away was another house of a more traditional seventies cut, perhaps the home of his brother Björn.

Rasmus Rönn returned. "Nice undies," said Sammy. "Where'd you get them?"

He disappeared again, and returned, now dressed in pants and a T-shirt.

"You're not working?"

"Sick leave."

"Where do you work otherwise?"

"It's none of your business."

"Tell me," said Sammy.

"About what?"

"What are you going to do with the Austrogel?"

"What the hell is that?"

Sammy had to admit to himself that Rasmus was good at keeping a straight face.

"Ten kilos. Tell me. I have no desire to drive to Almunge and bring in your brother. Not yet anyway."

Rasmus glared at him with animosity that would have made anyone hesitant or scared, but on the contrary Sammy was enlivened by tasting a little unmasked hate.

"He lives over there, right?" said Sammy, motioning with his head.

The blow, or more precisely the shove, put him off balance, but by reflexively waving his arms he managed to get hold of the railing and stay on his feet.

"Are you drunk or what?"

Sammy stared at the door that had been slammed in his face. Now there were two alternatives. Either he forced the door and confronted Rasmus or else he called for reinforcements; a patrol car with a few constables would make the whole thing easier. He did neither. Instead he started looking around. He took out his phone, pretended to talk, went over to the house where he thought Björn Rönn lived, felt the door, peeked in through a window, walked around to the back side and stayed there a couple of minutes, sauntered farther to the garage, slipped in between the double doors that were half open, lingered there a moment, went out and continued his performance by pretend-talking on the phone the whole time, and disappeared from Rasmus Rönn's field of vision as he rounded the garage.

There were piles of mixed wood and in the center was a massive chopping block. He sat down on it. It smelled good. He called Bodin and told him where he was, but nothing else. Bodin was busy trying to reach Lovisa's parents, who were apparently on a flight home, so he didn't have time to be curious. Sammy clicked off, looked at the time, 7:22. He thought he could wait up to an hour, but it took only thirty minutes before he heard a car approach. He sat there calmly, picked up the ax that was leaned against the block, weighed it in his hand.

The car, a Toyota with the NCC logo on the trunk, drove all the way up to the woodpiles. Björn Rönn got out, waited a moment before shutting the car door, as if he was thinking about whether he would have to revise the story he'd thought out. Sammy smiled at him.

"Rönn cuts spruce," he said. "You're Björn, I understand. Nice that you could come. Will you be done soon? A lot of rock in Almunge, huh?"

"What do you want?"

"You know. Your little brother told you."

"I don't know anything about the Austrogel that disappeared."

"Disappeared? Makes it sound like it was conjured away. 'Stolen' is the word."

"I don't know how it happened. I've explained this to the police. I wasn't responsible for the blasting, that was a hired firm."

"But someone must have tipped off the thief, right?"

"Go to hell!"

Björn Rönn showed all the signs of poorly controlled aggression. If he were to get violent Sammy's chance to assert himself was small. "Nice ax," he said.

"Put down the ax and get out of here."

"Gränsfors, those are the best. This is the big model, right?"

"Do you get to behave however you want? Come to folks' homes, peek through windows . . . and . . . make accusations."

"You in NRM, or whatever you're part of, probably make home visits too. With or without an ax. So skip the empty chatter, we know your type, what you're up to. Some of you actually talk with us, maybe they get scared, maybe they reconsider, grow up if one may say so."

"You're talking shit!"

"Why did I pick you out, do you think, when there are twenty others at the site to choose from?"

"You need to find a scapegoat. I don't give a damn that Nyllet is in trouble."

"Who's Nyllet?"

"Don't play dumb. If you don't find someone on the crew, then Nyllet will go to jail because he's responsible."

"Put him aside. Your little brother is involved in burning down schools and you're going to blow something up. What will it be this time, an organization, a mosque, or what? Tell me what has to be destroyed, how many have to die so that you'll be happy in this country."

Björn Rönn stared at him before he turned his eyes away.

"Rasmus was not involved in the fire," he muttered.

"There are those who say he was."

"Then they're lying."

"We'll probably have to bring him in."

Rönn made a motion with his arm, as if he was aiming a blow, but changed his mind at the last moment. Sammy almost wished that Rönn would attack.

"My mother is sick," said Rönn. "She would be completely crushed . . ."

"How is she sick?"

"Cancer."

"I'm sorry. And she'll be crushed if we bring Rasmus in?"

Björn Rönn struck his hand on the roof of the car.

Sammy leaned the ax against the chopping block. "Do you have your own forest?"

"Yes, on a little waste land. Everything else we sold off when my old man died."

There was something in Björn Rönn's behavior, a tone of voice, that Sammy really wanted to build on, but he didn't quite know how. He sensed that the construction worker, who had become boss for twenty or so others, was far from stupid after all.

"It's nice here."

Rönn grunted and looked around.

"It would be a shame to risk it," Sammy continued.

"What do you mean?"

"If Rasmus goes in for arson and you for theft at the job, who'll take care of the wood? Who'll take care of your mother? How will you find a job when you're released from the pen?"

"I have to get back to work."

"Okay, but think about it. Here's my number, when you want to talk, call and tell me where we can find the explosives."

Björn Rönn took Sammy's card, inspected it, and put it in his chest pocket.

"Forget about Rasmus. He's a little stupid right now," he said and slowly went his way. Once by the car he lingered a second, turned around and observed Sammy.

"How do you think we could live together in peace?"

"By blowing them to bits, maybe," said Sammy. "Kill everyone."

"I'm really not a racist," said Björn Rönn. He looked sincerely mournful at having to say something so obvious.

"How did it start?"

"What's that?"

"Your hate. I saw what you've written on the internet. Did it start here at the woodpile? Who threatens you here, in Rasbo?"

"I have to get to work," said Rönn and jumped into the car.

Sammy sat down on the chopping block again and stayed there a long time. The smell of wood, sawdust, and bark made him both dejected and satisfied. It had been a long time since he'd held an ax of such quality. "Hickory," he said out loud and stood up. By his feet was a troublesome piece of gnarly spruce. He set it on the block, got pitch on his hand, took a step back, seized the ax with both hands, inspected the contrary wood, measured, raised the ax over his head, swung it around in a magnificent arc, and hit the piece with all the force he could muster.

"Nice," he heard someone say, and he spun around. There stood Rasmus Rönn.

"You have to try," said Sammy, kicking the half that lay to the right of the chopping block. It would need to be split in at least two more parts. "You'll have to take the rest," he said and made a gesture with his hand over the drifts of uncut wood, set down the ax, and continued. "Tell me what happened on New Year's Eve."

At nine o'clock he turned onto the highway. The radio news spoke about opinion poll numbers before the election. The party Sammy voted for, mostly out of old habit, was in trouble, "historic low level," and he understood very well why.

He turned off the radio, called Angelika, but without real hope that

she would answer. "I'm in Skåne, you know where and you know why," she had in obvious haste jotted down on a slip of paper that he found on the kitchen table. And he knew very well, her damned sister had no doubt made a bed for her in the guest room with the "amazing view." He hated Mölle. He hated Skåne. Maybe not all of it, but Mölle. Her damned brother-in-law could be added to that, the amateur psychologist, who hummed and nodded, and then added on with more crap. "You have to find the energy in yourself. Liberation comes from within."

If the party he'd voted for all those years was struggling with problems, he himself was in at least as much trouble. The woman he'd loved for all these years was foreign to him now. There was only one thing that could make him excited and satisfied. Work. The hunt. He was ashamed of how simple that insight was, but so it was. He'd seen it in colleagues, the symptoms were easily legible: a miserable morning mood, which as the day went on gradually changed to what could be perceived as joy in work, but which was mercilessly broken down the closer you came to the end of the workday. "I'll stay awhile" was an all-too-common statement.

He was there, shutting the door behind him was freedom. Had he missed her in the morning? No. On the contrary, the silence at the breakfast table was nice.

The church in Börstil looked as ample as usual, corpulent in an irritating way. He had time to spare, that was the reward for getting up at five o'clock, so he stopped there for the first time. The door was open. He hesitated but did not go in. Church sanctuaries were enticing, but at the same time in some vague way he was afraid of them. He walked for fifteen minutes in the churchyard, making one full round. He was reconciled with Börstil and its annoyingly ample church.

He knew that Therese Andersson would be at home. "I'm not presentable at work," she'd said, without explaining why, but when she opened the door Sammy understood what she meant. She looked miserable, swollen around her eyes, flushed, and with a runny nose.

"Pollen," she said sadly, but smiled.

"Everything is blooming."

"Without the romance."

This girl, thought Sammy, *is dangerous.* They sat down in the kitchen. *Pedantic* was his next thought, neatness and order, everything in its place. They made small talk about May, everyone was talking about May and the heat. He declined coffee, but regretted it immediately and said yes. Therese fetched two cups and a shiny stainless-steel thermos, took out a plate, set out homemade cookies. He observed her, her posture, the bare shoulders. Shoulders were important to Sammy, he thought it was there that a man could decipher not only a woman's attitude, but also her character. He was not ashamed of the thoughts that passed through his mind, but would never reveal, not to anyone, what he was thinking. Well, perhaps to Ann. He turned his head and observed the empty chair by his side. When he and Ann had coffee together, back when they were colleagues and perhaps more than that, they always sat next to each other, seldom across from each other. Sammy had a hard time with her gaze.

"Would you like milk?"

He nodded. Even though his wife had run away and the night had been terrible, he felt content. After that they talked about everyday things and each had a cookie. Sammy asked if she and Andreas had a steady relationship. "Sort of," she answered, taking a tissue from a holder and quietly blowing her nose.

"How long have you been together?"

"We met at a party, it was Christmas lunch, last year. It was mostly men, some kind of gathering within the construction industry. His brother drives a truck too, and he thought I should come along so it wouldn't be so heavily male."

"Tell me about last Saturday. I know that my colleague Brundin has asked, but we have to be absolutely certain about everything, about all the details. This concerns arson and murder."

"Andreas came here, we'd decided to talk a little. He helped me carry in a few packages that I bought at IKEA, and then we drove to Öregrund. There's a fairly new restaurant there that I wanted to check out. It's called Bojabäs."

"Why did you want to check it out?"

"I work at a company called Windwave, it has to do with energy supply and control systems for wind and hydropower, and we have some customers who come for visits. Customers who perhaps like to eat. My job in part is to take care of the logistics, arrange the details, make sure they're comfortable."

"I'm sure you do that well," said Sammy but immediately regretted his flattering comment and hurried to ask another question. "You got there around six, six thirty?" Therese nodded.

"What did you have to eat?"

"Fish stew," she said with a smile.

"When did you come back here?"

"Eight o'clock maybe."

"Who drove?"

"Andreas."

"And then you were here for the rest of the evening and night?"

She took out another tissue.

"I don't know," said Therese, blowing her nose.

"How is it that you don't know?"

"I was asleep, I was really tired, I was taking medicine. For allergy, that is."

Sammy waited with a new question. The silence in the kitchen chafed. He tried to imagine the two together in bed.

"You think that Andreas took off during the night," he said at last.

"I don't know," she repeated.

"Is there anything that suggests that he didn't stay here the whole night?"

"He . . ."

"I mean, why are you unsure?"

"It's more a feeling. I thought . . . maybe I was dreaming. He was cold."

"What do you mean?"

"At night when he crawled in next to me, his body was cold."

"As if he'd been outside, you mean?"

She nodded.

"He wanted . . . but I think I pushed him away from me . . . maybe it was a dream."

"Had you been drinking?"

"Wine."

"How much?" he asked, even though he knew. Brundin had checked with the serving personnel at Bojabäs.

"Quite a bit."

A whole bottle of white wine, Brundin had said.

"What was he like in the morning?"

"Normal, I think. He left early, so I don't really know. He'd parked the truck in Österbybruk, a friend of his was going to do some work on it, if I understood right."

So many threads to pull on, so many people who are dragged along, thought Sammy, feeling for the first time the effects of the restless night and early wakening.

"Would you like more coffee?"

"No, thanks. One thing, it pains me to ask, but I'm compelled: Have you seen any violent tendencies in Andreas?"

Therese squeezed the tissue in her hand, giving him a quick glance before she looked down at the table. Sammy immediately sensed that the question was troubling to answer.

"I've met him and he seems to be a good guy, but you know him better, of course. People do have many sides."

"When he gets stressed . . . not that he's ever hit me, but I get scared anyway. He moves aggressively, raises his voice, shouts out things."

"Has he been stressed lately?"

"A little. I think it has to do with the farm. He doesn't get along that well with his father."

"How is that? Tell me."

"I don't really know that much, Andreas is quiet about that sort of thing, but it's about what will happen with the farm, the agriculture that is. Now it will probably get even worse, with Daniel gone."

"Is Andreas not that interested? Maybe he would rather be diving in tropical waters."

"You know about that?" said Therese.

"Did he ever argue with Daniel?"

"They were different, as different as brothers can be. I think their father wants too much."

"Does he ever discuss politics?"

"No, never. He turns off the TV whenever that comes up. The other day he said how boring Sweden is going to be now that there'll be an election."

"Are you interested in politics?"

She shook her head. "Should I be?"

"Thanks, Therese, for . . . Now I have to get going."

She looked up in surprise. "You don't want to ask any more questions?"

He shook his head. "Do you have anything to add?"

"No."

"You can always be in touch. You have my number on the card. Whenever you want."

She smiled and inspected the card.

"Can I email you?"

"Whenever you want."

Knock it off! thought Sammy. *She's a lot younger, and you're married.* Or was he, hadn't Angelika run away? With a few quick steps he left Therese on the stairs, as if to show that he really was in a hurry, but then stopped by the gate and turned around. She was still standing in the doorway, with a cautious smile, as if she didn't know who she was saying goodbye to: a police detective who might arrest her boyfriend or a middle-aged man who clearly was interested in her.

In the car came the anger. *What a fool you are!* He struck the steering wheel and momentarily inspected himself in the rearview mirror. *You miss the most obvious questions, the ones that have to be asked, and why? Did she fake you out? No, you missed because you're afraid, afraid to no longer have anyone to curl up next to. You're a bad policeman, you're a pathetic man who's been abandoned by his woman, by his child's mother.* He kept intoning his self-pitying litany. He drove off but could not keep from placing his hand on his crotch.

"You're thinking with your dick," he said, but knew that wasn't the whole truth.

✦

Twenty-Six

"I knew it would turn out bad, but not that Lovisa would have to die."

Kalle Friman looked unusually healthy and tanned, his body sinewy and flexible in a way that Sammy could envy. But that was on the outside.

"She was supposed to go with you to the Caribbean?"

"That was the idea, or Malin and I thought that. . . ."

Friman continued his restless promenade around the yard, and Sammy simply had to keep up, even though he would have preferred sitting down somewhere to talk.

"When she was little she wanted to be an archaeologist. She made her own artifacts, which she dug up and displayed." He threw out a hand toward the remnants of a vegetable patch, and Sammy guessed that was where the excavations had taken place.

"What made her join up with the right-wing radicals? She associated with people from the Nordic Resistance Movement, is that right?"

Friman stopped, appeared to consider a response, but shook his head.

"Deep down she was a nice girl."

"When did it start?"

"In high school. She met a guy she worshipped, but he was probably moderately interested, so to get closer to him she read his lips and then repeated his racist nonsense. Today he's some kind of *Sturmführer* in Dalarna, Ludvika I think. I saw his name and photo in a report that *Expressen* did. He already had a lengthy record with you all."

Kalle Friman mentioned his name, and Sammy took out a notepad and wrote it down, even though it probably had no significance for the events in Tilltorp.

"She talked about the threats against Sweden, but she had everything a young woman could . . . I mean, what was threatening her? Is it the immigrants who shut down everything reasonable, the post office and the railways and all that sort of thing, you know, healthcare, not to mention the retirees?"

Sammy had heard that argument previously, but it was as if it didn't take with Sweden Democrats and others. Common sense didn't always get across.

"She was deceived."

"But every person must make their own choices, right?"

"She was kind. It was that goddamned Nazi who stuffed her full of shit."

"When you're not out sailing in the Caribbean, what do you do?"

"I was a survey manager at Svevia, site measurements and precision leveling. Now I don't know anymore. I thought when I was on the plane here: Sell the shit in Sweden, stay over there."

"Your son then, Sam?"

"What about him?"

"Will he stay here, in Sweden?"

"He doesn't fit in the Caribbean."

"He's not your son, if I understood the matter right?"

"A so-called bonus child," said Friman, making no effort to conceal the sarcasm.

Sammy told him that someone had been staying in the cellar during the winter. Kalle Friman looked perplexed, but didn't seem particularly upset.

"Did you hear anything from your bonus child while you were sailing?"

"No, nothing, and we didn't expect to. Maybe Malin had some email contact, but she didn't say anything about it. Sam is special, but you've probably understood that."

"I got the impression that he was afraid of you, that he would get yelled at if he was in the house too much. Was that the case, do you think?"

Kalle Friman did not reply, instead directed his attention to a rusty hedge trimmer he found in the grass, no doubt left behind since last fall. He threw it aside, indifferent where it landed, and it reinforced Sammy's impression that Friman had mentally already left the house in Tilltorp. Now that his daughter was dead there was nothing that connected him to the village, or Sweden, he had hinted several times.

"They're beautiful when they blossom," he said, pointing toward a carpet of sturdy leaves growing in the shade from a hedge on the north side of the house. "But they spread like crazy. Comfrey."

Sammy had to walk faster to keep up when Friman set off again. "Have you questioned Sam?"

"About what?"

"Whether he set fire to Mattsson's house."

"You think that?"

"He hated Lovisa and he's crazy enough to do such a thing."

"What does your wife say about . . . such a scenario?"

"She doesn't say anything. She just grieves."

"How long will you be in Sweden?"

"No one knows."

"Why did he hate his half sister?"

"Because she was smarter."

Was she? Sammy had that comment on the tip of his tongue, but kept it to himself.

"Sam thinks shallow. He has his little den and his bloody zoo that he builds up, he's on that level. He's never had a further thought about what happens in the area, or even a few kilometers away, never expressed a single dream beyond getting more rabbits and all that other stuff, peacocks and donkeys, as if he doesn't understand that Route 288 leads farther out into the world. Maybe he's happy there, in his little world, what do I know? Sometimes he takes the moped and drives to Gimo to have pizza! Then he feels adventurous."

"He mostly seemed scared, if I'm going to be honest," said Sammy, who was starting to get tired of the self-important sailor.

"Yes, it's clear, he thinks that you're going to blame him."

"Did you usually blame him?"

Kalle Friman gave him a look.

"What do you mean?"

When Sammy did not answer immediately, which was perhaps his all-too-common tactic, Friman laughed. But it was a dry laugh, free of all affection, and for a moment Sammy could glimpse something in his facial features that Bertil Efraimsson had talked about, which made Friman not treat Sam Rothe well, but sadistically instead.

"Sam knows he's not very bright, he knows that he constantly messes up, makes mistakes, says wrong things, misunderstands. Of course he's scared. It's only the rabbits he's not afraid of."

"Did you hit him?"

"You can go to hell!"

"I will, but I really don't like your way of describing your stepson. Perhaps he's not the smartest but he is a person. You look down on the weak."

Friman looked at him with indifference.

"Just like Lovisa did," Sammy added, and left Kalle Friman. In the future Bodin could handle any talk with the Caribbean.

"Are you some kind of bloody thought police?" Friman screamed after him.

At Lindell's things looked calm. *Maybe she's working with her cheese,* thought Sammy, but he drove into her driveway anyway. There he stayed in the car. He wanted to think, wanted to be logical, but he was too tired. What he did understand, however, was that a breakthrough would be needed soon. The fire in the smithy was the key, he was sure of it. The motive was obvious: Daniel Mattsson, considered by most to be one of the perpetrators behind the school fire, would be punished, his house would be burned down. Whether the arsonist knew that Daniel, and Lovisa, were actually in the smithy was unknown. The house would be burned down as a warning, or as an outburst of desperate, misdirected lust for revenge. It pointed in a single direction. One of the refugees had returned to the village to take vengeance.

Or! He struck his hand on the steering wheel to underscore his opposition to overly quick and simple analysis. Or else the target was Daniel, and for quite different reasons, and Lovisa became an unexpected victim, or else maybe she was the target, for unknown reasons, and Daniel was simply finished off in the process.

Sammy closed his eyes and leaned his head against the neck rest. A buzzing fly was his company in the car. He was aware that his trains of thought were miserably primitive and one-track, that he was only repeating what he and Bodin had already thrashed over. Sometimes repetition was required, but shouldn't he be able to add some new idea or angle?

"Angelika," he said out loud. "What are you doing?" *Mölle, who the hell wants to live in that hole?* Her sister and brother-in-law evidently. Sammy loathed people from Skåne, and the only reason was the bona fide couple on the Bjäre peninsula. Now he could add additional demerits as far as Sweden's southernmost province was concerned.

The night before he had spoken with his daughter. As usual she was calm and collected. It was impossible to understand where she got that characteristic from, and she thought that Sammy just had to wait. Angelika would come back, or not, was her laconic comment. "And what do you yourself want, you haven't seemed that engaged?" she'd added. Where did she get all these words from?

So wrong and tiresome, he thought, *that the two of us are on the brink of divorce like so many others our age, as if it were built in.* Some of their acquaintances still stayed together and would probably do so for the rest of their lives, the way it's said when the promises are made.

What do you yourself want? If he only knew. The fly buzzed, moving restlessly around. Sammy opened his eyes and found himself being observed by Ann. She looked worried. He opened the car door.

"Are you just tired or are you not feeling well?"

"Both," he said, laboriously getting out of the car.

"Has she left you?"

"Skåne."

"Come," she said, almost lovingly, and took his arm. For a moment he wanted to put his arms around her. "Let's sit down, I'll fix something."

He trudged after her; she definitely smelled of cheese. "Sit down in the hammock," she said, pointing, as if he'd forgotten where it was. He obeyed. It already felt better. Solitude was not good. Even so he was a lone wolf, he had realized that more and more, but now he wanted someone to listen to his lamentation, because he wanted to complain. It wasn't his fault that frost had crept into their marriage. Hadn't he always been there, been her confidant all those years?

Ann returned with two mugs. The policemen's cure, coffee. The stomach's curse. Coffee.

"Tell me about it," she said, and he talked, and talked.

"Get a divorce," said Ann mercilessly when he had come to the end of their story of suffering. "It's been going that way so long."

"You've never liked her."

"It's mutual. She was, and I'm sure she still is, too smart, too cool. I'm a country girl, from Ödeshög besides, which won a competition on which town was the most boring in the land. She comes from a fine neighborhood in Copenhagen."

"Outside Copenhagen, Hørsholm is the name of the town," he corrected her.

"She's a fine lady, a lady with roots in upper-class Denmark, and you know that. And you liked that. You liked her manner, her well-groomed exterior, as it's called, always fresh, a decoration. You were enticed, weren't you? She's a Krabbe, and let the rest of us understand that the name had a considerably better ring to it than many others. Lindell, for example."

"I'm a Nilsson. She married me."

"But kept her maiden name."

"Say that you were jealous."

"I was jealous," said Ann. "But that went away pretty quickly."

Sammy Nilsson got up.

"She is so much more," he said, more vehemently than he had intended. "She has a big heart, even if maybe it's not noticeable. I still like her, I think."

"If you have a big heart, and it's not noticeable, then what use is it? There's a major risk that those around you only see the cool smile and the beautiful nails."

"Maybe you're right. My daughter thought it was better that we got a divorce, even if she didn't say that flat out."

"Speaking of which, I found a dead badger in my bed."

"What?!"

Ann told him in detail about the stinking animal carcass and how she felt compelled to change all the bedding.

"You didn't report it, I understand."

"No, but it's getting a little repetitive, first the doves, then the badger, and now the board through the window."

"What doves?"

She told him about the doves with the broken necks that someone had left in her mailbox.

"Carrier pigeons," he said with a grin.

She didn't smile.

"That fell at their post."

She smiled, but it was only to be friendly, he understood that very well. Lindell was not much for wordplay.

"Who?"

"No idea, but the Vikings Ottosson and Sanberg are probably a good tip."

"Shall we bring them in?"

"On what grounds?"

To stir the pot, he thought, but did not say anything. Instead he made a gesture that could be interpreted as indifference.

"Doves and badger," he said, sitting down again. "Were they ordinary doves?"

"I don't know," said Lindell. "I'm not a zoologist."

"But you are a former police officer. You didn't spend much time on the doves, threw them away, and then there wasn't any more to it, right?"

"I took pictures of them."

She picked up her phone, browsed to the pictures, and held up the screen.

"These are no ordinary pigeons that sit and shit on the roof of the cathedral."

"Aren't they stock doves?" said Lindell.

"Yes, but these are foreign."

She looked at the pictures, five in all.

"I understand," she said.

"Send the pictures to me," said Sammy. "I'll check around a little. Maybe there are unaccompanied doves from Farawaystan."

Lindell made a face that only expressed tedium.

"You're like old Berglund," he said, "judging people by name and origin."

"He didn't judge, but he was attentive to names and origin, as you call it. That made him—he noticed that many people wanted to come from nicer homes, wanted to be a little superior, like a sickness. He didn't want that."

"Yes, he was a good policeman, a good person," Sammy said. "I know."

"Sure, I'd also like to be a millionaire, have a classy apartment in Copenhagen and a small estate on Jutland," Ann said.

"Drop Angelika now!"

"Whatever."

"She's probably the one who's going to drop me."

They looked at each other. No longer young, but not yet decrepit. Colleagues, but somehow not. Loving, but never completely with each other.

"The two of us are probably not just friends," said Sammy, "but allies."

"We've both lived in an illusion," said Ann. "Me with my Edvard and you with your Angelika. So different, but there have been parallels anyway, don't you think?"

"You make cheese. That's why he comes here. Cheese makes him calm."

She held up her hands in front of him. He took them and brought her palms against his cheeks.

"That's the nicest thing you've said in a very long time."

✦

Twenty-Seven

Two days in May passed. The sun was a searchlight and the fields were crackling, smoke blew in from the north, but this time it wasn't arson, but a forest fire near Andersbo. Two days in May, when the investigation of the arson and murder of Daniel Mattsson hung in the balance.

Sammy Nilsson was working from his side. He had seldom if ever been more focused. He refused to think about Angelika and Mölle, he didn't call, didn't text, didn't think about the marriage that threatened to go under. Instead he compiled what they'd arrived at so far, printed out, rewrote, and read again. In the center to start with was the Mattsson family, as if it was all a traditional homicide investigation, but the perspective shifted more and more to apply to Tilltorp as a phenomenon. The village emerged organically; it was as if he could touch it. Sammy had always been good at visualizing. Now he constructed the landscape, populated it and gave the various actors roles, let them speak and improvise, filled in himself where they hesitated or kept silent. The whole thing became a drama that he staged in his mind. He liked that, it livened him up, and during these two days he became, if not a better person, then in any case a better detective.

Ann Lindell worked from her side too, even though she was off for two days. There was a fervor in her thoughts and body. Every time she stepped out in the yard she looked toward the potato patch to see if any small shoots had appeared. She had to wait. So much joy in one place. She pulled the garden hose over and set it down. "Downpour" was a word that came to her. Had she ever used it before? She didn't need to stand there and watch the water as it worked its way ahead, flooded, "pearled" as Edvard expressed it once. She would never forget it, that time on Gräsö when together they planted a vegetable garden for Viola, the archipelago woman that Ann came to love like a wise grandmother. Now the water pearled, and was sucked in, down in the light soil, which before her eyes changed character, dampened, saturated, darkened. She did not need to stand there and watch over it all, but the longing was too difficult. For a couple of days she was expectant, she wanted to see Edvard, hold him, wanted to feel his hands, or at least hear his voice on the phone, and she told herself that it wouldn't be long. Everything she did aimed ahead. *It's spring I guess,* she thought, but understood that it was so much more. It was life, suddenly so urgent, so short.

"The doves," said Sammy.

"Google it," Bodin said with a smile.

"They're diamond doves, I've already figured that out, but who the hell has such a thing at home?"

"Sam Rothe," Bodin spit out, as if it were the most obvious thing in the world, and Sammy saw that his colleague was as surprised as he was.

He entered the name in the computer and at the same time picked up his phone.

"Hi, this is Sammy Nilsson from the police in Uppsala. We met, as perhaps you recall."

Bodin made an attempt to imitate Rothe's stupidly bewildered expression, but could not keep from laughing.

"I see, it's cool, I have a question that's outside of work. The daughter of an acquaintance really wants to get a rabbit, and then I happened to think of you. You sell them too, don't you?"

Bodin drew a rabbit on a confiscation report that was on Sammy's desk.

"How nice. Do you have other animals, I was thinking about birds?"

The pen stopped and Bodin looked up.

"Nice . . . funny . . . even guinea fowl. Good! Maybe I'll stop by later today." He ended the call.

"It's Friday," said Bodin.

"He has different kinds of doves," said Sammy. He already knew how it fit together.

"Are you going there today? I promised to come home at a reasonable time."

"I'll drive out myself, no problem," said Sammy. "I'm a bit curious about this guy. He even has a donkey."

"Greetings to it in particular," said Bodin, whose mood had steadily improved during the week.

Ann remembered Astrid's party. It had taken a backseat during the last few dramatic days. What present do you get for an eighty-year-old? Flowers was the obvious answer. Five kilometers away was a little nursery. She had bought things there before and was comfortable with the eccentric gardener. He was talkative in an undemanding way, and very knowledgeable. She walked around the garden to see if there was anything she needed to add to her flower beds, locked the door, and then took off.

Gösta was standing by the road with his hand on the mailbox. Ann stopped and told him where she was going. "Should I buy something for Astrid from you too?" Just as she said that, her body was permeated by a wave of pure delight. It must have been noticeable, because Gösta observed her with a perplexed look before he answered.

"Buy something beautiful" was all he said, reaching for his wallet and taking out a hundred-kronor bill.

"The weather should be nice," she said.

"If that's good I don't know, it hasn't rained for a month."

"I watered the potatoes today."

"What kinds have you planted?"

"Maris Bard, and now I'll see if the Hungarian has any Asterix left." It gave her a rare satisfaction to be able to speak that sentence.

Gösta grinned. "See you," he said.

Ann drove away, but immediately met an oncoming vehicle and moved to the side. A truck squeezed past, and as it did she glimpsed movement outside Efraimsson's workshop. It was Bertil, who stood with his arms crossed, a somewhat strange pose for him, she thought. And then a younger man who was gesturing. It was Andreas Mattsson. He was angry, you could not interpret his body language any other way. They were the same height, and resembled a couple of boxers who were puffing themselves up at the weigh-in before a title match. He was good-looking, she observed, before a thought struck her. "Of course, that's how it is," she mumbled, and some of the question marks were straightened out. "That's how it fits together," an insight that opened new perspectives where village life and what had happened the past few months were concerned. Ann stayed where she was, and so that she wouldn't seem too intrusively curious she picked up her phone from the passenger seat and put it to her ear, pretending to talk while she studied the two. The conviction that her suspicions were well grounded grew when Andreas Mattsson turned around completely and headed for his BMW. Bertil remained standing outside the workshop. *Nothing seemed to upset that man*, she thought, *not even Andreas Mattsson's obvious fury.*

Bertil followed the yellow car with his gaze, and caught sight of Ann. She raised her hand in a greeting and continued her charade. The BMW darted away in the opposite direction.

The master gardener's name was Istvan, naturally, like all Hungarians. He was a bachelor, about seventy years old, marked by a life of physical labor in all kinds of weather. His skin was like an alligator's, his back bent and his hands strong, even if somewhat crooked from rheumatism, and he was apparently equipped with an unshakable stubbornness. He had a limp, which he tried to conceal. His most prominent feature otherwise was gentleness in dealing with his customers, combined with sternness when it came to the care of plants.

The nursery was small and outdated; even the old hotbeds remained and were used for propagation and as a stopover for summer flowers. Ann enjoyed his company. He was generous with information and advice, and for her he represented a kind of faith in people's ability to overcome difficulties and unexpected setbacks in life, which had been bestowed on him in large measure. He had lost his family in Sweden, his mother and an older sister, and the few relatives in Hungary had been decimated. There was a solitude around Istvan that moved Ann deeply. There was of course no possibility for confidences, or for her to say something more openly consoling. She was one of many customers, not particularly regular besides, and his attitude where personal things were concerned marked a distance that could not be bridged so easily.

The choice was a blue-flowering African lily in a pot, not cheap, from herself, while on Gösta's behalf she bought a white hydrangea. Gösta would have to add a few more tens.

"Very good choice," said Istvan. "The lily must be brought inside during the winter," he added.

"I'll have to do an internet search," said Ann.

Istvan wrapped the plants with great care. It turned out that he knew Astrid Efraimsson very well. He sent along a greeting to the birthday girl.

"Come by and congratulate her, she would be happy," Ann encouraged him.

"That's not possible on a Saturday in May," Istvan replied, and his parting words as Ann stood by the exit were that he hoped for rain. "At least twenty millimeters."

I shouldn't shop there, she thought on her way home. She loved the garden and the flowers, and liked Istvan a lot, but there was a sorrow about him, a sometimes poorly concealed melancholy, that she was drawn into like a moth to a lantern. Perhaps the run-down environment contributed, the carpet of moss under the homemade greenhouse tables, crooked and in some places rotten gables, the dripping faucets and leaking water connections, the yellow reminder notes on the old cash register, notes that had paled and lost their relevance, and over all this the greenhouse roof's shadow color of chalk, which created a ghostly feeling of white blood that had run down the patched glass panes. When Istvan could no longer manage, all this would deteriorate very quickly and definitively, and as a destructive finale the facility would be razed, perhaps by machinery from Mattsson's fleet, hauled away in containers to make room for two or three single-family houses.

She wanted to shake the old man, hug him, and even stroke her hand across his rough cheeks. There was so much to say to a man of his caliber, there were so many questions to ask, about his childhood in Budapest, what happened to his father in 1956, a man in the government, Istvan had only hinted that his father had difficulties, how and where his sister had lived, and not least where his love for plants came from. Plants were the light in his life, that much she understood. With people he had signed a kind of peace treaty.

"Are they edible?"

Sammy Nilsson understood immediately that the question was an unkind slap in the face of the breeder, and made an attempt to smooth it over.

"I mean, sometimes you see rabbit in stores, and in southern Europe . . ."

"What stores?" Sam Rothe whispered.

"City Gross," Sammy improvised.

Rothe shook his head. He didn't look well. Even the straggly wisps of hair seemed affected by some complaint.

"Which rabbits are the most popular?" They were walking along rows of hutches where the poor things were kept. There were small ones with soft, wooly pelts, Sammy thought they resembled toy animals that he'd once bought for his daughter. Others were fat and rough, and gave an aggressive impression.

"It depends," Rothe answered after a while. "How old is the girl?"

Sammy was completely nonplussed, before he recalled that he had fabricated a daughter of an acquaintance, as a pretext for going out to Rothe's mini-zoo.

"Twelve," he answered, wanting to get away from the stinking gnawers. "Do you have birds too?"

"That's a different thing. Not as easy to care for."

"Yes, that's clear, but I'm just curious."

They rounded a building and in a courtyard a large enclosure for ducks, chickens, and what Sammy thought were geese appeared. Some looked extremely gray and plain, like on any Swedish farm, others more spectacular in grand colors and strange plumage. It looked professional and well-ordered. In the middle was a pond with a little island, on which there was a little house. Cackling broke out as they approached.

Rothe now showed a completely different side. He was active, laughed and shouted things incomprehensible to Sammy to his wards, and the din increased. Sammy praised the facility. If Rothe had problems in his contact and interactions with people, this was where he came into his own.

"You mentioned that Lovisa was here and wanted to buy meat to grill."

"Buy? She stole. She never bought nothing her whole life. They took a miniature pig and some doves. Someone in her gang was French or something, I think, and he liked doves. Lovisa just laughed when he walked around in the aviary."

"What kind of doves?" Rothe did not reply, but instead devoted all his attention to dragging a water hose to the pond, but Sammy knew that he was on the right track. "Was Daniel Mattsson with them?"

"He's not a good person."

"Should I turn on the faucet?" asked Sammy, who realized that a dialogue with Rothe was not like a normal conversation.

"There's no rain coming," said Rothe.

Sammy took out his phone, browsed to the pictures of the doves Lindell got in her mailbox. "Was it ones like this they swiped?"

"Where'd you take that picture?"

"Doesn't matter, were they like this?"

Rothe nodded. "I recognize Betsy."

"Do you have names for all of them?"

"Of course."

"Thanks," said Sammy, and he meant it. "This is really sad for you, I get that. Did you recognize anyone who was here and stole your animals, other than Lovisa?"

"There were so many. Some of them live in Tilltorp."

"Have you seen them in your parents' house?"

"Maybe."

"Sebastian perhaps? Or Stefan?"

Sam Rothe did not answer immediately. "I know that I'm a little . . . but when I came there they called me a lot of things. Lovisa was drunk. I never drink, but she does all the time. And the others too. I have my animals. I don't want to be with anyone. Maybe they'll beat me."

"You have it nice here," said Sammy.

Rothe nodded. "I'm nice. They know that. You have to be nice, otherwise they quarrel."

"The rabbits you mean? Can't they run loose like the birds?"

"Then they bite. Rabbits can be mean to each other."

"Do you want a rabbit?"

Sammy held out a box which at one time had been used for clementines from Morocco. Between the laths a nose was visible.

"What would I do with a rabbit? Did you buy it?" Ann asked.

"You have a fence, it can run loose."

"No, thanks. I've had enough with pets, living or dead, and that poor thing is going to eat up my flowers and then die during the winter."

Sammy told about his visit, that now he knew where the doves in the mailbox came from. "Rothe is afraid, he definitely recognized one or more of the intruders, but doesn't dare talk."

"Good," said Lindell. "Then I know, but I think it's best to drop the whole thing. We'll have to see it as a boyish prank. They are young men, but more like boys. If there's more, we'll have to call in the cavalry and strike back."

"A dead badger in the bed," Sammy reminded her.

"Haven't you ever had one?"

Sammy grinned, but despite her carefree attitude, Ann could keep from laughing. She didn't want to tell him how dead it felt. The village had changed with that "boyish prank," worry and uncertainty had crept in. Murder and arson she could take, even explain, but the meanness in the attacks against her house and peace of mind undermined the basis for her life in the village. Who could you trust? Even the increasingly waffling carpenter Gösta seemed like an unsure card. She did not want to openly account for the uncertainty to Sammy, even if he could certainly guess how it felt.

"Tomorrow there's a party at Astrid's, the woman who lives on the other side of Ottosson's cottage. She's Bertil Efraimsson's sister. She's turning eighty, and I'm going. It will be fun, gossip a little, have cake."

"Then you can keep snooping," said Sammy.

"No, I'll eat cake."

"There will be grilling," said Sammy.

"You can check one thing: Mattsson's family background."

"What do you mean?"

"The population register can provide information, but I can't call and ask."

"Why?"

"We'll have to see," said Ann, seeing how irritated he got.

"Monday," he said.

"Is she back?"

"Still in Mölle, or Copenhagen, I don't really know."

"How does it feel?"

"Good," said Sammy. "I have time to think."

"So are you doing that?"

He shook his head. "Are you sure you don't want a rabbit?"

✦

Twenty-Eight

Gösta Friberg stood on the front stoop, dressed up in a blazer and a pair of freshly ironed trousers, and as he approached, Ann caught a whiff of cologne. In one hand he was holding the wrapped hydrangea. She had the agapanthus in a box.

She said something about how nice he looked, and he seemed visibly pleased. He took her hand and for a moment she got the idea that he was going to kiss it, but he was content with a cautious squeeze, and countered by saying something about her dress. This was a different Gösta than the irritable one she had encountered recently.

"I don't often wear a dress," she said. It was new, simple and flowery like spring.

It was an amazing day in an amazing month of May. Doves and badgers were forgotten, she was going to a party. She only wished that Edvard could be by her side. She had tried to get Erik to come out, but he'd laughed and said something about pensioners meeting. He was mistaken! The first person to meet them was a young woman, Ann thought she was around eighteen, who was greeting guests by Astrid's gate. She was almost too perfect, as if styled for a TV commercial.

"Welcome," she said, opening the gate. "It has to be kept closed because of the dogs," she explained when Gösta suggested leaving it open.

"Who are you?" he asked.

"Naomi, Leo's daughter, Astrid's granddaughter."

"But my goodness how you've grown!"

"You're the one who's the policewoman," Naomi said to Ann.

"Not any longer."

The young woman observed her with a serious expression for a moment, before she resumed her smile. In the garden half a dozen pieces of garden furniture were set out. Astrid must have borrowed them, and there were already a lot of people sitting in chairs and couches even though it had just turned twelve. In the village you arrived on time, preferably before the designated time, she'd learned. It seemed that everyone knew everyone.

They went together to a table where Matilda and Anders from the creamery were sitting. She stopped. It felt good.

"Where's Astrid?"

"In the kitchen, of course," said a woman whom Ann vaguely recognized from a meeting at the historical society. Then it had been about cable for the internet. The woman had ardently and verbosely opposed the whole project.

"A little something," Astrid had said, but it was already clear that there would be quite a lot to choose from. On two tables in the shade under an apple tree were numerous plates covered with plastic wrap, from a grill came the aroma of meat, evidently Andreas Mattsson would take care of that, and in plastic cases were bottles and cans submerged in ice. Party.

She did not want to talk cheese with Matilda, or greenhouses with Gösta either, which he'd brought up on the way there, and definitely not the events at Hamra farm, or dead badgers. But, it struck her as she let her gaze sweep across the party attendees, what should she talk about?

"I'll go in and see if I can help out with anything," she said.

The front door was open and Ann went right in. A roomy kitchen was directly to the right and it was full of activity. Astrid caught sight of her and came up, giving Ann a quick hug. "Congratulations! I thought I could carry a few things out." On the kitchen table were trays with plates and silverware.

"Is the boy here? No? What a pity, I thought he could spend a little time with Naomi."

Ann took hold of the tray, heavier than she'd expected, and lugged it out to the garden. There was Bertil, who without a word took over the load. "Have you gotten anything to drink?"

She let herself be passively led around by chance, talked a little here, a little there. She did not want to sit down at a table, only to get stuck in a limited company where the conversation perhaps went on idle. Most seemed to be village residents, some she was acquainted with, others she recognized, and everyone seemed to know who she was, as shown by greetings and comments. It felt good, if a trifle frustrating, as if everyone had googled her in a kind of network of curious local historians and gossips. This was white Sweden at a party, the whitest of all conceivable parties, freed from fifty years of demographic change.

She was one of many, there was no noticeable expectation about her conduct or what she said, no demands were made, simply questions about how she was doing. She was free to talk with anyone at all. She could behave, more or less knew the codes for socializing. Occasionally Bertil passed by and put on his best smile.

This is the village, she thought, leaning against a pear tree with a glass of punch. *It's probably good, but not completely free of anxiety.* Could she see herself celebrating her eightieth birthday here?

At a nearby table sat an elderly woman. By eavesdropping Ann understood that she was an old schoolteacher who was temporarily visiting the village. The woman radiated a rare mixture of authority and warmth. A schoolteacher to respect and love, as Gösta explained when she stopped him to confirm her theory.

"She's writing a book," he said. "She interviewed me." *You pompous geezer,* Ann thought, but with the lowest conceivable level of aggression. Ann headed for the punch bowl and filled her glass, observing the inhabitants of her village.

The Mattssons from Hamra were of course not there, but their son Andreas appeared to be content by the grill. She went up to him. They had only said hello to each other from a distance, but no more than that. Now it was time. She introduced herself and mumbled something consoling.

He just shook his head. "Is it possible to live and be content here?"

"You know more about that," said Ann. "But there are those who are doing everything to make me feel uncomfortable."

Andreas looked up from the steaks, which in Ann's opinion had already been on the grill too long.

"How's that?"

She told him that she'd been harassed, mentioned the doves and the piece of wood that had been thrown through the window, but said nothing about the badger.

"I'll be damned" was his only comment.

"Let the meat rest," she said with a smile. "Set the steaks to the side."

"Well done, or well burned, is what counts," said Andreas, and evidently did not realize what was macabre about his words.

There were many things Ann wanted to ask about, but she realized that then she would reveal she had information that she shouldn't have access to. Instead she pretended to be curious and gossipy.

"I heard that Sebastian Ottosson is going to start raising goats."

"I see, who said that? I have a hard time believing that, he doesn't have any money. I don't think old man Ottosson had many pesetas in the bank."

"Matilda at work mentioned something. There's some consultant who is helping with the plans. He'll get a subsidy and a favorable loan, if I understood it correctly. Goats are good and we need milk for the creamery, but of course it costs."

"My God! There's nothing but subsidies in this country!"

"Of course it's strange," said Ann. "But you get quite a bit of EU subsidy too, don't you?"

He gave her a quick look while he added meat to the grill.

"I don't get involved with the farm."

"How does that feel?"

Ann's question was direct, as if they'd been friends a long time, but it was also deliberately unclear. Did it concern his presence at the party and the grilling, or was it about his situation in general, and perhaps the situation at Hamra in particular? Andreas stared down into the bed of coals, hung up the tongs on a hook, and wiped his hands on a flowery apron.

"I shouldn't be here but I promised Bertil to help out. And you're a former police officer who can't stop asking questions?"

Ann nodded. "Do you have the keys to what's happening in the village?"

Andreas was about to say something, but looked around and kept his reply to himself.

"I heard that you constructed the grill," Ann said to Bertil, who had come up to them, "and put the meat master to work."

"Is it working?" Bertil said, putting his arm around Andreas's shoulders.

"The police are helping me with good advice."

"Do you want a replacement?"

"Have you ever grilled anything in your whole life?"

Bertil smiled. "It may have happened."

Ann observed the two tall men and slipped away before she was tempted to say something unconsidered. She sensed that the duo in front of the grill had many of the answers to the questions about what had happened and was happening in Tilltorp that occupied her, the village, and the police. If not unambiguous answers, then in any event the psychological and material background for what had occurred. It struck her, while she aimlessly wandered around Astrid's yard, that many things were ridiculously trivial when it came to people's maneuvering and bargaining. It became even clearer in a small village, where much of the noise in more expansive, and therefore more complicated, environments was filtered away. The events stood out as natural, even necessary. That was a crude simplification, a kind of vulgar deterministic psychology, she realized. The people in the village were, like everyone else, reflective, often wise, and responsible, with choices to make. It was not fated that the school would burn, nor that Lovisa would die in a fire and Daniel be clubbed down. But there was a bit of *Midsomer Murders* about it all.

How many think they know, or at least suspect? she thought. *Astrid, perhaps. Gösta, doubtful, he's so occupied by his own demons. Waldemar Mattsson, probably not.* And what did Sammy know or guess? The impatience sat like a spear in her chest. How she longed for Sammy! If she called him, would he come? It was Saturday, his wife had run off to the upper class in Skåne, and he'd never had any extensive connections or specific recreational activities that could occupy his weekend. And above all: He was just as crazy and eager, just as merciless to himself, as she was. As she'd been before anyway.

"You're having a good time, I see," said Gösta, who had slipped up by her side. She gave him a smile in response.

"The mood is a bit subdued. Astrid thought for a while about canceling," he said.

"I think it's a little strange that Andreas Mattsson is here. His brother was killed a week ago."

Gösta leaned forward. "You're not the only one who thinks that."

"Perhaps they weren't such close friends?"

"They've always been very different. Andreas the quick-witted one, Daniel a little slower. Waldemar saw that too, but despite that he always talked about the youngest."

"Maybe Andreas is too independent, or what do you think? And he's quite unlike Mattsson."

"That may be so," said Gösta. "Have you gotten anything to eat? I'm going to help myself anyway."

Ann made her way closer to the table where the old schoolteacher was sitting. She was an interesting person, Ann had already gathered that by eavesdropping.

"And now they're free to choose. But I think it's a deceptive choice. Because who chooses actively? And chooses what? Who can drive their kids to the other end of the municipality?"

"Isn't there school transportation?" someone around the table objected. The teacher's gaze rested for a moment on her opponent before she answered. "Ulla, you're still living in the sixties, and in a way you're right to do that, but think about it, who is in a position to choose actively? Would your parents have done that in 1960? You must excuse me, but I don't think so. They were the most honorable people imaginable, but in today's race they would have come up short. You studied, you were successful, weren't you, and you can thank primary school for that, which I actually think your parents voted for."

The conversation at the table, which was attracting more and more participants, continued. Bertil stood by Ann's side.

"I came here in the fall of 1945, when the Nazis were beaten and the war

was finally over," the teacher said. "The same year Astrid started school. And now we're sitting here, on her eightieth birthday."

"She was born in 1923," Bertil whispered, "and didn't retire until 1990."

"It's a birthday party, but at the same time a funeral, isn't it?"

Bertil started as if he'd been struck, but Ann saw in his eyes that she had hit the mark, that he understood and accepted her statement.

"The village is a sinking ship," he said. "We're the last ones." He looked around before he continued. "Do you see him over there?" Bertil pointed to a middle-aged man, Ann thought she'd seen him before. By his side stood an aged woman bent over a walker.

"His son was involved in setting fire to the school."

"Who is he?"

"Allan Sanberg."

"And Stefan is the son, I understand. Are you certain?"

Bertil Efraimsson hesitated, closed up. Ann recognized the signs.

"Tell me about Allan."

"He's self-employed, carpentry, foundations, all that sort of thing, all-around. Capable, but a bit hot-tempered at times. He's going to work himself to death. Has problems with the pump. Grew up a short walk from here. His mother, a magnificent woman, is in a nursing home these days, about the same age as Alexandra Gauffin, married to Sixten Sanberg, a navigational engineer who was from the village. He's dead now. One of the men I admired when I was young, one of them . . ."

Ann saw that it was hard for Bertil to continue, the memories overcame him.

"And the son, Stefan, I've met. A real charmer. What do you know? How certain are you?" she asked.

"Not a hundred percent, but almost."

"Have you mentioned anything about your suspicions? To the police, I mean?"

"No."

"Do you want to talk with a detective?"

"No, not really. I don't believe in revenge."

"It can also be called justice."

"I didn't believe it to start with, but then . . ."

"Then you talked with your neighbor, Gösta."

"You think so."

"Gösta is like a restless hen, and I think it has to do with the school fire. He said something, didn't he?"

"Ask him."

"Who do you want to protect?"

Bertil did not answer immediately. He looked around with a distracted expression, as if he didn't care about her anymore and was looking for new company.

"I've learned not to run around with speculations, especially in a village like ours. It only leads to discord. What happened is frightful and sad, human lives have been lost, hope has been wiped out, and what's left is we who are assigned to live, and judge. But I can't, I no longer know what road to take."

"Is it the case that besides Stefan Sanberg, Daniel Mattsson was there and set the fire, and now you don't want to add to the burden for the family? That some kind of justice was served when he was killed."

"That would be a grotesque justice. It's not up to us humans to . . . I think God is going to mete out the punishment."

"Can't we help God get started?"

"I have to talk with Astrid, she probably needs assistance," Bertil said and left. *You run off when things start to heat up,* thought Ann. She had little use for that talk about God, and Astrid had a whole platoon helping refill, set out, and clean up.

Coffee and cake came to the tables. The mood rose, the sound level was high, the spiked punch bowl had certainly done its part, and there was lots of laughter. There was singing and cheering. Sherry was sipped. Astrid shed a tear, thanking everyone, and the guests applauded.

People started to take off, but latecomers replaced them, perhaps those who had to work on this amazing party Saturday. In the background, between tender birches and blooming lilacs, Ann glimpsed the blackened chimney on the school property, but there were few or none who registered that, she believed. From having been a visible monument to fire and destruction, perhaps evil and hatred, now the sooty brick had become a part of the village that few took notice of. But if you thought about it all, it was a bit like the old hovel on the long curve, or the junk cars on

Edström's property; the chimney ought to be taken away, it's an eyesore, people in the village said.

Ann decided to slip away without any ceremony. The greeter, Astrid's granddaughter, was still standing by the gate to welcome guests and say goodbye.

"Are you leaving already?"

"Yes, unfortunately, I have to get going," said Ann, untruthfully but completely honestly. She didn't have to do anything, but at the same time she felt compelled.

"Maybe we'll meet again," said Naomi. "After school is out I'm going to help Grandmother with cleaning, 'death cleaning' she says, but I think that sounds gruesome. I'll be here for a week for sure."

"Erik, my son, will be here then, maybe you can get together," said Ann, and suddenly became envious of her youth, her skin, the peach-colored tank top over her shoulders and her young breasts, and the optimism her whole figure radiated. She had to subdue the impulse to lean forward and let her lips touch Naomi's throat.

"Grandmother said something about that. She's probably afraid that I'll be bored with all the old people here."

Ann left the partying behind. She didn't feel particularly intoxicated, but it was as if her vision was partly sidelined, the road and the edge of the ditch were blurry. She was having a quiet late-spring cry. The absence came over her. She stopped abruptly and checked her phone, but there were no messages, no missed calls. *I'll call*, she thought, suddenly clear that spring had caught up with and passed her, and that she stood as if nailed to the spot. Soon high summer would come galloping and quickly be over.

✦

Twenty-Nine

The message came in while Ann was standing in the screened outdoor shower, which was next to Erik's cabin. She had it installed so he could take care of himself. Maximum independence was something he appreciated. She loved showering outdoors, the open sky and the sometimes chilly experience reinforced the sense of rural freedom.

She read it in the hammock. Sammy would stop by. I'm taking a chance that you're at home, he'd written, and managed to make three typos in that short sentence. *A knight in shining armor,* she thought, went back in with her wineglass and set it covered in the pantry. A system she used to try to fool herself, but the fact was it did hold down consumption. She gave it one last look and played with the delusive thought that she would forget the glass, smiled to herself, because she knew that the day she forgot wine it would be time for an Alzheimer's examination.

Sammy Nilsson came half an hour later, and sat down beside her. "You smell like a party," he said after a while.

"Punch."

"Punch, it's been a while," he said.

Sammy had many faces, and over the years she'd seen them all, but the expression he showed now was new. He looked wounded, as if he was unhappy about not being able to be there and party and drink punch. It was an expression that didn't suit him. Ann understood that it was about his relationship with Angelika, perhaps the solitude that he'd been forced into for a few days. Then it's easy to take to punch, she knew all about that.

She chose not to ask about the situation on the home front; if he wanted to talk, he would.

"I've got photos of some of the country youth," he said, "if Rothe is eager to identify any of them."

"I told you to drop the dove story."

"I want to get Rothe to talk."

"You want to talk doves, so he'll start to like you."

"Something like that. If he points out Sanberg, maybe Ottosson, then I have a reason to go after them."

"Two arsons and at least one homicide, and you're going to investigate the theft of a dove, well thought out," said Ann, mostly to provoke, because she understood his tactic well.

"At least one? Have you heard something in the village?"

"The refugee kid who disappeared, maybe he was killed and disposed of. In this village anything can happen. No, no one has said anything."

Sammy grimaced and shook his head.

"Daniel Mattsson, Sanberg, and then a third one, who is that?"

"Ottosson, the future goat farmer," said Ann.

The discussion slowed down, and they fell silent.

"Have you talked any more with Andreas and his girlfriend?"

"I thought about going to Östhammar later today."

"How does she seem?"

"Credible," said Sammy.

"Is she good-looking?"

Sammy sat with his head tipped back, as if he wanted to take a nap, but opened his eyes and peeked at her. "Good-looking," he said and quickly got to his feet.

"How old?"

"She's older than Andreas, closer to forty, I would think."

"And you're going there on a Saturday evening."

"She was the one who called me."

"Jesus. What does she want?"

Now was when something more might be said, but Sammy held back. "Talk," he simply said. He stood turned away with his head lowered, his hands in his pockets. "I'm heading for the rabbit man."

"Can't you stay and tell me a little?"

"Don't have time," said Sammy, and Ann felt a stab of something that could be interpreted any number of ways. Perhaps jealousy, but did she begrudge him some flirtation in Östhammar?

"I think she wants a divorce. Angelika, that is. I think she's met some-one."

"Is it that bad?"

"Snow-in-summer is pretty," he said, pointing toward a stone fence surrounded by white flowers.

"The things you know."

"Too bad it stops flowering so fast" was Sammy's parting line.

He nodded and went his way. Sneaked away. Ann understood. He didn't want to empty out his grief before her. And even more, he was sensitive enough not to talk about infidelity, and what that could lead to. He had followed her journey from close up after all.

She went inside to get the wineglass and returned to the hammock. The thoughts of Naomi, the girl by the gate, returned unbidden. There was something there, youth, her obvious openness, innocence many would say. She stood out as innocent, naïve even. Naturally, she was a teenager, and what did Ann have to do with it? Should she be in a constant state of jealousy about everything and everyone? But the fact was that she felt a kind of longing for the young girl, her downy neck and small ears. And then the smile, which promised to overturn everything musty and enclosed.

At the birthday party, surrounded by the old people of the village, Ann could feel relatively young, but that feeling collapsed like a soufflé at the encounter with Naomi. That was why she'd wanted to lean forward and sip her youth, draw off a drop, a scent.

The narrow, winding gravel road that led up to Sam Rothe's house and animal-breeding operation followed the edge of forest and meadow, with open pastures and small fields on the other side. There were no other houses, and the only sign of life was grazing sheep. A single blue sign for a turnout, which looked misplaced, because how often would you encounter anyone, but it was evidence anyway that there was a kind of consideration in an otherwise desolate part of Uppland.

In another time perhaps Sammy Nilsson would have stopped, gotten out of the car, and enjoyed spring more directly, but now it was with a sense of suppressed desperation that he observed the pastoral views. Unconsciously he started driving slower and slower, and it was only when he glimpsed Rothe's barn that the paralysis eased up somewhat.

Rothe was standing in the farmyard, he must have heard the car coming. It was to some extent a different person who met Sammy this time. He extended a hand and looked Sammy in the eyes, which hadn't happened before.

"Was she happy?" he asked. It took a moment for Sammy before he understood that Rothe meant the fictional young girl for whom Sammy claimed to have bought the rabbit.

"Of course!" he confirmed. The rabbit was still in its box, loaded in the trunk of the car. Sammy had completely forgotten the critter. "She was really happy."

"Yes, all children need something soft," said Rothe.

"I've brought some photos with me. Maybe you'd like to look and see if you recognize anyone who was here and stole your animals."

Rothe slowly browsed through the dozen photos that Sammy handed over. "The French guy isn't here," he said. "But him and him were involved." He pointed, not completely unexpectedly, at the pictures of Stefan Sanberg and Sebastian Ottosson. "I recognize a few more, but they weren't involved."

He spoke without hesitating, without his gaze wandering, gave back the photos, and then said something that Sammy didn't really understand. "They're murderers."

"Do you mean . . ."

"I mean the school," said Rothe.

"Do you know? Did you see it with your own eyes?"

"Stefan bragged about it."

Sammy put the pictures in a folder while he thought about how he could go further. This was as close to the crime and the perpetrators as they'd come so far.

"When was that?"

"When he was here, and once in the house. It was when Lovisa had come home and they were partying. I came to . . . I didn't know that Lovisa had come home."

"And Omid was still in the cellar?"

Sam Rothe looked down at the ground, and nodded at last.

"You came there to give Omid food, or something?"

"You know his name?"

"Everyone has a name, and I remember his," said Sammy. "We've wondered where he went. Some believed he froze to death in the forest and was eaten up by wolves and lynx."

"Ridiculous," said Rothe, smiling for the first time.

"Where did he go then? He couldn't very well keep living in the house when Lovisa showed up?"

"I don't know. He was just gone."

Sammy put his hand on Rothe's shoulder. "You did the right thing," he said. "He really needed help. He couldn't come here?"

Rothe shook his head.

"He was never here to visit?"

"No, he didn't dare walk on the roads, and the road through the forest doesn't work in the winter."

"He didn't say anything about where he might think about going? He didn't mention any friends, any town?"

"He talked about some people he knew in Gävle, but he didn't know where they were."

"Did he know what happened to his cousin?"

"He asked and I had to tell him. I lied at first, but he understood, and I had to."

"What else did Stefan say about the fire? There were two others who set it, did he say who?"

"Daniel was involved."

"Sebastian Ottosson too?"

"I don't know."

"That's okay," said Sammy. "I have to get going, but don't say anything about this to anyone else."

Rothe nodded, but his facial expression had taken on the fear and oppression that dominated him before.

"It was good that you talked with me. Thanks."

They shook hands. Sammy felt solemn in some unfamiliar way. He walked slowly back to the car, suddenly uncertain whether it was right to go to Therese in Östhammar. Maybe he ought to stay awhile with the rabbit man. He turned around, gave a thumbs-up, but he would have liked to have done something more, or rather: said something more. What he'd seen was a remarkable change in a young, oppressed man. It was as if Sam Rothe had grown several inches before his eyes. He'd spoken out, admittedly in a quiet way, but nonetheless with a clear purpose. The question was whether he would be able to testify, repeat those two names.

✦

Thirty

It was a flea market Saturday in Hökarängen town center, and uncommonly lively on Peppartorget. The explosion occurred at 4:10 P.M. A boy, who would be starting first grade in August and who had spent a lot of time riding back and forth on his new bicycle, died immediately when he was slung into the low wall that surrounded the square. An elderly couple, who had lived on Tobaksvägen since 1952, were both conscious as Henny bled to death before her husband's eyes. The man was seriously wounded, with fragment injuries in the abdomen and right arm, but would, against his will he later maintained, survive. Never could John Einar Gulbrandsen have imagined such an end for his wife.

After the explosion absolute silence prevailed for a moment, before wailing and screams filled the square. This happened on a daily basis in Syria, Afghanistan, and Iraq, but not in Hökarängen. Until this sunny Saturday afternoon in May.

Six persons killed immediately and twenty wounded, one of whom died after a few hours, was the outcome of the worst terrorist attack in Swedish history. A success, thought Frank Give, who monitored it all from Hökis restaurant a hundred-some meters away. Maximum destruction was maximum confusion and terror, and therefore maximum success.

The phone buzzed in his hand. It was Lena: "What was it that exploded?" was her question. "Some darky set off a bomb on the square," he answered.

That was also the version he later told the reporters who came to the scene. Give made sure to be witness number one, the one who'd seen the whole course of events, and could describe how two men, right after the explosion, ran from the square in the direction of Fagersjövägen. He stood calmly before the cameras and microphones, recounting factually and in detail what had happened.

This was an observation that no one else could confirm, but was the image that came to mark the reporting the first few hours. Two men, two dark-skinned men, two young dark-skinned men, who leave the crime scene running. That was the term he used, "the crime scene." "It was like in Kabul," he said to make an international association, but was careful to appear collected, and endlessly sad. "I think about all the fine Hökarängen residents who died, my neighbors, what have they done wrong? Isn't it enough now?"

It was a performance as good as any.

✦

Thirty-One

On the bumpy road it was just as slow driving back, and it wasn't until the straightaway before Tilltorp that he picked up speed a little, and once out on the county road returned to his usual driving style.

It was a Saturday at the end of May and it was noticeable. People were out in their gardens, he saw grills being lit, a badminton net being tested, a party tent set up in Hökhuvud, children playing soccer on the greenest of all grass. It was unusually warm, almost continental. It promised to be a fine evening. The Swedes came to life. Sammy likewise, tense about meeting Therese, mainly a witness in a homicide investigation, but also something more, he was uncertain what.

Therese met him on the stairs, as if she'd been standing there since his last visit. The swelling in her face had gone down, maybe medication had helped. "Nice that you could come," she said. "Shall we sit outside?"

Sammy thought about Ann and her hammock, but there was no such thing here. They rounded the cottage to a traditional piece of garden furniture, painted green with lots of laths. They drank white wine. Therese hadn't even asked what he wanted, if wine was okay, but instead resolutely

poured a glistening golden liquid in two glasses and set the bottle in the wine cooler on the table. Maybe a bit too sweet for his taste, but it was good anyway, refreshing and promising, that perhaps it would be a good summer. Despite everything.

It felt like he was taking back some of what he'd lost the last few weeks. The dissatisfaction he'd felt, the anger that had built up, was scattered. The thought of Angelika subsided, in reality hardly existed at all, more like an irritating insect that was buzzing in one ear. She had deserted her home and was no doubt drinking her wine with a view of the sea, together with her tight-assed sister and their mother, in her blindingly white pantsuit, a garment that he'd always associated with upper-class old ladies.

Therese was no old lady! Her parents came from Gräsö, and Sammy could not keep from laughing. "Then they know Edvard," he said, "and they must have known Viola, an amazing old woman." Suddenly Edvard was an ally in the struggle against the Mölle mafia and all sorts of misery. He took a sip of wine. *I should eat something,* he thought.

She looked at him with surprise, an expression that after a moment changed to amusement. "Naturally," she said, "I don't really know, but of course they probably do. I know who Edvard is."

He told her about Ann and Edvard, mentioned things that not even Angelika had heard, as if it were the most natural thing in the world. Therese observed him as if she took him seriously.

"I'm hungry," he said just like that.

"Shall we grill?"

She made it sound like "Shall we go to bed?" in his ears anyway. He set the wineglass down and looked at her. *What is going on?*

"Let's grill," he said.

"The au gratin potatoes are already done."

"I love au gratin potatoes."

"It's a gas grill. Just one thing: Turn off your phone."

Sammy obeyed.

She went to get the meat to grill, entrecôte from Lövsta, it turned out. He put his index finger on the meat, room temperature. *I want to grill with this lady,* he thought while he investigated how to work the propane grill, the size of a small aircraft carrier.

They didn't say much while they ate, now and then giving each other a quick glance. The wine was now a red from Tuscany.

"He's lying to me," she said suddenly.

"Why is that?"

"Maybe he killed his brother."

A gull came flying out of nowhere, screamed out a warning, and sailed away just as quickly as it appeared.

"You think that he went . . ."

"I wasn't sure, but then I saw the key cabinet. I always hang the car key, my key, on the same hook, but that morning it was hanging on a different one."

The wine was making Sammy a little less quick, but then he understood what she meant.

"He took your car."

"Everyone recognizes his BMW."

"And you have a nondescript Japanese car," Sammy observed.

Therese took another sip. *Can she be like Lindell?* he thought. Obviously she liked swilling wine.

"He didn't have anything to drink in Öregrund, otherwise he usually has a Hof beer or so when he's driving, and he didn't have anything when we came home."

"He had to get up early for work, maybe that was why."

"That was just what he said, but that hasn't stopped him before from having at least one beer."

"Are you sure?"

"I keep track of my things, almost phobic. I keep track of keys especially."

He thought about the meticulous order in the house, which he'd noticed immediately during his first visit. Everything seemed to have its obvious place, like in a little dollhouse.

"Is that why you asked me to come, to tell me this?"

"Yes, I needed to talk."

She looked at him. Her gaze was serious.

"I need attention, a little tenderness," she said. "Andreas is cold. I'm just a way station."

Like I am for you, thought Sammy.

"I can take that," she continued, "if he didn't say one thing, but think another. He just wants to escape. He hates Sweden."

"Why would he drive to Tilltorp in the middle of the night?"

"I don't know, but he was mentally absent when we were at Bojabäs, otherwise he likes going out to restaurants. He had something on his mind that he was brooding about."

"Something he later wanted to check at home on the farm, even if it was the middle of the night, is that what you mean?"

"I know that he had a relationship before with that woman who died in the fire."

"What did he say at the restaurant in Öregrund? Anything special, I mean?"

"He talked about the Philippines, as usual. He'd checked houses to rent, and said that he'd found affordable airline tickets. He never got so enthusiastic about anything on the home front."

"Are you interested in going with him?"

"No, not at all," Therese said in a voice that revealed that the question had been up for debate earlier.

"Did he say anything about Hamra farm?"

"He seldom does, you can't be less interested in agriculture than he is, but now if I remember right, he talked about Waldemar, 'that old jerk' he called him. They've never really gotten along very well, but recently it's gotten worse."

"Why 'old jerk'?"

"No idea. I've stopped listening."

"Property is never good," said Sammy, thinking about Angelika and her sister in Mölle, and their endless arguments about the farm in Jutland, the parental home in Hørsholm, and "the apartment" in Copenhagen, which the sisters owned together. It was a soap where the scenes and loyalties changed from time to time. There were faithless cousins, a demented aunt, and not least their own mother, a world-class schemer, schooled in the mendacious postwar Danish bourgeoisie.

"Shall we go in?"

In response Sammy started wordlessly gathering plates and dinnerware. He felt a strange emptiness inside, as if he'd lost the exhilarated tension he'd felt earlier in the evening, but now there was no return. He'd been drinking and in that way painted himself into a corner. He had to spend the night, even though that certainly wasn't a brilliant idea. He carted his load to the kitchen counter, turned down a whiskey, and tried in vain to find a way out. There was none. Now he couldn't start babbling about Angelika and that "it wasn't right."

"I've got to fix something in the car," he said, making it sound like he was going to check the ignition or the oil level. Standing for a moment on the steps it occurred to him what had created the sudden onset of discomfort: Therese's irrevocable rejection of Andreas Mattsson's plans in Asia. She was as little interested in the tropics as he was in agriculture. That wasn't what he needed to hear. Not now! Like the maladjusted farmer's son, he wanted to be transported, to the Philippines, Bali, Svalbard, or anywhere at all.

In the glove compartment was the minimal toiletry kit, the one he always had with him. Angelika had joked about it as the "kit for precipitous flight," a joke that he actually hadn't heard for a long time. Now both of them were in flight. Her kit consisted of two suitcases.

He went back in, ill at ease but nonetheless not as anxious as perhaps he ought to be, experienced as he was in the studied art of performance. Therese apparently was soothed by his smile; she gave the toiletry kit a glance and stroked his back. He let go, convinced that he would pull through it all. He would have to process the self-contempt later.

"Are you armed?"

"Yes," he said.

The look he got he perceived as desirous.

The text message read simply "Our dynamite guy?" with Ann as the sender. It was sent the day before, but it wasn't until eight o'clock on Sunday morning that he read it. He turned on the TV in the kitchen: special broadcast because of an explosion in Hökarängen.

"My God how awful," Therese said behind his back. He hadn't heard her approach. *It's the age of bombings,* he thought, and thought about telling her about the theft in Almunge and Björn Rönn, but did not say anything and instead drew her to him. She felt different than Angelika, but he already knew that since the night before.

"I have to make a call," he said. "There'll be work to do."

"But that's south Stockholm," she said.

He stood up and went out into the yard. First he called the station to get the private number of the colleague who had investigated the theft of Austrogel. It was Nils Stolpe, whom he'd known during his entire police career. Sammy thought Stolpe was a good policeman. They talked for ten minutes. It was a little sensitive that Sammy had visited the Rönn brothers and intruded on his colleague's investigation in that way, but he could point to the connection to Tilltorp. Revealing Ann Lindell's source and the tip she'd received in the Linnaeus Garden about Erland "Smulan" Edman was thornier, but he told the truth, that she'd called him immediately, but that he later forgot the whole thing. "That was when everything was happening in the village, and I forgot to call you."

"The informant has been involved with us before?"

"Yes, as the son of someone who was murdered," Sammy explained, and told him about Lindell's role in that investigation, the murder of Little John many years ago.

"I remember some of that," said Stolpe, who seemed to be taking it with equanimity that he hadn't been informed earlier. "Maybe it's time to bring in this Erland Edman?"

"I'm a little unsure about that. It would be stupid in any event to disclose where the tip came from," said Sammy. "Can I go to see Rönn today? What do you say? Somehow we made some sort of contact."

Stolpe thought about it. "I'll have to discuss this two floors down, there are others who are rooting in this as you understand. It's a fucking witches' cauldron," he said at last. "But if you don't hear anything within half an hour, then go. Just one thing, can Rönn be volatile?"

"Don't think so," said Sammy, who remembered the ax on the chopping block.

They ended the call, but Sammy remained standing with the phone in his hand. It felt as if he needed to make more calls. "Others who are rooting," Stolpe had said, that could probably only mean that the security

service was involved in the game, and surely not just them. A bomb produced rough seas.

He saw a movement in the window; his chain of thought was broken.
Now he just wanted to get away from there, and he could sense that Therese
wanted him to leave.

✦

Thirty-Two

Bertil Efraimsson was affected, but still not drunk. It was the second
time in his life, and this time too it was eau-de-vie that was the agent.
He'd bought the bottle on Friday, perhaps with his sister Astrid's birthday
party in mind. It felt right somehow, he'd had an idea that the two of them
would make a toast, but the bottle was stored away and not brought out
until Sunday morning, when it was opened without further ceremony.

The Pentecostal blacksmith could no longer make sense of existence. For
some twisted reason he thought that alcohol could adjust his attitudes to
life, a quarter-turn here, a half-turn there, as if consciousness were a mechanical apparatus that needed to be prodded like an old mill. Resorting to
a sledgehammer was too crude, there had to be fine calibrations with more
elegant instruments. He played with his thoughts like that, saw it all like a
day in the workshop, a day with detail work, with the magnifying glass set
up over the workbench. It amused him, more than he cared to admit.

He drank deliberately. Was it good? Yes, maybe. He sat quietly on the
garden chair, with the bottle by the table leg and the glass on the table.
The sun was shining. He drank the brandy unmixed, just like his father
and uncle had done.

Perhaps it looked idyllic, but he was basically becoming more and more
terrified. He called Gösta, asked him to come over. Bertil's voice must
have betrayed the seriousness of his request, because his closest friend
in all respects hurried over after only a minute or two. When the situation was clear to him he sat down. Not because he was particularly in the
mood for alcohol in midmorning, but two were required for that bottle.

They carefully clinked their glasses. Gösta became exhilarated at once.

They talked about the birthday party, who had been there and who was absent. When that subject was thrashed over there was silence. A single car passed now and then. The wagtail, which Bertil called Britta, came flying in a beautiful swoop and settled down on the sundial. In other words it was as usual, like before, except for the brandy.

"Did you see the news yesterday?"

"A real explosion," said Gösta.

"Who does things like that?"

"Someone said it was that ISIS. There are lots of those swarthy types at the square."

Bertil filled the glasses, which were small and neat.

"We have to talk," he said. Even though Gösta understood very well what this concerned and that it was necessary, especially if their friendship were to continue, his mood was deflated. Why not just sip a little carefully from the water of life, and like Britta enjoy spring? Maybe he could go after the pot of meat soup he'd prepared a few days earlier, then they could have lunch together.

"This has been a strange spring, don't you think?" Bertil said in his congregational voice. "I distrusted you when you said you hadn't seen anything when the school burned, and I also suspect why you kept quiet, but we can put that aside. I haven't been honest either."

Gösta reached for his glass, but it was already empty.

"The glasses are from my grandmother and are probably meant for something sweet," said Bertil.

"Maybe we should take it a little easy," said Gösta. Bertil stopped his movement, straightened his body, leaned back, and nodded.

"The boy who disappeared came to me in March."

"The cousin?" Gösta felt himself collapsing, like he was being emptied of air. The nightmare would never end.

"Exactly, the cousin. Where he'd been staying for over two months he didn't want to say. He got to stay with me, but now he's disappeared."

"Was he staying . . . ?"

"In Sigvard's old room."

"That explains a few things," said Gösta, who thought about Bertil's mysterious behavior the past few months, the shopping trips to Uppsala and the late-evening habits.

"He was sad, of course. Omid knew that his cousin had died. I don't know how he found out."

"Does he speak Swedish?"

"Pretty well, and he's quick-witted, he learns really fast. He is extremely technically oriented."

"When did he disappear?"

"A day before the smithy burned, on Friday," Bertil said, reaching down for the bottle by the table leg.

"Oh my goodness," said Gösta, pushing his glass forward. "Was he the one who set the fire?"

Bertil carefully poured the brandy, screwed in the cork, and set the bottle back before he answered.

"What should a person think?"

"But how did he know . . ."

"Omid saw Mattsson's boy from the window, and asked who it was. I think he recognized him from New Year's Eve."

"And you told where he lived?"

"That was thoughtless. He asked about a lot of things and I was used to answering most of it. He wanted to talk with Daniel, he said, but I knew that the whole Mattsson gang would be gone that weekend, so I said that there was no point in going there."

"But he went there and set the fire?"

"I don't really know."

"Did he kill Daniel?"

"He wasn't like that," said Bertil, and Gösta had seldom if ever heard him sound so helpless.

"But in those countries you resolve conflicts by killing each other."

"He wasn't like that," Bertil repeated, as if he wanted to convince himself that it was true.

"You can go to prison," Gösta said, not displeased to have a certain advantage. "You've held back information."

"I don't care about that. I helped him and I don't regret it. He was in need. Imagine yourself, Gösta, being so vulnerable in a foreign country. Reaching out a helping hand is never wrong."

Gösta felt Bertil's gaze, but chose not to say anything.

"And that applies to you too," Bertil continued. "Have you told every-thing you know to the police, about what you saw?"

"Does a person have to be open about everything?"

Personally Gösta felt no need to always be honest. There must be a place for deceit and self-deception, otherwise life would be unbearable, like an endless revival. Once he'd gone with Bertil to a camp meeting, a guest preacher had come to the area, a tent was raised, folding chairs set out, exten-sion cords laid. It was simple and functional, Jesus doesn't need more, Bertil explained. They were very young, Bertil had been saved for a year or so, and he himself was curious. Bare lightbulbs dangled from the ceiling, there was a smell of trampled-down grass, cheap perfume, and sweat. The congregation was dressed up, expectant, many ecstatic. The preacher started carefully, but quickly and expertly revved up, thundered, and waved his arms. The excite-ment rose. A few fell like bowling pins and were expertly caught. He saw Olofsson, who normally was a sensible plumber, burst into tears. The Berg-mans in the old cabin were speaking in tongues, perhaps with each other.

Then there was witnessing. One by one the congregants stepped for-ward; everything should come out in the light. No one could escape questioning and judgment. Gösta was bewildered. He didn't want all the sincerity, didn't want to hear about all the filth, about sins and mistakes real or imagined, he didn't want to see acquaintances exposed. He broke out of the collective madness and ran off to his moped. Bertil, who had ridden behind, had to manage as best he could. As someone newly saved he was surely able to fly.

"What will you do?" Gösta asked.

"I thought about talking with Ann."

"Why is that?"

"She's a police officer, or was, maybe she knows what to do."

"There's no point," said Gösta, but did not explain why. He felt increas-ingly displeased. *Since the refugees came here everything has gone wrong*, it struck him, but he held his tongue. Bertil always knew better, always had something to say.

"I never heard him laugh. What I thought at first was laughter, was weeping instead. Can you understand? It was at night, he wept in his room. And it sounded like laughter somehow, concealed despair."

Like a hyena, thought Gösta.

"It sounded uncanny in the dark, as if all the world's sorrow had taken over the house. A few times I went up to his door, but I never knocked, never opened it. I prayed to God that He would console the boy. And maybe it helped sometimes. There were moments when he smiled. We used to sneak out to the workshop, he was comfortable there. I taught him to weld, the basics anyway. When he put the pieces together well he might look a little satisfied, and that made me smile too. It had been a long time since I had a companion in the workshop."

It struck Gösta that it had also been a long time since he'd seen his neighbor smile, much less laugh. And didn't that apply to Gösta too? They were on the downhill side of life and there wasn't much to be happy about. Nowadays.

"I told Astrid. I had to."

But you didn't trust me was on the tip of Gösta's tongue.

"He could become a good machinist," Bertil continued. He looked content, apparently unaware of Gösta's increasingly dogged expression. Maybe it was the alcohol that led them in different directions? It was as if Bertil became inattentive to the brandy's effect, he simply let the intoxication come, while Gösta, who was a considerably more experienced drinker, kept an eye on himself and the other man.

When Gösta had gone home Bertil heard the blackbird sing for the first time. It was sitting at the top of the old larch tree. The tree that he had decided to cut down several years ago, but which still stood there, mournfully scrubby. Now he was glad he hadn't chopped it down.

He conversed for a while with the blackbird, which so unexpectedly found its way home. Bertil took that as a sign that there was still time, not hope exactly, but a reprieve anyway, together they would get to experience one more spring and summer. His anxiety subsided a little. He saw his neighbor disappear into his house. *We're relics,* he thought, *old-timers on the way out. One morning we will no longer exist, but that will be in the winter, when the birds have fallen silent.* No one would sit with him, he would die alone, he understood that, it was as if inlaid in his system. No one would keep him company once he'd grown cold, the way people did before.

Of course there were things he regretted, but it wasn't possible to put things right after the fact. Astrid had been saying that for decades. His sister knew, had always known, but loyally kept silent. She was actually the wisest person he had encountered in the village, not counting old schoolteacher Gauffin.

"I'll go to the police," he said out loud to himself, stealing a glance at the bottle, but let it stay there. Perhaps he would finish the day by emptying the last third. On the other hand he did take the glasses in and washed them before he got ready in the bathroom.

✦

Thirty-Three

When he was passing Hökhuvud he called Ann. He heard the news blaring in the background. *The whole country probably has the TV on.* She sounded tired, but wished she could go with him to the Rönn brothers, like before, when she and Sammy were a couple, as she put it.

Ann thought a solo raid was a dumb idea. "A SWAT team would only make matters worse," said Sammy, even though he wasn't sure of that. "And I want something to happen."

They talked for several minutes. He was happy that she didn't ask where he'd spent the night.

After clicking off the call he phoned Bodin. His colleague listened and then said that they could meet at the church. Sammy was about to decline the offer, but something in Bodin's voice, a new sharpness, changed his mind. He only had to wait twenty minutes, Bodin must have put a heavy foot on the gas pedal. In the meantime he called Angelika, who had taken the leap over the sound and was in Hørsholm, north of Copenhagen. She complained about the heat, her sister's unpredictability, and that the garden was in bad shape; the garden help had been missing for a month. He was silently happy that the poor Bosnian had finally fled. Sammy had never met a more timid person. He always dutifully performed his tasks with stoic calm, but Sammy had seen the mutiny in his eyes. Perhaps Angelika would drive over to Jutland. She had nothing more than that to say, and Sammy, what could he tell her?

"I'm standing in a graveyard," he said at last.

Bodin showed up, reported that the day before he had visited Norberg, his hometown. It had evidently done him good, because despite the circumstances he looked rested. They discussed how they should proceed. They agreed that Sammy would visit Björn Rönn alone. They wouldn't bother with the younger brother. His time would surely come. A hundred meters from the farm they drove the cars onto a forest road, where a spruce plantation concealed them from the house.

Bodin got out. Sammy explained where the houses were in relation to each other. Bodin pulled on a jacket. "They're violent," he said. "Are you armed?"

Sammy nodded and tried to smile, as if that were routine.

"I'll follow you, go around the houses, so that I can keep an eye out. Take your time so that I make it there," Bodin said, pointing with his whole hand. He was showing a new side, more decisive than Sammy had ever seen him before.

"I hate Nazis" was the last thing Bodin said. Sammy smiled to himself as he walked up the gravel road. His colleague was more and more surprising. He had some of the temperament that Sammy himself had once had, the drive that had once made him a good policeman. Later he'd settled down, disarmed, as it felt, become one of many, slowly, with soul-deadening routines.

Sammy found Rönn where he'd left him before. He was standing with a bare torso, his T-shirt hanging over a sawhorse, and had just set a massive piece of spruce on the chopping block. Sammy could see how it already put up resistance, twisted and straggly. It was evident that he spent quite a bit of time chopping wood; there were drifts of freshly cut logs. He was sweaty and his hair was standing on end, giving him an almost wild impression. He did not look surprised, calmly set aside the ax, grabbed the T-shirt and dried off his face and chest, as if someone had called him in for a bite to eat.

"Better than spinning," said Sammy.

"I'll get a fresh one," said Rönn. He disappeared and came back after five minutes, dressed in a loosely fitting Hawaiian shirt. In the meantime Sammy had inspected the edge of the forest to catch sight of Bodin if possible.

"Hökarängen," said Sammy. "Have you ever been there?"

He saw immediately that the shot hit the mark. Björn Rönn's character was such that he had a hard time concealing a lie; Sammy had already understood that the first time they met.

"At least seven dead, two of which were children."

"I saw the news," said Rönn, focusing on buttoning his shirt.

"Is that how the struggle will be conducted?"

"I don't know anything about this." He ran his hands through his hair.

"You're chopping wood in sheer desperation," said Sammy, making a gesture over the quantity of wood.

"I don't know a thing."

"Sometimes you have to be unfaithful," said Sammy. "Last night I was for the first time."

Björn Rönn looked straight at Sammy, which he hadn't done before.

"It was necessary to be able to go on. You have to realize when life takes a turn in a direction you never could foresee, maybe not even imagine or want, but that nonetheless becomes the only conceivable thing to do. It's time for you now. Be unfaithful."

Rönn did not say anything. Sammy waited.

"You lose something, but—"

"I know what you're trying to say."

"If that's the case—"

"You're so fucking predictable," Rönn hissed.

Sammy felt a cramp in his crotch, like a forceful contraction of the muscles. Therese had not been gentle and he was out of practice.

"Who did you call?"

"Huh?"

"When you went to get your shirt."

"Am I under arrest?"

The question was so horribly American that Sammy could not keep from laughing.

"You'd like that, huh? Become a martyr. No, you're not, but you will be. It's a matter of time. The question is how many more innocent people are going to die before that. You have a single chance, and that's today. Now. Talk with me. Now. Then it's over. When the SWAT team comes."

"I don't know anything," Rönn said quietly.

"You don't want this," said Sammy after a long silence.

In the distance church bells were ringing. Rönn gave him a quick look before he took off the shirt and reached for the ax. At the same moment branches were snapping and Bodin was visible in the thicket. He mostly resembled a lost mushroom gatherer who was forcing his way forward, until you could make out his facial expression. Rönn straightened up. "Who the hell is that?"

"It's Bodin from Norberg, the one who hates Nazis. The one who's going to torment you, pick you up from jail, again and again, make sure that you get nausea, diarrhea, and heartburn from your anxiety. He's going to talk with your brother and your sick mother, your relatives, neighbors, and coworkers. The policeman who acts folksy, but hates Nazis. The policeman who's going to see to it that you end up in the big house for ten or fifteen years."

Bodin came up to the woodpile, observed the surroundings as if he were trying to work out how a raid could be set up, sent a demonstrative gob of spit in the direction of Rönn before he left the yard without having said a single word. Sammy was astounded, but at the same time impressed by the performance.

"My wife has left me, I don't know if it's for good or not," Sammy said when they'd returned to their cars. "So I'll keep going. There's no one waiting at home." He felt a need to talk about it. With all due respect to Lindell, but he needed to talk with a man, wanted to hear a male colleague say something, maybe offer something strengthening and edifying, something along the lines of how "they" could never understand how "we" were doing, all the shit "we" were forced to see and experience.

"My wife came back," said Bodin. "So you never know."

"Capricious," said Sammy, but Bodin didn't take the bait, so Sammy told him about his visits with the rabbit man Sam Rothe, that there seemed to be an opening, in any event where the school fire was concerned.

"Then maybe it will be possible to wrap the whole thing up, I mean the school fire too," said Bodin, who followed up Sammy's own train of thought.

"What do we do with Rönn?"

"We have to talk with our colleagues in Stockholm, of course. And then we'll bring Rönn in first thing tomorrow and maybe that guy Lindell was tipped off about."

"Let's bring in both of the Rönn brothers," said Sammy, who felt ill at ease. He would like to have a Björn Rönn who, if not innocent, was nonetheless unaware, who hadn't realized what the theft at his workplace would lead to, if it was the Austrogel after all that exploded in Hökarängen.

"We don't know if there's any connection," he said.

Bodin gave him a look before he got in the car. Sammy was not capable of reading what it expressed. Was it sympathy or contempt?

"I'll talk with Stolpe first, he's the one who's investigating, and then we'll have a chat with Stockholm," Bodin said. "I think a morning raid would be good here, maybe at five o'clock. I'm sure he goes to work early and I like waking people up."

"Maybe he'll take off before that."

"Wouldn't think so," said Bodin, who was starting to get insufferably sure of himself. Sammy exerted himself not to show his irritation, and simply nodded instead.

"Maybe I'll bring in the lads Ottosson and Sanberg, exploit the situation so to speak. Frighten them, suggest that they're bomb terrorists too."

"That's probably a good idea," said Bodin. "I'll talk with Stolpe about putting surveillance on Rönn's house. Now when we've scared them a little, maybe he'll think of something. Maybe he'll get a visit."

"The phones? Listen in a little," said Sammy.

"Thought about that too, and it shouldn't be any problem. Seven dead. But it takes time to arrange."

Their eyes met. Sammy wanted to be just as effective as his colleague. He would like to believe that Bodin was the one who could drag him up out of the mental and professional ditch he seemed to have driven into.

"Forget about your old lady now," said Bodin, and it was so unexpectedly and pointedly brutal that Sammy started.

They separated, each in his own car, and when they reached the highway they drove in opposite directions, Bodin toward Uppsala, Sammy northeast.

The landscape was smiling at him, which despite his quandary he had sense enough to see. The morning gave a promise of a beautiful day. Sammy got the illusion that he was on an outing in the Uppland landscape, perhaps one of all those rounds to exhibits and artisans that he and Angelika had made over the years. Not everything was good, many times he'd been bored, even angry, but there had been many professionals who passed muster. He remembered in particular a blacksmith who could tell about the old ways, the regional tradition he worked in, and the new, which actually was the same, but under quite different working conditions. The blacksmith had radiated something that Sammy lacked, but had a hard time putting into words. Joy in work perhaps, and the will to communicate a thought about the iron in his hands, but there was also something else, something more subtle, which had strongly moved him. Angelika had not been as affected as he was, that was noticeable when he later tried to talk about the visit. She thought his work looked "heavy," whatever she meant by that. He sensed that she wanted to say "clumsy." Iron did not speak to her.

He had an impulse to turn off the highway to look for the blacksmith, but put that out of his mind. Maybe he would be disturbed on a beautiful Sunday in May, it was different to open up his smithy and studio in an organized art tour, and Sammy had work to take care of. He felt alone and abandoned. The meeting with the alert Bodin had not improved his condition; on the contrary. And even worse, the visit to Therese had not healed anything, instead it had opened up wounds, old as well as new. Both literally and figuratively he had been disrobed. She had desperately ridden him through the night, perhaps just as exposed and alone too. He tried to see it from outside, tried to factually examine what had happened, but his crotch was still sore, as well as his shoulders that she gripped during her violent ride. And it would surely get worse, when Angelika

returned home and the nagging aches would assume other proportions and occupy other places in his challenged body. Deep down he knew, there wasn't much to think about. He'd been unfaithful, he'd betrayed his wife, it was that simple. He could close and archive that investigation.

It was with a feeling of loss and emptiness that he drove into the village. Several cars were parked by the creamery. He knew that they were open on weekends to sell their products directly to customers. They had opened a little café too. The creamery had become a popular destination, Ann had told him. "How people carry on," Sammy said out loud to himself. Some children were racing toward some swings mounted in an old tree. Their shrieks of delight could be heard from far off. There was a stab in his chest. Much of what he loved in life was over. The blacksmith had demonstrated something different. Over the years he had not only refined his professional knowledge, but also captured a sense of peace in his life, a kind of meaning with the passing years, that stood out clearly to Sammy. The craftsman had used his years well, stored them, while he had used his up. Maybe that was what he'd seen in the craftsman's studio, a view and an impression that made him dejected, envious, and exhilarated all at once.

I should have become a blacksmith, an unreasonable and almost ridiculous thought, for that reason possible to express.

He drove past Ottosson's house without giving it a look, sneaked a glance at Efraimsson's, came up to Ann's, drove in through the gateway, parked, and got out. The snow-in-summer was still blooming. It pleased him to have learned a new word, and the name of a flower at that. Ann was visible through the window. He sat down in the hammock, and cautiously started it swinging. She came out with a thermos and two mugs, dressed in an improbable yellow rag decorated with fire-breathing dragons.

"Tea ceremony," said Sammy.

"Be my samurai," said Ann.

They rocked, drank coffee, conversed about Rönn.

"Angelika then?" she interrupted, when his discourse about the woodpile at the Rönn brothers' was idling.

"It's probably over."

She did not comment on that. He tried to empty his mind of thoughts, let go of Rönn and the blacksmith, start over. He glanced at Ann, who had done just that, started over. It was a long time since he'd seen her so balanced.

"When you mentioned that I should contact the Tax Agency and check up on the Mattsson family background, what were you thinking about?"

"Something's not right," she said.

"There's that in all families."

"I don't think Andreas is Mattsson's son."

Sammy smiled to himself. If it hadn't been for Daniel Mattsson's death, maybe he would have laughed out loud. The thought passed quickly that it serves them right, the rich farmer Mattsson and this bloody village too.

"Who's the father? Do you have any idea or are those only loose thoughts?"

"It struck me when I was at Astrid's birthday party, Andreas is indifferent about the farm and it's not only because he doesn't like agriculture."

"He's completely uninterested, according to Therese."

"He has no peasant blood in him," Ann said with a smile.

"What kind of blood does he have?"

"Who does he resemble?"

"How should . . ." Sammy fell silent. Who does he resemble? The answer was obvious, there weren't that many to choose from.

"Bertil Efraimsson, our local preacher."

Ann nodded. "Similar body build, aquiline nose, they even have a number of expressions and gestures in common. It became so obvious when I saw them together."

"Does Mattsson know about it?"

"I have no idea about that. But Bertil knows, of course, or it would surprise me greatly if he didn't."

"In other words Andreas was conceived in sin."

"That can be shown in the family background. Or else everyone, above all mother Mattsson, kept quiet, pretended. That's not to say that Mattsson knows, maybe he thinks he's the father."

"Did everything that happened, the fires and the murder of Daniel, affect that?"

"Maybe not," said Ann. "But it creates bonds, loyalties."

He wondered whether he should tell her about Therese's suspicion that Andreas made an outing the night the smithy burned, but preferred not to talk about his own adventure in Östhammar. He stood up, took a few hesitant steps.

"What is it?" Ann asked. Sammy grinned, and then told her what Therese had said.

"When Erik and I drove to the fire, a car disappeared in the other direction," said Ann. "I didn't think about it then, I was so focused on turning up toward Hamra, taking the right driveway."

"What model?"

"Not a clue. A small personal vehicle, not a pickup. I only saw the rear end of the car disappear. It was maybe a hundred and fifty meters away, and there was semidarkness."

"The rear end." Sammy sat down, took out his phone, and tapped in a text message. "A picture is coming," he said.

They waited. Had Andreas really driven to Hamra? And in that case, why? Sammy stood up again, wanted to stretch his legs, actually wanted to set off on a fast march.

"That thing with the hammock," he said. "Is it really a good idea? It gets damned restless."

"You're the one who's restless, not the hammock."

His cell phone peeped. "Was it one like this?" He held out the screen in front of Ann.

Ann studied the picture that Therese had taken of her car. "Think so."

"Think so," Sammy repeated. "Maybe better to bring the car here, so you can see it in the environment and at the right distance."

"Maybe so," said Ann in an unusually defensive tone.

"Should I bring in Andreas and question him again?"

"You smell different. Is it her shampoo? Is she good for you?"

Sammy did not answer immediately, gave Ann a quick look as if to check how much room there was for waffling. "What do you mean by good? No, maybe not, to be honest. But you know how it is."

"No, you'll have to tell me how everything is. The only thing I know is that it's not that smart to sleep with a witness in a homicide case."

"One time," said Sammy. *You weren't always that smart either,* he thought, with some bitterness in his mouth. How many times hadn't he cleaned up after Lindell's drunken maneuvers, protected and defended her?

"So many dead," she said, and he understood that she meant Hökarän-gen. They looked at one another. He understood that it was her signal that the criticism would not be more extensive. Not after one time. Not today.

"So many dead," he repeated. It was dizzying, he was involved in the investigation of the worst act of violence in the country's history, and he was the one who could help solve it all. There was no time to rock in a hammock in the country and chew the fat with an old colleague, and there was definitely no time for personal travails.

"I'll let Tilltorp go today," he said, but corrected himself immediately. "I'm just going to check one thing."

Nils Enar Andersson seemed to have been waiting for him. Sammy parked the car beside a rusty Mazda 323, which did not appear to have moved recently.

"You're from the police," the old man commented immediately. Coke-bottle glasses, Bodin had said, and it was true. Through the lenses Nils Enar's eyes were unnaturally enlarged, which gave an almost surrealistic impression to meet his gaze, as if he were a lizard from outer space.

He was properly dressed in a pair of polyester trousers, white shirt, and a striped vest that had been around a few years. Sammy thought that perhaps he was going to church.

"That's right," said Sammy. "I was in the neighborhood. My colleague talked with you about Lovisa Friman, and now it's clear that she was the one who perished in the fire."

"Poor girl" was Andersson's brief comment.

"And Mattsson's boy," Sammy added.

"Yes, he lost his life too."

"Did you know Daniel?"

Andersson hummed. "I've seen him grow up. He got what he deserved.

They say that he was a Nazi, but he was really not a bad person. He became one. It's as though the world is upside down."

He fell silent, and Sammy found it good to wait.

"I was at the farm for over forty years. The one crazier than the other, mostly the old man, Albin that is, Mattsson's father. But it was work as good as any, and I did my job."

Sammy wished that he had Bodin's insights about farming, but discovered that he didn't need to say much, the old man was self-propelled. He talked about how he started as an animal tender, and ended as a jack-of-all-trades, the final years the only employee. "Then the boys grew up, and I retired. That was fifteen years ago."

"And now, what do you think is happening?"

"I don't give a damn," Andersson said frankly.

"You're right in that," said Sammy.

"Yes, what should I do, a mossy old man, what should I say? Everything's upside down. And the school burned, I went there in the fifties, not because I got so much wiser, but I learned to read, that was the most important. You have to be able to read, without words you're lost. I read a lot." He pointed at the piece of furniture that was set up outside the veranda; on the table was a book. Sammy understood that he'd been sitting there reading and stood up when he heard the car.

"There is one thing," said Nils Enar Andersson. "Something I've been wondering about. That night."

Sammy waited for him to continue, and it took some time. "I'll take the book inside, it might rain."

"What are you reading?"

"About war. I only read about war these days."

The old man picked up the book and went inside. Maybe he needed to think a little. Sammy wondered which night he meant; there were probably only two alternatives, New Year's night or the night when the smithy burned.

"You never know," he said when he returned, making a vague gesture toward the clear blue sky.

"Which night?"

"He's old now and barely wants to move, lies down most of the time, but he heard something, Bronco that is, and barked. We've been comrades for fifteen years and I understood that it was something important, something unusual, something extraordinary, if one may say so."

Nils Enar fixed his eyes on Sammy, as if to check whether he believed the statement. Sammy nodded. "You understand such things," he said.

"It was cold, but I shuffled out onto the front stoop. He doesn't care about deer at all, they bleat and hiss sometimes. It was something else, that I understood."

He pointed toward the road that led up to the neighbor.

"And there was something in the dark. I actually got a little shaky."

"What was it?"

"It was someone laughing," said Nils Enar Andersson. "Can you understand? In the middle of the night, dark and raw, cold, and someone is laughing. I knew that the Frimans weren't here, so of course I started to wonder."

"Laughing?"

Nils Enar nodded. They observed the road, the old man to recall the memory, Sammy to try to visualize, understand what might have happened. Was the old man mistaken, perhaps it was an animal anyway? He suspected who might have passed by in the dark, but there was nothing to laugh at that night.

"I thought it was a lunatic. I actually loaded the shotgun."

"It was a boy from Afghanistan," said Sammy. "He came from the school, ran away from there. Perhaps I shouldn't tell you this, but you probably need to know. I understand that you've wondered."

"From the school?"

"He's a cousin of the boy who froze to death in the car. I can't say more than that."

The old man digested the information. "Thanks for that," he said after a while.

"But I don't think he was laughing. Perhaps he shouted something?"

"It was laughter. Perhaps he was crazy?"

"I don't think so."

"Was he the one who set the fire?"

"No, he was a victim of arson. He ran to save himself."

"That was the damnedest thing. And where is he now? Is he alive?"

"I don't know," said Sammy.

"I think he's dead," said Nils Enar after a short reflection.

When Sammy left the old animal tender and drove a kilometer or two, he remembered. He stopped the car, got out, and opened the trunk. There it lay, the rabbit he'd bought from Rothe. Dead.

✦

Thirty-Four

"The three wise men," said Bodin. Nils Stolpe did not look amused. *He's probably not a morning person,* Sammy Nilsson thought. Not even the sight of the SWAT team from the capital could noticeably liven him up.

The trio of detective inspectors—Stolpe, who in no way lived up to the title, Bodin, who had brought a thermos, and Sammy—stood at a comfortable distance from Björn Rönn's house, squeezed between bushy clumps of what Bodin had said was blackthorn.

The time was 4:52. The weather was as predicted, clear and a little chilly, but during the day the temperature would approach twenty-five degrees Celsius.

"Strange that there isn't a dog," said Bodin. "They should have a dog."

"They probably don't hunt," said Stolpe.

Sammy wanted to move around, but of course it wasn't possible. Partly because of the bushes that surrounded them, but primarily because the slightest movement could jeopardize the effort. The idea was that the Rönn brothers should be taken by surprise, and so far nothing indicated that they were aware that it was crawling with police around their house.

"Goddam thorns," said Sammy. He glanced at his watch: 04:53.

"A lovely morning," said Bodin.

"My God," Stolpe muttered. He'd been grumpy ever since they met up in Uppsala.

"We can have a cup later," said Bodin.

"This is not a goddam moose stand," said Stolpe. Bodin chuckled.

"Did you make sandwiches too?" Sammy asked.

"Now they're starting to move," Stolpe whispered. Two dozen police, equipped with bulletproof vests and helmets, advanced crouching in defined positions. They had automatic rifles in their hands. They moved ahead soundlessly, as if, despite the massive impression they gave off, they were hovering over the yard. A few headed for the barrack where the younger brother lived, while the majority aimed for Björn Rönn's house, all in a coordinated movement.

Sammy could not help thinking that it was impressive, in a frightening way. The choreography was studied, the police were coordinated in the slightest forward movement, and communication was wordless. The threat of violence, deadly if such was required, was inscribed as an obvious part of the scenography. They surrounded the two buildings, they took their positions, everyone had an assigned place.

A half dozen of the police made their way to the front door. No time was lost, the door was forced open without any ado, and the first police stormed into the house. At the same moment a couple of windowpanes were broken and smoke grenades thrown in. "No knocking here," Sammy Nilsson whispered.

Everything then happened very quickly. The police streamed in with gas masks as protection against the smoke. Very soon Björn Rönn was dragged out coughing, in his underwear. The house was secured. Everything was over in a minute. All the same it felt like an anticlimax, as if the whole thing were a rehearsal.

The arrestee stood completely still with his hands behind his back, guarded by two policemen and a dog. He stared down at the ground, coughed a few times. Stolpe and Bodin stumbled out of the thicket while Sammy hesitated and stayed behind. The dominant feeling was not relief, but shame, as if he'd violated Björn Rönn's rights. That was wrong, very wrong, he knew that; it was highly probable that Rönn was involved in the theft of explosives at his workplace. Whether he'd had knowledge of, or was even involved in, the massacre in Hökarängen was less certain, but regardless the crime was such that finesse and kid gloves could be set aside, a few windowpanes had to be broken. Rönn was, or had been, a member of a neo-Nazi organization, which had hate and threats of violence on the program. Then you had to count on a punch in the jaw.

Sammy finally followed his colleagues and went up to Rönn, who gave him a quick look. "You had your chance yesterday. To talk, I mean," said Sammy. Rönn paid no attention.

"Were you involved in Hökarängen?"

Rönn shook his head. Sammy sighed deeply. He registered that Rönn had similar underwear as his brother, blue with yellow hearts.

"Where's Rasmus?"

Rönn shrugged and looked around, as if he was saying goodbye to the farm. "He's gone on vacation," he said after a while, but by then Sammy had already lost interest in the brother. He observed Rönn, who was standing with bowed head. It looked like he was steeling himself against the morning chill. *He'll get at least two years,* thought Sammy, *maybe even up to ten, depending on the degree of prior knowledge and collaboration. Life sentence, if he's been active in setting out the bomb.*

A gust of wind blew in between the houses, bringing with it a smell of bark and resin. Who would use all the wood that had been collected?

"Unnecessary, huh?" said Sammy, and gave the foreman Björn Rönn one last look before he walked toward the car. Stolpe, Bodin, and the colleagues from Stockholm could take care of it all. *My God,* he thought, *to wrap this up.*

Once at the car, he hadn't said a word to his colleagues, he was angry at himself: Feeling sorry for a Nazi, that was probably the lowest anyway! Then it occurred to him what it was. It wasn't Björn Rönn he felt sorry for, it was his mother, sick with cancer, who was haunting him in his mind. He could picture her, in a sickbed at oncology at Uppsala University Hospital.

Laughter was heard from a group of SWAT police who were standing by a black van. They were probably relieved, the mission was completed without complications. Now they could pack up, drive back to Stockholm, stow away their equipment. Call it an evening, as Sammy's father had said. There was something extremely artificial about their figures, cinematic maybe, as if they put on different roles. It was probably the uniforms, the equipment and the purely physical aspect, as if they were taken from a comic book or computer game. They stuck together, they were compelled, it was in the nature of their mission; if one responded, everyone responded, if one laughed, then they probably all laughed.

Sammy observed them for a few seconds, did not want to stare, did not want them to think that he was overwhelmed by their performance. By necessity they were cast in the same mold, and therefore dangerous, it occurred to him. Effective, but dangerous. When he and Bodin responded it happened at a slow pace, in haste perhaps at times, but unsynchronized and spontaneous, their feet stumbling a little as it were. He smiled to himself. He had never been a commando, and naturally never would be either. "Cheese," he said, out loud and clearly. One of them looked up. Sammy nodded toward him and mumbled a "thanks for the help," then got in the car. Would he get any credit? It was actually his work that led to the raid. Or should Lindell get the credit? He wondered how it went picking up Erland "Smulan" Edman.

His mouth was dry, there hadn't been any coffee from Bodin's thermos. Forget about that, forget about Edman, stop by Gränby Center and have a coffee, mix with the crowd, ordinary people, unarmed consumers, go into the liquor store. He looked at his watch; it would be a while before it opened. Probably not until ten. Wonder if Angelika was awake? Was it too late to repair their life together? There was a cottage at the Krabbe family's farm in Jutland, a kind of gatehouse, where one of the farm laborers lived before, but that he and Angelika now had use of. They had experienced good times in it, they could be by themselves, shielded from the outside world as the cottage was increasingly bedded in vegetation. It was still clean, not soiled by their endless petty arguments. A fairy-tale castle only for them. He could breeze down there in a day and a half. *Should I go on sick leave? I can certainly get time off, I've put in so much overtime.*

His thoughts were running like lost sheep, bleating dejectedly, as if they'd ended up in the wrong pen. He did not move, just sat there in the car. There was nothing strange about that per se, policemen spend a lot of time in cars.

Then he pictured Rönn again, awkward, maybe scared, maybe cold, just in his underwear, on his way toward his own downfall, a pitiable figure. It was an image that would return in his mind, he understood that. He'd seen something similar, maybe it was a photo from the Norrmalmstorg drama in 1973, when the perpetrator, what was his name now, Olsson? was led away from the bank he'd tried to rob. Or was he recalling a documentary on TV? Then it struck him. It was a picture from the extermination camps of the Second World War he'd seen once many years ago. A liberated man, but dressed in a single rag, a kind of bodice that went down to the knees, skinny and miserable, Poland, early spring 1945. A group of Soviet soldiers in the background.

The pictures changed, the contexts likewise. A Jew in a death camp, a neo-Nazi in his yard. He struck the steering wheel with one hand. "That's good," he said to himself. What that was he didn't want to dwell on at the moment, but he knew inside that the contact he'd made with Björn Rönn was true, but dishonest.

He put the car in first and drove away. After a couple of hundred meters there was a car from Swedish Television parked on the side of the road. If he wanted to put himself in the spotlight, to get attention and credit, he could stop, get out, and give the journalists exactly what they wanted. Such a segment, with connection to Hökarängen, would definitely be shown on national television, perhaps even in other countries. He slowed down, rolled ahead, stopped. *Perhaps Angelika would see me on TV, perhaps our daughter? I could not care less what Ann says. I could not care less what Bodin and Stolpe say too.*

"Hi, are you looking for . . ."

"You're a police officer, right? This concerns a connection to Hökarängen, right?"

The journalist, a young woman, looked eager to say the least. *Calm down,* he thought.

"My name is Sammy Nilsson, with the Uppsala police, and I can give you some info, maybe not everything, but enough that it will be good, but we have to do it here. It's cordoned off farther ahead and I have to leave. Then you can drive up and film the barricades if you want."

"Okay," she said, taking a deep breath and signaling to the cameraman to leave the vehicle. She smiled to herself, and Sammy was forced to hide his own smile at his whorish behavior.

✦

Thirty-Five

"Are you Andreas Mattsson's biological father?"

Bertil Efraimsson observed her with an amused expression, but there was no mistaking either that he signaled danger and vigilance. *No one in the village can beat him at arm wrestling,* it occurred to Ann Lindell, an unmotivated but completely understandable reflection.

"Why do you ask?"

"Because I'm ungodly curious."

He did not react, his facial expression was unchanged and he said nothing. She hated these kinds of situations, when she had to explain herself, start over, talk at length. In her previous life she had mostly avoided that sort of thing; a police officer has an advantage from the start. It was only the most hardened, or disturbed, individuals who could circumvent that advantage by consistently keeping their mouths shut.

Now Bertil was a true man of God who did not want to feast on the quandaries of others, so he broke the stalemate. He led her to the bench, mounted on the wall, not the garden chairs where they'd sat before when Ann came to visit. No, the bench, where you didn't have to look each other in the eyes and thus could toy with the truth more freely.

"Yes, if such were the case," he said at last. "If such were the case, it doesn't change a thing." He fell silent just as suddenly as he had started speaking, sighed deeply. Ann hurried to add something.

"If it doesn't become public, that is."

"Public," he repeated. "That's another way to put it."

"Publicized sounds so . . . what shall I say . . . like advertising in the newspaper."

"It definitely does not change my life. I'm at the tail end." He went on about this, how everything leveled out, how old grudges and vexations faded away, how the desire for peace and calm shifted your perspective and attitude to life. "I don't wish for anything, my desires are limited, basically always have been, but it's become increasingly clear with the years."

The old men in this village take empty talk to a higher level, she thought, but she could see herself in what he was saying. She was a cheesemaker, no longer a detective inspector. This was no interview room, this was a simple bench where you sat and told tales, and where her jurisdiction was apparently limited.

His smile was ambiguous. He turned his hands and observed them as if he was examining a pair of new bargains he'd found on a shelf at the hardware store in Uppsala.

"It may be so, it would be strange to deny," he said. "I think he understands, neither Wendela nor I have talked with him, and now, why should we dig up the past?"

"But—"

"I know what you're going to say: Everyone has a right to know, not just suspect, but know who one's biological parents are. Maybe so. If Andreas really wants to know, get it certified, so to speak, what deep down he's already understood for a long time, well, then he can ask. Ask who his real father is."

"Who knows?"

"You think this has something to do with the fire in the smithy? If not, there's no reason to root in this."

The admonition was clear, even though he flashed his parish smile.

"How does it feel for you then?"

"Good."

A shadow passed unexpectedly across the farmyard, but the sun returned just as quickly. Ann looked up; the clouds sailed ahead at a significant speed, as if a heavenly regatta had been organized. It made her feel dizzy. Nothing was fixed, everything was in motion, it occurred to her. She could see herself and Bertil Efraimsson clinging firmly to the bench, whirling in an earthly course around their own axis, around the sun. It was only the law of gravity that prevented them from being slung out into space on a path toward eternity.

She mentioned something about this, it wasn't that easy to formulate, but Bertil was a good listener, she already knew that from before. She could never talk about this with anyone else in the village. Carpenter Gösta would certainly burst into laughter. With the right of old age Astrid would scrutinize her with that mildly critical gaze, which would say: *Don't show off.*

"Yes, it's dizzying," he agreed. "But I have it arranged. Already at a young age I took out insurance. My journey goes on without great surprises and I know the destination well."

"No turbulence, no air pockets?"

"It happens."

"The police think that Andreas visited the farm the night of the fire."

"What would he have done there, you mean?" Bertil said after a moment.

"I don't mean anything, it's what my former colleagues are thinking," said Ann. "What do you think?"

"I think it's talk. They're grasping for straws, but there's probably no evidence, right?"

She understood that he was fishing for information.

"And if such were the case, what does that say? That he visited Hamra for completely sensible reasons, perhaps."

"I don't know," said Ann. She was satisfied, now worry was planted in her otherwise so secure neighbor.

"There may be lots of reasons, maybe he needed to retrieve something from the machine shop, something he forgot. He works all the time."

"I know no more than you do," said Ann.

She heard for herself how false that sounded.

"You have the same gestures. Andreas makes that movement with his hand too. And you both have that slightly dismissive expression."

"Dismissive?"

Ann smiled. "Yes, when you slightly disapprove of what's said."

"Yes, we're alike," said Bertil. "But he has a more restless mind."

"Is he going to take off?"

"I know no more than you do," he said, repeating her words.

A glass of wine would sit nicely, she thought, but without being controlled by the torments that took her hostage before. Then she could feel the grip harden, how she was slowly but mercilessly driven toward the edge of the precipice, where she had to stare down into the abyss, toward her own dependence and degradation. She relaxed, leaned against the wall, and let the wood siding warm her back.

Learn to keep quiet, she kept her inner monologue going, *then the thoughts and answers will come to you.* She stole a glance at her neighbor. He was still attractive, admittedly graying but still forceful. She understood very well why Wendela Mattsson had fallen for him. How did it happen, was it a one-night stand or did they have a longer relationship? Maybe still? No. Of course it was impossible to ask and had nothing to do with the arsons, but it was still a little exciting to speculate about.

"I've never talked with anyone about what happened," Bertil said, and Ann almost started laughing. "It feels strange and distant, as if it didn't concern me, my life."

"I'm as silent as the grave," Ann felt compelled to say.

"Yes, now I don't want to make a confession here and now, but perhaps we can reason a little with each other in the future."

"Let's do that," said Ann. "We'll reason a little with each other."

"I talked with Naomi, Astrid's granddaughter. She said that the two of you met at the party."

"A fine girl."

"She's Astrid's joy. She's in high school, some kind of theater program. It doesn't sound all that serious, but she speaks good English and that's important. At the school twenty percent voted for that Åkesson. One-fifth. In Gimo the Social Democrats probably had an absolute majority at one time. I wonder how it will be this fall."

"I remember that there was a lot of coverage about the refugee facility in Gimo. It was closed down, right?"

"That was years ago," said Bertil. "There was a lot of ruckus and protests. They tore the buildings down too, no one wanted to live there. There was so much sorrow in the walls."

"You're thinking about refugees?"

"I'm thinking about people. They are people."

"Was Andreas there raising a ruckus too, ten years ago?"

"He was in school then. It must have been fifteen years ago. Of course he was influenced. Bullying has probably always existed, I remember it from the school here, and then a lot of Iraqis and Syrians come, of course they're bullied."

The TV in the kitchen ground on. It was a bad habit she'd started when she moved there, shamefully aware that maybe Erik would spend a little more time with her if there was a screen in the vicinity. Something cultural was on, or maybe a travel program, it was about the city of Dubrovnik, and she stayed seated. In front of her she had a little wine. Should I travel there? She followed along in the narrow alleys, enticed by sidewalk cafés, and marveled at all the stone that had been heaped together to build the city. So much work, it struck her, and then she smiled to herself; that was a typical Edvard comment. Would he go with her to Dubrovnik? *I have money, enough that I could invite him.* "I have the money," she mumbled, stealing a glance at the wineglass. How much had she saved the past two years through her reduced consumption? It was thousands of kronor.

The last sweeping images showed sea and beaches. *It will have to be something like that,* she thought, and her already good mood was reinforced. *I have command over my life. Edvard, come with me, don't be silly, relax, you like the sea.*

Dubrovnik was followed by Sammy Nilsson's mug on the TV. The shock—it was nothing less, astonishment and surprise were words too feeble—the shock was immediate and total. A special segment from the news studio showed a tousled Sammy talking about explosives. The vein that ran along the side of his left eye was pulsing, like it always did when he got going. He did it well, there was a drive and a drama that was unrehearsed, and for that reason so good. His dogged expression, the tone of voice, his gaze fixed in the distance, consistently looking to the right, as if he was still on his guard, all of it was authentic and stylish. Ann understood why they chose the clip as an introduction to the story.

She took a sip, turned up the volume, and felt the excitement grow. *That he dared* was her next thought. Normally a media spokesperson or someone higher up in rank would have that kind of first talk on TV in such a serious investigation, but she also understood why he could take the risk. He was untouchable in a way, it was his work that led up to the raid in Rasbo, how could he be seriously criticized? There was nothing spectacular in his action, he'd done the right thing, led the SWAT team to the right place, to the right person, and then left it all. But had they arrested the right person? Time would tell. That was naturally the weak point. Sammy could be adventurous, but he wasn't stupid, and he'd maintained that Björn Rönn knew about what happened in Hökarängen and that the construction worker almost blurted out that he knew. Ann believed Sammy on that point. If he'd seen it, then it was so.

She took out her phone, pressed speed dial 2. Busy. She wanted to know if Erland "Smulan" Edman had also been brought in. She left a voice message, began with congratulations and was on the verge of ending by saying that she and Edvard were thinking about going to Croatia, but left it at a traditional goodbye.

Should she call Justus? Maybe a little later when he was home from work. She stood up, walked over to the window and peeked out, glanced

at the wineglass, empty, left the kitchen without knowing what she should do. Days off during the week were not a good idea.

"Think," she told herself. She opened the front door. *Think, like you did once upon a time, many times when you were ahead of your colleagues, when the unit boss Ottosson looked up during the morning meeting and gave you that look that seemed to say: I'll be damned, of course that's how it is.* She recalled the good memories, expertly suppressed the less good ones.

"Who benefits from Daniel Mattsson's death?" The most obvious answer was probably his brother, or more precisely his half brother, Andreas. He was now the sole heir to the Mattsson empire, unless there was something deceptive in the line of succession at Hamra Farm & Contracting. She didn't really know Mattsson, hadn't been able to study and assess him, and definitely not after the smithy fire.

On the other hand, Waldemar Mattsson could live another thirty years, and if he threw in the towel earlier, then Wendela would surely be sitting on an undivided estate. Was Andreas prepared to wait for his inheritance until he was over sixty? Wouldn't he want to realize his dreams of a life in the tropics before then? Okay, he could probably do it on his own, without inherited money, and see the farm as pension insurance when the heat got too heavy and healthcare too primitive in Southeast Asia.

She returned to the kitchen, pulled the laptop to her, and googled pictures of various Toyota models. Therese owned a twenty-year-old metallic-gray Corolla, Sammy had told her. Of course, it could very well have been one like that she saw the night of the fire. Her inattentiveness was irritating, but her focus had been on the flames. "Bloody amateur," she muttered and closed the computer.

Was it Andreas Mattsson who took off after setting fire to the smithy and killing his half brother? If he was returning to Östhammar he was heading in the wrong direction, but he had probably seen her headlights approaching, and the fact was that it was possible to come out on Route 288 from that direction too, even if it was a few kilometers longer.

Her testimony would never be enough, she understood that very well. There would have to be other evidence to link Andreas to the scene, but that was not something he needed to know. In an interrogation Sammy Nilsson and Bodin could maintain that he was recognized at the scene and at the right time, in order to undermine his defense in that way, get him to wobble, start lying, start wrapping himself in explanations that would not appear credible.

You could convict a perpetrator in that way, but Andreas Mattsson seemed to be made of sturdy stuff. If he were wise he could simply flatly deny it, maintain that Therese was really intoxicated that night, where the waiter and the bill from the restaurant in Östhammar would support his description, and add that she was filled with a desire for revenge because he wanted to abandon Sweden and her as well, and for that reason wanted him to go to prison for something he hadn't done. An attorney would crush her testimony; an assertion that a car key is hanging on the wrong hook in a key cabinet would not hold up in court. And could Ann herself swear that it was a gray Toyota she'd seen in the semidarkness? No, she would be forced to answer in a courtroom.

Had Andreas observed the speed limit? There were probably at least a couple of speed cameras that he must have passed on the way to Östhammar. But were they activated at night? Sad to say she didn't know, and most likely he drove lawfully. He knew the road well too, knew that there were cameras.

Ann worked through the arguments, for and against, testing different perspectives. Now she was at her best, with a glass of wine, and only one, pumping around in her body. It struck her that she had met all those involved except one, Sam Rothe, the rabbit man, as Sammy called him. He would also benefit from the smithy fire, if you could put it like that. His sister died inside, and he too would become a sole heir. That was a horrible thought, but reality was that brutal, after many years in the police force she had no difficulty realizing.

From what she understood the two of them, Lovisa and Sam, had not been particularly close. On the contrary, Sammy had hinted.

If she hadn't been drinking wine, she would have gotten in her car and visited him. There was a reason, or rather a pretext, and that was the dove that ended up in her mailbox. That was an entry as good as any. She decided to wait an hour or two.

✦

Thirty-Six

"It's your damned fault, Nilsson," the disembodied voice hissed out of the speakerphone. He was a boss of some kind, a boss somewhere, no doubt in the capital. Maybe they'd been introduced. Sammy did not recall. There were too many others in the room, a tumult almost, before it gradually calmed down a little.

His voice was like a snake's avatar, cold and slippery in that deceptive way that now seemed prevalent among the higher command. *Maybe there were courses for that sort of thing too,* Sammy thought, or else they were influenced by Netflix, an idea that Lindell had tossed out, that the schooling of the big bosses happened outside the actual legal system.

Sammy did not reply. Bandits and commanders were vulnerable to silence, that was generally known. Åhlander stared at him, the whole gathering glowered. "Well? Do you understand that?"

Sammy cleared his throat, but did not say anything. His own phone beeped, but he ignored it. It beeped again. "It's probably a reporter," he mumbled and sheepishly pretended to smile. The segment on TV had opened a floodgate. Sammy had become popular.

Vidar Stefansson, police master in the city, stood up. He was known for speechifying, often with formulations so far-fetched and provocative, deliberate or not, that they could be misunderstood and misused by colleagues as well as the media and general public. "We have an arrest, we have a confession," he stated for the third time in ten minutes. "And that's more than what Greinefors achieved, wasn't that his name, that guy who was shouting out of the speakerphone? Where is he anyway, at a conference in Andalusia? I thought I heard flamenco in the background."

A virtually general guffaw erupted, because the gathering was relieved, and in somewhat high spirits. Naturally there were those who were not so easily amused, but they were clearly in the minority, because this was truly a breakthrough. The Uppsala police had shown initiative and force at a time when the whole world was wondering what was going on in the kingdom of Sweden, where street markets were as dangerous as in Baghdad or Kabul.

"It's your fault," Åhlander repeated, "that continued surveillance is compromised. Using TV to make yourself known in the media, that's not police work."

"Change detectives," someone in the gathering tossed out. "So far we here in Uppsala have managed ourselves well."

The meeting on late Monday afternoon, where prosecutors, various experts, and a motley group of police officers from widely separated areas and authorities were gathered, rationally got no further than that. Everything had been plowed through, accusations and gibes had been delivered, and nevertheless a kind of order had been established.

Björn Thomas Rönn had confessed that he, and he alone, was behind the theft of explosives at his workplace in Almunge. It had happened on March 3. It was a "mission" he had been given.

The statement was deemed credible, even if there were question marks. He had access to the workplace but had nothing to do with blasting work, which was managed by a different company, and the safety procedures were rigorous. But sure, it had been possible to carry out the theft.

He did not know who had given him the mission. It had been communicated personally at an auto parts store in Uppsala, where Rönn was going to buy a car battery. Two strange men stopped him and told him what he had to deliver.

Sammy Nilsson was sitting alone in his office. He'd turned off the sound on his phone and announced that he did not want to be disturbed. Fatigue had come over him, the certainty and lightheartedness from the meeting had vanished. The fact was that he felt lousy. He held up one hand in front of him. It was still motionless, even though he felt shaky. And alone. It was a strange feeling, but he understood that it was a reaction to everything that had happened the past few days, both personally and at work. He was alone.

He gasped for breath, collected himself, and turned back on the recording of the interview with Rönn. He had followed it in real time, but wanted to see it again. Stolpe led the questioning. Nisse Hjelm from the intelligence service was by Stolpe's side, likewise a colleague from Stockholm, Erik Miid. Rönn had refused any assistance from an attorney. He was wearing prison clothing, had eaten lunch, and looked more or less stable compared with his early morning appearance.

"I must have been shadowed," he said.

"You had never met the two men before?"

"No, never."

"Why didn't you come to us, why did you carry out the theft?" was Inspector Stolpe's obvious follow-up question.

"They threatened me," said Rönn. "They said they would burn down the house."

"Your house in Rasbo?"

"The whole farm."

"How did they know there were explosives at your workplace?"

"I don't know."

Hjelm leaned forward.

"Isn't it the case that you may have met those two before? I mean at one of those gatherings you've attended."

"What do you mean by gatherings?"

Hjelm glanced at his notes. "In October last year one was held in Tierp where you and thirteen others were present. Nine of them are known to us, all convicted of various offenses and crimes, everything from illegal driving and narcotics crimes to felony assault. Were those two men perhaps at that meeting?"

"No."

"What was the Tierp meeting about?"

"I don't remember."

"In 2014 you were on a municipal list for the Sweden Democrats, but not before the election this fall. What has changed, don't you like them any longer?"

"I don't have time for such things."

"It's said that the gathering in Tierp was about a march, a kind of national parade that would pass through north Uppland."

"I know nothing about that."

"There was no march, instead it became a bomb at a square," said Stolpe, who visibly wanted to retake the initiative. From what Sammy had understood he was not terribly interested in the political background, he wanted to see the theft and the bomb as just another crime.

"I don't know anything," said Rönn.

"Have you ever been in Hökarängen?" Miid asked.

"No."

"Never visited Peppartorget?"

Rönn looked directly into the camera but his gaze was neutral, as if he didn't really understand what had happened, and what was happening. It was clear that beyond the shock and confusion Rönn understood, he was no numbskull, but nonetheless Sammy felt a growing discomfort. Three against one in the interview room did not feel just.

"No."

It was a ridiculous feeling, he understood that. Rönn was an accessory to a massacre, nothing less, there was no room for the slightest bit of sympathy. He turned off the recording when a cautious knock interrupted his train of thought. It was Nils Stolpe. He looked worn out.

"That Erland Edman has been swallowed up by the earth. According to his wife he's working for a scaffolder in Landskrona, but when I checked with his buddy down there he was completely puzzled. He hadn't heard from Edman for a couple of months."

"Brother Rönn, then?" Sammy asked.

"He's said to be in Thailand."

"Why am I not a bit surprised? Unemployed, he said, but can afford to travel abroad."

"According to the travel documents we found on his kitchen table he should be at a hotel in Phuket. We have colleagues on the scene as you know, they can question him and make an assessment."

"Bring him home," said Sammy. "Scare the shit out of the little Nazi."

"I have nothing against that," said Stolpe.

"Has Rönn's phone given us anything?"

"Not a bit. Nothing has been saved since last winter and the recent calls are reasonably uninteresting. They have a connection to work, to Uppsala University Hospital, his mother is apparently there, and to other relatives. He doesn't seem to have much of a social life."

"Maybe he has a concealed prepaid phone."

"My thought too," said Stolpe, who unexpectedly sat down in the visitor's chair. It creaked under his weight.

"What do you think?"

"The colleagues in Stockholm are checking surveillance cameras. Maybe we can produce something there."

"Around the square?"

"In part, but also stores, subway, and so on."

"Can it be the case as Rönn says, that he turned over the dynamite and then didn't stick around any longer, didn't know what would happen?"

Stolpe sighed.

"It's not a hundred percent certain that the connection exists, I mean between Rönn and Hökarängen. Or what? We don't know."

"The white supremacy movement," said Stolpe. "That's where we're moving, and it's where he has been involved. He must have understood."

"But we have nothing on Rönn other than the theft in Almunge. He has confessed and he'll be convicted, of course, but he continues to flatly deny everything, so we have nothing."

"The connection exists and we'll find it," said Stolpe, but did not sound especially convinced.

"It's crucial to find Erland Edman."

Stolpe sighed again.

"Go home," said Sammy.

"You know that's not possible."

Sammy smiled. He felt a splash of collegiality, even warmth, an increasingly rare sensation.

"We can celebrate later, have a beer."

Stolpe looked up; the surprise in his eyes was impossible to miss.

"Maybe so," he said and hauled himself out of the chair. "And the smithy fire?"

"We'll solve that," said Sammy.

"How are things with Ms. Lindell?"

"I've never seen her so content." It gave him a rare delight to express those words to a colleague, one who'd seen Ann in other forms.

"She's helping you, huh? A little private detective work. I've heard the talk."

"She lives in the middle of the village, so of course she's listening," said Sammy.

"The new guy then, Bodin?"

"An annoying dialect, but he seems good."

"How long have you been a policeman?"

"Twenty-four years," Sammy replied.

"You didn't need to count," Stolpe observed, nodded, and left the room.

✦

Thirty-Seven

Erland Edman wiped the sweat from his forehead. His cold would not go away. Eight floors. Five left to go. In his hand he had a sports bag that threatened to fall apart, no doubt some damned Chinese who cut corners, he thought, wrapping the handle around his left hand. He held his right hand compulsively around the railing, more or less dragging himself upward, but stopped again after three floors. Two doors, it said *Suarez* on one mail slot, *Lee* on the other. He cleared his throat and fired off a thick wad of spit that ended up on the wall in between. Someone had scribbled *Fack jo* there.

Edman trudged on. The sweat felt like a cold carpet against his back. *This isn't real,* he thought, and for a microsecond he saw himself as the striving little ant he was. He experienced no triumph when he reached the eighth and final floor, only sheer exhaustion, perhaps a little fear too. A handwritten piece of paper read *K. Olsson.* Edman exhaled, tried to get his breathing back to a more normal rhythm, and wiped his forehead with the sleeve of his jacket. He knew that he looked terrible, but there wasn't much to do about that. The only thing that would help was a few days in peace and quiet, preferably in a bed.

He poked up the paper. Under *K. Olsson* it said *Sven-Olof Granat* on a brass plate. The doorbell didn't seem to work, so he knocked carefully. The door was opened by a man that Edman had never seen before.

"Erland's my name."

"Let the piece of shit in!" he heard someone shout. The voice was not to be mistaken, it was Frank Give.

He was reclining on a dark brown sofa, the only comfortable piece of furniture in the room. There were also a half dozen plastic chairs, a table, and a TV placed on an old beer case. The TV was on; there was a special news broadcast. The crime in Hökarängen had messed up the program schedule.

"My God how they talk, they don't know shit," Give said and laughed. He looked up and inspected Edman. "Did you swim here?"

"The flu," said Edman, clearing his throat. "The elevator isn't working."

"It's those goddam gypsy kids. They grill in the elevator."

Edman closed the door behind him. "What the hell is it?"

"We have to talk."

Give only sneered in response, but eased up into a sitting position. "Would you like a beer?"

"I'm taking aspirin. What about that kid who was killed too?"

"I knew it! I knew you'd bring that up!"

"It was a little boy."

Give leaned forward and took a can of beer out of a cooler.

"That's just because you have one yourself, but there will be those kinds of losses."

"He was a Swedish boy. His name was Jonathan."

"I damn well don't want to know what his name was. I don't give a damn. A gang of Abdullahs and Alis died too, that's more important. Don't you understand, you see!" He made a motion with his hand. "We've made history!"

Edman glanced at the TV. Once again the destruction at Peppartorget in Hökarängen was shown, and how people flooded the square with flowers and lit candles. He had seen it any number of times. The sound was fortunately lowered to a minimum.

"He was riding his bike on the square."

"We'll do as we've said, if you had the idea now that we should cancel."

Edman crossed the room and sank down on one of the chairs. "I'll probably have a beer," he said. Give fished up a can and tossed it to him with a grin. "Smart," Edman said tiredly, setting the beer on the table so that the carbonation would settle down.

"Do you think Björn will talk?"

"Never," Give affirmed. "We decided that if he got caught, he would admit that he swiped the goods and then keep his mouth shut."

"He's going to be in prison for a few years."

"He knows that. He'll go in for theft, no more than that. He has himself to blame. He could have done as we said."

"He could have left with his brother, but he didn't get away."

"Amateur," said Give.

He took a sip, observing Edman.

"His life is destroyed. His mother is dying, how nice is that for her, do you think?" said Edman. He carefully opened the beer. The sweat had subsided, but despite the medicine the oppressive feeling in his head and the aches in his muscles had not been relieved.

"Listen! Don't sit there and regret everything! You knew like everyone else what would happen, so don't come now and complain."

"Does your lady know about—?"

"Lena doesn't know a thing, and damn you if you say a single word."

Edman shook his head. "Why should I do that? Killing a seven-year-old is nothing to be proud of."

Frank Give was not a powerful man, but when he stood there was something alarming about him, as if he could detonate at any moment. Edman knew that, he'd seen it. Give was a field full of undetonated mines, where no one could walk safely. The fragment injuries could be extensive in an explosion.

"It's just that she's anxious by nature. She takes it all in, feels so strongly," said Give, unexpectedly conciliatory, and sank back down on the sofa. He closed his eyes and took a few deep breaths, mumbled something while he fumbled for a fresh beer. That didn't make Edman less nervous, but he hoped that it was all a part of some kind of therapy. Give had gone to a neurologist, that was known in a smaller circle of his acquaintances, even if he himself denied it.

"So it'll be Alby on Saturday?"

"You bet!"

Edman was actually feeling ill. Maybe he had to vomit. He followed what was happening on the TV. People were asked if they were afraid. An elderly man in Skarpnäck was quivering with rage, he wished the terrorists a painful death. People screamed their agreement in the background. The reporter looked a bit terrified. Then came representatives of various religions, the Catholic bishop, likewise an imam, a minister from the

Church of Sweden, and a representative from the Jewish congregation in Stockholm. They were obviously on the same page.

"All four of them have beards," Give snorted from the sofa. He seemed to be getting more and more drunk.

How can I block him? thought Edman. But he knew that the only person who had any power over Give was his Lena.

"Jesus H. Christ, the way they babble. But that's good, let them carry on about humanity and that kind of shit, so the Swedish people know what traitors they are."

Edman stood up and went over to the window. The view was magnificent. He stood like that for several minutes, counting lighted windows on the buildings right across the courtyard, following the lights of airplanes across the dark sky, counting the sequence on the blinking radio masts, but nothing could push away the image of Jonathan's crumpled bicycle on Peppartorget in Hökarängen. There was no light in the world that could brighten the world.

He thought about Li'l Erland, how he would remember his father. What made him better than those crazy ISIS fighters with their sabers? *I have to talk with Lena,* he thought. *She must get Frankenstein to stop.*

"Who was it who answered the door?"

"Olsson," said Frank.

"Does he know about . . . ?"

"He knows."

"How many know?"

Frank turned his head. He looked at Erland Edman and smiled. "Are you starting to get nervous?"

"No, I just want to know how many there are who can snitch."

"Olsson, you, me, and Nyström, you've met him. And then Rönn, of course."

Jimmy Nyström was the one who had constructed the bomb. After two tours of duty in Afghanistan, he was good at that sort of thing. A warrior, Frank had called him, someone who liked to kill Islamists.

"Five," said Edman, "one of whom is behind bars." But he suspected that Björn Rönn had talked with his little brother. They were close.

"But there are many who back us up. Thousands."

"I need more ammo," said Edman. "I've been shooting a bit," he continued, when he saw Give's surprised expression. "And you know that I don't like pistols all that much. Maybe I need something more powerful."

"Not everyone can run around with automatic weapons, but Olsson takes care of all that," Give said at last.

"Good," said Edman, trying to look content.

"But don't shoot a cop for God's sake!"

Edman finished the last of the beer. "Why should I do that?"

"Because you've always hated cops, right?" Give sneered. Edman could see now that he was drunk, perhaps under the influence of something else too.

"I should go home and go to bed," he said, but the mere thought of making his way down the stairs, out onto the street, up to the car, and then the long trip home, made him sink down on the chair again. Or "home"? He couldn't drive to Uppsala. He had to hunker down in a dilapidated forest cabin outside Gimo. Rönn had passably equipped the place, and now it functioned as a retreat site for the band of warriors.

"Olsson!" The door opened immediately, as if he'd been standing at the ready. "Arrange an AK-5 for Erland."

Olsson observed him with eyes that sat very close together, which gave a slightly stupid impression, even more so as he was slightly cross-eyed. He did not say anything, but Edman understood from his expression that he thought it was a bad idea. *Is he mute?* he thought. The discomfort took a new form. Olsson was a soldier, one of Give's men. There were a few that Edman had met and had a hard time with, but he knew that he just had to go along with it. Olsson, however, seemed more than allowably disturbed.

Olsson nodded at last. "Rimbo," said Give. Edman knew where he would find the carbine. They had a dozen places, caches, where weapons and ammunition but also information and instructions could be set out and picked up. "Tomorrow, eleven o'clock at the earliest." He liked his role as commander, you could hear it.

Edman stood up. He had nothing more to say. There was no point in nagging Give about the explosion in Alby. If he had decided, he was impossible to budge. Unless Lena could get him to change his mind. That was the last chance.

He left the apartment.

✦

Thirty-Eight

The message was written, but not sent. Her phone felt warm and sticky, as if the words generated heat. Ann stared at the display again. She wanted to reword the short sentence, but it couldn't be expressed in too many different ways, unless she wanted to be false, keep using euphemisms.

She stood up, indecisively set the phone on the kitchen table, opened the pantry door but immediately shut it again, went up to the window. Shouldn't they be peeping up soon, the shoots from the potatoes? "A light soil," she said, echoing Edvard's description.

The almost physical sensation that time simply passed, running away at an ever-faster tempo, came to her again, this constantly recurring feeling. As if everything was in vain, all conviction, all the goals she had set up and struggled to achieve. "Then you have to water." "Claptrap" was a word she had inherited. Everything is just claptrap, her father's humorless and self-abasing phrase. "Then you have to mound." *Yes, but what then? Then and then! I want to mound now!* She turned around, picked up the phone and pressed "Send" on the message, opened the pantry, took out a glass and bottle but felt such terror that she was incapable of pouring the wine. It was as if the bottle had taken on a life of its own, it shook in her hand, and the glass fell out of her other hand and shattered. She took a deep breath, breathed slowly, closed her eyes, did as she was told by the woman at the clinic that she'd gone to two years ago. There were so many methods, five steps, twelve steps or however many there were, to get over, go past, move forward. She breathed until the oxygen around her was used up. That was her method.

The hammock received her, gave her the movement she craved, sent her thoughts like arrows in all directions. They struck apple trees, the fence, gables, Erik's cabin, woodpiles, and sheds. Everything was here.

Don't skimp. Hold on. Pick up the pieces. Shower away the anxiety, let the pheromones work, waken him from miles away, lure him to you like a moth to the twilight lamp.

Get dressed! Now in size 38! Get dressed. Undress! She pushed with her feet and the hammock got renewed speed. *Surround yourself with scents. Let summer come, open everything wide, air out the room, let the wind fill the rooms with the smell of yellow bedstraw and honeysuckle. Get drunk, have a third glass! Breathe in. Breathe out. Mound the potatoes. Let his hands cup themselves around you, dampen you. Breathe out. Live a little longer. Caress him. Give him all the love that's built up, let the floodgates burst.*

She put a hand on her left breast. The nipple was stiff under the bleached fabric of her shirt.

"Sammy!" She heard for herself how that sounded, challenging like at an agility class for puppies.

"Yes, my dear."

"Are you drunk?"

"Are you?"

"Knock it off. Finally you answer. I've been thinking about something. What makes a man get out of bed in the middle of the night and get in the car to drive forty kilometers?"

"I understand. I've researched the subject, if I may say so. Therese couldn't give a reasonable explanation, there was nothing that Andreas had said that would explain it. He had basically been distracted and absent that evening, but no more than that."

"Love and jealousy," said Lindell. "That can explain it. Think about it, a lot of other things you can think away, sleep away, drink away, but if you're possessed by jealousy it sits deep, you don't get rid of the thorn that easily."

"You mean that he was still in love with Lovisa?"

"It's not for certain, you can be jealous anyway. We know that he talked with his brother that evening. Therese said that, didn't she? Andreas knew that Daniel wouldn't be going with his parents to Stavby, and maybe Daniel told him that Lovisa would be coming to visit at the smithy. Maybe he said that just to annoy Andreas, some kind of competition between them."

"And when he was tossing and turning in bed with Therese, he couldn't stand it any longer, but instead felt he had to go and check, is that what you mean?"

"Something like that," said Lindell, who had no problem whatsoever picturing it all. "Unreasonableness wins over logic."

"Why did he take Therese's car?"

Sammy's question remained unanswered, even though there was only one reasonable explanation. Lindell felt how she was running on idle. As long as you couldn't show that Andreas had actually been at the scene, there was nothing to move ahead with, which Sammy no doubt also realized.

In that way the call ended itself. Ann had unconsciously walked around the property several times. Now she was standing by the potato patch, staring at her phone. *Why snoop?* it struck her. *You've left that behind.*

Right before the regular news broadcast was about to begin, Bertil Efraimsson came slowly walking across the road. It was actually the first time, besides during Astrid's party, that Ann had seen him outside his own property. It struck her how homebound he must be. She had seen Gösta out on all kinds of errands, often with his little cart where he stored his tools. Bertil didn't go anywhere, people came to him and his workshop.

Bertil took his sweet time, and he walked slower and slower the closer he came to her driveway. There he stopped. Ann could observe him from the outdoor shower. She had just cleaned up after a brief but intensive duel in the garden. She had carted away excess stones from a failed attempt to build a rockery; it most resembled a distended fruitcake with stones sticking out like raisins. She had never seen a more unnatural structure. Now she had picked away the stones. The work had done her good. She had released her thoughts about bombs and arson. Now she would be reminded without having to turn on the TV.

The gravel crunched under his feet. Halfway to the house he shouted out a "hello." Ann stepped out. *If you were fifteen, twenty years younger, Bertil* was a thought that flickered past.

"Am I disturbing?"

"Not at all."

She went up to meet him, pointed at the hammock but changed her mind when she noticed that it was in the shade. A pale evening sun was still shining over the back side of the house, and she piloted him there. He said something complimentary about the flowers. They sat down. He turned down coffee.

"Reason," she said, getting right to the point. "You said that we could reason together."

"I have to confess something," said Bertil. "Perhaps I've made myself guilty of an earthly crime, and that may have happened. What's worse perhaps is that . . ." He fell silent. Ann waited. She could sense his indecisiveness and tension.

"Omid, the missing boy, stayed with me for a couple of months. I hid him."

"The cousin of the one who froze to death?"

Bertil turned his face up, breathing in air through his aquiline nose, as if to gather strength. Then the whole story came out. Ann chose not to interrupt with questions, but instead waited until he was finished.

"He disappeared a day before the fire in the smithy, you say? Did he set it?"

"No," said Bertil, but without the customary force in his voice.

"Where is he now?"

"No idea."

"Have you talked with Sammy about this?"

"Only with Gösta, that was the other day, and Astrid knew that the boy was with me. And now you know. Soon the weekly paper will be writing about it."

He gave her a crooked smile. She wanted him to leave. She had all the information, now she needed to think in peace and quiet. Bertil stood up hesitantly, as if there were still things to add.

Ann followed him with her gaze until he rounded the corner of the cottage. She perceived his smile as false, even if she was convinced that

he had an honest intent. But it was nonetheless a church smile, a mildly indulgent, slightly dismissive, smile.

She had missed the news broadcast and checked the latest developments on the internet instead. No progress in the investigation was reported, but that didn't have to mean a thing. She tried to imagine the activity going on in both Stockholm and Uppsala, but without any success, she knew too little about the approaches and ideas that applied in her former colleagues' hunt.

Sammy's phone was busy. She left a voice message that briefly relayed what her neighbor had just said.

✦

Thirty-Nine

Tuesday started with a gentle spring rain. It was over in twenty minutes, but the freshness it brought with it seemed to have affected everyone at the creamery. Even Anton looked energized.

Matilda and Ann helped turn cheeses in the ripening room. It was physical labor, work that Ann liked, the smell, the coolness, the rows of magnificent cheeses. She was still fascinated by the massiveness of their rounded forms and the silent sequence that slowly but surely changed the consistency, color, and taste. There were no guarantees in which direction the process would go. Mostly it went as calculated, but sometimes something unexpected happened. Not even two such experienced dairy people as Matilda and Anders could be absolutely certain.

Ann wanted to talk about what had happened, both in Tilltorp and in Hökarängen, but Matilda had made it clear that she wasn't interested. That was the advantage of going to a job completely separate from what had occupied her thoughts the past few days. The police officer in her had to give way to the mysteries and labors of cheese making. And that did her good.

She worked a half day and could go home at lunch. That had been decided a few weeks ago, her new slimmed-down schedule. Matilda had apologized and said it was temporary, but Ann was worried that it was the start of even more reductions. The creamery's products were doing well, but the investments had been major, the payments heavy, and now they needed to expand further. "I don't want to, but Anders says it's necessary. It seems as if this kind of small-scale operation isn't sustainable. And now, if we're going to start selling in Finland, maybe it's needed." Ann knew that Anders was in Holland to buy more equipment, among other things a new cheese vat was on the wish list.

On her way home she thought about Matilda's words. It worried her; she didn't want to lose that job for anything in the world. What would she do then? And it was so close, just over five hundred steps. She could no longer imagine having to get in the car and drive for miles every day to work.

Sebastian Ottosson was perched on a scaffold, scraping paint. Ann stopped by his mailbox. She raised the lid carefully; nothing in the box. He pretended not to see her but instead continued working. The flakes were dancing.

"It will be nice!" she shouted. Sebastian lowered the scraper and turned toward her. She understood that he was trying to evaluate her words, what they stood for.

"We need milk at the creamery. When will you start with the goats?"

He climbed down and went up to her; only the gate separated them.

"Has Anders talked about that, about milk?"

"Of course," said Ann. "Milk and cheese are all we talk about. Get going with goats!"

He shifted his feet.

"Are you alone? No one to help you?"

He cast a glance toward the house. "Not today." She suspected that he was lying, because an older car was parked by the back of the house. She didn't recognize the make, but out of habit memorized the license plate number.

"I'm going to put up a fence next week," he said. "I've already bought a tribe, in any case the start of one."

"Have you worked with goats before?"

"In Sörmland, when . . . there was a job I got, or I lived there, you know . . ."

There was something tormented about Sebastian Ottosson, something unexpressed. He gave her a quick glance. "Granddad believed in it, the goats that is."

Ann wondered where his parents were. Had he been placed on a goat farm in Sörmland? Could she ask? No. Would she check on that some other way? No.

"I talked with Anders and Matilda, but they didn't know. Have they talked with you about buying milk from me?"

"They have a lot going on now, but sure, they need more milk. Now we only work with cow's milk, and goat's milk would be a good addition."

He looked toward the creamery, then gave her a quick glance, as if to figure out if she was serious.

"You live here in the village, your family is from here. I came here recently, but we have to get along, don't we?"

He nodded mechanically without any great empathy. For a moment Ann had the idea that he agreed simply because in the future he wanted to sell milk, as if she could decide that. To check his reaction she told him about the harassment and the threats she'd received, the doves in the mailbox and the piece of wood through the window. The badger too, but not that it was in her bed, that felt too embarrassing.

"Who's behind it?"

"I don't know."

They observed one another. She believed his quiet denial.

"I think it was Stefan, your buddy. And he was probably involved in setting fire to the school too. He's not a good person. You'll live here with your goats. Good. I'll walk past here on my way to the creamery and see to it that the milk becomes good cheese, and for many years at that. Good. You have to choose who your friends will be."

"It's cool," he said while his increasingly stressed appearance contradicted that message. Ann waited, but when he remained silent she said goodbye and left.

The first thing she did was to check on the car on Sebastian's property. It was an Alfa Romeo, a model unfamiliar to Ann, registered to a certain Rasmus Rönn. She ought to have been more surprised, but it was as if the information only confirmed what she had already taken for granted, that everything fit together.

"Take your fucking goats," she mumbled and felt her mental blood pressure rising, a feeling of equal parts disappointment and fury. Was Rasmus in Thailand, as Sammy had said, or in Tilltorp, which the car suggested? Rasmus, an ugly name besides, like a treacherous cocker spaniel.

She sent a message to Sammy about the Alfa, then placed herself in the therapeutic outdoor shower, after which she sat down with her new diversion maneuver, a pitcher of lemon water with a lot of ice, which she pretended was a discolored sangria. She sipped and thought, but shoved aside everything that had to do with creamery or murder. "Dubrovnik," she said quietly. She knew inside that Edvard could imagine coming along, while she could also hear him say something about work, that it was crucial to be available during the summer, the summer guests on Gräsö always needed help, and they paid well. Was he a bore? She, and her girlfriends, had asked that question for all these years. The answer was an unambiguous "yes." Even so she'd loved him, and thereby blocked everything and everyone, gave up several possibilities to seriously get to know other men, men who would not hesitate for a second to go to the Adriatic coast or Trinidad, or anywhere at all. Romantic men, talkative men, lighthearted men. There were such men, weren't there?

No, it had been Edvard who counted. A masochistic attitude. But loving a bore must say quite a bit about herself, right? She didn't want to complete that thought. Could he change? She really wanted to believe that he could, not least after his latest visit, when he had demonstrated a kind of newfound levity.

She sent a text message, told him about Croatia. It felt as if she was making an ultimatum, even though in no way could that be read in the short message.

✦

Forty

"Congestion tax," Stolpe said with a grin. "Do you know how many entries there are into Stockholm in May?"

"Over forty million," Sammy answered immediately.

"I think I got there before our Stockholm colleagues, but it wasn't easy to get the Transport Agency to move their asses."

"Who passed?"

"You exaggerated a bit, but there are over eight million entries. They take in more than a hundred and forty million in tax in May alone, did you know that?"

"Naturally," said Sammy.

"Seven hundred thousand decisions are going to be made on tax, one of which applies to our friend Rönn. He doesn't even know about it yet."

"When, last Saturday?"

"Congestion tax isn't charged on Saturdays."

"When?"

Sammy felt his irritation growing, against his will however, because he had no problem identifying Stolpe's satisfied expression. Sometimes things cruised ahead, and then even a simple detective inspector must get to savor it.

"Monday, May twenty-eighth, at five thirty-eight P.M., at the Kristineberg interchange."

"How did you manage, or did you threaten someone at the Transport Agency?"

"I took a chance that he drove in the NCC car. They have some kind of company agreement, don't ask me how it works, but it facilitated the search. Now we'll go ahead and check backward."

"When did he drive back?"

"That we don't know. The fees don't apply in the evening, but I know that he worked the following day."

Stolpe got up from the chair, hoisting his pants up over his bulging abdomen. Sammy thought he reminded him of some movie character from the forties. He grinned.

"Of course, sometimes things fall into place," said Stolpe.

"And now you're going to pick him up from the prison hole?"

"It's already done. He's been sitting in room five for at least half an hour. Now he wants a lawyer, and one's on their way in. Will you be there?"

Sammy considered for a moment but declined. He didn't want to see Rönn ground down, so that was enough.

"I'm going out to Tilltorp," he said. "Little brother Rönn's car is there."

"You see" was Stolpe's insipid comment, before he took in what Sammy had said. He looked up. "We'll probably get to have a damned beer sometime."

"That we will," said Sammy.

"Are you going alone? Bodin, then?"

"He's checking Rönn's contact network in his phone and computer."

"How are things on the home front?" Stolpe removed his jacket from the chair and pulled it on in a surprisingly smooth motion.

There was clearly talk in the building. Sammy forced himself to smile. He wasn't particularly surprised but a little disappointed at Stolpe's insensitivity, and he left his colleague with mixed emotions.

As he headed northeast from Uppsala in his new, leisurely driving style, thoughts of Berglund, his old colleague, returned. Perhaps there was a connection, his driving style and what Violent Crimes looked like ten or fifteen years ago. *Old man thinking leads to old man driving,* he thought, glancing in the rearview mirror and seeing half a dozen cars behind him. When the road opened up to two lanes all of them breezed past him, and a couple of the drivers gave him a look.

Without Sammy registering it he had arrived in Gimo. He turned to the side of the road, stopped the car but let it idle, sat completely still for a few minutes before he took out his phone and called Ann. She answered immediately. "We're on a coffee break," she said, and he understood that she was at work. "But I can wave when you drive past."

"We'll talk later," said Sammy, clicking off the call. On the way out from Uppsala he'd had an unexpressed feeling that together they would visit Sebastian Ottosson. It wasn't the first time he'd had the idea that they were still colleagues, although it happened less and less often, but he understood how significant she'd been. And still was. If he ever were to flee to work out the tangles in his life, it wasn't Therese in Östhammar or anyone else who mattered, it was Ann.

Maybe she and her coworkers were still sitting against the wall of the creamery, having coffee, sunning themselves and waiting for the cheese to behave. He drove past without waving. He parked across from Sebastian's house. There was plenty of room, the fence around the school property had been removed, and he could drive up on the lawn in front of the ruin. It no longer smelled of arson, but summer. A scrubby gooseberry bush, perhaps a remnant from the school garden, had already blossomed over and Sammy could sense the minimal unripe fruits.

He crossed the road. Sebastian was nowhere to be seen. The Alfa was still there. It was a clean Giulietta, six years old, Sammy had checked. He had no relationship to Italian cars, but it appeared to come from there, from the south. The doors and hatch were locked. The interior was well-cleaned, the only loose object was a pillow in the backseat.

"What do you want?"

The voice came from above. Sebastian Ottosson's head was sticking out from a window on the top floor.

"I'm looking for Rasmus," said Sammy.

"Why is that?"

"You know."

"He's in Thailand."

"Why is the car here?"

"I drove him to the airport. The car gets to stay here."

"When did he leave?"

"Saturday evening."

"Can you come down? It feels a little crazy to talk like this. We can sit down out here."

Sammy thought about Rasmus Rönn, his immaturity, as if he hadn't really grown up. The shove that he delivered on the stairs and that almost made Sammy fall down had been an expression of that, like something on the schoolyard, as if he hadn't understood that it wasn't a great idea to shove a policeman. If it had been someone else Sammy would have taken him into Uppsala, scared the shit out of him, but he hadn't really taken Rasmus seriously.

They sat down on the back side of the house. Between the bushes they had a partial view toward Bertil Efraimsson's house and workshop. Sebastian was dusty with plaster, with impressions from a mouth guard that covered part of his face. His hands and forearms were stained with paint.

Sammy started by talking renovation. Sebastian answered willingly but briefly. "You're keeping at it," Sammy observed.

"I want to get the house fixed, because I have to get started outside, have to make a fence for the goats soon." He told him about his plans, now more expansively. Sammy had seen the pile of fence rolls. "I have some buddies, and Bertil will help out. He has a little tractor too." Sebastian looked at Sammy a bit defiantly, as if he wanted to say that he had friends, a plan, a life.

Sammy nodded. He would have liked to help out, in another context, in another world, but he couldn't say that. The kid would certainly not understand.

"I've helped drive fence posts," he simply said. "Grandpa had a little place."

They sat silently for a moment. *It's strange,* thought Sammy, *what country air does to a person.*

"But I mostly got to carry the mallet," he added, before he started on his actual errand. "You know what happened last Saturday. Hökarängen. Is Rasmus involved?"

"Do you mean—?"

"Exactly, seven innocent people died. Has he bragged about dynamite, and what you can do with it? Did he set off a bomb and then run off to Thailand? Did he tell you anything?"

Sebastian shook his head.

"Was he shaky last Saturday? Maybe a little speedy? You know that his brother Björn stole explosives at a construction site?"

"It's not my thing."

Sammy took that as an admission that he knew about the theft.

"I want to work with what's mine. I don't give a damn about anything else."

"What's wrong with you? What in the hell is wrong with Tilltorp, with Gimo, with this fucking Nazi countryside? You don't give a damn about anything or anyone. Okay! Who'll buy your goat cheese, have you thought about that? Will Stefan, your buddy? Rasmus? Your racist friends who vote for SD and burn down schools? Your neighbors? Not likely. They don't care about fine cheese for two, three hundred kronor a kilo. Cheez Doodles maybe, but not goat cheese."

Sebastian gave Sammy a quick look, there was a hint of fear but also doubt that he'd really heard right.

"If I burned down your house because I didn't like your hairstyle, or because I hated goats, would you be happy?"

Sammy stood up, incapable of sitting still. He kicked at the ugly IKEA table. A type of table that was on each and every balcony in the city. It fell over and Sebastian threw himself forward to catch it.

"What the hell," said Sebastian, but without sharpness, picking up the table.

Sammy walked away a few meters, afraid that he might also attack Sebastian. *Take him into Uppsala, pick that bastard to pieces,* he thought.

"Do you think I like . . . ?" Sebastian began, but fell silent when he saw the policeman's expression.

Sammy walked away, stood so that he could look out over the ground where goats would soon be grazing. The thoughts of Angelika returned, they had been germinating in the back of his mind ever since he woke up, maybe he had dreamed about her, and now they blossomed out. *I'll escape to Denmark,* he thought, the idea that had taken hold, even though he suspected it wasn't worth the trouble. He would be rejected. And Skåne or Denmark was not the right environment for reconciliation. True, the gatehouse on Jutland where they'd had such a good time was still there, but the thought that they could re-create some kind of trust there was stillborn. Something more was required to rescue their marriage, they needed a miracle.

"I don't want to," he mumbled and turned around. Sebastian was still sitting there, observing him, probably unsure what was happening, perhaps aware that he had gained an advantage.

"There's been a lot going on," said Sammy.

"I don't think he went to Thailand. I drove him to Arlanda, but I don't think he got on the plane." Everything came as in an exhalation.

"Why do you think that?"

"It was something that occurred to me."

"Did he say anything?"

"He talked about his brother, that he was worried about him."

"Worried about what?"

"He didn't say it directly, but that Björn had changed, gotten nervous. I've met his brother and he's never been the nervous type. On the contrary: He's the one who always had to calm Rasmus down. They were supposed to go together to Phuket, they got a charter at the last minute, you know, but then Björn backed out. He said he had to work, but what the hell, he'd already gotten the time off. And if there's anyone who's worked, it's him, he probably has who knows how many hours of overtime."

That the Rönn brothers would travel together was news to Sammy. He left Sebastian, went around the corner of the house, left a voice message for Stolpe and told him what he'd found out. He then called Bodin, who actually answered, and repeated it all. "Pop down, maybe Stolpe is still questioning Björn Rönn. And you can probably check the flight last Saturday, if both were supposed to go, and if Rasmus Rönn really left."

Bodin did not seem to be in his best mood, perhaps he was grumpy because Sammy had taken off alone, but he did not protest, simply couldn't. They ended the call, despite Sammy's attempt to prolong the conversation. He wanted to keep talking, hold up the damned cell phone, which he usually despised, as a shield against the reality he was forced to subdue. He had Sebastian to relate to. The goat farmer.

"How old are you?"

"Twenty-four."

"When it was burning and you understood that people would die, what did you think then?"

"Mostly later," Sebastian answered after a few seconds of silence. "Then I thought, *Nice to be rid of those darkies.* They were right across from where I was going to live. But it's a shame about the ones that died."

"And then?"

"I talked with Granddad. He was actually crying, it was the first time I saw him cry. He went to that school. He told me that his dad had been a foster child at several places and had to move around all the time. He was like one of those refugees that you see on TV, Granddad said. With no peace, as he said several times. That was what he said: 'With no peace at all.' Several times. Granddad got a little gaga at the end, he babbled on."

"And your granddad then? What was it like for him? Did he get any peace?"

"He did well, because his father and mother . . . They built this house and they could live here their whole lives."

Sammy turned away. A car went past.

"So you started to think."

He sensed more than saw Sebastian's nod.

"Gaga. But he was nice, Granddad. He believed in me."

Sammy did not want to ask about Sebastian's parents, where were they? What was it like for Sebastian as a child?

"You're not on Facebook?"

"Nah," said Sebastian, looking embarrassed, as if he'd been caught with something shameful. "For a while before, but it takes so much time. You have to sit and 'Like' all the time."

"Or dislike," said Sammy.

Sammy was convinced that Sebastian knew who set fire to the school, but this was not the time to pressure him about that. Maybe he also suspected where Rasmus Rönn was hiding out, if he wasn't sitting by a pool in a tropical country. Instead Sammy, himself surprised at the quick turn and choice of subject, told Sebastian about Ann, what a capable police officer she'd been and how much she liked living in the village.

"She'll probably be off work soon."

"She usually walks past," said Sebastian.

"I'm going for a drive," said Sammy. He wanted to add something, but was aware that it could go wrong when many thoughts and notions crossed each other. Sometimes it was better to keep your mouth shut.

He stopped anyway. "Listen, Sebastian, you know that the owners of the creamery, I don't remember their names, but—"

"Anders and Matilda," said Sebastian.

"They were really upset about the fire. I heard them the following day. They would never forgive you if you were involved in setting it."

"But I wasn't involved—"

"They would never buy any milk from you, not even a deciliter."

"But I wasn't there!"

"They don't know that."

"What the hell do you mean?"

"If anyone tells them that you were involved, then it's over for you and your goats."

It took a moment before Sebastian Ottosson understood the meaning of Sammy's hint, but by then Sammy had already disappeared around the corner of the house.

He didn't know where he should go, so he stayed standing by the car. Maybe he ought to take off, but it was as if he'd gotten stuck in the village with the beautiful fields and the ugly name. That was what Bertil had said when he described Tilltorp, and it was true. In a way it was an idyll, but under the surface it was ugly, even repulsive. *Like Jutland,* he thought and smiled to himself. Like fucking Jutland!

When he turned around, his thoughts disturbed by a noise from the other side of the road, he caught sight of Bertil Efraimsson. He was rolling a sheet-metal barrel across the ground, kicking it with his foot and following behind, giving it another kick. It looked as if it amused him. The barrel hit the wall of the workshop and stopped. Bertil arranged what Sammy thought was a kind of base, where he raised the barrel and measured so that it stood right under the downspout.

Sammy crossed the road and onto Bertil's property. "Now all that's lacking is a little rain."

"This may be the last barrel I set out," said Bertil. "They usually last for ten years before the rust gets them."

"When I was little my dad set out barrels to collect rainwater. There were probably bugs in them."

"Divers," said Bertil, "who breathe with their rumps."

Sammy remembered this very well, how they floated up with the back end first, as if gasping for air, to then take off down into the darkness.

He could never kill them, like he did with other beetles, in glass jars with cotton swabs drenched in ether. When they'd quit twitching he ran needles through the ring sheath and body, and then mounted them in boxes. But the divers he left alone. He became their friends.

Sammy cursed himself for starting to think about his macabre collection of insects. There was so much there, in the years between eleven and thirteen, that was heavy, and that he tried to dispatch to oblivion.

"There are divers in the barrel over there," said Bertil, pointing toward one end of the house. Sammy went there, while Bertil went into the workshop.

It was a two-hundred-liter barrel, no more than half full. A wood stick was driven down into the barrel. He understood that it was because of the squirrels. The water surface was smooth, dark. In the depths a beetle was visible. It moved leisurely at first, to then pick up speed, as if it discovered that it had an audience. It floated up, exactly with the back end first.

Bertil, who had rolled out a new barrel, joined him. Together they observed the diver, who took a few strokes.

"Do you know that the wake after a beetle who swims in water is always at thirty-nine degrees? That also applies to tankers, sailboats, everything. Always thirty-nine degrees. The laws of physics."

"God's order," said Bertil.

Without anything else being said they started walking, heading for the slightly sloping pastureland that was squeezed like an arrow between workshop and forest.

"Here my old man had pigs that rooted around, long before they started talking about free range and all that organic stuff. As far as I know they never ate anything artificial."

Bertil swept his gaze across the ground. Groups of boulders rested like mossy gray flocks of prehistoric animals between the scraggly tufts of sedge, a single rough-hewn fence post stuck up like a beacon that searched for its missing comrade, and scattered rowans, grown crooked in the inhospitable soil, struggled on stubbornly in a kind of resistance movement.

"This is my land," said Bertil. "I could never leave it."

Sammy had nothing wise to say, however much he tried, he knew that deep down. There were stories that touched what he thought Bertil wanted to express, but they weren't suitable for the moment. *The last barrel,* he thought, *was that what called forth this unexpected melancholy in Bertil?*

"Then we ate them up."

Sammy understood that he meant the hogs, and that it was a very conscious statement to break the mood, put a stop to it. They turned back, and remained standing outside the workshop.

"The boy was capable, and people are lacking who have the patience. He had that. And the eye."

"You mean Omid?"

"Just him. The only boy who has worked in this workshop, since I was that age myself. He would have done well for himself."

"Is it profitable?"

"Can be," said Bertil. "Now it's in demand again, handiwork."

"You wanted him to stay here?"

Bertil's facial expression changed character for a moment, a hint of a smile was visible, but also a hasty glimpse of pain, as if he'd clearly seen the possibility of a still-living workshop, but at the same time understood what was unrealistic about such a thought. Then he took a deep breath.

"He'll be sent away, the politicians have decided that."

They parted. Bertil returned to the last barrel, Sammy walked away toward the car. He felt as if the village had invaded his brain. He was put under the influence, as in all investigations of serious crimes, where people always exposed themselves. Murder had that effect. What had happened was no ordinary shooting in an area that in the media was proclaimed a no-go zone, even if naturally there were points in common. If he could explain Tilltorp, then he could explain and unravel the skein that was called Sweden. That was perhaps why his thoughts, and he thought Ann's too, often returned to Berglund, the old fox at Homicide who without having wished it or even understood had come to influence a whole generation of younger colleagues. But Berglund's conclusions had also led him wrong, that life, and the mechanisms that guided people's doings, were simpler before. That thought was false. It wasn't better before, it wasn't easier to understand your time before. It was simply that the tools for analyzing and understanding seemed to be frittered away, like when you lacked that Phillips screwdriver in your toolbox.

When did I last hear someone figure things out in understandable terms? Sammy asked himself. He had arrived at the car but remained standing with his hand on the door handle. *When did I last hear a party leader give a context, a perspective, and a reasonable way forward?* They were all bewilderingly alike, except one, the Sweden Democrat. And he got sympathy! In the fall he would get the votes, Sammy was convinced of that. Maybe not Bertil's vote, but certainly Sebastian's and probably the retired carpenter's.

The school property was burned and deserted. Sammy saw it as a symbol for what was happening in Sweden. It was as if a gang of arsonists was advancing across the country.

His thoughts were spinning. "I'm starting to go crazy," he mumbled. "I'm starting to punish myself." Suddenly he understood that he had to rise up out of the apathy he had lived with so long. He missed so much. So much was missing. *I'll buy a lottery ticket, win a fortune, and become Ann's neighbor, retire,* he thought. Bertil could teach him to weld, something Sammy had wanted for years. He could help the goat farmer put down posts. And Angelika? He opened the car door. And Angelika? *I don't love you anymore.*

✦

Forty-One

Rasmus Rönn had not boarded the plane that should have taken him to Thailand. Bodin sounded pleased when he said that. Björn Rönn had looked genuinely surprised when he was asked why his brother hadn't checked in. Bodin babbled on. Sammy hummed.

"Maybe Rasmus was involved in Hökarängen," Bodin speculated.

"That may be."

"Maybe he got cold feet and thought we would bring him in at Arlanda."

Sammy stood leaning against the car. He had just finished a call with

Angelika in Denmark. It was all over, that was clear. She wanted a divorce. It felt like falling into the sea in November.

"Or else he didn't want to take off alone. Hello?" Bodin yammered. "Are you there?"

"Yes, just thinking," said Sammy.

"Just don't think too long, then maybe there'll be time for another explosion."

"I'm in the middle of something, I'll call you later," Sammy said and simply clicked away the call.

Sammy slowly walked around the school property, indecisive, hesitant, as if he'd suddenly realized that he was missing something essential but couldn't grasp what it might be. Was it something Angelika had said, was it about Rasmus Rönn, or what? A motorcycle thundered past. The speed and noise decimated the rural peace and shook him out of his paralysis. He saw the driver's bent back and the way he leaned into the curve that led toward Lindell's house. Sammy wished that he could move ahead like that, put everything behind him.

He stood there knowing that he was being observed, surely by Sebastian, perhaps by Bertil Efraimsson, but it didn't bother him that he openly demonstrated his slowness, his dithering. He knew that a resolution was not far off. He didn't base that on any solid facts, but on a feeling. He knew from before that a sneaking insight in a difficult investigation always made him worried and a little doubtful, like a confused older person. It was as if he needed the disorder before everything could be sorted out in the right sequence. It reminded him of a summer job he'd had as an assistant mail carrier, the disarray with all the letters, cards, and bulk mail before everything was in the right compartment, the supervisor's raspy voice in the loudspeaker, and it was time to depart, the liberation of getting to straddle the bicycle and pedal away to his route.

It struck him that this was why it was so hard to live with him. And Lindell! It occurred to him a moment later. They were children of the same spirit, so often, much too often, with their thoughts somewhere else, on their way somewhere, many times with an uncertain destination, two target-seeking robots with an unforeseeable path.

The job as a detective inspector had taken hold of him, like a predator tearing his body and mind to pieces. Now he, and Angelika, had to pay the price. He shook his head as if to be rid of the insight, but also knew inside that there was no alternative. Or was there? This was him, Sammy Nilsson, for good and bad. He had met hundreds of enterprising colleagues, grindingly boring, but effective, systematically predictable, often blissfully unaware of their healthy capacity to separate work and free time. Perhaps Bodin was one of them. Berglund had been something in between.

"I am who I am," Sammy mumbled, unimaginatively and doggedly, a culprit's feeble defense.

"First and foremost: Forget Hökarängen," he encouraged himself. "Others have to solve that. It's this peasant hole that's your job."

He looked around, let the thought sink in, returned to the car and drove off, passed Lindell's house without a glance. "The smithy," he mumbled, but drove past the lane to Hamra, and turned instead onto the road toward the farm where Sam Rothe was living.

It was silent there. As if a neutron bomb had fallen and eliminated all life. Not a single rabbit, not a single colorful or cantankerous duck. The dovecote was deserted. Aviaries were open. A few paper bags that perhaps had contained feed blew past. A wire gate was swinging back and forth in a monotonous rhythm. Sammy hooked it shut.

"Sam!" he called, and it felt a little strange, like searching for yourself. He got a reply in a drawn-out bellow. He understood that it was the donkey, which had greeted him the same way at the previous visit. It came plodding between two sheds, followed by Sam Rothe. He was dressed in light green overall, at least a few sizes too big, and for that reason made a pitiful impression.

"Do you have a gun?"

"Where are the animals?"

"I've sold them. Most of 'em. Some I let out, mostly doves, species that can survive here. Can you shoot Ares? No one wants a donkey."

"That's probably not legal," said Sammy.

"People put down their dogs and cats when they get too old or sick. There can't very well be any difference with a donkey. Or what do you think? You're the law, after all." Rothe sounded cantankerous.

"Why is he called Ares?"

"He was called that when I bought him. It means war god."

"He doesn't look that warlike."

"He's sad. All his friends are gone."

"You want to shoot a donkey because it's depressed," Sammy observed.

"Shoot me too."

"Can't it go around and graze among the cows?"

"Have you seen any cows around here? Or livestock? Everything is shut down."

"Would goats be okay?"

Rothe didn't think so. "Ares is too nice." Sammy tried to get him to drop the thought of the depressed war god, and asked who had bought the other animals. Rothe told about his contacts, especially the rabbit club and the local association for birds. This was an unknown world to Sammy, and perhaps he was not all that interested, but he let Rothe talk on, it surely did him good.

"I've got a good reputation, they know that my animals are healthy. I've bred parrots, mostly gray parrots and cockatoos, all with breeding certificate, in case you're wondering."

"I'm not wondering about anything," said Sammy, who found the whole thing increasingly absurd. "Why are you getting rid of everything?" he asked.

Rothe refused to talk any more about his deserted farm and how he imagined his future. Surrounding himself with animals had been his life, Sammy understood that. Now he was alone. He had no family to speak of. No neighbors. The rabbit club's members would probably come to visit less and less often.

He needs help, professional help, Sammy thought when he saw the lost little man in his outsized overall. But nonetheless he couldn't keep from pressuring him a little.

"I think you know where Omid is."

Rothe stared stubbornly down at the ground.

"He's no rabbit that you can sell or a donkey you can shoot. He's a young person who's in trouble right now. Help out and rescue him," Sammy continued. It didn't appear to bite. Rothe had perhaps experienced too little empathy and consideration to be impressed by Sammy's argument. He had gained the animals' trust and given them love in return. "You helped him before."

"Then there was snow," said Rothe. "And now I'm going to move," he interrupted Sammy's further attempt. "I have to. They're going to sell this too."

"Who?"

"Mom and Kalle."

"So they're the ones who own—"

"They bought this 'cause they wanted to get rid of me. Now they're going to leave Sweden and need money."

Sammy was struck by the cruelty in the mother and stepfather's behavior. They knocked the legs out from under Sam, surely they understood that. Where would he go? He'd been able to live cheaply at the Rabbit Den, breed and sell animals, he had a place, he had contact with other nerds. And now?

"Damn, how sad," he said.

"Shoot me too," Rothe sobbed. "It doesn't matter if I live or die. Why should we live and be tormented? You've hunted him like an animal."

"Who do you mean?"

"Omid."

"As far as I'm concerned they can gladly stop."

The donkey screeched. Rothe responded with a movement of his arm and a clicking sound. Ares moved away a little and started frantically tearing at grass and plants, which grew lushly around the abandoned pond. Could he shoot the war god Ares? No, he didn't think so.

"Humans are strange animals," said Sammy.

"Omid probably isn't around anymore."

"What do you mean?"

"He's probably dead. He said that he came here to remind me about how everything . . . I don't remember what he said, but he got so depressed. He talked about bad people."

"Do you think he committed suicide?"

Rothe did not answer immediately. It looked as if he was digging in his memory, and Sammy waited him out.

"I don't know, when he couldn't live in the cellar any longer he just disappeared."

"He hid in the village," said Sammy. "Someone helped him."

"Who was that?"

Sammy pretended not to hear the question. "He came here a while ago, is that right?"

Rothe was getting ready to formulate a lie, Sammy saw that immediately.

"Is he here now?"

Rothe shook his head.

"Did he set fire to the smithy, do you think?"

"I don't want to talk with you anymore."

And why am I talking with you? thought Sammy. *We're not getting anywhere; on the contrary, I'm just getting depressed.* There was something unpleasant about Rothe. Sammy did not want to believe that it was due to his emaciated appearance and often half-witted image, but rather an increasing irritation at the unrelieved dissatisfaction that marked his whining and suffocating pleading for sympathy. *Get away,* Sammy wanted to exclaim, *help yourself, you zero, don't blame others all the time!* But he regretted it every time those thoughts bubbled up. The rabbit man had all the odds against him, probably always had. How much love and understanding did he get while he was growing up?

Sammy walked slowly toward the car. It was probably the last time he would visit the farm, perhaps he would never see Sam Rothe again. It was like signing a report, setting it on top of a bundle of papers, closing the folder to then send it into the archive of oblivion. Now it didn't work out that way, a lot was handled electronically, everything could be brought up on a screen in seconds with a few taps, but Sammy liked the image of dusty file cabinets in a cellar far down in the underworld, where the text slowly faded.

He brought his hands to his face, held them there, as if to hide himself from the world or perhaps to rub away the images of dreariness and misery. His palms gave off a foreign smell, almond perhaps, something moisturizing, creamy white, but also mildly spicy. Where did it come from? It felt peculiar in the context, shouldn't he smell like farm and donkey? Was it a memory from Jutland, wasn't this the way Angelika smelled at one time? Didn't she have a cream, maybe a perfume, when spiciness was popular? Musk, was that what it was called? He knew that he was on the wrong track, but he liked the word as such, short and mysterious. He associated it with bodies.

Or was it Therese in Östhammar who through a synapse in his brain reminded him of the vague promises they had given one another?

Then it came to him how it fit together. It must be the flower baskets he unconsciously rubbed against on the school property that deposited their scent traces, and which were able to eliminate the faint but clearly identifiable reminiscence of arson. The next image that fluttered past in his brain was the memory of Ann crouching in her flower bed. She was slowly but surely creating a world for herself. It felt both good and bad to him to think that. Good, because she was the closest to a dear friend he had; bad, because she was leaving him behind. He was still stuck in a life he should have left long ago, she in her idyll, with cheese and flowers and now perhaps also an Edvard, heavy and boring to be sure but like an extended pier against a high sea.

He looked around. Rothe was still standing there, with the donkey's heavy head close to him, as if they were exchanging secrets in a whisper. The rabbit man observed him with a puzzled, indolent expression on his thin face. *How pale he is,* it struck Sammy, *even though he lives here, as if the sun doesn't shine on him.*

"Listen!" Sammy shouted. "Ask Omid to come out, so we can talk."

He didn't know where the impulse came from. Rothe remained on the same spot, only the donkey reacted with a bellow. Sammy waited. He knew deep down that the Afghan was hiding in the house. Where could he have gone otherwise after he disappeared from Bertil Efraimsson?

A window opened. There he stood, a dozen meters away. They looked at one another. He looked different from what Sammy had imagined, older, more robust. Perhaps it was the beard that contributed to that impression? His face was otherwise neutral, with a stiffness in the features that Sammy recognized from interview rooms at the police station.

Now Sammy would get answers to some of his many questions. Omid wanted to talk.

✦

Forty-Two

Forest croft, he thought. That was before. Then there really was a forest. What now surrounded the road up to the little red cabin was a plantation, spruces perhaps forty years old stood in straight rows in a gigantic parade. Branches caressed the pickup's roof and windows with an eerie rasping sound. It was dark, even though the sun was shining. There was nothing of value besides a certain amount of cubic meters of timber, which was still too little to justify a final logging. Perhaps it would wait for just as many more years, if a powerful storm didn't sweep in and transform it all into gigantic jackstraws before then.

The house had once been the center of new cultivation from the mid-nineteenth century, and over fifty years ago the small parcels were still being worked by one Albin Pettersson and his family. Erland Edman had read about that on a small plaque that was hanging above the sideboard in the little room. The old gray Ferguson tractor, which the crofter Pettersson was able to buy in the early fifties, still stood in a shed. Björn Rönn claimed that he'd gotten it started. The present owner, a distant relative of the last farmer, had moved to Henderson, a little town somewhere in the southern United States, Erland didn't remember which state, because Björn had been unexpectedly verbose when they visited the place together the first time. How Björn knew him he didn't know either. Perhaps it was just as well. He wanted to know as little as possible. In any event they had access to the house, which they called "the Cape," and they would not be disturbed. The nearest neighbor was kilometers away.

There was only one access route, the narrow road, which was blocked by a locked boom. That was both good and bad, in Erland's opinion. Every time he left the hiding place he placed a slender thread straight across the road about five hundred meters from the cabin. If someone were to make their way around the boom and approach the house in a car the thread would break, or in any case be pressed down into the ground. So far this hadn't happened. A drawback was that he was caught in a dead end. Björn and he had examined the possibilities of clearing a provisional road out to the forest road in the vicinity, but it was too extensive a project to get started, and perhaps not that smart either, as it was too conspicuous.

If the police or any other unwelcome party were to show up, then you could simply go into the forest. They had placed a lightweight motorcycle behind the woodshed to enable a quick retreat. Erland had kick-started it more than once to take a short test drive, most recently on Saturday when the news about Hökarängen was broadcast. Would he ever be forced to take off on the thirty-five-year-old Yamaha dirt bike?

He drove the car into the shed and locked up after himself. The loneliness that he felt came not only from the fact that the silence was deafening. No birds seemed to thrive in the monotonous environment. "There are probably plenty of Russulas in the fall," Give had said with a grin. How could he know about such things, and who could socialize with mushrooms? Above all he missed Li'l Erland. He'd told his wife that he had a temporary job in Landskrona that he couldn't say no to. It was a lie with some plausibility to it. An old buddy, whom Mirjam despised and for that reason would never contact, had run a successful company for many years providing scaffolding and construction-site facilities. Erland had helped him before, and he was familiar with Landskrona and the surrounding area and could lie credibly about his stay in the south.

If only I was in Skåne, he thought. He had toyed with the thought of going away, but now it was too late, he was hopelessly stuck. They had decided that everyone in the group would go underground. Only Björn had refused, and how did that work out for him, Give had asked. "Stay there in the cabin. We'll lie low. It will blow over."

Blow over? As if this concerned a minor assault or a robbery. People had died, Swedes had died, a little boy had died. It would not be forgotten. Especially not if Give continued with Alby and other squares he talked about.

Erland Edman wondered whether he could be stopped. That was the thought that was grinding in his skull. Give had Olsson, if that was really his name, and Jimmy Nyström. Olsson seemed a little crazy and Jimmy would never be budged. After coming home from Afghanistan he was a different person. Erland thought Jimmy needed professional help. Instead he had taken off for another tour. Don't they have psychologists in the military? You could see just by looking at him that he was cracked in the head.

No, only Lena could stop her husband. Should he contact her? If it reached Give's ears, it was equivalent to a death sentence. He didn't know her well enough to assess the risk that she would immediately tattle.

Now in any event he would get a real weapon. He should have gotten it sooner, before he came to the forest cabin. An AK-5 was a good choice. Late in the winter he had test fired it in Dalarna, when he and some patriots from the Svealand division were there for discipline and training. How much ammo would he get? A magazine held thirty bullets, he already knew that. Nyström had been their instructor, he knew about the gun since Afghanistan. Erland had wanted to impress the war veteran. He was ashamed of that now, after he saw how nutty Nyström really was.

It must have been then, after the visit to Ludvika, they decided that he would be involved in the action against the mullahs on the square. Who made the decisions? He didn't know, and really didn't want to know. Now it was too late to back out.

A wind passed through the spruce plantation, reached the three apple trees and the little farmyard where Erland had been standing. It was a strangely warm gust. He longed for a little more rain to freshen up the air. There had actually been a cloud of dust behind the car as he drove on the forest road. He longed for so much. Not least Li'l Erland, and maybe Mirjam a little. When would he get to see them again?

He could not say that he was surprised, it was as if the wind had forewarned that he would get a visitor. The man came walking on the road, and he must have noticed Erland by the house. He was casually dressed, that was the phrase that popped up in Erland's head. Boots, green pants with pockets on the thigh, jacket of the same color and style, and with a cap on his head. He had a backpack. In his hand he was carrying an oblong case, which Erland thought at first concealed a rifle, but then realized must be fishing gear.

He walked without hesitation toward the house and called out a "Hello there" already from a distance. They shook hands, the man introduced himself as Lasse, he himself mumbled Patrik, the name they had agreed that he should use.

"I see, are you staying in the cabin?"

"Temporarily," Erland said.

"I've walked past many times, but never saw anyone here."

It appeared as if he was waiting for an answer, an explanation, but Erland remained silent.

"But the house looks reasonably well-kept. Nice location here in the forest."

"Yes, it's good," said Erland. He did not want to be drawn into a conversation with a stranger for anything in the world, but felt compelled anyway to let loose a little information.

"I'm staying here temporarily, a week, maybe two. I'm going to rest up. They told me to."

The man nodded in sympathy, as if he supported that idea completely.

"I was in an accident . . ." Erland continued, sticking to the script. "I'm not feeling too well, but here it's good, if you understand."

If you encounter anyone it's better to act a little crazy, Frank Give had said.

"I see, accident . . ."

"I'd rather not talk about it. But it's good here. Not so much noise."

"I can agree on that," said Lasse, who still looked sympathetic. "We'll probably have to form a club, because I'm on medical leave too, but today is the last day."

"Do you live in the area?"

"I have a summer cabin on the other side of the forest. I like to fish here, in the tarn without a name, as I call it. Have you been there? It's no more than ten minutes away."

Erland shook his head.

"I park on the forest road and walk through the spruce here. I could drive around, if it wasn't for that gate."

"The last day," said Erland.

"There are crayfish too, but perhaps I shouldn't say that out loud."

In another life perhaps Erland would have kept on chatting, he liked to fish, but now he just wanted to be rid of the intruder.

"I'm a little tired," said Erland. "They say that it's good if I sleep a lot."

"Yes, of course. You have to rest up sometimes . . . sleep well then," the man said, firing off his good-natured smile again.

He started to leave, but stopped after a few steps and turned around. "The fish are free, if you want to try, I mean."

Erland kept silent. That was what you did when you wanted to play a tired and confused lunatic. It was easier than he could have imagined.

"Five hundred meters, if that," the man said and pointed with his arm outstretched.

It did not feel good to have a person so close. Erland Edman felt that he was in the process of losing control, not because the man showed up, he was certainly inoffensive, but instead for his friendliness and smile. That was a life Erland had left behind. It was only in his contact with Li'l Erland that he could feel the old life, the thought of optimism and a kind of trust between people. When did life change appearance? He looked after the man, how he marched away between the trees with his rod and his fishing gear.

Suddenly his stay in the macabre forest felt unbearable. He was seized by the impulse to run after the fisherman, either to implore him to stay or put a bullet in his head, and out of pure reflex he took a few steps before he came to his senses. The pressure over his chest that he had felt the past few days forced him to take deep breaths, and the sweat broke out on his hairline. He leaned forward and rested his head on his knees. The image of the little boy's bicycle on the square in Hökarängen flashed past in his mind.

Tomorrow he would retrieve the weapon outside Rimbo. He looked forward to feeling the weight of the carbine and firing it. He peered after the good-natured man, but he was swallowed up by the spruce trees.

✦

Forty-Three

Omid was a young man, considerably taller than Sammy had pictured him. Sammy's first impression was that he moved self-confidently, but was also prepared to take a step to the side, back off.

His first words were: "That man saved my life." He meant Sam Rothe.

"I know," said Sammy.

"If he's done wrong, I'm the one you should arrest."

"He's from the police!" Rothe shouted.

"Shall we talk?" said Sammy, who up to now had not moved at all. Despite the tension—this was a breakthrough—he tried to keep his voice collected and calm.

Omid nodded. "It's been a long time since I talked with a policeman, and then it didn't go too well," he said. *He has a sense of humor,* Sammy thought, *that makes it easier.*

They sat down right next to the abandoned duck pond. Rothe had arranged a couple of chairs and a cracked bench under a flapping canopy of green fabric. There was also a round metal table with a bush-hammered top, what Angelika would call a smoking table. On the ground there were raffia rugs that had started to get moldy. Sammy got the feeling of being in a degenerate Bedouin environment. The shriek of the donkey, which seemed to sense the unease in the air, reinforced that image.

Rothe stood apprehensively a short distance away, and that was good. Sammy wanted to have Omid to himself. He started with his sympathy for his cousin's death. The Hazara made no comment.

"Tell me what happened. I'm thinking about the fire. What did you see?"

"I saw the ones who set it," said Omid.

"Would you be able to point them out?"

"One is dead. The one in the fire. Sam showed me a picture in the newspaper."

"Daniel Mattsson," Sammy stated. "Two others."

"I don't know their names."

"Would you be able to recognize them if you saw pictures?"

"I think so. It was dark, but it had started to burn. I saw them in the window, back side of the building. They were laughing."

"Why have you been hiding? You should have talked with us right away."

"No one believes a Hazara."

For Omid that was a truth, just as much as that the earth is round. It was there in his tone of voice, but it was not an accusation hurled out, simply a statement.

"Tell me what happened after the fire."

"I ran," Omid began. "I ran from Hamid." He looked at Sammy as if to underscore, imprint, his words. "Every day I see it, I'm running, it's cold. It's dark. I ran from Hamid. He is dead."

"But you didn't know . . ."

"No, I didn't know that he . . . but if I'd stopped . . . Why in a car?"

How many times must he have asked himself that question.

"You ran to Sam's house, right?"

Omid explained how he'd made his way in. The cellar door was unlocked. He found a sack of old clothes that he used for bedding, and even what Sammy assumed was a roll of insulation that he spread out on the floor. He curled up there. The next day Sam came to the house. He saw the tracks in the snow that led down to the cellar, and there found an exhausted Omid frozen stiff.

"He didn't ask anything. He helped me."

"Why, do you think?"

Omid looked over toward Sam Rothe, who was crouching by the pond, like an emaciated smallholder in a foreign country, a man who had just lost his harvest. It looked like he was considering drowning himself. Whether he heard what they were talking about was impossible to say.

"Where I lived with Hamid was a man, Hazara. One foot was missing, but he had a wooden one. He sold tea and small cakes with nuts, others with no nuts. They were cheaper. His sister baked. He poured tea in small cups. People drank and paid, he moved on. Every morning he poured a cup for a man with no money, gave him a cake with nuts. Not to everyone, there were so many poor people, but every day one man, one poor man. It can be cold in the morning."

"Was that in Afghanistan?"

"Iran," said Omid. "We had fled there."

"You can weld now," said Sammy.

Omid smiled. "Bertil taught me. He is like a book. He knows so much. He wanted me to try different things, in order to understand my hands. He bought airplanes and boats I should build. Small, small things, with glue."

Sammy understood that Omid meant models to put together.

"Patience, he said. I learned that word."

"Those two who are still alive, do you want the police to take them?"

Omid nodded.

"Do you want to look at the photos?" The binder with the pictures he had shown Rothe earlier was in the car. He retrieved them. Omid studied each photo carefully, as if he wanted to imprint the appearances. Without a word, without changing expression, he went through the binder, before he shut it again.

"Two," he said and without hesitation opened to the picture that was marked "3" and which depicted Daniel Mattsson, and went further to the last of the dozen that were in the binder. It depicted Stefan Sanberg.

"One is missing," said Sammy.

"Not there."

Sammy felt relieved in a way. Sebastian Ottosson was not pointed out. "Number three and twelve," he said. "Look one more time." Omid shook his head and handed back the binder.

"Did you set fire to the smithy, the building at the farm?"

Sam Rothe let out a sound that could have been made by one of the animals he sold or set free. Omid rested his laced fingers on his lap, mumbled something inaudible. Sammy got the idea that he was invoking a god. *But Muslims don't pray that way, do they?* Omid was probably a Muslim, Sammy assumed. He ought to ask.

A minute passed, a long minute, where the second hand hesitated before every movement. *Perhaps I'll never get an answer,* thought Sammy, and without a confession the Hazara could never be convicted. There were no witnesses, no technical evidence. There was motive, as well as opportunity, but that would not go far in a trial. Assumptions would be an attorney's obvious objection, and a court would agree.

"It may be number seven," Omid said at last.

Sammy opened the binder. The picture depicted Rasmus Rönn.

"Put them in prison," said Omid, and Sammy understood that it was a prerequisite for Omid to speak openly and honestly about the night when the smithy burned.

When Sammy Nilsson opened the car door for Omid, a flock of doves flew over the farm. They came in a beautiful long curve from the forest, describing an arc before they landed gently on the roof of the old barn.

"Coming home again," said Omid. Sam Rothe stood as if paralyzed, still by the pond, still silent. He had not said a word about the fact that Omid would be transported to Uppsala. The doves celebrated their newly won freedom by observing the abandoned aviaries. They strolled across the tile roof, amused themselves, socialized awhile, before as if at a given sign they lifted again and disappeared behind the jagged outline of the forest.

Sammy jumped into the car, locked the doors in childproof position. Omid met his gaze in the rearview mirror. Sammy said a silent prayer that the transport would go well, that Omid would not get any ideas. He should have called for backup, but did not want to subject Omid to that. This was perhaps the last time the Hazara could travel with a feeling that he was doing so voluntarily.

"I trust you," he said, putting the car in gear. "We'll take the back roads. It will be a little longer, but you won't have to see the village."

✦

Forty-Four

Say what you will about Frank Give, but he was effective. That was what Erland "Smulan" Edman thought as he stood in front of the cache. There were several, spread out around Mälaren Valley, but the one in the forests north of Rimbo was used the most. In an old root cellar by an abandoned croft a hole had been excavated, and a plastic case put down there. It was covered with a layer of dirt, gravel, and stone.

Erland Edman had been there and retrieved something previously. He had no idea who made the delivery, but guessed it was the man they called "Olsson." With an army spade with a short shaft he shoveled away the gravel. A black beetle rushed away in terror. He immediately bumped against the treasure chest. He took off the cover and there she was, black, glistening with grease. He picked up the carbine. There was something extremely secure in holding such an efficient weapon. A pistol or revolver was not the same thing at all. There was weight in the AK-5. Firepower.

Erland put the gun in a plastic sack and placed it in an old backpack, restored the hiding place as if it were a revered family grave, and returned at a rapid pace to the car. He could have driven all the way up to the deserted cabin, but he had followed instructions and parked the car a ten-minute walk away. Maybe Olsson was lying in the bushes keeping an eye on how and when the retrieval happened? It wouldn't be surprising. The suspicion in the group, and between the different battle groups, had increased. Maybe it was due to the media's rising interest, maybe because the level of ambition had been raised, more was at stake. Now it was no longer a game, now it was war, against the state, against the Jewish scum, against the blackened mob that had invaded the country, against the mullahs, against the newspapers that only spread lies, against the traitors to the people.

He left the area heading north, toward Rånäs. He had picked mushrooms with his parents in that area. He drove at the speed limit but slowed down anyway, felt he recognized a rest stop, or rather a glade, where they used to stop and have coffee. Now the glade continued into a logged area, like a sharp wide incision many hundred meters in, where mushrooms had grown before. A few seed pines were still left. Mossy stones wallowed in despair, exposed as they were to the tormenting sun. He increased speed and after a few kilometers turned straight east toward Almunge. It occurred to Erland that it was near there that Rönn had swiped the Austrogel.

It became an odyssey through a landscape he knew well. His mother was born in the area around Stora Väsby and his father on a smallholding in the middle of the spruce forest. Erland did not really remember where, and that pained him now. It was years since he'd visited the small villages, driven on the gravel roads through a landscape poor in arable land but all the richer in bogs, expansive forests, and isolated cabins. As he approached Tuna the landscape opened up, and he relaxed somewhat, drove up to Route 288 and turned northeast.

It felt good to think for a while about what had been. There was something inside him that gnawed and moaned, a sense of loss. He was often good at suppressing what he'd never fully understood and what was for that reason hard to combat. If you had a headache you took a pill, but what did you do with a sick feeling that concerned life? He was actually doing well! Mirjam was fine, the boy was healthy and growing as he should, they lived reasonably well in Sävja, even if there were starting to be quite a few darkies. The fact that he lacked a job at the moment meant nothing, he could get one tomorrow.

Sometimes he felt like kicking and hitting, even killing, like when he kicked at the young woman outside the ICA store in Nåntuna, the one who sat there month after month, no doubt a Gypsy, not because she was in the way, simply because it occurred to him. She'd shrieked, perhaps mostly from surprise, but no more than that. Maybe she was used to getting beaten by her clan. Next time he passed, then with the boy in tow, she had tensed her body, prepared for another kick.

"She's hungry," Li'l Erland had said and lingered by the entry, staring at her.

Why did he think about the Romanian bitch? If anyone were to kick at Mirjam he would kill that person. Now he had the chance to kill, and efficiently at that. The automatic weapon, with the three magazines, was in the trunk. He smiled to himself. *Just so I don't get like Give, or as disturbed as Olsson seems to be. I'm not like those nutcases. But I wouldn't hesitate to kill a policeman,* he thought. *I want to kill a policeman. It's my right.*

At three o'clock he was back at the Cape. The first thing he did was to check the thread across the road and then all the other security arrangements, small sticks and threads he set out in front of the door or mounted in the windows. Nothing had been moved. He placed the backpack with the carbine in a closet, he filled the coffee maker and watched the water gurgle out through the holder and down into the carafe. He sat down at the table in the little kitchen with the cup. "On Saturday it will explode," he said, out loud and firmly, as if to state it once and for all. He didn't want that, but knew that it was impossible to change. Frank Give wanted to move ahead hard, he understood that, ramp up the struggle, make the resistance clearer. Spreading flyers and marching around book fairs was not his thing. He wanted to create terror, it was that simple, and then victims were necessary, that was easy to understand. Give often returned to Italy in his reasoning about strategy and tactics. Their friends there had broken down society through terror. The leftist idiots had been crushed in the offensive that the police and military had initiated. The bombs that had been placed by the Fascists, sometimes disguised as left-wing activists, had been the pretext. Italy capsized, demands for law and order were heard more and more often. Now the left was crushed, hate against the immigrants so great that they were murdered in broad daylight by true patriots, and the people's trust in a democratic state and a functioning legal system was equal to zero. Out of this, Fascism could once again grow strong, Give thought, and Erland was prepared to say he was right.

Victims were necessary, he understood that, but the thought of that little boy on Peppartorget ground in his head. He drank his coffee. He ought to eat, but felt no hunger. The isolation in the cabin made him increasingly restless. He lay down on the old kitchen sofa. The closet with the gun was in his field of vision. The desire to test fire it became increasingly insistent. He shouldn't, but it was several kilometers to the nearest neighbor, now that the cheerful fisherman had gone home.

Loneliness. He thought about his father, whose name was also Erland. He'd looked up what the name meant, and it was a little embarrassing—"foreign" or "unfamiliar"—but it was the male name in the family that had persisted since the nineteenth century, and he had not hesitated to give his son the same name. The meaning could just as well have been "lonely," because that had marked his father and grandfather, and now himself. Whether his great-grandfather had been lonely he didn't know, but there was much to suggest it, it seemed to be the family curse. Because it was a curse! Being surrounded by people, but still solo. It was a condition that was invisible, and could often be concealed, but the aches were there.

You could only speculate on how it would go for Li'l Erland. Erland observed him and sometimes wondered, but he seemed quite normal. He had plenty of playmates, both at day care and in the neighborhood where they lived.

His father had died alone, suffocated by his own vomit in a cell. Can there be a more wretched death? His grandfather hanged himself two years later. In that action you are always alone.

How would he himself die? He got up from the sofa. There was still radiant sun. He ought to go out. He knew that it was that cursed glade, which no longer was a glade, that haunted him. It had been during a happy period, his father had been sober for a year or so, and he loved the forest, picking mushrooms and berries. There he was in his right element. If he was happy, the whole family was happy.

Erland went into the living room and up to the closet. He shouldn't, but what the hell, no one needed to know anything.

There was an ideal place a hundred meters or so into the forest. It was an old sandpit that the former crofters had made. Through the years they had dug their way into a low ridge, and in that way created a natural back-stop. Erland had test fired his pistol there. The ridge, which surrounded the place, created an arched noise barrier that to some degree dampened the sound.

The distance was short, perhaps only fifteen meters, but that didn't matter much. It was the feeling that counted. He raised an old pallet on end and set a rusty bucket on it, and slowly walked back. He unfolded the buttstock and put in a magazine, nowadays transparent plastic. He thought it felt a little shoddy, but it was clearly more practical and certainly cheaper. Thirty shots, 5.56 mm. Steel tip. The gun had open sights, no telescopic sight, but that wasn't anything Erland missed.

He laughed to himself. The feeling of loneliness had been blown away. He wished that Li'l Erland had been along so he could see his father so alive. He got ready, breathed in and out, the calm came over him, the bucket in the sight, and he squeezed off in the firm certainty that he would live a long time. He would not die in a jail cell, or hang himself in a dilapidated garage. No, he would die in a bed surrounded by love.

The recoil was mild. The bucket flew away with a bang, rolled a few times, gave up, and lay still. The shots echoed between the sand walls. A short salvo was enough, it was stupid to challenge fate. He stood there a few seconds, however, with the carbine resting against his shoulder, felt its weight, rocked with his knees. Everything felt good.

A snapping movement, as if a branch was broken off, made Erland instinctively crouch down. He ran over to the sand wall, curled up behind some brush, listened, peered. In his hand he held the AK-5. Was it an animal? Could it be a moose? Probably not, they didn't thrive in this terrain. The low ridge was surrounded by dense spruce forest. He thought about wild boars, which he'd seen traces of, moss that had been torn up, but that was by the boom where there were some damp areas.

Then the spruce curtain was parted by a movement. The happy fisherman came walking, dressed like the day before with a rod in hand and equipment on his back. He came from the east, he must have visited the tarn, and was walking in the direction of the logging road he'd mentioned, where he parked. He strode at a fast pace, not looking to the side. Erland was perhaps thirty meters away, partly hidden, but if the fisherman were to look in his direction the risk of discovery was great.

Hell, he was supposed to work today. Erland tried to remember what the fisherman had said the day before, didn't he say that it was his last day on sick leave? He was immediately swallowed up by new spruce trees. Erland remained seated. Had the fisherman heard? The tarn was not far away. Had he understood what it was? Not a given. He seemed to be the carefree type, who perhaps didn't reflect on the fact that there was a little shooting in the forest. Had he said anything about hunting? No, he had only talked about fishing.

After a couple of minutes Erland stood up and walked back to the cabin. He looked around constantly. The euphoria over the test shooting had been replaced by worry. He was seized by the thought of running after the fisherman, Lasse was his name, and silencing him for good, but obviously that was an idiotic idea. The fisherman would soon be missed, and the area around the summer cabin was probably the first place they would search for him.

✦

Forty-Five

Before Bodin and Sammy went into the interview room, they had a discussion about the fact that Omid Hayatullah had declined any assistance from an interpreter or representation by an attorney. *That wasn't good*, Sammy thought, but Bodin seemed indifferent. They went into the room with divided understandings.

"You're a Shia Muslim, from what I understand," Bodin said after the introductory formalities and condolences that Omid had lost his cousin. The Hazara nodded. "You have to speak up, so that it gets on tape," said Bodin, pointing at the recording equipment.

"Yes," said Omid. "I'm Shia, like almost all Hazaras."

"That's good. You're a minority, in other words," Bodin observed.

Is that good or bad? Sammy wondered, who was poorly informed on that subject.

Omid smiled. "Often," he said.

"In the cellar at Sam's parents' there was canned meat, do you eat that kind of food?"

Omid shook his head. "Maybe Sam thought so."

"Can you tell what happened when the smithy at Hamra farm burned down?"

Sammy's question came a little too soon, they had agreed to start cautiously, but from what he'd seen of Omid he thought that the Afghan could take it.

"I don't know," said Omid.

"You were there," said Bodin.

"I slept that night. At home with my friend Sam."

Sammy wondered whether he should resort to a lie, to the effect that Sam Rothe had suggested something else, all to wear down Omid's resistance, but decided that was a bad idea. Omid would surely see through the trick.

"You stayed with Bertil Efraimsson from the tenth of March until the day before the fire at Hamra. Why did you run away?"

"Bertil was nice, but perhaps he wanted to be left alone."

"You didn't tell him anything, that you would disappear?"

"No. He would have said stop."

"How did you find the way to Sam Rothe?"

"He told me."

"When you were staying in his parents' house?"

"Yes."

"You recognized Daniel Mattsson, is that right? You saw him from the top floor at Bertil's house."

"Yes, I saw."

"And Bertil told you where he lived?"

"Yes."

"You believed he was one of those who set fire to the school?"

"I know," said Omid, who did not seem nervous at all.

"You saw him outside the school, you say?"

"I saw, together with two others. They had set the fire, looked really happy. One had a gas can in his hand. They were drunk, all three of them."

Sammy took out the pictures he had previously shown to Omid, but he had supplemented them with another handful of photos.

Omid leaned forward. His dark hair had a peculiar whirl at the top of his head. He had recently had a haircut that was not particularly professionally executed. Sammy guessed that it was Rothe's work.

"Him," Omid said immediately, pointing at the photo of Daniel Mattsson. "And him." It was Stefan Sanberg. Omid looked up, as if he had to decide to continue or not, before he returned to the pictures on the table. He swept his eyes over the three rows with seven pictures in each. "And him too," he said at last, striking one picture with his index finger.

"Omid Hayatullah points out three pictures of individuals that he thinks set the fire at the school in Tilltorp the night of New Year's Eve between 2017 and 2018," Sammy said. "The pictures depict Daniel Mattsson, Stefan Sanberg, both from Tilltorp, and Rasmus Rönn, registered in Rasbo." Sammy illustrated by pointing out the three in order and at the same time saying out loud what he was doing. "Is that correct?"

"It's true," said Omid. "I saw them."

"And when you found out from Bertil Efraimsson where Daniel Matts-son lived, you decided to set fire to his house," Bodin said.

"No" was Omid's curt response.

"But it is correct that Bertil told you that the smithy was Daniel's residence?" Sammy asked.

"Yes, he pointed at it."

"What did Sam Rothe say about the idea of visiting Daniel?"

Bodin's question was presumptuous, but Omid showed no irritation.

"Did he go with you to Hamra?"

Omid did not answer, but Sammy saw something in his eyes. Bodin was on the trail of something.

"Sam Rothe would never let you go out alone at night. He likes you."

"He's nice."

"Sam has a moped. Have you driven it?"

"I have."

"From Sam Rothe's place to Hamra it's not far. There's a path through the forest, isn't there?"

For the first time Omid turned toward Bodin. "I don't know," he said.

"We believe that you set the fire, but that you didn't know Daniel was at home. Bertil probably said that he was gone that night, is that right?"

"I don't remember."

"You didn't know either that there was a woman in the house," said Bodin.

For the first time during the interview Omid reacted. He gave Sammy a quick glance before he looked down, rubbing his palms against his pant legs.

"You didn't know, right? Sam hasn't told you that a young woman died in that fire."

"No, I didn't know that a woman was dead."

In the way Omid said that, Sammy was convinced of his guilt.

"It was Sam's sister."

That was the death blow to the defense that Omid had decided on. He closed his eyes and let out a barely audible sound.

"I set the fire," he whispered. "I alone."

"You have to say it out loud," said Bodin, and Omid repeated the words that would give him a prison term for many years.

Sammy perceived the silence that settled in the interview room as a devotion. He was eternally grateful to Bodin that he had the sense to keep quiet. After a confession it was easy to get carried away in the euphoria. Sammy had experienced that himself so many times, but here there was no reason. True, an innocent woman had died in the fire, and as a result of it a presumably less innocent young man had died, but it was part of a series of incidents. It was a tragedy that could not be placed in an ordinary sequence where violence and brutal, serious crimes occurred. Sammy would never admit it, perhaps could not even explain it, because it would surely appear as if he wanted to relativize what had happened. Lovisa had been a full-blooded Nazi, and she had died what was surely a painful death in the flames. Daniel had been a racist and arsonist, and was beaten to death like a brute animal in the forest. Perhaps there were those who would maintain that justice was served. Sammy was not one of them.

"What happened with Daniel?" he asked at last.

Omid did not answer at first. The presence he had demonstrated until now was gone. He moved restlessly. The whirl on his head was joined by several more, as he pulled his hand through his hair. Perhaps they ought to take a break to give him the opportunity to recover, but that would amount to dereliction of duty. It would give Omid the possibility to collect himself and build a new line of defense, with silence and new lies or half-truths.

"What do you mean?" said Omid.

"What happened with Daniel?"

Omid looked completely perplexed.

"Did he run after you?" said Bodin.

"I don't understand."

"Daniel, did he run after you? Did you knock him down?" Bodin illustrated with his arm and clenched fist, as if he was aiming a blow.

Omid looked even more confused.

"He wasn't there."

"Let's take a break," Sammy decided. "Perhaps you want to take a shower?"

A strangely metallic smell of sweat had spread in the interview room.

The two policemen went to Sammy's office, while two jail guards took care of Omid. They would arrange food and a shower, and after a couple of hours lead the Hazara back to the interview room.

"What should we believe?" said Sammy.

For the first time Bodin looked reflective, and did not answer right away. That pleased Sammy, who was happy to wait out his colleague.

"The little bastard didn't know that Lovisa died in the smithy," Bodin said at last. "And Daniel 'wasn't there,' what does that mean?"

"He doesn't seem to be the type who lies so flippantly."

"We'll have to go out and bring the rabbit man in too," said Bodin.

✦

Forty-Six

Erland Edman loathed uncertainty. The feeling of being exposed, or not, was frustrating. It paralyzed him, made him incapable of doing anything. Had Lasse the fisherman heard the shot, perhaps even seen him fire the salvo? He'd been restrained, even though he wanted to use up the whole magazine. The question tormented Erland, making him pace around in the cabin like a ghost. The cabin was no longer a sanctuary. On the contrary, he was caught in a trap.

The feedback in his thoughts was interrupted by the phone, the one with a prepaid card, vibrating on the table. There were only two people who might call, and one of them was locked up at the police station in Uppsala. Erland understood that this meant problems. Give would never call to hear about how things were in general.

"Now it's time to step out of your baby shoes and put your best foot forward," the resistance cell's leader began with a limping metaphor. That could mean just about anything, but the tone confirmed that it surely

meant trouble. Erland went out on the porch and peered, thought he heard the sound of a car.

"You were talking about a place in Uppsala," Give continued. "That's where it's going to happen, the next date."

It took a moment before Erland understood. "Have you changed your mind? But it won't work! There's a hell of a lot of people there on a Saturday."

"I'm sure it will work as good as anything, if you just take care of your-self. They're coming up to the Cape this afternoon."

There was no doubt about who he meant.

"I've been discovered," said Erland, aware that this would trigger a landslide. "A fisherman came past."

"A fisherman! That's in the middle of the damned forest!"

"There are lakes, and tarns," said Erland, and it was the word "tarn" that triggered an inner stream of associations and memories. He sank down on a bench. *Get me away from here,* he had time to think before Give exploded.

Between the verbal assaults from Hökarängen, Erland had to explain as best he could. He even told Give about the test shooting, although he had decided not to say a word about it. Perhaps it was unconscious, in order to underscore that it was not a good idea for Olsson and Nyström to show up, that the Cape was ruined as a hiding place, that an attack in Uppsala was out of the question.

"Did the fisherman see anything?"

"Don't think so."

"Did he hear?"

"Maybe."

"We're going," Frank Give decided after a few seconds of reflection. "You have a buddy in Uppsala, right? Someone we can trust. Does he live alone?"

"Yes," Erland answered, cursing his loose tongue, that he had babbled about his only friend.

"Good! Then we'll assemble at eighteen hundred hours at meeting place three."

"And then?"

"You'll have to crash with your buddy."

"It won't work. He doesn't know anything."

Meeting place 3, that was the east end of the parking lot outside IKEA in Uppsala.

"The others will do reconnaissance, then we'll lie low. You'll have to take care of chow and the rest."

Everything was decided. What "the rest" was, he didn't understand. But Nyström probably knew, he always did.

"We can't drag him in, he's innocent" was Erland's final resigned objection.

"Just keep your mouth shut now," said Give, but with a laugh.

"Psychopath," Erland said in a whisper.

"Quite right," Give answered and clicked off the call.

When Erland "Smulan" Edman was eleven years old, he got a kitten. He missed it now, how it rolled up on his lap, purring like a low-pitched sewing machine.

Later it disappeared, maybe run over, maybe stolen, maybe simply longing for freedom. In moments of worry he would think about the kitten.

He understood that there was no turning back. Olsson and Nyström would set out the bomb, many people would die this Saturday too. Erland wished he was dead himself, but immediately thought about Li'l Erland. It couldn't end like this.

✦

Forty-Seven

Bodin started talking about Norberg as they passed Gränby Center and continued past Rasbo. There he fell silent. Sammy heaved a sigh of relief.

"You understand," Bodin said, resuming his hometown inventory as they passed the approach toward Upplands Tuna. "North-Jonsson meant a great deal to my family. He played accordion and fiddle equally well, had a pretty good singing voice and he was loyal."

"Was there a South-Jonsson?"

"Damn straight there was! But he wasn't too bright and sank himself in the lake, but had sense enough to take enough scrap iron with him so that he stayed there." He went on like that, about country characters and fiddlers, wise old women and fools.

"Are you nervous?"

Bodin smiled. "Is it noticeable? I guess I take hold of things that I can understand, clarify, what happened one time, what I'm used to" was the explanation he gave. Sammy nodded, thought he understood. He got the impulse to tell Bodin about his shipwrecked marriage, Jutland, and the whole thing, but decided that it was too soon, it could wait.

They turned off of Route 288 and were silent until they saw the *Welcome to Tilltorp* sign.

"That probably doesn't apply to everyone," Bodin observed.

The narrow gravel road that led up toward Rothe's abandoned animal farm was very dusty. Had he ever visited the village when it was rainy? He said something about that, and Bodin hummed in response. "We're visible from far off," Sammy continued, who also felt a growing worry.

The first thing they saw was the donkey. It was lying by the pond with its legs outstretched and the ungainly head close to the edge, as if it was reaching for water, but the poor creature would never drink again.

The two policemen stood side by side and observed him, the half-closed eyes and the open wound in the throat, where the blood had coagulated. It was as if their worry was materialized by the cadaver.

"Murder," Bodin said unexpectedly hard, as if he were spitting out the word. Otherwise he had no problem talking about hunting and butchering.

"Where's Rothe? This must be his work." Sammy sensed the worst, but called his name anyway so that it echoed in the farmyard. The desolation could not be illustrated more clearly. Bodin walked toward the house as if on a given signal, while Sammy chose the barn.

Sammy opened one half of the door, which actually smelled of fresh paint, in an environment otherwise dominated by the onset of decay. It reeked of urine, like cat piss mixed with the acidic odor of silage that had seasoned.

Against the far wall net cages were piled, mesh rolls and fence posts were in a muddle on the concrete floor. On the other short wall rope, loops, and chains were hanging in a certain order. That was probably where Rothe retrieved the rope that ended his life.

He was hanging from a beam in the roof. A short distance from his feet was a rabbit hutch, which he must have climbed up on and then kicked away to dangle freely. Sammy saw immediately that there was nothing to do. Rothe had succeeded in his effort.

It was not the first time that Sammy had seen a suicide, but it was definitely the most damaged and mournful figure he had seen dangling from a noose.

"Do you think he knew that his half sister was in the smithy?"

Sammy turned around. Bodin stood in the open doorway, and in the light that came into the barn's dusty darkness his profile looked slightly satanic.

"Impossible to know," said Sammy.

"Did he kill Daniel Mattsson?"

"No idea, but I would like to believe so."

"The laughing Hazara will go free, in any case in the question of homicide or manslaughter," said Bodin, and Sammy did not know his colleague well enough to decide if he thought that was good or bad.

"Now the Frimans can sail alone," Bodin observed.

"Will you call?"

Bodin left the barn immediately and without objections. It was the kind of trivial thing that made Sammy like his colleague. He sat down on the rabbit hutch, sneaked a glance at the body, and gave Sam Rothe a kind of posthumous justice. No other services would be read over him.

✦

Forty-Eight

Lars "Lasse" Henriksson was worried. He didn't like trouble. He was a simple man, with straightforward thoughts and an open mind. That was the image he tried to project anyway. He had a hard time with irony and mixed messages, as well as violence, trickery, and meanness. A nice man, who wanted to see good in everyone. He thought that way about the man in the forest too. The one named Patrik.

His wife Eva-Britt was of a different sort. "Of course you have to call the police," she said, without hesitation. She mistrusted everything and everyone. The immigrant who passed out flyers in the town house development where they'd lived for twenty years was likely a presumptive, even hardened burglar, whose only goal was to look for suitable targets. The cashier at the ICA grocery store who counted out the wrong change had a system for her deceit, that was obvious. The postman surreptitiously read their mail to get at family secrets.

"Not a soul has lived in that cabin for years. I'm sure some gang has taken it over."

"On the contrary, he seemed extremely lonely and a little confused. I think he's unwell."

"A dangerous gang," Eva-Britt repeated, and for once she was right in her suspicions.

Lars Henriksson called at last. What settled the decision was that he had heard a salvo. It was an automatic weapon, no doubt about that, and what recreational hunter or pistol shooter had such a gun?

Finally Lars Henriksson was transferred to Nils Stolpe, who immediately realized the significance of his observation: mysterious man in the forest, not far from Rasbo where the Rönn brothers lived, staying in an isolated cabin, and as frosting on the cake a salvo from an automatic weapon. He asked the witness not to say a word about what he'd seen, not to anyone. "What about my wife?" Henriksson objected. "Ask her to keep quiet." That gave Henriksson a good laugh.

They ended the call. It struck Stolpe that it could be the missing Erland Edman who was nesting in the spruce forest. According to his wife, Mirjam, it was as if he'd been swallowed up by the earth, and she'd started to get really worried. She'd tried to reach him several times, but Erland hadn't answered. When at last she called his acquaintance in Skåne, he denied any knowledge of a scaffolding job for Erland. Early in the morning Stolpe and two colleagues, Eva Briis and Hampus Book, made a visit to the Edman home, and that had not made Mirjam any calmer. Nothing of interest was found in the apartment. Nothing that could link Erland to missing explosives, Hökarängen, or contacts with radical right-wing groups.

Eva Briis, who according to Stolpe was a good police officer despite the fact that she was a woman, sat down with Mirjam in the kitchen and tried to coax something out of her that could lead further in the search for her husband. In vain. The only thing she could say was that he would never do anything "criminal" that would risk his contact with Li'l Erland, their son. She said that with a tone of defiant pride in her voice, and Eva Briis really wanted to believe her, but was too experienced to accept that.

Stolpe first called Sammy Nilsson, and then Bodin. The three met in the command room. Stolpe had set up map sheet 70 in the Sweden series, "Gimo," and pointed out where the cabin was located. "Isolated to say the least," said Bodin. "I had no idea there was so much forest in Uppland." Sure enough the map was dominated by green, with only small sections of yellow that indicated an open landscape.

"That was where the riches came from," Sammy explained, who during his trips in north Uppland with Angelika had read up on this. "The mines needed wood and the iron processing needed charcoal."

"It sounds like at home in Norberg," said Bodin.

"And Saturday nights needed keyed fiddles," Stolpe added. "Took a course many years ago. It was exactly in Gimo."

"That's not far from our old colleague Lindell," Bodin observed. "Who said that the countryside is boring? Charcoal kilns, keyed fiddles, blue cheese, and arsonists."

Sammy never ceased to be amazed by some of his colleagues.

"We'll go there," Stolpe decided, who gladly saw himself as commander, Sammy realized that. "We'll need assistance, but for one Edman we don't need a SWAT team."

"He's armed, if that information is correct," Bodin objected.

"Henriksson was certain. He's been in the civil defense and ought to know how automatic fire sounds," said Sammy.

Stolpe took no notice. "A patrol at the forest road that Henriksson talked about, it must be here," his meaty index finger finding a point on the map. "And two carloads of alert constables at the entry road to the cabin. Dog too. If we can get a helicopter in the air it would be good. That's enough for one 'Smula.' Vests on and reinforcement weapons too."

Bodin and Sammy gave each other a look. Sammy smiled, but had a nagging thought that someone would have to pay for this arrangement.

An hour later they were on their way. It had taken a while, and some difficulty, to anchor the response. There was a lot of nervousness in the building. Everyone wanted their rear ends covered in case anything were to go wrong, but Stolpe's enthusiasm was boundless.

Another forty minutes later everything and everyone was in place. It wasn't possible to scare up a helicopter, however. Sammy picked up Henriksson to serve as a guide. It was deemed necessary to find the right location as quickly as possible, if Erland Edman, or whoever it might be, were to get the idea to flee on the worn path which according to Henriksson ran from the cabin to the forest road. After having performed his mission as guide he would be brought back to civilization, that is, the police station in Gimo, which now suddenly, and to the Gimo residents' surprise, was heavily manned. Gimo experienced some excitement, and Arnold, a notorious blogger from Ytternuttö, had already thrown out wordy speculations and honed drastic formulations, convinced as he was that the crowd of police officers was connected to the invasion of darkies.

Stolpe and Bodin, who were positioned at the approach to the cabin, made a final review before they moved ahead. They were prepared to be met by a locked gate, but they had equipment to force every obstacle. They had discussed bringing a wheel loader or tractor, which could simply push aside boom and posts, but that was judged too noisy. The decision was to advance from the gate on foot, to attract as little attention as possible. Once the main force of thirty police officers, one of whom was a dog handler, reached the cabin, the gate would be removed and a police van and two ambulances would be brought in.

It was about eight hundred meters to the gate. During the slow advance they had radio contact with Sammy, who was by the forest road with the guide and half a dozen uniformed colleagues. Everything seemed to be working.

"What a hell of a forest," said Stolpe.

"It's no forest," Bodin muttered. "But this is how it looks these days."

They reached the boom, left the cars, and continued on foot. Stolpe lagged, but Bodin, who was used to moving in the woods and fields, had no problem following the more energetic uniformed colleagues. They sensed that perhaps they were writing crime history, drawn into the country's most extensive terrorist investigation, and they were eager to get there.

Sammy heard the crackling in the earbud before Stolpe's hoarse voice reported that they were at the cabin. The guide Henriksson had just returned to the logging road with a policeman as escort. The cabin was visible between the trees. It looked like any other cabin: stone foundation, red siding, white corners, brick chimney, and a small porch. Sammy answered Stolpe that he too was on the scene and that the place looked completely dead. The curtains were drawn and there was no smoke from the chimney.

All according to plan, so far. Was there an Erland Edman, and was he a terrorist bomber? Were there others? Somehow they had assumed that Edman was alone, perhaps based on Henriksson's testimony. Sammy tried to follow the advice he had once received about how he should breathe in pressure situations. Maybe it was humbug, but the mere idea made him relax.

"Nisse, no car is visible, but it may be in the barn," he whispered to Stolpe.

"It's a shed," Bodin interjected.

"I love you," Sammy whispered. "I'll go up and check from the back side. Wait here for now."

It took him a couple of minutes to make his way there. First he was forced to walk back a little, then sneak ahead in a crouch, screened by a low boulder and thicket of bushes he identified as waxberry. Hidden by a root cellar he peered ahead; no fluttering curtains from the windows. For two or three meters he was almost unprotected, only a few scrubby currant bushes passably covered him. He wriggled slowly forward, centimeter by

centimeter, thinking that any rapid movement would more easily be noticed from the house. The overgrown grass smelled like Jutland, a Jutland that he would probably never experience again, and he had to suppress the thought of digging in and staying there.

"Shed," he mumbled and breathed out. He had managed the maneuver. There was no window but some wide cracks between the wallboards worn from age. He peeked in, at first seeing nothing before his eyes got used to the darkness inside. The gleam of sheet metal and a faint reflection of a headlight. The discovery created a double feeling: the croft was occupied, and could house a bomber or something as simple as an ordinary bandit who was in hiding, or even more likely, a lonely man, perhaps slightly deranged as Lars Henriksson hinted, who amused himself with a completely legal weapon. All alternatives involved hazards on a sliding scale, from mortal danger to discomfort.

By moving a little he could see in between a wider crack and read the license plate. He reported the letter and number combination to his colleagues. After a minute came the answer; it was a Volvo V40 and Erland Edman was listed as owner.

Mortal danger, in other words. Sammy was struck by the thought of a booby trap. He knew very little about explosives and had never heard of Austrogel in particular before, but the mere thought of what Peppartorget in Hökarängen looked like made him report his suspicion to the others.

"Roger," said Bodin.

The stillness was broken by Stolpe's voice, amplified by an honorable old megaphone with 1.5 volt batteries. Sammy happened to think of an old American TV series, *Hill Street Blues*.

"This is the police, the house is surrounded," Nils Stolpe intoned.

Half a minute passed. All that was heard was a crow cawing. Sammy glimpsed it sailing across the sky.

"Erland Edman, we know you're in the cabin. Do the simple and right thing: Come out with your hands in the air." No reaction. The crow's call faded out in the distance. Sammy peered at the gable of the shed.

"We have to talk," continued Stolpe, who had put himself in what was surely an uncomfortable crouching position. He held the megaphone in one hand. "General Patton," Sammy mumbled, forgetting that it was broadcast in everyone's earbuds. Faint giggling was heard.

"Come out, we have to talk," Stolpe repeated.

The response was a salvo of automatic fire through a broken window. Sammy saw his colleague being thrown backward. The megaphone made an arc in the air. Furious activity broke out over the radio. Several of the uniformed colleagues answered the fire, without any order being given, peppering the house so that chips flew in all directions and glass shattered. The war had come to the Gimo forest.

A new salvo came from inside the house. For a moment Sammy thought he saw a barrel sticking out through a window. Could he crawl closer? That would surely be madness. Erland Edman was serious. He could quickly change windows, and then Sammy would be easy prey on the open space between shed and house. *Where is the SWAT team?* Sammy had time to think before a motorcycle was kick-started behind the cabin, he recognized the sound. A man with a bundle on his back, leaning forward over an old dirt bike, lurched off between the thickets and trees, almost drove right into a large stone but at the last second made an evasive maneuver, skidded, but managed to thunder on. Sammy could not help but admire how capably the driver made his way in the difficult terrain.

On the back side four men were placed, and Sammy heard how at least two of his colleagues opened fire. He screamed into his microphone. The motorcycle was swallowed up by the curtain of spruce. Bodin's voice was heard over the radio: "Fuck, fuck, fuck this all to hell!"

✦

Forty-Nine

Many years ago he'd driven the Novemberkåsan motorcycle race in Rasbo. It had been pouring rain for over a day and it was a few degrees above freezing, in the forest it was muddy up to the hub, and treacherously slippery stones and roots were sticking up everywhere. He wasn't among the leaders, but he made it through the course. It was a feat, something to tell Li'l Erland, when he could understand such an effort.

So it would be a hell of a thing if he couldn't make his way out of this goddam stick forest! There were no cops chasing after him. He heard a dog barking at a distance. But none of that actually worried him. He drove ahead, filled with adrenaline he whipped himself farther, had to get off the bike at one point and walk it over a V-shaped ditch that cut straight through the spruce plantation, but otherwise he was a winner who drove on. He was soon at the forest road. He stopped indecisively, trying to picture the map that was nailed on the wall in the cabin. He should have taken it with him! There were three directions: to the right, which led out of the forest to populated areas, that is, police; due north, which involved denser forest, certainly more impassable but on the other hand a completely unexpected choice; and then left, perhaps not as surprising but enough that he could gain time. But where did it lead? Could he come out in the direction of Morkarla? In that case maybe he could steal a car and make his way out of the area, either on Route 290 toward Uppsala or on side roads southwest toward Alunda.

He chose the latter alternative, for several reasons, mainly because of the risk of roadblocks toward Gimo, but also for the uncertainty of how long the gas in the tank would last. He told himself to drive calmly, not least to make as little noise as possible. The road was in reasonably good condition, the weather had been dry a long time. He kept looking toward the sky, a helicopter would be the primary threat, it could search considerable areas in a short time.

After a kilometer or two the road ended in a turnaround. A little timber of poor quality was lying there, perhaps an abandoned surplus. An opening in the forest, which now resembled a forest with a more varied appearance, suggested a path. He took it, content that the stately spruce gave him some protection from being seen from above, and he relaxed a little. Had he hit that fat policeman with the megaphone? He probably had. Frank Give had always nagged that Erland would really like to shoot a cop. Now it was done, and it was actually not anything that worried him. If he went to prison it wouldn't matter when a sentence was pronounced. And wasn't that his right? Li'l Erland's grandfather had died because of the nonchalant carelessness of the police. Now they were even. He would explain that to the boy one day.

He cruised ahead daringly, at times on difficult stony ground. All his skill and dependability had to be put to use. It was like a reprise from the practice of his teenage years.

Gradually the landscape opened up, small meadows of partly over-grown hayfields came more often, scattered drying sheds appeared, a rot-ted fence ran parallel with the path. These were remnants of the peripheral fields of smallholdings he saw. Here there were moose in the fields and certainly mushrooms in the fall, he thought.

In the distance he saw a farm, grazing horses, and a tractor that plod-ded ahead pulling a wagon. Everything seemed peaceful. He scanned the sky. No helicopter. How long had it been since he left the cabin? Maybe twenty minutes. Before too long every road would be crawling with cops, both on 288 and on the road between Uppsala and Österbybruk. It would take a while for them to come out from Uppsala. He didn't think there would be cops any closer. The small police stations were shut down or unmanned.

He drove on, now on a winding gravel road. There were scattered houses. He passed an apparently abandoned chapel and came up to an old workshop, where decades of scrap had collected on the yard in front. A rack for pipes, ventilation drums neatly arranged in declining size re-sembling a gigantic organ, steel plates leaned against the wall, and an old Saab 95 that was parked for good. He turned as if on impulse behind a rusty container, left the motorcycle, and started looking around. Behind the dusty, stained windows of the large entry something large and white was visible. The door was closed, but on the back side was a door that with some difficulty he could force open. It was as he thought, the building was used as a storage space for campers and recreational boats.

Most important, however, was a Saab 95, the same shade of blue and the same model as the one outside, but in considerably better condition. It was parked in front of the entry and looked drivable. Erland searched on a board above the extended workbench, where keys were hanging in rows. *This is truly the boonies,* he thought, when he found the key to the Saab.

It started right away, purring like a cat, obviously happy to be put to use. He checked the fuel gauge, half a tank, let the engine idle and contin-ued his inspection. The key to the entry was in the lock. The Saab could in other words be driven out. He got an idea, after having determined that the car was equipped with a tow bar. The oldest of the campers was a so-called egg, probably from the early sixties. The hitch looked sturdy. He released the brake, prized the camper forward, and hooked it up on the tow bar.

In a space that functioned as a combined break room and changing room he found an overall, worn and gray, ideal in other words, and a cap hanging on a nail. In a washroom there was a yellow, single-use razor stuck in a dirty glass, and with that and some soap he peeled away the mustache he'd had a long time. He quickly outfitted himself in overall and cap, and went out to the motorcycle, which he managed to prize up into the container and cover with a little scrap metal. It looked as if it had been lying there a long time. Back in the workshop he dirtied his hands with a little oil and put a stripe on his left cheek too. The smell triggered a vague memory of the past and he stopped for a moment.

After listening and taking one last look around, he drove the vehicles out of the building and onto the road.

✦

Fifty

"Which side is the liver on?"

Bodin did not reply. Maybe he hadn't heard the question, maybe he didn't care, or else he didn't want to show his ignorance.

"An injury in the liver and . . . you remember Anna Lindh? One stab and then she was on the floor. It can look ever so innocent, but when the doctors start poking around then there's blood gushing, and you go into shock and all that."

"If you're so fucking knowledgeable, then you should know which side the liver is on. And what the hell is 'all that'? Bellyache?"

Sammy did not respond. He knew that he was babbling.

"He'll survive," Bodin said after a while.

"You think so?"

"Yes, with that layer of fat."

"But he was bleeding heavily. And then those hits in the groin."

For over two hours they had waited, looking up every time the swinging door opened, but they'd stopped getting up and asking. They understood that they would get word when there was something to report.

Sammy thought about grass, the odor he'd sensed so strongly as he was crawling forward outside the cabin in the woods. It was such an unexpected feeling and reaction, not only because the circumstances were special, that returned him to an existence so separate from what he was living in now. As if the grass wanted to remind him about life, but it was probably only children and people in love who drew in the healthy aroma of fresh grass and aromatic herbs, and in a state of undisturbed curiosity and happiness at that.

He let out a deep sigh. Bodin looked up.

"I didn't know he was divorced," said Sammy.

"We're the closest next of kin," said Bodin.

"There's a son, he's on his way."

"'Closest,' I said. Stolpe Junior lives in the marshes in the far north."

"It was Vidsel."

Another hour passed before word came: "Your colleague came in with life-threatening injuries in the abdomen and groin," followed by the classic formulation: "His condition is stable but still very serious."

"Is he going to survive?"

"It's too soon to say."

The doctor could say that much, before with an apology he disappeared just as quickly as he'd shown up. The two policemen sank down on the chairs again, but Bodin stood up again immediately.

"You stay, the two of you have known each other for many years, right? I have to go and bring in Edman."

Sammy nodded, content to be left alone, even if it was in a kind of waiting room before the end of life with rows of impersonal chairs and institutional light fixtures that made it feel like a morgue.

The door swung one last time after Bodin. Sammy stood up and took out his phone, turned it on. He always felt guilty using it in a hospital setting, as if all the sensitive apparatus would shut down, but he had to check missed calls and messages. There were quite a few, but nothing from Jutland. He called Lindell.

She answered right away. "What's going on?" she asked without any introductory small talk.

"Have you heard? Stolpe had surgery, they don't know how it's going. I'm at the hospital waiting. If he wakes up I want someone to be here."

And even if he doesn't, Sammy thought.

"Is it Edman?"

"Seems to be."

"I heard about the rabbit man. That's so sad. Did he commit suicide?" It was Lindell in fine old form. No evasions. The emotions could come later.

"He hanged himself."

"And how is it going with Edman?"

"At large," said Sammy, who felt some discomfort even though he wanted to talk, maybe because she was so on while he himself had settled into reflection.

Lindell was silent, waiting him out, he understood that very well.

"I'm thinking about resigning," he found himself saying at last. "This thing with Angelika, and now Stolpe." These were unspoken secrets, but Lindell caught on right away.

"I understand," she said. "You can come out here. It's fine to sleep in Erik's house. You need a little country air."

As if I haven't been in Tilltorp enough, he thought, but mumbled something that could be understood as a weak affirmation.

They ended the call. He got a crazy impulse to go to her directly, but naturally that was impossible, and he sank listlessly down on the chair. He turned off the phone.

Just then the doors opened. It was the doctor. Sammy feared the worst.

"We estimate that your buddy will wake up in an hour or so. You might as well go down and have some coffee for now, and come back later."

Sammy stood up, nodded in thanks, and left the depressing corridor. To get a little exercise and to avoid any other passengers on the elevator he took the stairs. The doctor had said "buddy" and not "colleague," and that made Sammy stop on the third floor and take a deep breath, before he continued his clopping downward journey. Stolpe had been in the building, that was when they were still on Storgatan, when as a young, unnecessarily daring candidate Sammy started his employment. Sammy hadn't thought about it that much, but Nisse Stolpe, no taller twenty-five years ago but at least twenty kilos lighter, had overlooked Sammy's somewhat cocky attitude. Even though other colleagues had been offended by the newcomer's conduct and treated him accordingly. So he and Stolpe were probably not just colleagues, but "buddies" too.

"I don't understand, why would he..." Mirjam Edman twirled an index finger in her dark hair, which fell freely over her shoulders and framed a fine-boned face.

Eva Briis observed a woman whose life had been smashed to pieces, and who also looked completely worn out, slouching and with her hands constantly searching for distraction. But then she got up quickly from the couch, went up to the window, turned her back on the policewoman, and looked out over a sun-drenched courtyard, where the lawn had already started to turn yellow. Briis waited, sensing that Mirjam had already started planning for a life without Erland.

"He doesn't have any real friends, and actually no real acquaintances either," she said without turning around. "Where will he go? He only has me and Li'l Erland. He had a dog when we met." She told Briis about the collie, how it got sick and one night simply died. Briis, who felt like she was sitting on pins and needles, let her talk.

"Does he have good contact with Li'l Erland?"

"The boy is his great joy. Maybe his only love."

She turned around. Briis could see how anger was slowly building up. "Where is he? Why did he lie?"

"Has he mentioned someone named Björn Rönn?"

Mirjam shook her head.

"Does he have any connection to Hökarängen outside Stockholm, acquaintances or relatives there?"

"No, not as far as I know."

"Does he have someone else? Is that why he lied?"

Mirjam took the question with unexpected calm. "I've had that thought but I don't think so. Actually I'm sure he hasn't met anyone else."

Briis went through the obvious questions, about his recent behavior, if he'd shown interest in firearms, if he had any phones other than the Samsung that Mirjam knew about, and anything else that might give an opening in the search for Erland Edman.

After half an hour, when three officers simultaneously searched through the apartment once more, for the moment there was nothing to add. Mirjam had been ignorant of her husband's activities, and that felt like a relief. Li'l Erland would not have both his parents under lock and key.

"Where is the boy?"

"With my sister."

The mood was subdued, to say the least, in the command room for the search. It was now confirmed that it was Erland Edman. Henriksson the fisherman had pointed him out without hesitation on a picture from the portrait collection. Fingerprints also tallied between the cabin and his home, and his car was parked in the shed.

So far it was probably good. You knew who you were hunting. It was worse that they had no idea where he was. He had slipped out of the net. Calculations were made on how long a full tank for that type of motorcycle might last. It was clarified that it was a lightweight; a policeman placed on the back side of the house was a former member of a speedway team, and he was sure of that. On the wall was a map with the cabin marked with a pin, surrounded by a circle of conceivable distance, assuming that the tank was not refilled. The area was a sizable piece of north Uppland.

They also knew, through Mirjam Edman, that her husband was an experienced motorcycle driver, which had become clear to them when they saw him in action.

According to Mirjam, as far as she knew he had no acquaintances in the area where he could conceivably hide. She could not name any really good friends whatsoever of Erland, any he could rely on under any circumstances. According to Briis he stood out as a loner.

There was no immediate explanation for how and why he ended up in the forest cabin, other than that he obviously wanted to hide out, and that reinforced the suspicions that he was involved in the bombing in Hökarängen. In jail Björn Rönn had denied acquaintance with Edman. "Maybe I've seen him on a job, if he's worked for NCC," he'd said, noticeably uninterested in the question. He didn't know the cabin and the surrounding area at all, and he hadn't seen any automatic weapons "for years and years."

The owner of the cabin was identified but not reached. His name was

Sven-Erik Andersson and he had moved abroad many years ago, according to a distant relative probably to the United States, but there was no address, not even a city. Who had access to the cabin, not least for upkeep and inspection, was unknown, but obviously someone had to take care of the ongoing maintenance. There were signs of recent repairs and improvements. Questioning of neighbors had not produced anything in that respect.

In other words the forest cabin was an ideal place to stay hidden. A salvo fired from an automatic weapon with 5.56-caliber ammunition, and a recreational fisherman, had put a stop to that. That Lars Henriksson's first workday in a long time turned out to be a scheduled day off was the coincidence that created an opening in the investigation.

"So much damn forest," said Briis, who together with Bodin was staring at the map on the wall. "What do you think, is he camping out under a downed tree?"

"He was heading for Uppsala," Bodin decided. "Maybe he happens to have a buddy, even a like-minded Nazi lunatic, in the vicinity."

"Then it will be hard," said Briis. "But I also think that he headed for Uppsala. He wants to be close to his son. I got the impression that he's a very lonely person and the only thing that means anything is his kid. I actually got the feeling that his wife was jealous."

The barricades that were placed on routes 288 and 290, in both directions, had come up too late and produced zilch. A warning to the general public that an armed man was being searched for had gone out via the broadcast media and over the internet, and a photo of Erland Edman was shared frequently on the net. The phone lines were burning up at the police stations in Gimo, Tierp, Östhammar, and Uppsala.

A press conference was planned, but few specifics could be reported.

A man with no real friends and few acquaintances, and with no interests other than motor sports that he practiced in front of the TV, a man without fixed points, clubhouses, pubs, or restaurants that he often frequented.

"But what the hell!" Bodin exclaimed. "How can we be so dense! Who gave us the tip about Edman to start with? It was that woman in Tilltorp, the former colleague."

"Lindell?"

Bodin took out his phone and entered a speed-dial number. Sammy did not answer. Bodin left a voice message. He thought Sammy would have his phone turned off as long as he was at the recovery room where Stolpe was.

Bodin knew that Ann Lindell couldn't be searched for in open sources. He called "the grunt," the trainee he got so much use out of.

"Find the unlisted mobile number for Ann Lindell, former police officer living in Tilltorp, Östhammar municipality" was his brief instruction. The grunt had the reasonable characteristic that he didn't need long harangues to understand. A few minutes later he reported the result. Bodin called immediately. It was as if Eva Briis did not exist, but evidently he registered her smile because he gave her a quick look and smiled back. No answer from Lindell either. He left a message that she should call back "at once," an order that could not be misunderstood.

"What do we know? Through the fisherman, the car, and fingerprints, Edman is linked to the cabin, and we know that he was a champion at making his way through the forest on a bike, but that doesn't link him to Rönn or to the bombing in Hökarängen."

"No," said Briis, who'd had the same thought. "But he lied to his wife, claimed that he was at a job in Skåne. Why?"

"Maybe he's tired of her."

"That may be, but you don't usually need an automatic weapon for that."

"We have to find the motorcycle!" Bodin exclaimed. Many of their colleagues looked up. A few smiled, and they were the ones who could identify a policeman who cared. According to Bodin, that was no longer a given.

✦

Fifty-One

He knew where he was. He'd been to a wedding in Morkarla. It felt like long ago, even though it was only three or four years ago. The couple who had promised each other eternal fidelity, the bridegroom was a cousin of Mirjam and the bride from Thailand, had already separated.

To the north, Österbybruk was not far away, but that was not a good

alternative, and south the road went to Ramhäll, the old mining community, and farther down toward Lyan and Route 288. He didn't want to go
there either. He had a feeling that he should be able to work his way up
to Route 290 by way of side roads. Didn't the cousin live in some place
called Flymyra or right near there anyway? He took a chance, drove south
and then turned west on an insignificant gravel road. It had to lead somewhere, he figured.

The Saab coughed occasionally, but even so ran admirably well. It must
be at least twenty-five years old. The camper egg hung on. The tension had
eased somewhat. He was on his way. The vehicle was a good camouflage.
Who would believe that a cop killer fled with an aged Saab and an antique
camper?

When he got to Flymyra he felt a bit triumphant. Now he had a chance
to get away. Just north of Kungstomt he came out on the highway and
drove south without hesitating. After about five kilometers he met the first
police car. There would be more.

Erland understood that roadblocks were being set up.

It was almost four o'clock in the afternoon before Ann Lindell called
Bodin. If she'd been a reporter it would be possible to refuse, she thought,
with reference to source protection. Bodin waited, she heard his breathing
and the noise in the background. She could easily picture the situation at
her old job, and was once again struck by the thought of how good she had
it, before she gave Bodin the name he wanted: Justus Jonsson.

"I have the phone turned off at work."

"So you say," said Bodin.

"It's a benefit we have in the dairy industry," said Ann. Bodin clicked
off. She could not be angry. He was in a terrible spot. The pressure on the
agency had probably never been greater.

Even so she wanted to be there, in the midst of the mess, and yet not; in
the midst of the decisive spurt, as it's called in middle-distance running,
and yet not. The police occupation was like alcohol. A hellish poison, which
knocked you out, paralyzed, but also often refreshing and good, alleviating
and conciliatory. After that came the aches, the anxiety.

In the evenings she drank ginger tea. She was the ICA store's biggest customer of the shapeless roots, which she cut a piece from every evening and peeled, sometimes with a smile on her lips, sometimes more dogged. She pretended that it helped. Her stomach at least became harmonious like never before.

"Sammy," she said out loud and smiled. If he were to show up in the evening anything at all might happen, she understood that. That thought made her happy in an unfortunate way. Happy, because she was still a woman that Sammy, as a man, could *desire*, that lovely word. She didn't need to feel guilty about her lust, as she had before. One reason was probably the police environment, so infantile and toxically male, so oppressive. She remembered Beatrice, her old colleague at Violent Crimes, how she struggled. Impudent, many thought; excessive, others said, but no doubt she'd been right.

She didn't need to be ashamed of her body, as she had been before, as she stretched her hand across her thigh, belly, and breasts, assessed, compared.

"It's the cheese," she mumbled. That was what had liberated her. The 528-step method, it worked! She laughed at her craziness, which was the truest and wisest thing she'd experienced in years and years.

She called Erik. "It will be Dubrovnik," she said as soon as he answered. He started to laugh. Then it struck her, that was how his father had laughed, that one night. After that Erik had been conceived, who in flight had taken with him that good laugh. What else had he inherited? She didn't know.

They talked awhile. He must have noticed something in her mood, because gradually his voice wilted.

"I haven't been drinking, I just got home from work," she said. "I'm just happy. That's why I called you, do you understand?"

"Got it," he said.

"What are you doing? Have you . . ."

"Mom, go to Dubrovnik, promise me that."

Ann took a breath, suppressed a sob, and promised.

✦

Fifty-Two

The moment Justus got out of the car on Molngatan the phone vibrated in his pocket. Unknown number. Worries, he just knew it, and stared at the display until the phone fell silent. Probably the cop. Otherwise there weren't many who called, it was often about work, or Berit who needed help with something, sometimes an old buddy from the Aquarium Association who wanted advice or tips. Justus had partly taken over his father's role as expert on tropical fish. It wasn't strange, having grown up in front of an aquarium. Cichlids were what bound him with Little John, then and for always. It wasn't a role he strove for, or even wanted, but now he was established and in demand and didn't think he could refuse people, some of them old friends of his father, when they got in touch.

He suspected what the call was about. His old friend Erland was in a really bad way, the bombing in Hökarängen and the raid in the Gimo forests, and the subsequent hunt for one of the "terrorist bombers" had been the major topic of discussion at work. Not just there, the whole nation was following the development of events. The tragicomic element was that the previously withdrawn, not to say insignificant, Erland "Smulan" Edman was at the center of attention. A few at work recognized him from before, one had been a coworker with Erland at a job in Björklinge, and could testify to an extremely reserved mason.

During the day Justus had thought about calling Ann Lindell, which she had encouraged him to do if he found out anything new. He hadn't really, but he was curious. He wondered where Erland had gone just as much as everyone else.

The phone vibrated again. This time he answered, and said exactly that, that he didn't know anything.

"No, Erland hasn't contacted me."

Justus regretted having sought out Ann before, because now the crowd of cops came running again, just what Uncle Lennart had warned him about once upon a time: "If they get a hold, they never stop." And Lennart knew, he was one of those the cops always went after if anything happened, a car theft or a silly break-in at a store.

"I've been at work the whole day," Justus said with a sigh.

He walked slowly toward the entry. The tiredness struck him doubly.

"Yes, you're welcome to check, if you want to get the gossip started at work."

He clicked off the call. Inside the entry to the stairwell two men were standing. Cops, he understood that immediately. He knew that he would never get rid of the connection to the bomb in Hökarängen. There would be talk at work and the neighbors would look at him suspiciously. No smoke without fire, it was called.

"You all should have checked up on him then, when I called," he said. The men didn't say anything, but instead followed him up the stairs.

He opened the door, aware that there was no point in arguing. Both policemen pulled out their guns, pushed Justus aside, gave a sign that he should stay in the hall, and slipped into the apartment. Justus shut the front door behind him. At the same moment the phone vibrated again. This time it was a known number. He quickly clicked off the call.

The policemen came back. "If he gets in touch, you have to call us. Understood?"

Justus nodded. "He's not going to be in touch."

The older policeman observed him. There was no friendliness in his gaze. Justus understood that he knew about his family background, perhaps he'd even been involved in the investigation of the murder of Little John, maybe he'd put Uncle Lennart away some time.

"We haven't seen each other for a long time. Why should he contact me?"

When they left the apartment he took out the phone again. Did he have any choice? He opened a can of beer and sat down in the kitchen, wondered what he could do, must do. Actually, being passive was also an alternative. He stared at the number. Where are you, Smulan? It was unforgivable to blow people up, if he really had been involved, but at the same time Justus could feel for his old friend who was now being hunted by everyone.

As long as he didn't answer, or call back, he himself went free. No one could accuse him of anything. The phone was set on silent. It could be his explanation if the cops started snooping in call lists. He threw the phone on the kitchen counter.

✦

Fifty-Three

"Cable tie, it can be traces of a cable tie," Wikman said. He stood with the report from the medical examiner in his hand, read the final comments, and set the papers aside.

"What in the name of hell," Sammy said, but weakly, more like a prayer for an end to all the infernality that was pouring in across his desk.

"And a few bruises on both arms, right under the elbows, as if he'd been tied up from behind."

"The rabbit man was no thug," said Sammy, who could easily imagine how Roth was overpowered and tied up without any great difficulty.

"His wrist was broken," said Wikman.

That decided it. They looked at each other, the technician and Sammy, reading each other's thoughts and mood. Wikman pushed his glasses up on his forehead and shook his head.

"I felt sorry for the boy," Sammy summarized.

"And even more now. Imagine being hanged."

"Can we be completely sure?"

"Hard to believe that he would have his hands tied behind his back in any other context," Holm, the other technician, said unexpectedly. Wikman was usually the one who did the talking. "In theory you can hang yourself with a broken wrist, but . . ."

"The medical examiner seems to be quite certain," said Wikman.

"Who?"

"Hjortsberger."

Sammy nodded. Fredrik Hjortsberg was levelheaded and reasonable. The two technicians left his office. Their work was over and the medical examiner and pathologist had had their say. Now this concerned a homicide and then the case ended up on Sammy's lap.

He picked up the report, exemplarily concise and specific, and read through it before he started thinking about a motive. In reality there was probably only one. Someone, or more than one, was afraid that Rothe would start talking about things he'd seen or heard. The risk was probably even more imminent after he'd gotten word that he had to move from the farm. After that there were no bonds of loyalty whatsoever to the village and its inhabitants.

"Let's take another look," said Wikman, who had come back into the office. Sammy looked up, partly absent in his own thoughts. "Now that it's murder." The technician carefully shut the door behind him.

The exhaustion pulsated like waves through his body. First the hours at the hospital, and now this. There didn't seem to be any end to the misery.

The brief conversation with Nils Stolpe, who was in a borderland between life and death, had sapped the juice out of Sammy. If you could even call it a conversation, Stolpe had mostly spluttered and raved; Sammy was not even sure that he recognized him. Stolpe would survive, Sammy had decided, but the doctors were not equally sure. "Things can happen," one of them said, but did not explain what. His son, strikingly like his father, showed up later, and Sammy briefly explained what had happened. *Your father is a harebrained cop who made a fool of himself*, he could have summarized, but refrained from any emotional expressions and turned the baton over to the worried and stressed son.

Sam Rothe had always, in one way or another, taken beatings. His childhood could not have been fun, several people had hinted. That thought tormented Sammy Nilsson, as always when children and young people suffered. Had Rothe ever been in love, gotten to taste love; had anyone ever pressed his body next to theirs?

What did a lack of love do to people? Some turned violent, some developed more acceptable, albeit trying, methods to assert themselves and their worth, others became compliant to the point of erasure. Rothe had seemed that way, afraid of beatings and therefore a little slow-witted. He had certainly not been at the head of the class, but subordination had reinforced that slightly stupid characteristic, and then the hamster wheel was in motion. One thing led to another. His death, roped and hung like a brute animal at the slaughterhouse, was in a way a consistent end point to his life, but where the animal's body had a value, Sam Rothe was worthless even in death.

Sammy felt nauseated, about to vomit, and that could not be blamed on the lousy coffee at the emergency room and the police station. He shuffled some papers listlessly on his desk, printouts of the interviews that had been held with a couple of the young men at the New Year's party in Tilltorp. That was where it started, that was where the thought of fire and death took shape.

He decided to go there again. He couldn't remember how many times he'd already done that, but now he was determined that something decisive had to happen.

✦

Fifty-Four

"Where are you going?"

He answered with a truth and a lie: that he was going to the creamery to discuss goat's milk. The destination was correct but the purpose a different one. He wasn't sure that the "bitch cop," as they called her, was working. He knew that she didn't work every day, and he hadn't seen her walk past, but he had to take a chance. Going to her house was not a good alternative, there was no good way to explain that.

It was a workday for Ann Lindell, more than usual. Matilda was "indisposed." Ann thought she was pregnant. Matilda was known for being sensitive, often for no reason, but in this case Ann bought her absence. The

This has gone well so far, thought Ann. "We can . . . I can call a couple of former colleagues who will pick him up. He's wanted, after all. Then you can go home and work on the house and think about goats."

Ann let the silence do its work, wondered whether she should call Uppsala directly, but there was probably no great rush. Rasmus probably didn't have many places to flee to, and it amused her to play cop for a while.

"I believe you," said Ann, "but you have to be honest."

"There's so much," Sebastian said again. "They're my friends. Some of them anyway."

"They'll go away," Ann said immediately, perhaps a bit harshly, because Sebastian looked up.

"Daniel is dead."

She waited patiently for him to continue.

"You didn't come here to talk about the dead," she said when he hesitated too long. "This is about those who are still alive, isn't it?"

"There were three that night. The idea was Stefan's. Daniel was pretty drunk, but went along. Then he fell asleep on the floor at my house, and that was when the fire was burning the most."

"And the third one was Rasmus, is that right?"

Sebastian nodded. "He's almost the worst. He laughs when people die."

"Like in Hökarängen the other day?"

"Not just that."

Ann recognized the signs of when they were starting to approach the core, when the words became important, but so hard to say. That applies to most, but for some it was like opening the floodgates completely, everything came rushing, where sometimes it was hard to understand what was important and what was surplus information. Sebastian was not that type, he struggled with the words.

"I was thinking about the guy with the rabbits, Lovisa's brother."

"What do you mean?"

"He died."

"And then Rasmus laughed?"

Ann wondered what Sebastian wanted to say, but was not really sure what this was all about.

"There was a gang there stealing animals. I wasn't with them."

creamery owners had wanted a child for several years, and it was under-standable that she was worried about the slightest stomachache.

It was calm and pleasant in the creamery; she was the only one there. She stood awhile and observed the equipment in the cheese-making room. You could see your reflection in the stainless steel. Now it was the floor's turn. She opened the faucet and let the water flow through the hose, seized the scrub brush and let it work. It was a job she liked, to get to splash without reserve across a floor where there were a couple of scuppers that greedily captured the water.

The melody sounded from the wireless box on the wall. Someone was at the door. Ann turned off the water, stepped out of her boots, and went to answer it. She was sure that it was a customer, someone who could not or did not want to understand the sign with the store hours.

She opened with a ready answer on her lips, but Sebastian Ottosson was standing outside the door. During her years as a police officer Ann had seen numerous physiognomies that demonstrated various signs of worry, anxiety, guilt, and shame, and Sebastian was expressing all of them at once.

"Come in," she said, and he was not slow to slip in and pull the door closed behind him.

She took him to the break room.

"This isn't about cheese, is it?"

"I walked here, thought maybe you were working."

She nodded, understood what he meant. "Here we can speak freely."

"Rasmus is with me. He's hiding."

"From the police?"

Sebastian nodded.

"Why? Is it because his brother has been arrested?"

"That too."

"Tell me what you know. Even if it's hard. I understand that you want to talk, that you want to get rid of your worry, right?"

"There's so much," said Sebastian, and Ann thought for a moment that he would burst into tears.

"Start somewhere. Start with what hurts the most."

"Then I can't go home. Rasmus is going to figure out that I told. I have a hard time lying without it showing."

This has gone well so far, thought Ann. "We can . . . I can call a couple of former colleagues who will pick him up. He's wanted, after all. Then you can go home and work on the house and think about goats."

Ann let the silence do its work, wondered whether she should call Uppsala directly, but there was probably no great rush. Rasmus probably didn't have many places to flee to, and it amused her to play cop for a while.

"I believe you," said Ann, "but you have to be honest."

"There's so much," Sebastian said again. "They're my friends. Some of them anyway."

"They'll go away," Ann said immediately, perhaps a bit harshly, because Sebastian looked up.

"Daniel is dead."

She waited patiently for him to continue.

"You didn't come here to talk about the dead," she said when he hesitated too long. "This is about those who are still alive, isn't it?"

"There were three that night. The idea was Stefan's. Daniel was pretty drunk, but went along. Then he fell asleep on the floor at my house, and that was when the fire was burning the most."

"And the third one was Rasmus, is that right?"

Sebastian nodded. "He's almost the worst. He laughs when people die."

"Like in Hökarängen the other day?"

"Not just that."

Ann recognized the signs of when they were starting to approach the core, when the words became important, but so hard to say. That applies to most, but for some it was like opening the floodgates completely, everything came rushing, where sometimes it was hard to understand what was important and what was surplus information. Sebastian was not that type, he struggled with the words.

"I was thinking about the guy with the rabbits, Lovisa's brother."

"What do you mean?"

"He died."

"And then Rasmus laughed?"

Ann wondered what Sebastian wanted to say, but was not really sure what this was all about.

"There was a gang there stealing animals. I wasn't with them."

creamery owners had wanted a child for several years, and it was understandable that she was worried about the slightest stomachache.

It was calm and pleasant in the creamery; she was the only one there. She stood awhile and observed the equipment in the cheese-making room. You could see your reflection in the stainless steel. Now it was the floor's turn. She opened the faucet and let the water flow through the hose, seized the scrub brush and let it work. It was a job she liked, to get to splash without reserve across a floor where there were a couple of scuppers that greedily captured the water.

The melody sounded from the wireless box on the wall. Someone was at the door. Ann turned off the water, stepped out of her boots, and went to answer it. She was sure that it was a customer, someone who could not or did not want to understand the sign with the store hours.

She opened with a ready answer on her lips, but Sebastian Ottosson was standing outside the door. During her years as a police officer Ann had seen numerous physiognomies that demonstrated various signs of worry, anxiety, guilt, and shame, and Sebastian was expressing all of them at once.

"Come in," she said, and he was not slow to slip in and pull the door closed behind him.

She took him to the break room.

"This isn't about cheese, is it?"

"I walked here, thought maybe you were working."

She nodded, understood what he meant. "Here we can speak freely."

"Rasmus is with me. He's hiding."

"From the police?"

Sebastian nodded.

"Why? Is it because his brother has been arrested?"

"That too."

"Tell me what you know. Even if it's hard. I understand that you want to talk, that you want to get rid of your worry, right?"

"There's so much," said Sebastian, and Ann thought for a moment that he would burst into tears.

"Start somewhere. Start with what hurts the most."

"Then I can't go home. Rasmus is going to figure out that I told. I have a hard time lying without it showing."

"He got really sad, I heard." Ann was fishing, but Sebastian did not take the bait. He stood up from the table.

"Cheese," said Ann. He took a deep breath, as if to gather strength, gather courage, and make a decision in which direction he would go.

"Cheese is life," she resumed.

He smiled faintly, and Ann answered it.

"What's his real name?" he asked.

"Sam. Sam Rothe."

"I probably need to talk with the police."

"I'll call right away," said Ann.

"Rasmus bragged that they killed him."

Ann took out the phone and entered the speed-dial number to Sammy, before what he'd said sunk in.

"Who?"

Sebastian shook his head.

"Hi," said Ann, happy to hear Sammy's voice even though it was marked by stress and fatigue. "I'm at the creamery. There's a guy here you need to meet. Are you already on your way? Good!"

✦

Fifty-Five

One thing he'd learned during the training in Ludvika about staying hidden: Move as little as possible. Often you did the opposite, under the illusion that movement made it more difficult for a pursuer. But that only increased the risk of being observed, the course leader had drummed into them. The idea of turning toward Skyttorp was good, in itself that was an evasive maneuver where he lost time but avoided possible roadblocks on Route 290. He drove by way of Viksta, and at Björklinge reached the old E4 and took it south.

He drove straight to Boländerna in Uppsala. First he disconnected the camper, parking it outside a store that sold sporting equipment. It was too conspicuous and attracted attention, he reasoned, which was why it was necessary to get rid of it. He parked the Saab on the outer edge of the agreed area on the IKEA parking lot. From there he had a good view of the approaches and could also see how several curious people stopped by the "camper egg," walking around it and trying to peek in through the small windows. Maybe someone was thinking about stealing it, the hitch was unlocked. It would be a blessing if a camper thief came by.

He leaned back in the seat, closed his eyes, and thought through the day. He had acquitted himself well, the flight from the cabin filled him with a bit of pride. He fell asleep within a couple of minutes. From outside he looked like a worn-out laborer or mechanic who was taking a nap.

An hour later he woke up. He pulled out the phones, first the temporary prepaid one, which showed nothing, and after that his own, with a long series of missed calls. It was not particularly surprising. He went through the numbers, three known, including Sigge from Landskrona; in other words he knew he'd been used as a cover. Mirjam had called eleven times, which wasn't strange.

Exactly at the agreed time Frank Give's car drove onto the parking lot. It cruised slowly in the middle row, made a turn farther up toward the IKEA colossus, and cruised back. Two rows farther down the Saab was parked. It struck Erland that he could curl up and hide. Give would never suspect that he was camping in a vintage Saab, but instead was certainly keeping an eye out for a Volvo. Give must have heard the reports on the radio about the hunt for Erland, and it didn't require much imagination to picture that Erland was hiding out somewhere in the forest, and for that reason couldn't make it to the meeting place. It was an enticing thought to make himself invisible. It could end right then and there. He hadn't been involved in Hökarängen, but the fact that he'd shot the policeman at the cabin could never be explained away. If he was dead, many years behind bars awaited him. Murdering a policeman wasn't popular, but he could not be convicted for little Jonathan's death.

Give's car approached. Nyström the bomb expert was with him. Erland slid down on the seat. He pictured Li'l Erland before him, and in a sudden insight he understood that the boy was lost, the great love in his life was thrown away. There was no forgiveness for what he'd been involved in. His posthumous reputation would be merciless. He reached down and fumbled under the plastic bag on the floor on the passenger side, where the AK-5 was hidden. A new magazine was in place. Thirty shots would be enough if he wanted to put a stop to the two psychopaths who were approaching. He slid farther down on the side. If he did put an end to his two companions now, which was an easy match, what would he do then? Put the barrel in his mouth? Roar off in the old Saab? Where to?

Give turned between the last two rows of cars. The Saab was parked almost farthest south, flanked by a Ford and an Audi, in an otherwise sparsely used parking lot. There was still time to quickly slip over into the backseat and curl up on the floor.

When they had a few car lengths left he opened the door to make himself known. At the same moment it struck him that maybe they wanted to kill him. After the police raid in the cabin he was a burden, a possible snitch. He pulled the automatic weapon to him, but concealed it behind the car door.

Give was leaning back nonchalantly with his left arm resting on the window, smiling his infernal smile. It was as if nothing affected that guy. Beside him Nyström's indifferent mug was visible.

"Traded up, I see," Give observed.

Shoot him, an inner voice whispered. Li'l Erland would remember that, and nothing else, that it was his father who killed the bombers.

"My dad had one like that."

"Have you ever had a dad?" said Erland, and it was the closest to a protest he had ever made against the leader of the group.

"What happened?"

"The cops came. It must have been that fisherman who snitched."

"He didn't snitch, you do that if you belong to the organization. He was just doing his civic duty."

"Is he dead, the cop I mean?"

"Not as far as I know. They said on the radio that he was alive, but in critical condition."

Kill that bastard!

"But you can check the news on the phone."

"I forgot that," said Erland, who in reality had been afraid of listening to any news.

"Have you talked with your buddy?"

Erland shook his head.

"But you know where he lives?"

Erland nodded.

"Then let's go," said Give, jerking his head to show that Erland should get into the van.

"I have to get something," said Erland, bending down and sheathing the AK-5 in the plastic bag, pulled on the backpack, an old Fjällräven that could hold ninety liters, and pushed the gun down. His pistol was already there, a toiletry kit, and a change of clothes. He looked around the inside of the car. He would miss that old Saab. It felt as if the car, the brand and year itself, the décor, the panel and upholstery, were the last contact with a life that had been lost, a life that he now definitely said goodbye to.

"Nice outfit," Give said when Erland was done with the farewell and closed the door behind him. Erland looked down at his overall. He liked that too, the slightly sweaty and oily odor.

"What do you have in the backpack?"

"Some clothes and a few things I've prepared for escape."

"Is the AK-5 in there?"

Erland didn't need to say anything, the answer could be read on his face.

"Take the gun out and leave it behind in the car. We can pick it up later."

They parked by a gas station on Årstagatan, which was next to a McDonald's. Erland saw people coming out with hamburgers in hand, thought he detected the aroma in the air. He was really hungry.

"Can't you buy something?" said Erland. "I don't want to show myself unless I have to."

"Okay," said Give, and Nyström left the car without a word. He came back with three bags. They ate in silence. Erland observed the customers at the outdoor tables. They were living, laughing, and chiding their kids. When had he last laughed? Only a week ago he'd been there with Mirjam and Li'l Erland. At the table where they'd sat was another family with kids.

Give broke the silence. "What happened?" Erland told them about the arrival of the police, the exchange of gunfire, the flight on the motorcycle, and where and how he acquired the old car. They neither interrupted nor commented on his detailed account. Give hummed a little and smiled a few times. Erland took that as approval. The disturbed Nyström showed no reactions at all. He had probably murdered Taliban and civilians in Afghanistan with the same indifferent visage.

"Smart to shave off the mustache" was Give's only comment.

They left the car. Give and Nyström each carried a sports bag, Erland brought his backpack. He felt vulnerable, exposed, while they waited for the green light. They made their way across heavily trafficked Vaksala-gatan and into an area where the streets had weather-related names: there was rain and storm as well as sunshine and thaw. And then Molngatan, where Justus lived. Nyström was sent off to look for patrol cars and plain-clothes police. He came back and mumbled something that Erland understood as a military term for "the coast is clear." The army veteran was getting more and more ridiculous.

Erland took the lead and guided them to Justus's entry. It was open, as if they were expected. A cleaning woman was mopping the entry level. She looked up in fear, as if she instinctively understood that the three of them could be a threat. They walked up the two flights of stairs. It said *Jonsson* on the door. Erland remembered the housewarming party. There had been complaints. The next day Justus went around to the near-est neighbors with flowers, and in that way turned a bad thing into a good one.

"We'll go up one flight while you ring the doorbell."

"Is that smart? The cops can be waiting inside the door."

"Yes, and then you're caught," Give observed.

Justus Jonsson was tired of cops. Actually he always had been, that was probably implanted since childhood. In his family the legal system had not played a positive role. You should always avoid, always fear, and sometimes despise cops, he'd heard from his father, Little John, and his uncle Lennart. They'd both had scrapes with the law. It was basically their own fault, they realized that, rarely blamed anyone else. There was the whole scale of misdemeanors, from youthful sins such as shoplifting and public intoxication, to more serious matters: car theft, a couple of minor assaults, fencing, resisting arrest, and threatening behavior. They had calmed down with the years, but the suspicion remained. The only police officer that Justus could come to terms with was Ann Lindell. Maybe it was something she'd said during the investigation of the murder of his father, he didn't remember exactly, or else it was simply her whole attitude that he liked.

Now he was thinking about contacting her, stood with the phone in his hand, entering the number he'd received.

Instead his doorbell rang. He was convinced that it was the police who'd come back, with new frivolous questions. He opened the door with the hope that someone would get it in the forehead.

"What the hell!"

"Are the cops here?" Erland asked.

Justus's bewilderment was answer enough. If the police were hiding in the apartment, his expression would have been different. "We have to come in," Erland said. Give and Nyström came down the flight of stairs.

"Let us in," said Give, exploiting his psycho look to underscore the order.

✦

Fifty-Six

A creamery. The break room at a creamery, a somewhat less common type of interview space. The smell was different too. The coffee fumes were basically the same as at the police station, but the slightly tart smell of cheese was new and a bit odd to Sammy.

"The cheese folks," he said. He felt relaxed for the first time in quite a while. Maybe fatigue played a part, but more significant was the feeling that the Tilltorp tangle could be unraveled. The village had been an open wound for six months, with the terror of New Year's night and then the fire at the smithy, topped with what was probably the murder of a harmless young man.

"Do you understand that I have to record this? No one's going to come later and say that I made things up. It's your own words that matter."

"It's cool."

"And one more thing: I thought you were part of the Nazi gang, but I was wrong."

"It's cool," Sebastian repeated.

"Tell us about Rasmus," Sammy encouraged him after having turned on the recorder and stated the time and place, and who was present.

"He's at my house. I don't want him to be, but he's out of his mind."

"Have you told him that you don't want him at your house?"

"He doesn't give a damn about that."

"Do you feel threatened?"

"Not exactly, but if he knew that I talked with you he'd go crazy."

"He didn't go to Thailand, even though it was all paid. You had to drive him back here instead, is that so?"

"Yes, he wanted to stay at home for his brother's sake."

"Because we brought Björn Rönn in for questioning?"

"Questioning," said Sebastian. "That sounds good."

"Tell me what happened on New Year's."

He repeated what he'd said to Ann, but this time in more detail. Three of the partyers, whom he listed without hesitation, set fire to the old school. "I wasn't drunk. It was Granddad's house after all."

Sammy milked out even more details, not least that there were others who had witnessed the same thing. Sebastian listed half a dozen names. Sammy recognized them all from the list of the partygoers. He wondered whether they used any flammable fluid to get the fire going, and Sebastian thought that maybe they had retrieved a can of gasoline from one of the cars, but he hadn't seen anything.

"You said something to me about Sam Rothe. That Rasmus laughed when he died. Why is that?"

Ann's interjection made Sammy jump. Obviously she didn't know about the medical examiner's report.

"He's sick. And Stefan too. They went there, said that they were going to break him."

"Do you think they killed Sam?" said Sammy.

"Rasmus said that they did. He said that Rothe pissed on himself."

"Why would they kill him?"

"Stefan said that Lovisa's brother killed Daniel."

Sammy sat silently a moment, tried to digest this.

"Where did he get that from?"

"Daniel's brother told Stefan."

"Andreas Mattsson said that Sam Rothe killed Daniel Mattsson, have I understood that correctly?"

"Yes, Stefan said so anyway."

"Did Andreas see that with his own eyes, or hear it?"

"I don't know."

Sammy gave Lindell a look.

"Have you told us everything?"

Sebastian Ottosson nodded. Sammy pointed at the tape recorder.

"Yes! Now I just want to be left alone."

"One last question: Where is Stefan Sanberg?"

"No idea. Maybe out on a job with his dad. Maybe in Österby, where he hangs out with a girl."

"What's her name?"

"Madeleine. I don't know her last name. She works in a store, I think."

"In Österby?"

"I think so."

"Thanks," said Sammy, reaching over to turn off the tape recorder.

"Wait!" said Sebastian.

"Yes? Was there something else?"

"I regret that party. I want everyone to live, but now it's too late."

He stood up, gasping for breath. Sammy thought that he would burst into tears, but Sebastian steeled himself. Sammy turned off the recorder, gave Ann a look, nodded. The fatigue came again like a blow to his head. He closed his eyes. He could see Angelika, Jutland, and the whole mess. *How strange it is,* he had time to think, before Ann took hold of his neck, as if he were a kitten.

✦

Fifty-Seven

"What the hell are you doing here? And who are they?"

Erland sank down on the living room sofa. "Nyström and Give," he answered at last. The former was making a round of the apartment, while the one with the scar on his face stood by the window facing the street.

"Your buddies from Hökarängen?"

The one called Give laughed. A sound that didn't make Justus a bit calmer.

"We'll be here a couple of days."

"Never," said Justus. "You're leaving now. Erland, for Christ's sake, what do you have to do with these idiots? Think about your boy."

"Are you working tomorrow?"

The question was so out of context that Justus automatically answered yes.

"Call in sick," said Give. "You're going to help us."

"With what?"

"Practical matters, backup."

This was different from Uncle Lennart's petty gangsters, Justus understood that. He tried to make eye contact with Erland, but he seemed completely knocked out where he was reclined on the sofa.

"Can you make coffee," the leader said.

"Was that a question or an order?"

"Now you're starting to understand. Make coffee and keep your mouth shut for a while."

"Unexpected company," Justus said, going into the kitchen, which was directly connected to the living room. He took out the can of coffee and filters. He seldom drank coffee late in the afternoon or early evening, but now a cup was needed. He slowly filled the carafe with water while he looked for the phone. It was between the paper towel holder and the bread basket, and he reached out his hand and entered the code.

"Get going," he heard the other man's voice.

"Nyström, is that your name? Do you live in Uppsala?"

"Shut up."

"I know a couple of Nyströms."

Ten cups, he had never made that much before. The can was almost out of coffee. He opened the cupboard above the stove, rooted around, and found half a kilo of Zoegas Intenzo, at the same time as he managed to produce Lindell's number with his other hand.

"Only the best is good enough," he said and looked at Nyström over his shoulder, holding up the package.

"No knives," said Nyström.

Justus smiled and opened the package like he always did, with a tug. Out came a delightful aroma that he associated with early mornings and Little John. In contrast to Berit, they were morning persons. At the kitchen table they could talk about cichlids and anything that had to do with aquariums. They dreamed a little. About Africa. About the lakes in Africa, about the fish in the lakes of Africa.

"What the hell," said Nyström. Justus tipped the coffee into the can. He still hadn't had a chance to tap in the number. Instead he had to measure coffee into the filter under supervision and turn on the coffee maker. He was a prisoner in his own home. Captured by three terrorists. He leaned against the kitchen counter, hid his face with an open hand, as if he was struck by great despair. The other hand rested on the counter. The coffee maker started gurgling. What would they do in Uppsala? Blow something up? The mosque, maybe. If he remembered right it was the world's northernmost and had suffered some damage but nothing really serious.

"Are you all hungry?"

Nyström made a dismissive motion with one hand. Justus saw that two fingers were missing. "What happened to your hand?"

"Taliban," said Nyström.

"Ask Erland if he still takes milk in his coffee."

Nyström turned his head. That gave Justus the opportunity he'd been waiting for. He entered Lindell's number, saw that the call was connected.

"He never takes milk in his coffee, he says."

"Of course he does," said Justus. "Erland is a little senile," he continued, in a ridiculously loud voice, as if he wanted Erland to hear his banter. "That's why he associates with bombers like you all."

The question was whether she answered the call and heard his jabbering, but there was not much to choose from, so he continued.

"But what the hell, come home with me! Stay for two days. What the hell are you going to blow up? The mosque? You probably hate Muslims, huh? When were you in Afghanistan, Nyström?"

"Forget about that!"

The coffee maker let out one last death rattle. "And that Give, he seems more than disturbed." Nyström smiled.

Justus took down three mugs from the hooks under the kitchen cabinet, Moomin mugs that he got from Berit. He knew that she longed for a grandchild, maybe she believed that the Moomin motif in some unknown way would get him to start thinking about that himself.

It struck him that he would die in the apartment; there wouldn't be any Li'l Justus. What would they do when it was all over, when the mission was completed? Leave the city, of course, but leaving a witness behind was not a bright idea. He poured coffee, gave Nyström a mug, and took the two others with him to the living room.

Erland had fallen asleep on the sofa. Justus set the mug on the low teak table that Little John had bought once, and which now was stained by numerous rings from glasses and cups. He gave the other mug to Give.

"You're a bullshitter," said Give, but smiled when he saw Little My's gloomy expression.

"I think I'll have a cup myself," said Justus.

Erland had woken up, and reached for the coffee. "I've probably never had milk in my coffee." His voice was creaky like an old man's. Justus returned to the kitchen and unhooked the mug with Snufkin.

The call was ended. He stood there, resumed his pose with his hand in front of his face, tapped in a new call.

"What the hell is it with you!" Nyström had followed him and was standing in the doorway.

"I'm so fucking tired," said Justus. "Tired of violence and evil. What are you going to blow up?"

"A square, of course," said Nyström. "Vaksala, isn't that what it's called?"

"Vaksala Square on a Saturday! Is that why you're going to camp out here? You're out of your damned minds. It's Saturday market then. Any number of people."

Nyström sipped his coffee.

"You're going to kill however many people! Vaksala Square on a Saturday! Many people are going to die!" Justus screamed, leaning over the kitchen counter and taking the opportunity to click off the phone and put it in his back pocket.

✦

Fifty-Eight

Everything proceeded calmly. Resigned and quite passive, Rasmus Rönn was sitting at the kitchen table at Sebastian's place when two dozen police officers crowded into the house from three directions. One group had made their way up to the top floor by means of the scaffolding, and another had climbed in through a window in the old parlor where old man Ottosson had spent most of his time in recent years, a room his grandchild had so far not touched. A third group made use of the front door, which in the summer heat was wide open.

It was as if he'd been waiting to be picked up by the police. He had even just taken a shower and looked considerably fresher than the last time Sammy Nilsson saw him. He observed with enormous satisfaction how a couple of uniformed colleagues forced Rasmus up in a standing position and locked his arms behind his back. Sammy had an impulse to give him a sock in the jaw, but this wasn't an arrest in Alabama or Rio, instead in a village hole on the edge of nowhere.

Then he remembered what Ann had said after she'd been living in the village for six months: *Tilltorp and Gimo are the center of the world, do you understand that?* He didn't then, but now he was starting to sense what that might mean.

"You mustn't shove policemen, it always ends in handcuffs" was the only thing Sammy said in Ottosson's kitchen. Rasmus did not condescend to look at him. Sammy followed them out, saw how ungently he was stuffed into a van that had driven up. The back end of an ambulance disappeared in the birch grove that surrounded the highway north. A group of policemen stood by the old schoolyard. One of them pointed at the blackened chimney. Ann stood together with Bertil Efraimsson outside his house, and witnessed the undramatic resolution. Sebastian Ottosson was nowhere to be seen. Maybe he was still hanging around at the creamery. Rasmus Rönn would be reunited with his brother in jail.

Sammy leaned against the scaffolding, waved to Ann. His brain felt completely empty. He called the hospital again. Nils Stolpe was alive, but he could not understand much more than that from the strained formulations. He had asked to speak with Stolpe Junior, but it couldn't be arranged. The thought was that perhaps he could tell his father what had happened.

How to continue? Rasmus Rönn's companion was wanted. According to Bodin, who had visited Stefan's father, Allan Sanberg had no idea where his son might be. Should Sammy go there too? Sanberg lived half a kilometer away. Should he go in search of Andreas Mattsson? Sammy had tried to reach him several times, left voice messages on his phone and sent texts. The information that Andreas had said that it was Sam Rothe who killed his brother was sensational to say the least. It was an admission that during the night he left Therese in Östhammar and was outside the smithy when it burned.

Was that correct, or simply a way to push the guilt onto the defenseless Rothe? Sammy stood up slowly. The technicians had arrived and would start working in Ottosson's house. *What was there to search for?* Sammy wondered. Traces of a murder that happened several kilometers away? Had Rasmus dragged something with him from Rothe's, a souvenir from a successful lynching? Probably not. But it was a routine measure, nothing could be ruled out.

Sammy wanted to get away. He had a lot of paperwork to do of course, the sooner that happened the better, but did he have the energy to go to the police station and the computer there? He said hello to Evelina, one of the few female crime scene investigators. He thought he saw some sympathy in her eyes, but it was probably just imagination.

At that moment his phone vibrated. Incoming call. Andreas Mattsson.

"I heard that you're at Ottosson's," he started without any further ado. How he'd heard that was unclear, maybe Bertil Efraimsson had called and told him. "You wanted to talk."

"Where are you?"

"In the truck, on the way to Lyan with a load of dirt."

"Come here."

"I'll be there in ten minutes, and in Tilltorp in half an hour" was the driver's optimistic plan.

"We'll meet at Hamra," said Sammy. "It's good that you called," he added, grateful that any communication had functioned. "Do you have any idea where Stefan Sanberg may be staying?"

"Not a clue."

He walked over to the neighboring lot. Ann was smiling. Bertil observed him seriously. "Is this the center of the world?"

Bertil made a gesture that could mean: *Sure, it is.*

"I just spoke with your son," said Sammy, who in some way wanted to poke a hole in the workshop owner's liberal wall of probity. Naturally it didn't work. "He was at the farm the night the smithy burned."

"Yes, he told me just that. He wanted to talk with his brother."

"Half brother. And it went the way it did."

"You seem worn out," said Ann, and in that moment Sammy despised her supposed concern about his condition.

"Then he blamed Sam Rothe and sent that poor guy to his death."

"He wanted to talk with Daniel, not kill him," said Bertil.

Sammy turned away. He'd had it up to here with the village. How the hell could she live here? He left the two, walked to the car. He ought to exchange a word with Stefan Sanberg's parents.

Could he call Therese? Angelika? Was it there, in desire, in the need for intimacy and oblivion, that the answer was found? The tired hormones, and the once so proud and unreal plans about life itself, carried on an unequal struggle against the ennui in a worn, aging body. He was fumbling for answers.

Allan Sanberg was sitting in the kitchen. On the table was a cup of coffee that said WORLD'S BEST DAD. Beside it was a copy of *Aftonbladet*. "Yeah, I buy that rag out of old habit." The headline concerned someone who had lost seventy-two kilos. He looked tired, in that reflective, indolent way that physical laborers do after a long day, after a long week, after a whole life of physical work.

"That little shit is not too bright," he summarized.

"It doesn't look good," said Sammy.

"Mom is going to grieve herself to death. How can I tell her? Do you really think he was involved in setting the fire?"

"Looks that way."

"And then, that Rothe? Was Stefan there?"

Sammy nodded. "He bragged about it." There was no sense in cushioning the words, or using euphemisms. Allan would not go for such talk.

"When he was in his early teens I used to show him pictures. Mom had put together an album with things from the past. So that he would understand. My parents were heroes, do you get that? Personally I've cheated my way ahead."

"I've heard that you're a good craftsman."

"That's not so hard. It's just a matter of cleaning up after yourself. Now she'll have to hear that her grandchild set fire to the school she once attended. I did too. And the boy for a couple of years."

"You're most worried about his grandmother?"

"Yes, actually. She had dreams. I just wanted to work and make money. That's different, you know."

Sammy thought he understood the homespun philosophy.

"How many years will he get?"

"At least ten," Sammy guessed.

"I see. Would you like some coffee?"

"That would be nice."

Sammy glanced at the clock. Soon Andreas Mattsson would show up.

"He's missing something. We haven't been able to give him sense."

"I think you've done what you could," said Sammy, who felt a need to console the mournful figure who drank his coffee and read his paper in the kitchen he'd sat in for decades, his whole life really.

"Do you know a girl in Österby named Madeleine?"

"Stefan said something, but I don't know a thing about her. I think they met a couple of weeks ago."

"Maybe he's there," Sammy thought out loud.

"I've always voted for the Social Democrats," Allan Sanberg said unprompted. "It's been tradition. When I was a lad we marched in parades and that. Red banners. Once my father spoke in Gimo. He was in the road workers' union. It was the laborers who started it, but that was a long time ago, of course. People listened to the old man. He had a voice. Sometimes I still meet people who remember."

"I've voted for the Social Democrats too."

"A cop?"

"Yes, there are a few of us. Not many, but still. I got it from home. Also."

Sanberg gave him a look that was hard to interpret. Then tears started running down his cheeks. He just sat there and cried, did nothing to hide it or dry the tears. It was a frightening sight. Teardrops landed on the headlines of the tabloid.

"That business about cleaning up after yourself, what does that mean?"

"When you do a job, well or poorly executed, you have to clean up after yourself, pick up all the scrap, wipe off, sweep, and such. That's the sort of thing people notice. The rest maybe they don't understand that much, but if it looks tidy afterward then they're satisfied."

Andreas Mattsson drove his vehicle with great skill, a truck with a trailer. He backed up next to a storage building, turned off the motor, and got down from the cabin. These were practiced movements.

Sammy was sitting in the same garden chair at Hamra farm as before, where he and Bodin met Andreas the first time. He stood up, they shook hands, then sat down as if they were two chess players who had finally agreed on the conditions for a first match in a series that would decide the master's title. But there was no chess clock on the table, only a tape recorder. Andreas did not comment on that.

"What did you see that night?" Sammy asked, making a motion in the direction of where the smithy had once been. It was an offensive introduction, which didn't allow any objections or chitchat.

"I was at the farm office, and saw how it was on fire. It was actually a beautiful sight between the trees. Suddenly a figure shows up at the edge of the forest. He ran like a lunatic, right into where we have wood piled, I'm sure you've seen it."

Sammy hadn't, but he nodded.

"Who was it?"

"No one I recognized. This happened quickly too, and the smithy was burning. It was completely in flames, it could be seen from far off. I opened the window and jumped out from the office and started running. Then I caught sight of Daniel, he more or less crawled, stumbled along. Farther up, toward the road that we use for old pastures, another figure shows up. I recognized him immediately. It was so fucking improbable."

"Who?"

"Sam Rothe."

"You know that it was him?"

"He is, was, a couple of years younger than me. We've met quite a few times. He is just standing there, I don't think Daniel sees him, and when he comes closer there's an argument. I remember thinking: *Now you're going to get a beating.* Daniel could be really rough when he was scared. But it was the other way around. Sam swings something at him and Daniel collapses. Clubbed down."

Andreas fingered the tape recorder.

"Don't turn it off."

"Okay then."

"Did he die immediately?"

"I think so. The branch had penetrated his skull. Through the eye."

"What did you do?"

"I pulled out the branch."

"And . . . ?"

"I saw the lights from a car across the field, and understood that someone was coming, someone who had seen the fire. I thought it was Bertil. Never that the carpenter would show up."

"Why is that?"

"His mother died in a fire. That's what they say anyway."

"But it was Ann Lindell who came," Sammy observed.

"I found that out later."

"We didn't find a branch."

"I took it with me. I had it in my hand when I ran to the car. I just took it with me."

"You threw it away?"

Andreas shook his head. "No, it's at Therese's, in her shed. I don't know why I didn't throw it out the window on the road, but it was lying in the car, and then I had to hide it somewhere."

"What kind of branch?"

"Pine."

Sammy had a vague memory of a green-painted building on Therese's lot. Andreas described where in the shed he had stowed away the branch that killed his brother. He did it without showing any emotion, as if he were recounting something ordinary and trivial. In general his speech was marked by a dry factuality, something that Sammy had sometimes noticed during interviews. The common denominator was that those being questioned with this appearance demonstrated a marked strength of will, often combined with grandiose self-esteem.

Sammy interrupted the interview, walked a short distance away to call his colleagues in Östhammar. Fortunately he got hold of Brundin, who promised to immediately drive to Therese's and go through her shed. "I see, what do you know, a murder weapon," Brundin said dryly.

Then Sammy called Technical, got to speak with Wikman.

"Is it possible to secure fingerprints on a pine branch?"

"Possible, probably depends on the surface. What do you have going?"

"A murder weapon," Sammy said, repeating his colleague's words. "It's in Östhammar, I'm told. The colleagues there will take the branch to Uppsala. Okay?"

*   *   *

The interview resumed. The obvious question was asked. Andreas Mattsson fished a piece of paper from his back pocket, unfolded it, and set it on the table.

"It was because of this I drove to Hamra that night."

Sammy picked up the soiled paper, quickly read the text, which encompassed about ten lines and ended with Andreas's signature.

"You intended to show this to Daniel?"

Andreas nodded. "We'd argued a couple of days before. Completely unnecessary! It wasn't his fault that things were the way they were on the farm. We were both victims of that old bastard's greed and talk about inheritance, traditions, and how important it was to protect the farm. Sell the shit, was my suggestion!"

"It couldn't wait? I mean, showing the paper to Daniel."

"Nothing could wait. I'd waited long enough. The same day, before I went to Therese's, I called the old man and resigned! Can you understand? I resigned from the hauling business and the farm."

Now came the emotions. He stood up but remained by the table. Sammy gave him time.

"What did he say?"

"He just laughed. I think he was satisfied in a way, even though he lost a driver."

"You call Waldemar Mattsson during the day to resign, and that night you're going to show a paper to your brother where you renounce everything, all rights to Hamra Farm and Contracting, have I understood that correctly?"

"Exactly like that. I wrote it in the office and printed it out. Then I saw the flames. It was on fire in a few seconds. The smithy was dry as dust."

"I assume we can find everything on the office computer. There's probably a log for the printer too."

Andreas nodded. Now that all was said he looked indifferent.

"Why did you tell what you'd seen? At Sebastian Ottosson's."

"It just turned out that way. I was there and was going to talk with Sebby about fence posts. He didn't have enough, he thought. He's not that experienced."

"Who was listening?"

"Sebby, of course, and his buddies. I know Stefan from before and then there was another, Rasmus, I've only seen him a time or two."

"It just turned out that way? You didn't tell us, but three others, just like that."

"Sebby said something about Rothe leaving the village, and there was a little talk."

"You never confronted Sam Rothe?"

"Why nag about that? Daniel was dead."

"Explain!"

"It wasn't possible to do anything about it."

"It wasn't the case that you wanted revenge? He was your brother, after all."

"No, I just wanted out of here. And then I felt sorry for Rothe, that he would have to go to prison."

"You said nothing to the three at Ottosson's about . . ."

"I didn't say shit! Other than what I saw."

"How did they react?"

"I think they were shocked. Rothe was no killer exactly."

"And now he's dead."

"He probably had a guilty conscience."

"There are signs that he was murdered."

Andreas Mattsson's surprise could not be mistaken. "I'll be damned . . ." he blurted out, before he realized what Sammy was fishing for.

"You think I hanged him?"

"You let a murderer go free, but perhaps you had the idea to take care of it on your own? Or that some others could fix it. Maybe on direct order."

"Forget that. Don't you understand? I've left this. In two weeks I'm flying to Manila."

"A murder is a good reason to leave the country. I want you to get your passport."

✦

Fifty-Nine

After taking leave of Bertil Efraimsson, Ann Lindell walked slowly homeward, overcome by a peculiar mixture of satisfaction and despondency. The former came from the fact that the arsons appeared to be solved, and hopefully that would put an end to some of the talk in the village. She was satisfied besides at her own effort, and the department's. Sammy, Bodin, and the others had conducted themselves well. Finally, you might add. That gladdened an old police heart.

The despondency came from the fact that Tilltorp had been transformed, the tone had changed, trust had taken a knock, but also from the reactions of outsiders—many who had not even visited the village had strange ideas. At the gym in Österby talk had spread the whole spring, every time she'd gotten questions whether anything new had come out. "But you must know something!" a Zumba participant blurted out when Ann refused to speculate. Maybe they thought that as a former police officer she had access to special information.

As an undercurrent, mostly unexpressed, was the understanding that it was the fault of "the others." "What business did they have here, I mean from the start?" was a line she heard from a customer at the creamery. A plumber, a normally sympathetic and humorous man who lived in the neighborhood, and who helped out with some small jobs at work, had mentioned that they couldn't even speak Swedish. "They want subsidies, but don't want to learn the language" was his analysis. Would she ever be able to joke with him like she'd always done? Even her closest neighbor had undergone a metamorphosis during the spring, from cozy uncle in carpenter's pants to a real grouch.

Small displacements. Words that crept in. She looked around. A car approached, too fast and too close. She was forced to step down in the ditch. She hadn't seen it before, a dark BMW that skidded outside her lane. There were many passersby who didn't understand that curve. Before her time,

Gösta had said, a car had crashed right into the lilac hedge on the other side. She memorized the license plate number, a sheer reflex, and took out her phone to call and check who the owner was. That benefit, calling the station and quickly getting information, she still had. She still had friends left at the department.

"Missed Call," the display said. The number was known, but not listed in her contacts. She browsed back in her call list, had to browse a long time before it showed up. She wondered who it could be. She counted days, tried to put the number in a context, see which other ones were right before and after, but got no wiser. She opened Eniro and checked the number: "Justus Jonsson."

When she closed the browser she discovered two new voice messages. She listened. Clicked off, stood completely breathless, stock-still, before she routinely checked the time when they were entered, and then listened to them a second time. The words were etched in.

✦

Sixty

The phone vibrated. Justus took it out of his pocket.

"Don't answer," said Give.

"It's my mom. I have to answer, otherwise she'll come here. She lives in the area, and she's constantly worried."

They looked at one another. Justus wondered whether Give knew that Little John had been murdered, and how that affected Berit. Maybe Smulan had talked. He liked to lay it on thick about that. Give nodded.

"Hi, Mom, how's it going?"

He went up to the window, stood with his back turned to the trio who were parked in the living room: Give and Nyström on the sofa and Erland on the armchair.

"Of course I've heard. Everyone's talking about it."

Molngatan was deserted.

"Yes, Smulan has always been a little crazy, you know that, but I don't think he was involved in the bombing in Stockholm."

At the turnaround's parking lot, at the far end of the street, were two black cars, newly washed, both with tinted windows. A Volvo V90 and an SUV of a make and model unknown to Justus.

"Call Mirjam, I think she would appreciate it. Console her and that, but talk more about Li'l Erland."

Justus peered in the other direction. Gränby Bilgata, which ran perpendicular to all the various "weather" streets, was just as deserted.

"Maybe you can go there? Her mother is completely nuts and I think her sister lives in Enköping."

Vaksalagatan, one of the city's main arteries, which runs all the way from Stora Torget to the northeast exit and which on a late afternoon was always busy, was almost completely quiet. A couple of two-axle transport vehicles painted green with no company name passed going east. They gave the impression of belonging to the military.

"No, he hasn't called me."

The bus stop was abandoned.

"Of course, do you think I'm crazy? Call Mirjam!"

This is not normal, Justus thought, *it shouldn't be this quiet.* It could only mean one thing: Lindell had heard his message and understood, realized the seriousness. Soon the storm would come to Molngatan. He laughed.

"That's good, Mom, we'll talk later. Now I'm going to make an omelet."

He clicked off, remained standing for a moment by the window to collect himself before he turned around. He understood that he was in the eye of the storm, and what that could mean. Smulan met his gaze. In his old buddy's eyes was a mixture of defiance and loss, maybe a little hate too. He surely didn't like hearing Mirjam's and Li'l Erland's names. Justus lowered his gaze and went toward the kitchen. He had to think something over. The kitchen was perhaps the best place to be.

✦

Sixty-One

Wikman's message was brief but informative: "Print on the pine branch belongs to Sam Rothe. Blood and tissue fragments have been sent for analysis."

Sammy was divided. In a way a dead perpetrator was nice. *There's less paperwork* was his immediate, frivolous thought, but at the same time it was a shame that Sam Rothe's posthumous reputation was that of a murderer. It also gave support to the village's perception that he'd been a failed person, and also reduced Rönn's and Sanberg's crime of hanging the rabbit man from a beam. *They only demanded just revenge*, some would surely think.

Tilltorp would become a bit poorer without the rabbit man, it struck Sammy, a quality lost. There should always be eccentrics, those who deviated, walked to the side, who asserted their right to live a different life. They could be called village idiots or fools, but they gave the lives of the well-adjusted a necessary thorn. Wasn't Bertil Efraimsson also a village idiot in his own way? Both had also shown their generosity by giving the laughing Hazara a sanctuary.

Perhaps Andreas Mattsson would get his passport back and in two weeks be sitting on a plane to Southeast Asia, if he would not now be indicted for obstructing a homicide investigation. He had actually kept his mouth shut about his brother's killer. That in itself that was such strange behavior that with the help of capable lawyering maybe he could wriggle out of an indictment.

Hamra Farm & Contracting AB would never be what it had been. What would Waldemar Mattsson do? To an outsider his striving now stood out as meaningless, something that Allan Sanberg had mentioned in passing. "Like my life," he'd added.

It's hate that grinds down all efforts; to get to breed rabbits and other small animals in peace on an isolated smallholding in a backwater, or build a prosperous farm and haulage company, or as in Allan Sanberg's case be a small cog in the construction of society that assumes a kind of baton passed on by one generation to the next.

Hate crushes both the one who hates and the one who is rejected, scorned and despised.

Sammy sat in his office, which was a sanctuary in the chaos that had erupted, even if he kept the door open in order to catch some of what was happening.

The bombers were in the city! The siege of Molngatan and Gränby had started. Once again Ann Lindell had submitted the decisive information. How the hell did she manage? He could picture her rocking in her hammock in her rural idyll.

From there his thoughts went to Angelika. It's over, he'd repeated however many times the past few days, and nothing had happened to refute that assertion. On the contrary, Angelika had sounded even harsher the last time they talked. She was in no hurry to come back. *Does she have someone else?* The thought struck Sammy again, but he immediately dismissed it. She would have told him; she was that honest.

"Okay," Sammy said out loud. "Let it be that way." He'd gotten used to the idea. In any event during the day. At night she rode him like before. It felt like mockery. For the first time since his teens he'd had emission in his sleep. That made him furious in the night. "Danish bitch!"

The cautious knocking on the doorpost made him start. It was Bodin. "Stolpe is worse," he said. "Complications, they say."

"What kind of complications?"

Bodin shrugged.

"Is he dying?"

"I'm sure he will, but the question is when."

Bodin's comment brought Sammy to his feet. He rounded the desk and had time to perceive his colleague's terrified expression before Sammy slammed the door right in his nose. It was simply the case that at that moment he didn't want to have any colleagues at all, either living or dead.

✦

Sixty-Two

"Should we go and retrieve the weapons?" he heard Nyström say from the living room. Justus got up from the kitchen table and stood in the doorway.

Were they really not armed? That seemed unlikely, but not completely illogical. If they were arrested on the way, possession of weapons was not good advertising.

"There's no hurry," Give answered after a moment, as if he needed to consider the decision very carefully.

Erland Edman gave Justus a quick glance, then looked at the unwieldly backpack by his feet, and again looked at his old friend. What did he mean? Did he have a gun in the backpack?

"No knives," Nyström had said, that was ridiculous. Would he throw knives at three men? Was it possible to barricade himself in the kitchen? If he pushed a chair under the doorknob and overturned the refrigerator and freezer against the door it might work, but it would take more time than he had. He thought through the strategy: Pull out a chair, quickly shut the door and push the chair against it, jump up on the kitchen counter and overturn the fridge. And then call 112.

"I feel naked without weapons," said Nyström.

"I need to eat something," said Justus.

Give sat with closed eyes leaning back on the sofa. Justus would throw it out later, if there was a later. Give nodded.

Justus opened the refrigerator, pretending to inspect what was there, tried with his hand on the door to carefully tip the fridge toward him. It didn't move. But if he were to get up on the counter and take hold highest up on the back it should be a different matter. He took out the egg carton, looked around before he let the bottle of Hof follow. He needed a beer, preferably a couple, three. The three of them sat silently in the living room. He could feel their rising tension. Now was when they would start wondering.

He opened the beer with the ring pull on his right middle finger. He had inherited this from Lennart. Berit had always thought it was gangster style, but how many times hadn't he had use for it? He took a couple of sips.

"That sounds good," said Give. "But if you think you can drink us under the table you're wrong."

Justus answered with a belch and took out the frying pan and utensils for an omelet. Dinner often ended up being a quick egg dish. Once they'd stayed at a hotel, it was in Gothenburg in connection with a cichlid fair, and Justus would always remember Little John's delight at the breakfast including bacon and scrambled eggs. Berit had hardly eaten anything at all. Maybe she was ashamed of helping herself. Eating uninhibitedly was a sign of being lower class, she'd always thought. Bullshit, Little John had always asserted; "It's important to eat while it's there" was his motto.

He returned to the door. "Do you want any, Smulan?" He did not look at Erland at all but instead stared at the backpack to get confirmation that there really were guns in it. Erland Edman nodded, but then said no to the omelet. Hard to interpret, but it leaned toward a yes to weapons and a definite no to the omelet.

The question was whether he was prepared to make use of it? Justus whisked four eggs with a little salt. He was not really hungry, it was all theater, all to have something to do with his hands.

"Are you a patriot?" said Give.

"I don't really know what you mean," Justus replied. "But I suppose I am." He didn't want any political talk. Give had gotten up and was suddenly standing in the doorway.

"Then you understand what the struggle is about."

Justus nodded. The TV came on in the living room. It was a news broadcast, Justus realized that without seeing any picture. The reporter's excited voice cut through the apartment. "It is now confirmed that the policeman who was wounded in an exchange of gunfire outside Gimo in north Uppland has died from his injuries. In a press release . . ."

"What the hell!" he heard Nyström say. "The SWAT team is in Uppsala, do you see?"

"Damn it," said Smulan, sounding more terrified than convincing.

I guess I understood that, thought Justus, *that Lindell woman is smart.*

He felt a mixture of pride and fear. He had managed to get out a message, a call for help, but that also involved danger.

Nyström stepped up to the window, stood behind the curtain and peered out, and saw what Justus had already noticed.

"It's dead quiet," said Nyström. "We have to leave."

Give looked at Justus. "It's you," he said.

"They don't know that we're in town, it's that bastard they want," said Nyström, pointing at Erland Edman. "We're leaving!"

Do something, damn it! Justus wanted to scream to Smulan. "There is . . . You can take my car."

Give observed him. "You're dead," he said. "Maybe not today, but soon. And we don't need your fucking car. And you stay here, Edman."

Erland Edman pulled the backpack to him. Justus was surprised at how collected he appeared. "So you're leaving me here?"

"You killed the cop," said Nyström.

"You killed that little boy on the square."

"Bye now," said Give.

Erland Edman pulled a pistol from the inside of the backpack. "If I'm staying, you're staying," he said. Nyström reacted immediately like the trained soldier he was and threw himself forward with arm extended, but tripped over Justus's outstretched leg.

"Thanks," said Erland Edman, turning the gun toward Nyström and shooting him in the face. The bullet entered his right eye.

"What the hell!" Give shouted.

"There'll be no bomb on Vaksala Square," Erland Edman stated.

It was a macabre feeling, but Justus had a desire to laugh.

"Now you'll be famous, Smulan," he said.

Edman shook his head. Nothing seemed to bother him.

"Now it will be hard to sell the apartment."

"Who said that I want to sell?"

"You said that the last time we met. At the pub, don't you remember?"

Justus shook his head.

"Now we're leaving," said Give, who had collected himself.

Edman smiled. "You think so?" He raised the pistol a second time. "No," said Give, but Edman was no longer taking orders. He fired two shots in quick succession, both in Give's chest. The man with the scar was thrown backward against the wall and slumped down in a sitting position. He would be sitting there awhile.

"Go to Africa, like you talked about. That was probably what John would want. Sell the shit here and leave."

Justus observed his friend. "I'll make arrangements for Li'l Erland, you know that."

"Teach him everything you know about fish."

"Maybe bricklaying too?"

"Fuck that."

Justus nodded. He understood what would happen. "I'll call the cop," he said.

"They're sure to show up anyway."

"Would you like a rum before I go?"

"That would be good," said Erland. "Like before."

"Like before."

Justus went out in the kitchen, took out a drinking glass and the bottle that was in the pantry, poured a generous splash.

"You're not having any?" said Smulan.

"Not today. Berit gets so damned grumpy when I drink during the week."

He left the apartment. The shot came as he stopped out on the yard. At the same moment his call was connected.

✦

Epilogue

Tram 28 took them from the heights of Graça, skirting Alfama, to make its way creaking and screeching through the overcrowded shopping streets in Chiado up toward new heights. They got off at the end station, Estrela. There was shade under the trees by a modest outdoor café. They'd sat there a few days earlier, studied the pensioners, families with children, gangs of youths, and tourists. A generous, relaxed atmosphere prevailed in the park.

"The city has changed," said Edvard. Ann didn't like hearing that. It reminded her that he'd been there with someone else. That artist bitch.

When she suggested Dubrovnik he had immediately countered with Portugal. It turned out that way; for her it didn't really matter. He could have said Alvesta, Kil, or Älvsbyn. She would have gone along with it.

Now she was sitting in a park in Lisbon. Erik was in Berlin, and if and where he was sitting, she had no idea. The latest text message was consoling anyway.

"I'm going for a walk," Edvard said, getting up from the table without awaiting any response. That suited her fine. The message from Sammy had set the machinery in motion. On the park bench she could summarize the events of the winter and spring undisturbed. The investigation of the bomb in Hökarängen was completed. A Patrik Olsson had been arrested at Kastrup Airport for involvement in the bombing. As far as the colleagues in Stockholm and Uppsala could establish, he completed the quintet that was responsible for the crime. Three were dead—Give, Nyström, and Edman—and the fourth, Björn Rönn, was jailed. It had not been possible to establish whether his brother, Rasmus, had been involved in the plans.

In the little pavilion she ordered a glass of white wine. When she came back to the table the grilled ham and cheese sandwich was on the ground. A wild battle was going on over the remnants.

The man a few tables away was still sitting there. She had already noticed him when they arrived. There was something sly, that was the word that popped up, about him. Nothing threatening, hardly suspicious, simply sly. He was in his sixties, probably not Portuguese.

The pigeons flapped in front of her and she made a motion with one arm. They jumped a few centimeters. Oh how she hated pigeons. But these were Portuguese pigeons and she experienced a happiness that for a long time she hadn't believed was possible.

She leaned back, stretching out her legs. Her thoughts went to Erland Edman and what Justus Jonsson had told her. It didn't need to have turned out so badly for Smulan, he thought. Ann had heard that numerous times, but considering the nature of the crime and the fatal outcome there was reason to think a bit harder. She decided to look up Justus again. She wanted to talk. She wanted to know what happened to his childhood friend, what it was that radicalized Edman.

After the drama on Molngatan, Sammy had wanted to discuss what was happening in Sweden, but with a bitterness in his tone that Ann believed made reflection impossible, and she passed. The bitterness arose not least from the fact that his wife had met a British business attorney with a base in Copenhagen. He had already moved into the house in Hørsholm. The divorce papers between Angelika and Sammy were submitted. Moving van ordered. She wanted to leave Sweden. Ann was convinced that it was right, both the divorce and that they put seven hundred kilometers between them.

In Tilltorp the worst convulsions had subsided, but it was obvious that life would never be the same. The Mattssons would sell their farm and business. Ann did not know whether there were any prospective buyers. Andreas Mattsson was not allowed to leave the country as long as the investigation of the smithy fire and the murder of Sam Rothe was ongoing. Ann had run into him a few days before she left. He was thoughtful, calm in a way that actually was reminiscent of his biological father, Bertil Efraimsson. He was still driving gravel trucks, but wanted to get away as soon as possible. Whether he would be indicted on the grounds that he had not told everything he'd seen and knew about was unclear. He took it calmly and seemed to be the one of the two villagers who came out of this strengthened.

The other was Sebastian Ottosson, who little by little had started his operation. At the creamery a new cheese vat was installed and the goat's milk had started flowing in. Now new kinds of cheese would be made. Ann had made it a habit on her way home from work to stop by Sebastian's. He was an optimist. It was as if he'd been relieved of a great burden.

"What about the village?" Edvard had asked, and she had not immediately understood what he meant, but it was clear that Tilltorp must be reconditioned. A meeting at the historical society was planned for the middle of August. Strong emotions were involved but Ann believed that the biggest loudmouths would lie low. It was as if there was no space for hateful sermons. That quota was filled, and with such a mournful result for the village.

The processing of Omid's residence permit was put on ice awaiting the trial about the smithy fire. It could go in any direction. Sammy had spoken with him a few times, but that didn't produce much. Omid was constantly depressed, as if he'd given up all hope.

* * *

She took a sip of the wine, moved her chair a little so that she was in the shade again and at the same time took the opportunity to check whether the sly man was still there. Their eyes met. What was that about? He must have seen that she'd arrived in the company of a man.

Suddenly the stranger was standing behind her. "Excuse me," he said. She started, a little scared at first, then angry that he had surprised her. "We've met before."

Ann did not say anything. "We're colleagues," he continued, apparently unconcerned about the look he got. "Or were. I'm retired now."

Ann turned her eyes away.

"Folke Åhr, National Homicide," he said, nodding good-naturedly. Edvard came walking up. He looked amused.

"Yes, here comes your companion. Maybe we can exchange a few words regarding a common concern?"

Edvard sat down without a word. "An old colleague," Ann felt herself forced to explain.

"And you're Edvard," said Folke Åhr.

"Do we know each other?"

"No, not really, but I know who you are. You live in Viola's house on Gräsö."

"Summer guest?"

"Norrboda, not far from Nordh, whom you helped cut down a tree, if you recall," the retired policeman said, smiling broadly. "That pine."

Stop grinning, thought Ann, more and more embittered. "You said that we had a common concern. What might that be?"

"Cecilia Karlsson's disappearance from Gräsö."

"I have no idea who that is," said Ann.

"She's been seen here in this park," said Folke Åhr.

"And you thought that we were here to investigate," Ann commented. She suspected that the man had seen them in the park a few days ago too. "You put two and two together, a police officer, albeit a former one, and someone from Gräsö, in the same park the missing woman has been seen in."

The man nodded, pulling out a chair uninvited and sitting down.

"But you counted wrong, made it five," said Ann. "We're here on vacation, nothing else, not to search for a missing Karlsson."

"You mean this is chance?"

"When did she disappear?"

"On June twenty-fourth, 2009," said Folke Åhr. "It was a Wednesday."

"We have nothing to do with the case," said Ann. "We're leaving."

"You have wine left."

"We're leaving," she repeated and stood up.

Folke Åhr did not seem at all troubled. He followed her example, took a step back, pushed in the chair, and said goodbye. When he had taken a few steps he turned around.

"Perhaps we'll meet again," he said.

Ann Lindell sank back on the chair, took hold of the wineglass, and understood at that moment that it would be that way. They would meet again.